Shadow Over Avalon

by

C.N. Lesley

www.kristell-ink.com

Paperback ISBN 978-1-909845-24-4
Epub ISBN 978-1-909845-26-8
Kindle ISBN 978-1-909845-25-1

Cover art by Evelinn Enoksen
Cover design by Ken Dawson
E-book design by Book Polishers

Kristell Ink

An Imprint of Grimbold Books

4 Woodhall Drive
Banbury
Oxfordshire
OX16 9TY
United Kingdom

www.kristell-ink.com

This book is dedicated to my family, who put up with my scribblings over the years and offered their unfailing support.

Prologue

An ageless man sits in a cave, conjuring images in his fire. Weave a twist of fate there, pull the weft of compulsion here and the plan is ready to set into motion. He cares nothing about the misery and death he will bring to his victims; they are mere vessels to be used. A reincarnation will be born.

If only the original man had been more concerned with leaving an heir than with noble quests, equality for his knights, and the size of his round table, all the convoluted back-tracking of genetic material would not have been necessary. Still, he, Emrys, was in the very best place to guide the process through generations. He laughed at those he ruled, momentarily disrupting the careful illusion of a cavern that he had formed for his own comfort.

Soon, yes, soon he would have a real cave and be done with this tireless task. Just one more generation to bring the one. An ageless man sits in a cave conjuring images in his fire. Weave a twist there; pull the weft of compulsion there and the plan is ready to set in motion. Fortune twists in the strongest hands.

1

Earth Date 3892

ORB LIGHTS SUSPENDED over the buildings gave the plasglass dome of their 'sky' a blue glow against the fathoms of seawater pressing from above. Ordinary Submariners, people with real lives, hurried about their business like flows of tiny fish caught in a never-ending day. Initiate seers loitered at every junction. Serving as the eyes of the sentient computer, the Archive, these black-robed law keepers were as gloomy as their home, the dark towers of Sanctuary, which stood like rotted teeth amid the artificial brightness. Free at last from the grim place, if only for a short while, Arthur intended to enjoy his excursion into the city, his first since attaining the man-height needed to pose as an initiate.

He didn't see why seers forbade him when most other acolytes could visit their families on occasion. Surely he must have some kinfolk, and he thought his friend Ector, an officer in the Elite corps, would know. Ector had gone quiet every time Arthur tried to quiz him inside Sanctuary; something was being hidden and Arthur stood a good chance of finding out by visiting Ector at home. Aside from kin, he wanted more information about Shadow, the Terran Outcast who worked with the Elite corps on the surface world. He ached to know more about the place and the woman with a psi rating so similar to his own.

Two initiates turned in his direction. He attempted to stroll through the plaza with confidence, all the while giving off a mental signature of authority and right to walk from Sanctuary without the escort acolytes required. Their gaze rolled over him, moving on. Arthur heaved a sigh of relief. Ten more steps to a side street.

A black-clad form stepped into view, blocking the way. Arthur altered his direction, but everywhere he looked a seer stood, all of them focused on him. As one, they closed in on him. How had they known he wasn't allowed? He looked exactly the same as they did in his black robe.

Out-flanked, his mind caught in the crushing grip of two initiates, Arthur marched back into Sanctuary to explain his un-authorized excursion into the city of Avalon. He was now too busy shielding his mental abilities from his captors to come up with a convincing lie to excuse what, in his opinion, shouldn't be a crime.

The black doors of the inner sanctum hissed open to admit Arthur into the presence of a skeletal hag. As the matriarch of the seers, Evegena had the strongest mind of all. She didn't need any guards protecting her when she could squash the mind of another.

She looked up from her work interface, gray brows forming a harsh line over her pale eyes. "Caught in the city without permission and I see from reports you have willfully declined to gift your breeding mistress with viable semen. Explain yourself."

The power of her mind crashed against his barriers. Arthur adapted his outer thoughts to transmit frustration. "Why I can't visit the city like other acolytes?"

"They have family to visit, while you do not, and you have not addressed your other sin."

Hating her casual dismissal of his needs, Arthur shrugged. "Maybe I'm not fertile."

"Raising your core temperature before visiting Circe would ensure you aren't." Evegena turned her monitor to face him. "Look at your acolyte progress charts. Excellent in martial arts, weapons training, and you hold the record for submersion breathing. And then there is this—Telepathy and telekinesis scores border on a retarded bandwidth, results which don't match with your ability to destroy your own semen. Oh, and don't bother to lie to me. I can sense your barriers even if I can't penetrate them." She swung the monitor back and began tapping on the keyboard.

Caught. He should have aimed at scoring in the midrange, but it was too late for regrets. "I don't want to become a seer initiate. I want to join the military and use my powers to fight on the surface."

Evegena finished with the interface, splaying her fingers wide to stretch out the webbing between each digit. "As a ward of Sanctuary, you will follow the path I have chosen. You have ten days to bring your mental skills up to an acceptable level. During this time you will also provide viable semen. Should you decline, there will be consequences." She waved him out with a flick of her hand.

"I'm eighteen in two weeks, Matriarch. Legal age, and then you can't stop me." Damn her to the deeps. He looked down at her diminutive figure, his fury building.

Evegena's eyes narrowed, the gray-colored irises so light she appeared blind. "Don't imagine you can evade your fate."

Arthur bowed from the waist, his long seer's robes hiding his clenched fists from her as he departed.

*

A terrified scream wrenched Arthur through layers of sleep into heart-pounding darkness. At his side lay Circe, her naked body twitching in time with her nightmare; her ragged breathing warred with the thud and hiss of air changers in the corridor outside his room. Circe didn't get nightmares. Not ever.

A frightening, guilt-ridden possibility washed through him, since they had never spent the whole night together. Arthur had just woken from his regular nightmare. What if his sleeping thoughts bled into hers? He didn't want her hurt with his burden. Breaking all seer protocols, he pushed his thoughts past her mind's privacy barrier.

Breath scorching through labored lungs. Heartbeats thudding louder than footfalls. Darkness presses closer with wolves not far behind. The mournful wail of a hunter's horn sets the pack howling.

The faint light of a fire shines through dense forest. In the mouth of a cavern, a robed figure sits cross-legged beside the blaze. Within the depths of a cowl are eyes so black they reflect none of the flames, a predator's hypnotic link with cornered prey.

The dank smell of stagnant water mingles with wood smoke and lupine odor. The pack close for the kill, but the figure gestures, sending them slinking away into the night.

By the deeps! She continued the thread of his nightmare. His psi factor had slipped out of his control in sleep. What would the seer elders do if they discovered the product of a breeding program was defective? Keep alive the bits they needed and eliminate the rest?

He reached out with his mind to levitate an illuminator switch on his desktop across the room. A soft, golden glow lighted his simple acolyte cubicle and cast long shadows from his clothes chest. Light reflected through the plasglass surface of the table and chair. Circe lay curled, her hands over her wavy blonde hair. A single tear escaped to run down her flawless cheek.

Gently, he roused her, holding her tight in his arms as she awakened in a panic. "Now you know why I prefer to sleep alone." Arthur focused on the gray metallic ceiling of his cubicle, his lips set in a thin line. "I've had that dream every night for months."

Circe looked up at him with a frown, her blue eyes still wide with shock. "You raided my mind!"

"I don't like to see you suffering."

She stirred in his arms, shuddering. "Stop reviewing vids of the surface and maybe you won't invent nightmares around the place. Acolytes don't get permission to visit that primitive desolation, so why bother?"

"I haven't watched any vids. How can I dream up images of a place I haven't seen?" He rubbed his hands over his eyes. "Circe, I'm in someone else's body when I run from that pack."

"Racial memories? Thoughts from your time in gestation?" Some of the tension left her face.

Her delicate hands cupped his cheeks, and the soft webbing between her digits began to excite him. Arthur fought down the untimely urge. "Now do you see what you get for sneaking in here after hours?"

"I didn't have to sneak." Circe brushed her soft lips against his. "Had you accepted my invitation, we would be in my quarters, in my bed, with my cleansing unit a few steps away. Instead, we are in this bare room with no facilities." She grabbed the thin bed cover to rub him down. "And you stink."

He pushed her hands away, frowning and offended. "Go back to your room. You got what you came for."

"Did I? I felt the increase in your core temperature. I know I didn't get viable seed. Is this evasion an attempt to prolong your fun?"

Arthur stared, hurt that she would think he used her.

"Tell me about the dreams, then. Have you asked your parents if they run in your family?"

Harsh laughter burst from him. "Didn't you do your research? I have no parents—some nameless sire and a breeding mistress dam. The records are closed to me."

Her hands flew to her mouth. "I'm sorry. I didn't know. When Evegena gave me this assignment, she said she had already done the compatibility ratings."

"Our seer matriarch pokes her scrawny finger into my life yet again. Do you know how it feels to be an experiment in eugenics?"

Circe sat up, backing away from him. "Get an answer from the Archive. Acolytes have the right to access data."

"Easy words. We are permitted to research set subjects in the presence of a full initiate."

"You all wear robes of the same cut and color." She shrugged. "Who is to know if you are an initiate or not?"

He had managed to breach security earlier in the day, and no one would be expecting a second attempt so soon. Arthur smiled and reached for her in a gentle, loving way, putting every ounce of the skills she had taught him into the kiss he gave her. Circe responded for a few moments before she succumbed to the sleep command he slid into her mind. If he got caught by whoever spied on him the last time, he didn't want her blamed in any way.

*

Dressed in a clean black robe, Arthur stepped into the corridor. Like his sleeping area, no ornament, unnecessary furnishing, nor window relieved the bland grayness of a metallic thoroughfare designed to focus acolytes' thoughts inward. On the right and left, the doors of other sleeping rooms appeared at regular intervals. He ignored them, striding for a larger door at the end that gave access to Sanctuary proper. Air changers stirred to life with a soft whoosh, spewing dusty, dry puffs of air that made him cough, unlike the rich aromas of the dreamed surface world. The smoothness of his robe recalled memories of different textured clothes he wore in his nightmares.

He knew of one little-used outlet and headed there, not that the Archive had a physical presence. The sentient intelligence occupied all the data systems of Avalon, and was everywhere at once. Punishment for unauthorized access was the Hakara chamber, a pain amplifier known for breaking the spirits of its victims. But they'd have to catch him first.

Heart pounding, Arthur raised the hood of his robe to cover his head, aware that low psi-rated guards protected the privacy of seers during the resting time from the thoughts of others intruding on their sleep. The cowl shadowed his face to give him the anonymity he needed. If he were caught . . . well, he didn't want to think about that.

At the final intersection, before the corridor to the outlet, Arthur paused, caught with the thought that the Archive might hold no records of his parentage. Sanctuary might elect to hold paper copies rather than risk a raid by one such as himself. If that were so, he would have wasted his time. All he needed was a few minutes to browse records while the Archive's attention was elsewhere. It shouldn't take notice of an ill-used console with everything else it accomplished.

But then a new idea formed: rather than wasting the risky encounter with the omnipotent and invisible entity at a console location if the Archive was monitoring all outlets, a study of Shadow, the Outcast he had intended to ask Ector about, might confirm whether the reality of the surface world was in any way like his dream images. He knew she had first come to Avalon in the year of his birth. Maybe she knew of his parents. Arthur figured one or both might have been members of the Elite and therefore she would know. Questions about her couldn't worry anyone. Damn Evegena, he'd fight the invaders even if he had to steal a submersible to get there.

A cockroach skittered across the floor. Arthur caught the thing underfoot as it streaked to a small crack between the floor and wall. It crushed under his heel while he reflected on the Outcast, who represented an intriguing enigma for all acolytes. A surface dweller, the only one with cyborg implants and ranking in the Elite corps, made for a fascinating mystery, and then there was her psi power, unknown among Terrans. Maybe he could join her surface fighters?

He came to the door leading to the Archives, hesitating on the brink of sin, one step away from no return. The memory of his rapid capture outside Sanctuary returned to haunt him. Was it the Archive's doing? *Please let the thing be focused elsewhere.* His hand snaked around the open aperture to jam a thin probe behind the frame of a light switch, shorting out the circuit. Illumination activated by his entry died. A faint glow from the Archive console relieved the darkness.

"Welcome," the Archive's disembodied voice announced. "State your need." The doors slid shut.

Damn, he hadn't reckoned on the sentient being monitoring this output outside of waking hours for seers – so much for his plans to raid the database for his ancestry. On to his second option. "The Outcast. Why is she pivotal in this war with the aliens?" The question hung in the air of a darkened room – not one that he reckoned could give away his real intent. Against a far wall, a control panel gave enough light to stretch the shadow of a chair. Arthur, the lone corporeal presence, held his breath, willing the Archive to give him access.

"Change of pattern in most wars can be traced to one single act, which results in a cumulative displacement of events." The

Archive's now sibilant whisper hissed around the room, seeping into every corner.

"Just one?" Could a war start from such simple beginnings?

A sphere of light formed, suspended at head height and positioned three feet in front of him. It lit his seer's hooded black robe, but not his features, hidden deep within the cowl.

Don't breathe. Don't give it any chance to sample essence fragments.

"The extent varies according to the action." The machine's answer spread outward in waves of sound.

The sphere reformed itself into a resemblance of his face, floating at head height. *Deeps. A sonic probe. Oh squid shit.* The Archive projected full size holo-images of four potential matches, eliminating all except that of a young man of average height and build, high cheekbones and strong chin, deep-set violet eyes, and a straight nose. Dark brown hair fell to his shoulders in waves. Caught again, and furious, Arthur awaited the inevitable. He turned to repair the light source control, more as an escape from reality than for amends.

"Records indicate you are Arthur, a seer acolyte." The Archive speech pattern normalized. "There is no research permit issued to any acolyte at this time."

"I didn't ask. What's the point when the answer will be no?" He wanted to smash something, anything, to relieve his frustration. He wouldn't spend the rest of his life as a vehicle for the Archive in this sterile tomb of a place, like most of the initiate seers.

"Why make repairs when there are others more skilled in this task?" Curiosity colored the Archive's usually monotone mechanical voice.

"It's something to do while I wait for security."

"You intend to reduce the punishment by performing reparation?"

"Evegena"—he spat out the name of the seer leader—"does not clutter her mind with an acolyte's small doings."

Repairs to the light source completed, Arthur faced the general direction of his antagonist. "What meaning can the concept of punishment possibly have for a non-corporeal?" This outlet looked the same as any other console, a metallic gray back-plate, except all the touch controls shone like rows of parallel eyes. In this small room, even allowing for the reflective surfaces of the slick walls, the feeling of being a specimen preserved for study behind glass grew stronger.

"The absence of a feeling can cause as much discomfort as the presence. Your body language suggests you are either not afraid of punishment, or you have ceased to care."

"Does it matter which?" Arthur pushed back his hood, wondering at the absence of security, those ordinary people employed for night guarding. Most displayed an overzealous urgency, as if to elevate themselves into the ranks of the special by constant attempts to gain attention. He wanted this over quickly so he still had time to plan his future.

"Any individual choosing an unusual course of action is a source of concern. What motivates that individual is important. Come closer, Arthur. I need you to link." The Archive opened a port to release a metallic, snakelike appendage that wavered, swaying on the anchor of its roots.

"I'm not a full seer yet, I'm not trained for linkage." Arthur moved sideways to the door, but it remained shut.

"Security is not about to arrive, nor is that door going to open. I can access data from a conscious or an unconscious mind, Arthur."

A radiant force field behind and to both sides of Arthur pushed against him, moving inward by degrees to compel him to the console. Beaten, he edged over to sit in the chair, brushing his hair behind his ear to give the umbilicus easy access to the comm-link implant in his skull. A tingling invaded his body followed by a huge outrush, like cold water gushing inside him.

I see the concern you are hiding, the Archive supplied directly to his mind. *No, Evegena, in her capacity as seer matriarch, would not punish you by sending bad dreams. She has no imagination. What she will do is enforce celibacy while you are an acolyte if you continue to withhold viability when visiting the brood mothers. She will not let you treat such a serious subject as recreation. As for not wanting to become an initiate, you will change your mind if you see the surface world. It is a wild and primitive place, unsuited for one such as yourself.*

"I won't be a stud for them. I won't inflict my life on another." He didn't want to create others to live his artificial life, and sometimes imagined his unknown sire and dam coming together as strangers. Perhaps the elders had many specialized breeding programs to create the ultimate telepath? That thought made him feel like an old shoe, one awaiting a better, smarter replacement as soon as production improved.

Nor would you inflict your dreams on potential individuals, since the first part of your real question is already answered. I agree, the dreams may be due to psi-factor. The Archive paused, probing. *You have not undergone a rated psi-level test in the last six years.*

"Going to report that?" Deeps, if the elders found out they would try to force him to stand stud forever. He'd rather die.

Dreams are a means of release when escape from routine is otherwise impossible. The Outcast makes an excellent study example for this project. She is compatible to the primitive landscape of your dreams both by reason of her own natural environment, and by factor of her estimated psi-level.

"How can I know what the surface world smells like? I have read everything the seers will allow acolytes to know of the primitive outside without finding such a description." Why was the Archive allowing this exchange? Was he going to get away with his raid for data? He couldn't be this lucky.

Recreation of a different nature is best, the Archive advised, projecting a holo image of the Outcast, a young woman of medium height wearing an Elite uniform.

She had a look of death on her lovely face, some indefinable expression creating a chilling warning. Arthur studied the form. He'd never seen her likeness before, or been in a group allowed outside Sanctuary any time she visited Avalon. She looked so calm in this image, and yet she had started the war. Curling blonde hair outlined her face like a helmet. Under a short nose, her lips pressed together to form a harsher line than nature intended. Her eyes held him; their violet depths seemed to see into a distance filled with stark choices. This one factor confirmed her as a Terran Outcast from the surface world . . . they all bore the sort of gaze that made others think they could stare through rock.

In answer to your original question, pertaining to the part she played in starting this war, projection suggests 73.95 percent probability factor. One such individual affects ten more, who affect another ten on an expanding scale. Given the mobility of this subject, these statistics are exponential.

He knew she had interacted with many others, but not how, in the eighteen years since she had first joined forces with Avalon. Arthur wanted all the data downloaded on a portable tablet, since it seemed he might get away with his transgression.

Arthur, you will not be able to move in a few moments. Do not be alarmed. For a time setting of one standard unit, there will be full sensory playback of this subject's life.

Arthur struggled to free himself from the chair and dislodge the umbilicus. He fought to block the thought waves, and all the memories flooding into his mind. Acolytes never linked to the Archive for sensory playback. Only full seers possessed the training to meld in this fashion without becoming addicted, condemned to spend what remained of their lives in endless repetition of the recorded existence of another. *No, please not this. Anything but this.*

His body failed to respond; his trance deepened as blended memory pattern settings unfolded in chronological order. For one nerve-shearing moment, soulless black eyes stared at him from the reflective surface of the console, and then reality lurched sideways into a different dimension as time reversed.

2

Earth Date 3874

UTHER, DUKE OF TADGELL, signaled a halt at the edge of a wood with a stretch of grassland ahead. Thick dawn mist rose under a ruddy sun, giving the air a look of blood-tinged water. Sounds of movement distorted and magnified . . . of harness and hooves. A beat expanded into rhythmic thuds, the throb of a full gallop of a madman racing in mist over uneven ground. He backed his mount into deeper cover as the steady pound of hooves grew louder.

A horse and rider burst through the light-charged wetness, soaring over a low stone wall. The rider's laugh lingered in the rushing breeze long after her passage. As she rode the air, sunlight reflected against her bronze cuirass. Radiance made her flowing golden hair glow red and turned the animal's snow-white coat to molten silver before they vanished, shrouded by a sheet of mist, the drumming hooves fading.

A War Maid, riding without an escort, at a breakneck pace in poor visibility. His skin crawled with the fear he'd had another vision, for no ruler let female kin out alone. He turned, intent on pressing forward, to see night-colored eyes staring at him from the bark of an oak tree. Even as he reached for his sword, they disappeared.

A quick glance at his men, hidden deeper in the thicket, showed alert warriors, but not ones who saw a cause for concern. Another premonition after five years of peace, and why now, when he had no intention of going near Gold Band women, particularly War Maids?

*

Ashira rode into the natural gorge encasing her father's fort. The two narrow entrances to this valley ensured Menhill was impregnable, deterring even the flying lizards where limited wing-space wrecked their hunting.

A patrol approached, heading out to the main trail. Twenty riders drew near wearing brown tabards with sable, couchant polecats quartered with a single ram's head on their heraldic devices. One man in mismatched clothing rode rearguard. She guessed they tracked something dangerous, a mutation or a predator saurian, for an Outcast to be included. Ashira's curiosity stirred at the sight of this man. No, not man . . . creature. Sinners lost human status after the priest changed the color of their wristband to black. His expression was grimly fitting for a man with no home, no family and not even a name any longer.

As if aware of her scrutiny, he reined in his mount to circle around her. Light stubble peppered his cheeks and chin. Copper-colored hair hung in greasy waves to his shoulders. Violet eyes, a shade matching her own, raked over her. An old scar bit into his skin to weave from one eyebrow to the edge of his mouth, spoiling a handsome face. His once-rich clothes of gray leather and cream linens had patches, scuffs and dirt marks, and the breeze flapped the ragged green cloak at his shoulders. His one brown boot and one black cried of hardship, yet a fierce light kindled in the deep-set eyes. Ashira shuddered.

"Look well . . . sister." The voice rasped with disuse, chilling, flat, and made with effort. "You're coming within . . . my grasp soon."

"A raid?" Outcasts never lied when they struggled to talk past the vocal damage inflicted at the time of sentencing. "Speak, Black Band, or I'll have you questioned by our priest." Her brother always said these death-mongers considered themselves outside the concerns of humanity, caring for nothing except the thrill of battle-frenzy. Which fort threatened Menhill, since the Outcast thought to have her as his payment from the spoils? How dare he!

The Outcast rose up in his stirrups, made a sweeping bow in her direction, far too graceful for any former Bronze or Silver Band. "Not Brethren business . . . as yet. I see a shadow . . . hanging over you. Keep those blades keen . . . War Maid."

"You dare to threaten me?" Ashira rested her hand on the pommel of her sword. He'd never take her alive.

He smiled, blowing her a kiss before wheeling his mount to gallop after the other riders.

A gray cloud crept over the sun. In the distance, a priest had children sitting outside in a semi-circle, chanting morning prayers to the Harvesters. A sharp crack of the whip sounded, followed by a squeal of pain when the youngest misremembered. Ashira looked away, torn between disgust at the brutality and fear of her blasphemous thought that the priest enjoyed beating children. A shudder ran through her. Even her father, the king, couldn't help her if she angered the priest.

A wild merlin spiraled down with some bedraggled mess in his talons; a male bird, his bluish-gray back shimmering as he landed. The pair nested high up the gorge on a ledge created by a shaft mirroring natural light into the inner chambers. What would he think if he knew she could see each small fledgling from her room? Secure in his lofty position, he was unaware the place he had chosen resembled a wasp's nest beyond the outer shell, riddled with chambers, passages and halls.

Such a large and prosperous fort, and she shared her father's fierce pride in his domain. Why then did he dislike her so? Was it transferred loathing for Ashira's mother, the long dead second Queen of Menhill? This attitude of King Hald's was clear from the way he treated her half-brother and sister: Kieran, the all-important male heir and the eldest, then Syril, their father's favorite, and Ashira's responsibility to guard, the reason she must be a War Maid.

The last traces of exhilaration from the morning ride faded upon entering a ground level stable-cavern. A groom stepped forward to hold Storm for Ashira to dismount. She liked to tend to her own horse but must now stand aside for others to perform the task, after receiving her gold wristband in the ceremony marking her of the highest caste.

Horn calls from the heights warned of traders approaching. Ashira hurried into the fort to bathe and change. With peaceful company coming, she needed to dress modestly – not that she expected to see any of the travellers, but just in case they spotted her about her duties.

Once back in her own room, Ashira frowned at the sight of her hair. The untidy blonde curls, windswept from her ride, needed braiding. She had just finished weaving it into a coronet, pinned tight against her head when Kayla, aged servant to the women's quarters, shuffled into her room.

"His Majesty wants you in the audience chamber at once," the crone mumbled. Excited that punishment for Ashira was in the offing; a runnel of saliva wove down the network of lines crinkling her mouth.

That made three times this year King Hald had learned she rode out beyond her limits against his orders. She reached for a plain gray dress with long sleeves. Maybe he didn't know of her ride, but she laced up a pair of sturdy sandals for better balance in case of a whipping, despite the extra seconds this cost her. Before she could affix the face veil required for going into a general area in the presence of strangers, she lost her grip of the slippery fabric when Kayla tugged on her sleeve. No time to pick it up off the floor. He became more brutal when he had to wait longer than expected. Her back still hurt from his last rage.

"He said now. Leave it." Kayla led the way to the audience chamber where she bowed, to shuffle away before any more orders robbed her of time dozing beside a fire.

Her father, seated on a dais at the far end of the vast cavern, appeared flustered. His crown sat crooked, leaving his gray hair protruding from under the rim at one side. He wore a brown tunic over beige hose, his formal attire for important occasions. Kieran stood behind and to the right; her brother's straight red hair framed a sharp face that made Ashira think of foxes. His presence meant this wasn't a simple whipping for riding unattended, so what did her father want of her?

Hald's brittle smile reached his eyes without kindness. Every instinct warned her not to speak. Years of his indifference peeled away to reveal a single glimpse of loathing mixed with some expression akin to pleasure. Today, her father was a dangerous stranger. Icy fingers played over her flesh, raising each hair on her neck.

"Did you enjoy your ride?" her stranger-father enquired.

"Storm needed exercise." Damn, he knew.

"You could not wait for an escort, or stay in sight of the fort? You decided to risk Syril's safety by leaving her unprotected with an Outcast in Menhill. You were trained to guard her. Did you give no thought as to why I hired this creature?" Her father smiled.

"I learned of the Outcast's presence on my return." Ashira glanced at Kieran, trying to gain some clue from him. He had his gaze fixed on some far distance. Was this to be another whipping, or worse, loss of her horse?

"Had you chosen to obey my orders you would have known of the potential threat to Menhill, as well as why I employed an Outcast."

"Syril never . . . " Ashira bit back the rest of her excuse when his hand rose to silence her. She tried to swallow in a sand-dry mouth. Her heart pounded.

He raised his hand again in signal, and the tramp of feet sounded. Hald opened his other hand to reveal the crumpled scrap of a face veil, which he shook out to flick almost within her reach. Something heavy thumped down behind her, sending an echo booming in the great hall, but she kept her eyes focused on the face of her terrifying, stranger-father.

"Welcome, Traders," Hald said, his tone couched as a quiet threat.

A stolen glance behind revealed five strangers. Kayla hadn't warned her that these men would have an audience at once. Ashira didn't care if they saw her in uniform, but wearing this gown without a face veil, and unable to blend into the background like a Silver Band woman, embarrassed her. She knelt at her father's feet, her eyes fixed on that waving scrap of cloth outside her reach.

"I am in need of ore," Hald continued to flick the fabric near enough to torment her. "I am told yours is of good quality, but I am not certain I can trade for this much. What did you want in exchange?"

"The cattle of this region yield high quality milk," a deep voice answered from behind Ashira. "We will barter for four proven female breeders and one bull."

"It is true our beasts are valuable, so you understand their worth will be hard to match?" His lips stretched with a half-smile.

"The ore in exchange for one bull and four heifers, we will take our chances on fertility," the man with the deep voice offered.

She wondered at his sudden concession. He sounded relaxed, as if he didn't care whether he traded his valuable ore. What was she doing here while her father conducted his business?

"I can't spare enough cattle for a fair exchange." Hald's voice dripped pleasure. "However, I can supply other breeding stock of a sort you need, so I conclude these parcels of copper are meant as a bride price. My youngest daughter, Ashira, is six years into her second decade. Do you agree to the match?" The king gave a hand signal to his guards. A precise rustle sounded as they drew their swords in a unified threat to the strangers. Hald meant to keep the ore.

Ashira forgot how to breathe, unable to believe her father's decree. She turned at an angry rumble to catch a glimpse of four blank-tabarded soldiers surrounding one tall, black-clad man with a thundercloud expression. Outnumbered five to one, they faced bad odds in a fight.

"Did you really think I knew you not? Still hesitating? Doubtless overwhelmed by the honor," the king said, taunting them. "I will hear your consent, my lord." The trap snapped shut around the outmaneuvered men, echoing in the high-roofed hall like the dull thud of a coffin lid.

"Agreed." The dark man's voice grated. "I'm leaving now, Hald. Tell your men to stand aside."

"You all heard and witnessed?" Hald's smug tone aimed at his soldiers and Kieran, sealing the marriage. A roar of assent shook the air. He dragged Ashira to her feet, sending her reeling into the midst of angry, cheated men.

Strong arms caught her before she fell, dragging her along as the strangers made a swift retreat. This couldn't be happening. This wasn't real. Ashira was bundled astride a horse with the man mounted behind her, his arm like a band of steel round her waist when he spurred his steed to a gallop. The drumming of hooves echoed as the gorge that housed Menhill rushed past.

My father traded me. This thought went round and round in Ashira's head like a mad moth attracted to torchlight – traded away for a few parcels of ore, so he could keep his precious cattle. Why did he hate her so?

This morning's premonition took form. Outcasts lived so close to death some people believed they could see beyond the gray veil of time. Did Copperhead's vision include his own death when he said he would have her? Did he mean they would meet in one of the seven hells? Ashira didn't need foresight to guess her own fate. This ruler, forced into an unwanted union, would not show weakness to his fort by letting her live. Death it was then, but she'd fight through this hell for a chance to gain the Harvester's golden afterlife. But only those who died at peace with themselves reached the promised heaven; she needed to close off every bad thought this day.

Puffy white clouds hung motionless in an azure sky. A pheasant flapped from cover, squawking with fright, to clatter skywards at the thunder of hooves. Lush pastures peppered with cattle flowed by. They were headed south, away from higher sheep hills.

The company slowed on approaching a small thicket, and a whistle shrilled. Ten mounted soldiers in red tabards bearing a sable dragon device emerged to join the group. Each clean-shaven man also had his hair neatly trimmed to his shoulders, showing a disciplined fighting unit. They led five laden pack animals and two unburdened beasts. Every newcomer's face reflected disbelief, anger, and a trace of fear. Not one man dared look at the black rider behind Ashira.

When wild moorlands replaced meadows, the pace settled to a steady trot until the trail dropped down to wetlands showing signs of habitation. A small community of peat cutters had set up summer camp, plying their trade by carving into the brown, water-filled trenches. Marsh marigolds raised defiant heads, bright yellow sunbursts near the banks, and farther back, mounds of dark, rolled slabs dried in the sun, a source of sweet-smelling winter fuel much preferred by forts. Far above, a peregrine falcon spiraled up on a thermal, screaming his lonely challenge.

A peregrine for a prince, the order of falconry dictated. Hope flew with that bird for a second until she recognized it was a wild one without dangling jesses. Kieran wasn't looking for his despised half-sister.

The company took the trail into high moors visible beyond acres of coppiced willow trees. She craned round to see more, trying to guess their destination.

"Those are harvested for cane work," the rider said, his voice deep as he tightened his grip on her. "See that smoke over there? Craftsmen are boiling shoots for darker contrast shades. They'll be cutting withies all this month. We'll trade here. Know that I couldn't care less if you make a scene, but these simple folk will be embarrassed."

A few minutes later, the company reached a crude collection of daub and wattle huts thriving with industry. The man dismounted, giving his reins to a soldier. He stalked off without a backward glance.

Craftsmen brought finished cane-work out, and soldiers unloaded copper cooking pots from one packhorse before a rapid bargaining began. At the finish, two pots changed places for a wide variety of baskets and one screen. When the company set off, she tried to push aside thoughts of her fate, but it became more difficult with each passing league.

She no longer had a place at Menhill, her father having traded her in a bride price. This man, duped into the union, would lose face with fellow rulers if he kept her. If he looked weak, his fort would come under attack – that was a given. These wild lands they crossed held many places for losing bodies. Still they rode at a steady pace.

Sunset cast long shadows in a musty valley with ruins from ancient times. Most resembled mounds of rubble, but one large stone structure remained intact, except for the roof and half a wall. The horses trotted into one huge hall with symmetrical, smaller rooms against the two longer sides. At one end, a small opening gave access to a square chamber with higher walls than the rest. The tension radiated from the iron circle of her captor's arm around her.

Soldiers picketed their mounts at one end of the central portion and started to unload packs, all under the black rider's curt direction. When sentries began patrol, he dismounted, hauling Ashira down beside him. Grabbing a bottle from his saddlebag, he pushed her to that enclosed square room. Inside the roofless structure, the ground was studded with fallen stone blocks. One area by a corner remained clear, and here he threw her down. She lay still, sending a prayer to the Harvesters for this warrior to make a quick kill and not take time to pleasure himself first. During their journey, the hard muscles of a fighting lord had pressed against her; he would use a blade, not his hands, to finish her.

He took a long pull from his bottle, as if seeking an excuse to delay. Light shone on black hair, like a raven's wing at rest the way it hung down in folded waves. A straight nose jutted over firm lips, a strong square jaw beneath them. He towered over her, watching. His deep-set, pale blue eyes bored into hers. Here was a man who had treated her with respect up till now, but he was fated to be her executioner. She shuddered, praying he wouldn't force himself on her before he killed her. She would fight him if he tried, but would she risk the afterlife if she died in contention?

"Scream as loud as you please, girl. Not one man out there will interfere." He set the bottle to his lips again.

She closed her mind to the thought of him, of what he might

do to her. Sunset faded down through yellow to red. Pink-tinged clouds, shot here and there with gold, floated like fluffy down. A flock of geese flew honking, black and white, a homing arrow to their roost. Ashira took a deep breath, willing calm, savoring the smell of damp loam and crumbling stone. A faint whisper of honey-sweet scent rode on the air, and then his shadow fell across her as he knelt, bringing the aroma of horses, sweat, leather and liquor close.

Metal hissed on leather when he drew a short blade. He straddled her and, snatching up her right arm, he cut through the fabric of her sleeve. The dark-clad lord held her wrist to his, comparing status bands. Both gleamed reddish gold in the dying light, identical.

"I am Uther, Duke of Tadgell. Heard of me?" His eyes narrowed.

A sudden worm of fear gnawed at her vitals. This man didn't live by the rules. "I've heard stories." The Black Dragon Duke. Now she knew why he had hidden his identity. Some said he encouraged the dark Brethren to winter at Tadgell in exchange for weapons practice. He'd earned a reputation as lethal duelist, moving with a fluid grace found uniquely in seasoned Outcasts, or Brethren, whichever name they called themselves.

"So the weasel's get has a voice." He pulled on the liquor bottle again. "I thought Hald disposed of a bastard, but I see the gold band of a legitimate daughter. Why discard legitimate blood kin?"

"My father's device is a polecat, not a weasel." Ashira didn't care if she angered this man more. He looked as if he intended to drink himself insensible. Drunken soldiers made clumsy killers. She'd as soon goad him to act with speed before he had other thoughts.

"Weasel, polecat—stinking vermin, both. Did Hald have cause?" Suspicion or anger narrowed those ice-blue eyes.

She understood: rulers never traded daughters away to strangers. Marriages arranged for strategic alliance, to improve status, or for territory, were the way Gold Band ladies left their families. Clearly her father's hatred of her had become so bitter that he could no longer tolerate her presence.

The silence between them grew into a thing of menace. The duke's expression set into hard lines as he sheathed his knife. Every instinct warned her to conceal her battle skills from this ruler.

"You're what? Sixteen summers?" The duke's eyebrows rose. "Probably never let out of the women's quarters except by Hald's orders, judging by the lack of a face veil."

Still she stayed quiet, sensing he wanted something from her.

"Silence speaks louder than words. Do you know this, girl?"

His eyes returned to her band, and then narrowed as if beginning to question. Ashira balled her fists seconds before he caught first one wrist, then the other in an iron grip, forcing them together. His speed threw her off balance when he stood, forcing her to kneel in front of him.

"Swear an oath of fealty. Accept my protection, girl," he said. She would have to place her hands in his while she swore. An act to gain life would betray her training calluses when he felt her palms against his. Her fists remained closed; her head came up in a gesture of pure defiance.

"I could force you to repeat your defiance in front of my men. You do understand no other ruler could then question my right to order an execution?" The duke waited for an answer. "One last chance. Will you give me the kiss of peace?"

This vowed her not to harm him, and she wouldn't have to betray her sword calluses. She kissed his hands. The duke startled her with another swift movement, kneeling to join her, he forced her arms behind her back. Almost in a whisper, he said, "Girl, you've got a look about you. You remind me of someone I think I would do well to mistrust. I'll have the kiss on my lips."

Now Ashira could see his motives: this kiss would mean vowing to protect his life from enemies. He suspected treachery from Menhill. His arms tightened around her, bringing her into a rough embrace. His lips hovered over hers while he waited for her move. What did she have to lose? She closed her mind from the thought of what she did and just brushed his mouth. Moving away, she caught one of his eyebrows quirked up and the trace of a smile hovering.

"Such a vow holds true on our lives until we both agree to part company," the duke said. "I have your vow, and now you shall have mine."

Drawing her close, he kissed her. Ashira had not guessed a man's lips could be so soft. By the time he had finished, she was blushing, to his obvious amusement.

He became serious once more. "Speak the truth now, are you betrothed to another?"

She looked down and shook her head.

"Are you sure? Have you any pieces of jewelry you received from your father and not your mother that could be betrothal gifts?"

"None." Hald aimed high for Syril without stirring himself for her . . . until now.

"Then I have all that I need to know." Releasing her arms, he cupped her chin, compelling her to meet his eyes. "All arguments will be reserved for journey's end. You will obey my orders instantly, and I'd prefer if you could manage to uphold the dignity of our status by refraining from any whines, or complaints. The lives of all depend on strict discipline in the wilderness."

She nodded.

He let her wait, as if daring a stream of objections to burst forth. Hearing none, he released her, rising to his feet to execute a short, formal bow.

The duke offered his hand to assist her. "I think I will not permit Hald to reacquire you, whatever the outcome of this mess. Gold Band ladies are not treated thus. Besides, he doesn't deserve you."

Sympathy from this unexpected quarter chipped at her resolve. Her bottom lip began to tremble.

"No tears."

Ashira stopped at the savage tone. The Dragon Duke still sought to trap her off guard with his false kindness, a thin veil over anger and outrage.

"That's better. Now, are you composed enough to rejoin others, or do you need more time?"

"I'm ready." A shiver tingled through her. She no longer doubted he encouraged Outcasts for more than predator slaying. He seemed to have more than his share of their ruthlessness. The Black Dragon Duke operated by his own individual set of rules.

3

Earth Date 3874

A CAMPFIRE BURNED bright, the yellow flames licking at the laden spits sizzling and popping with gobbets of meat. The smell of smoke and roasting mutton wafted through the cool night air. Head held high, Ashira ignored curious men and the small pockets of nervous laughter. She stalked to the edge of the firelight to sit on a flat rock. The duke joined her, sitting close without touching, his look daring her to move away.

A soldier brought a water bottle, returning soon after with slices of roasted lamb resting on wedges of waybread.

"Hald raises good stock."

"He didn't trade with you except . . ." she started, aware far too late that this subject should be left alone.

"The beast tripped over one of my soldier's swords. It managed to impale itself through the heart. I'm sure every care would've been taken to heal it otherwise." He glanced down at her, a hesitant smile lighting his stern features. "We couldn't just leave it there to draw predators, could we?"

"That's theft. You should've given the animal a decent burial." She couldn't help looking at his lips, remembering how soft they felt.

"Oh but we do!" He laughed, taking a large bite out of his portion.

This was a show for his men; he played his part well. Hunger and thirst hit her after a full day of fasting. Ashira didn't care who had rightfully owned the animal, a prime specimen, and she hoped it had been valued breeding stock.

Some soldiers began a game of dice while others rose, stretching, to take turns on patrol. A few rolled up in their cloaks to catch some sleep. Ashira yawned as the events of a disastrous day caught up with her. She stared into glowing embers, getting sleepy.

The duke unfastened his cloak, lying down to cover himself with it.

"Lie beside me," he said. "I need you well-rested for tomorrow."

She settled as far away from him as she could while still sharing his cloak.

"Ashira," he said, quietly. "Did I mishear . . . is that your name?"

"Yes, my lord." She wondered at the hesitation in his tone. Her father never bothered checking details like a person's name.

"I'm not used to being around Gold Band ladies. I forgot how isolated you all are. Did I hurt you? Shall I order a litter made for the morning? You rode well for a lady, but must surely ache."

"I'll ride. I learned as a child." She wasn't going to show this man one trace of weakness, despite his apparent kindness.

A chill coming up through the hard ground seeped into Ashira's bones. Her muscles did ache from travel, despite her training. Without rest, she wouldn't last long tomorrow, and then he'd make her take a litter. She moved nearer, turning her back to him. The duke fitted to her contours. Warmth and a sense of safety seeped from him. Whatever his reputation, he had been honest with her so far.

Yet a feeling of a threat persisted, not from him, but from something else in the night sky, where two falling stars streaked from west to east. The sense of wrongness became unease. The Outcast and his warning swam across her mind. What had he meant by saying she would come into his grasp soon? Did he speak of a raid on this trading party, foreseen by one so damned that the future lay open like a fresh wound?

"What is amiss?" the duke whispered in her ear.

"Sentries will patrol all night?"

"We are safe enough here. There's not sufficient game to attract many predators." The duke reached up to grasp something from behind in the darkness beyond firelight. He thrust his liquor bottle in her face. "Drink. It'll bring sleep."

"I'm not permitted strong—"

"Hald has no authority over you now. It's my choice." His hand squeezed her shoulder in warning. Ashira pulled the stopper, propping up on an elbow to take a very small sip. The fumes went up her nose. She choked.

"Again," he said.

"It's making me feel strange. Why would anyone in their right mind want to drink this muck?"

"A criticism, lady? Very brave, considering your position. I imbibed because I've never killed a girl. I had no wish for a clear memory of the deed."

"Why didn't you . . . kill?"

"Let's say I prefer proof of ill-intent. Is Hald planning a night raid?" He took back the liquor, tensing against her as he waited for answers.

"He didn't tell me. I heard the horn calls to warn of strangers and was summoned into his presence, where he traded me away. I didn't see him outside of your company for more than a few heartbeats." Ashira didn't think Hald had any plan. She considered telling the duke, but decided against it. How could she tell him about the Outcast's threat without revealing that she was a War Maid? No other Gold Band lady was allowed outside the fort unless in the company of the ruling lord.

"Now I've unsettled you again. Still frightened by strange sounds in the night?"

"Something isn't right." Ashira examined her feeling of disquiet, wriggling a fraction nearer to him. Again Copperhead's warning stirred her. And falling stars meant death; each star took a soul into the great abyss. In the distance, a lone wolf howled a message, answered by a dreadful chorus.

"Night terrors," he said, tensing despite the calm tone of his voice. "The Wild Hunt rides."

"We're in danger?" Ashira said. "Will it attack? I once heard troopers talking of it. They went closed-mouthed when they saw me."

"I'm not surprised. The Wild Hunt is not a subject for ladies. Have no fear, we are not targets."

"It takes people, doesn't it?" Why the secrecy, if the rumors weren't true? Fear jangled her nerves.

"Ashira, if I tell you of this thing, it is not to be shared with other ladies, any females or children. Is that agreed?"

"Yes, my lord."

"I'll hold you to that." He paused as if collecting his thoughts. "Harvesters protect us, care for us and receive absolute devotion in return. Should any individual betray the teachings of priests, the punishment extends to both this world and the afterlife. Outcasts cease to be children of the Harvesters at the instant of sentence. When they die we assume they go to one of the seven hells."

"Don't they?" Ashira shifted in his arms so that she lay on her back.

"Being godless is a terrible wound. Some of them have

reverted to pagan beliefs. They worship the Horned One, a hunter riding at the head of a fearsome pack in the silence of night. Each kill made by an Outcast is dedicated to a god who wallows in blood. In return, they believe they will join the Wild Hunt in an afterlife. The pack is supposed to appear just before a dark one dies, if you want to believe that nonsense."

"Do you?" Relieved and curious, she tried to see his expression in the firelight. Too many flickering shadows spoiled her attempt.

"Were I an Outcast, I might be tempted. Now do you understand why this subject is restricted by our priests and why we are safe from harm?"

"Yes, my lord."

"Having humored you, I don't expect any nightmares. Go to sleep." He shifted his shoulder into a more comfortable position and closed his eyes.

Ashira obeyed the familiar male authority, letting sleep come in a fume-filled fog.

Cold dampness woke her the following morning, leaving the dregs of a disturbing dream like a bad taste in her mouth. A dark, damp, closed-in sensation and the sound of dripping, together with something malevolent that lurked just out of sight, teased at the edge of her consciousness. Whatever it was . . . hunted. She rubbed her eyes, trying to clear the memory.

The duke's cloak remained, a reminder of the night. Mist shrouded their camp, drenching her face with dew, and his deep voice shouted orders from nearby, jarring her aching head. Starting up, her hand touched something warm and scaly. A movement against her body brought her to her feet, forcing a cry of horror from her lips.

Men came running, the duke at their head. He looked around for a threat and finding none, raised his eyebrows in question.

"Snake." Ashira trembled, pointing at his cloak. She couldn't abide snakes.

The duke snatched at the edge of the garment to gaze in contempt at the reptile slithering for cover. He made a sudden grab, catching it just behind the head. "You fled from this?" He waved the thing. "Look at it. Can't you tell it's harmless?"

Ashira backed away shuddering, unable to take her eyes off the squirming reptile. The duke stalked off with the creature, throwing it outside their camp. Though he did not mention it again, his face still reflected irritation when they breakfasted on cold lamb.

Soldiers broke camp and the company prepared to set off without anyone finding a mount for Ashira. The duke lifted her onto his stallion and vaulted into the saddle behind her.

"Loosen up, girl. You're as stiff as a post," he said.

"I can ride. Why must I double? Since I am your possession, running back to Menhill isn't an option. Where else can I go?"

"I don't have any spare mounts, and you are light. Besides, it's easier to talk thus."

"More questions I can't answer?" Ashira sighed.

"No, teaching you sense." One of his arms wrapped around her waist. "The wilderness is not the place for frightened children. The scene you created back there could have alerted a predator. They smell fear. Lessons in wilderness skills will begin with that poor little reptile you scared. Grass snakes have black spots and a light collar, while vipers bear a distinctive zigzag along their backs. Snakes aren't a problem compared with saurians. They are the reason we must all be on our guard."

Instruction continued all morning, giving Ashira a new perspective on life outside a fort. Surprised at his detailed knowledge of nature, she began to enjoy his patient mentoring despite herself.

Just after midday, the company halted by a shallow stream

to water the horses. A quartermaster handed out rations of flat-bread and cheese to those not busy. Apparently more trusted now, Ashira was allowed to walk over to a flat rock slanting down into rushing water just upstream of the animals. She un-buttoned the top two fastenings on her gown to wash her face and neck, the cool water pleasant after the heat and dust of the ride.

A hand on her shoulder brought a stifled cry of shock. She hadn't heard the duke approaching. Her hands went to fasten her dress, but he brushed them aside, pulling down the neck of her dress to bare her shoulders. She flinched when his hand touched a sore spot.

"This wasn't my doing. These bruises are too old," he said, his voice quiet. "Women don't hit with such strength. That leaves your father as the only male permitted to touch a princess. Stay as you are while I get some liniment." He returned soon after, squatting down behind her.

He knew what he was doing with his massage. A warm glow from the sharp smelling potion began to ease the soreness.

"If I can devise some sort of privacy when we camp tonight, I'll treat the rest, the ones I saw lower down. Thrice damned weasel, there are other ways to discipline. You'll never feel my hand, I swear." Uther buttoned up her gown again to the highest bruise. His breath touched hot on her neck, and then his lips firmed against her skin in a swift salute.

"Maybe not your hand but I'll feel the point of your knife if I'm judged guilty of offending against you." Although aware of his right over her destiny, the memory of his kiss thrilled through her.

He nodded once. "Betray me and you will have a problem. Can I know why Hald was so brutal?"

She had never truly known. Maybe he had made her a War Maid because she resembled her mother; maybe so that she was in danger and might be accidentally killed without any repercussions. But now, had Uther's coming seemed like the perfect opportunity to dispose of her? She looked away. Certain men, like her father, bitterly resented having a War Maid as a wife. Once again, Ashira wondered why her father had ever married such a woman, knowing that he hated what her mother was – a thought brought on by her own swiftly arranged marriage, clearly motivated by Hald's own greed. What kind of bride-price had tempted him in overcoming his loathing long enough to convince the bride's family the match was good? It must have been huge.

Uther moved round to sit at her side. He washed his hands in the waters, wiping them dry on his cloak. "Then I must assume you were caught with some unsuitable man. Reason enough for a thrashing and swift marriage."

"I didn't," Ashira protested, burying her face in her hands.

"I am aware that someone who doesn't know how to kiss is a total innocent. I shall assume Hald forestalled a potential liaison." He slapped at a black fly on his cheek, squashing it, then cupped a handful of water to wash his face. A day's growth of beard hindered his effort.

"There's a bit by your nose still," she said, hoping to turn a delicate subject.

"Get it off. I don't want to look like an Outcast."

Ashira wet the edge of her torn sleeve and attended to the mess. There was a tiny line in the stubble by his lower lip. She scrubbed to find an old scar. Odd that Uther hadn't taken his wound to a priest for perfect healing. Only Outcasts bore battle scars, regarded as stigmas of evil, and yet he had just objected to looking as unclean as one of them.

When a soldier came to report all horses fed and watered, Uther lifted her onto his horse, taking care to avoid gripping her bruises.

Rain began to drizzle just as the trail dipped down from open moors into more wooded land. Uther called a halt to allow his band to change into wet gear. He wrapped his own cloak around Ashira, and then resumed his wilderness instruction when they set off once more. "See the sky? No birds or bird song are signs of a big predator."

At sunset, a bare hill circled with concentric depressions of ancient earthworks came into sight. It gave a clear view from all sides, but the duke appeared uneasy; Ashira sensed his tension on ordering a camp here.

Just as the company cleared the trees, a commotion behind brought the duke around. Ashira froze, horrified, catching sight of a saurian mutant – one of the dangerous flying lizards. It had a wingspan of twenty feet, a length of at least two horses combined with the hooked feet and the curved bill of a raptor. In those talons now hung a bleeding soldier plucked from his saddle by a gliding swoop none had heard coming. His screams shocked his comrades into action. Arrows pelted the lithe reptile, but fell back to earth, useless against its scaly hide. It flapped for lift, clutching its struggling trophy. A loud honking call announced both its victory and its indifference to the puny, creeping creatures below.

"Aim for the man, damn you!" Uther yelled. "Give him mercy!"

The screams ceased when a second flight of arrows found their target. Swearing, the duke urged the company forward.

A detail of silent soldiers closed off a deep trench in the hill for animals with another higher up, sporting a canvas stretched across the gap and pegged down for people to shelter underneath. It made a protection of sorts from attack or unkind elements. The duke left Ashira sitting under this crude dwelling while he detailed night watch.

After he'd gone, she unbound her sodden locks to towel the

wetness out on the hem of her shift. The sight of the screaming man impaled on talons wouldn't leave her. His death, a mercy killing, shocked her just as much. The thought that a flight of arrows from his comrades offered a better end than the saurian sickened her. She had just finished drying in the gloom when the duke ducked under the canvas, his dark hair curling from the rain.

"I'm taking first watch." He pulled a rueful face, looking at her exposed legs with regret. "Look lively, girl. You're with me. I don't intend to waste time searching for you if we're attacked again."

"Surely it won't come back," Ashira objected, smoothing down her clothing. She didn't want to stand in the rain after all her efforts to get dry.

"Saurians form pair bonds. At this time of year they'll have a nest of young. Our poor lad won't satisfy that brood."

Ashira sighed, clambering to her feet.

The duke positioned three men on the high side of the animal trench, taking the lower side himself with two soldiers and Ashira. "Sit here, but any trouble and you get down with the beasts. Keep low for safety," he said, already scanning the skyline. "Saurians make speed runs, bringing them in near the ground for a strike."

Rain pelted downward from the blackening sky. When a bright flash snaked to earth, all resigned themselves to getting soaked through. Thunder rumbled while the heavens opened in fury. A soldier grumbled about the weather to a comrade across the ditch. At least, he reasoned, they were safe from ornisaurs in this deluge. Seconds later a flapping wet-leather sound had them peering through blinding rain. The soldier stepped forward just as a huge shape swung over the crest of the mound, catching him squarely in the face. A sickening click sounded as his neck broke.

Uther swung his sword, aiming a mighty blow against one

huge wing as the saurian flapped for lift. The creature dropped its prey and landed, huffing in pain and frustration, jaws snapping at its isolated assailant. It stood a good four feet taller than the duke, an advantage offset by its clumsy movements on the ground, where it used its clawed wingtips both for balance and as weapons to keep all but its victim at bay.

Ashira grabbed the dead man's sword. A shout behind brought her about, blade held ready. Another saurian crested the rise in a killing swoop. She leapt, aiming for its throat. The next instant both crashed to ground. The beast's talons raked her arm when she struggled clear from under the astonishingly light beast. She blocked the pain, intent on the fight. The rank smell of reptile came to her with a hiss of agony from the creature as a soldier sliced into its neck. It shuddered from the mortal blow. She ran to the duke.

He circled, looking for an opening while he danced away from those snapping jaws. Ashira sliced into its tail. Using half-furled wings like another set of limbs, the beast turned to face this second threat, its breast exposed for Uther's deep thrust to the heart. It swayed, legs buckling and blood gushing from its beak, and then it crashed down, to twitch and spasm in death throes.

A warm wetness trickled down Ashira's arm as the thrill of battle ebbed. Uther strode to her side; he grabbed her shoulders and shook her. Men dashed round them, quieting mounts, making sure of kills, setting watch, leaving her isolated in an island of pain and angry voices. Uther's face to faded back into an incredible distance. His mouth moved, but she couldn't hear his voice. She stumbled, dropping her sword. Blackness dragged her down into velvet depths.

4

Earth Date 3892

CITY LIGHTS REFLECTED a blue haze off the plasglass dome separating Avalon from the ocean depths, his prison, the specimen jar where he would be studied until of no further value. Arthur settled down against an exhaust vent poking out of the flat rooftop.

Far beneath, railpods rumbled, ground runners hissed, intruding on his thoughts. Upon the rooftop of Sanctuary, the private citadel of the seers of Avalon, he sprawled in his place of refuge above the incessant motion. Images of the forbidden surface world mingled with the Outcast's history. Her world held the same sights and smells as his dreams of the land – a disturbing discovery.

A signature of thought-patterns alerted Arthur to a stalker. "Rooftops don't make good beds. Circe, your enthusiasm amazes me."

"Hiding again?" Her voice carried the overtones of hurt. "We had an appointment."

The skin-tight bodysuit she wore betrayed tremors in her delectable physique. She'd dressed to thrill: the emerald green color matched her eyes to perfection.

"Shall I ask Evegena to assign another breeding mistress to you?" Her lower lip sucked in, eyes brightened with unspilt tears.

Distressed to see her delicate features cast in such a sorrowful expression, Arthur opened his arms. She nestled down against him, her head over his heart. He stroked the smooth, golden hair that cascaded in waves down her back.

"How about we talk instead of arguing over my seed?"

Her eyes opened wide. "You want to talk? Other males prefer—"

He touched her lips with a finger to stop those ugly words. "I'm not others. I want your opinion on something."

Circe's brows drew together. She would have pulled away if he hadn't held her.

She's not happy, either. He offered comfort in the way he'd learned from her – not a sexual kiss, but a light touch that caressed, moving from her mouth to her neck for a leisurely return.

She turned away before he could recapture her lips. "Tell me what you wish to hear." The brightness of her tone sounded brittle to his ears.

"Honest answers, based on your own opinion."

She looked away. A single tear traced a path down her cheek. Arthur cupped her chin in his hand.

"Should I take vows to become an initiate?" He sensed her confusion in the peripheral thought-patterns streaming from her consciousness. In that moment, he was almost tempted to conform, until images of the surface world flooded his thoughts.

She raised one eyebrow. "Initiates can access the Archive at will."

"That's the catch."

"I know you wanted to find your ancestry. That is why you are accessing Shadow's records, isn't it? In case she saw one of your parents." Her brows drew together in a pretty frown. "Evegena's gifts are double-edged. Acolytes change when they evolve into initiates. You probably wouldn't be interested in who your kin are, or were, once you became an extension of the Archive."

"If I don't take the vows, I risk becoming addicted to sensory playback." He paused. "You didn't tell anyone I found a way to access the Archive, did you?" He had given up on finding his parents in the time he had left before Evegena's ultimatum expired. What he needed was an escape from Avalon that re-searching Shadow might provide. Circe's answer confirmed his fears and his resolution.

"No, but you must give up those sessions." She touched his cheek with her small hand. "Are you near finding answers to your ancestry, or are you drawn more by the outer world sensations?"

Arthur drew her against his chest, happy to be with her. He inhaled the heady aroma of her hair, and her skin. The Outcast study gave him a frame of reference to judge himself. Shadow was accounted stable, despite her elevated psi-factor. Could he walk in her path? In this moment, he wanted the impossible: a life with Circe, but a life in the outer world. He would have to convince her to come with him if he left, yet he feared she would never agree

"Circe? Would you like to spend the night with me, in my room?" She ran one finger over his lips in a way that fired his loins.

"I'll be prepared for the dreams this time."

Arthur fought to keep his tone level. "Not a problem. They haven't troubled me since the first Archive session." Her relieved smile thrilled through him.

Later, Arthur held her until she slept, her mouth curved up in a sweet smile that did things to his heart. She knew he'd with-held viability again, and yet she looked content. The thought of his continued deception troubled him. Evegena would reassign Circe if he refused to give viable seed. He didn't want to think of her with someone else, and yet neither did he want to give up a child that would be part of them both, especially now.

The Archive's call thrummed in his mind as if it had waited for this moment. Arthur intensified Circe's sleep pattern; she wouldn't know he'd left her for the hour a session would take.

He dressed in the dark and once more trod the path of temptation. However much Arthur stood to gain or lose, he deferred his final decision until he reached the small room and stood in the presence of the Archive, choosing to acquire more data in that moment. "How did the Outcast evolve into a war leader?"

"The human psyche can sustain a limited degree of misdirection." The Archive's vocalization echoed in an empty room. "Over-stimulation results in crisis."

"People heal." Arthur took his position. "It's in their nature."

"Biological intelligence is subject to change with each additional input of data, cause and effect."

His doubts surfaced. Personalities didn't alter overnight. He set controls for an interface link of one standard hour.

*

Earth Date 3874

A FAINT WAXY TANG of burning candles and the smooth crackle of clean sheets roused Ashira. Shadows danced on a high ceiling, strange leaping shapes on rounded buttresses. A black form unwound from a corner to stretch a terrifying height when illumination caught it, bringing the fragments of a dream memory into sharp focus.

"Welcome home," a deep voice murmured.

The threatening shadow made Ashira ball her fists.

"Easy, I'm not starting a war. I just didn't want you waking up alone in a strange place." The black form lit a brace of candles.

Now she recognized the duke, fear drained into urgent thirst. A pitcher and a goblet rested on a bedside table. He poured water for her, sliding an arm under her shoulders to raise her while he held the vessel to her lips. Blessed moisture flooded her mouth, but he forced her to take sips when she wanted to swallow a river.

"More." Her voice wavered, sounding strange to her ears.

"Wait a few moments, or it will revisit." He held the goblet out of her reach, frowning. "I thought I'd have to build a funeral pyre for a while, but my priest informs me that your fever has run its course. We were too late for him to prevent scarring, I'm sorry for that."

Ashira ran her tongue over cracked lips. Outcasts had scars. "Has the merchandise been spoiled?" Her voice croaked, an ugly sound.

He knew her for a War Maid and scarred. What happened to discarded possessions? Why did he bring her to his home?

"Someday, when you choose to be pleasant, I might show you all my scars." A quirky smile lit his stern features. He eased her back against soft pillows. "Meanwhile, there are clean garments on top of my clothes press. When you feel stronger, bathing facilities are through the entrance to your right. Try to get some more sleep."

Standing, the duke clicked his heels to execute a short, formal bow before marching for the door. Disappointment flowed through her at the sight of his departing back. Why didn't he shout at her for concealing her battle skills? *His* clothes press, he had said, *his* rooms and not the women's quarters. He wanted her to sleep. Her eyelids drooped already. What manner of man could permit her to live after the cruel trade her father had enforced? He hadn't tried to hurt her. He eased her pain. Why? Despite her questions, Ashira welcomed sleep's dark wings.

Consciousness returned by degrees. Warmth and then light made her aware of a throbbing ache in her arm. The room spun when she opened her eyes. She reached for more water, but the duke's advice made her sip rather than gulp. She'd no wish to have a return visit of the fluid, not with her throat already raw.

The smell of blood and sweat offended her nose. She became aware of her naked body under the bedding. A clean nightgown lay on top of the duke's clothes press. Lights danced in her eyes when she tried to stand and seek the bathing room. Walls slipped sideways. She crawled, ignoring the pain radiating from her shoulder to her wrist. She refused to look at the damage.

The cleansing room surprised her with a tub against one wall, but no pitchers of heated water nearby. Wheels attached to metal tubes seemed to hang over the structure. He wasn't cruel. He wouldn't have lied about this. Minutes later, she had her answer: one wheel, when rotated, provided hot water, and the other spewed out cold. A bench by the tub offered a selection of aromatic unguents in haphazard order, drying sheets stacked neatly on a shelf underneath. Ashira enjoyed the first hot bath she could remember.

Sliding back into bed wearing a clean nightgown represented bliss for her. Warm, comfortable and very tired, she slipped almost immediately back into slumber. A touch on her face wakened her to the duke by her bedside.

"Feeling better?"

"I thank you, yes."

His hand strayed to her tangled hair. "Will you let me make repairs? It would be a shame to hack all this off." Smiling, he reached to a shelf beyond her range of vision for a comb. A muscular arm snaked under her to lift her to a sitting position. She fought to stay awake as the walls began to move. "Just relax."

His voiced soothed her as he got to work. He didn't pull at her hair the way servers did, but held each lock while he teased out the tangles. Ashira marveled at his patience as she inhaled the faint hint of musk and leather coming from him. She closed her eyes.

"How many other Gold Band ladies are there at Menhill?" he asked. "Or were you the one and only?"

"My half-sister Syril." His closeness began to make her feel uncomfortable despite their now married status. It wasn't being alone with a man; War Maids held that privilege, deemed competent to guard their own honor . . . no, more embarrassment at the thought of why he visited.

"Younger?"

"Older by three years." Ashira answered, wondering at his interest.

"Did she receive beatings too? I took a good look at the damage while you slept. Hald's a cruel man."

Blood rushed to her face. He'd inspected the merchandise thoroughly when she couldn't object. "Syril is his favorite. As for me . . . it was almost as if I didn't belong to him."

"Were that the case, you would have been a Silver Band at best, if he had even let you live. So she wasn't pretty enough to attract admirers?"

"I am the plain one." Shame burned through her. "Syril has nice, straight hair, a lovely light red color."

Uther studied her face. One eyebrow quirked up as he turned her head to inspect her profile, making her blush again.

"Rusty hair, a beak big enough to make any goose envious and a dark mole by her mouth?" He laughed when she nodded. "I wouldn't give her bed room if I were a Bronze Band. I saw her spying from a doorway just before Hald turned up. She ruined her disguise as an unveiled Silver Band by making an important-looking server bow." He released her to finish combing another tangled strand.

"They all say I've got a commoner's face, and they're right."

"Different, in a very feminine way, but not coarse by any standards." He rotated her face to study it from every angle. "Tell me, did you always meet your lover at dawn, away from Menhill?"

"I am a maiden." Ashira met his eyes in angry challenge, daring him to deny her, and puzzled by his placement of her movements when his time inside Menhill had been so brief.

The duke frowned. "I saw a sight I will never forget on the day of our bonding, a War Maid charging through mist like a legend out of time. Know that I didn't connect a sad little girl with the earlier vision until I saw you fight. I might just decide to discipline you, since I gave you an order to run for cover during an attack." He glanced at her arm, his mouth forming a hard line of displeasure.

"Oath breaker." Ashira tried to pull away. "You swore no hitting."

"That was then." He put aside the comb, satisfied with his efforts. "I came to tend the wound."

Ashira bristled at the suggestion. "I wasn't meeting any man that day. I just like riding." She settled back to endure the area being treated. His hands applied the ointment in the same gentle way he had administered liniment to her bruises.

"For the present, rest here until you feel the need to explore. I grant you free run of my fort, but no going outside without my permission." He fingered the neckline of her thin nightgown, one corner of his mouth lifting. "I ordered you a dress to be made by the morning, so no pilfering of my clothing, War Maid. Is this clear?"

"Yes, my lord." Ashira caught her breath. She was not confined to women's quarters. She could go where she wished as long as she stayed inside the fort. Where was the worm in this apple? "Am I required to wear a veil, in case I should want to sneak off for another assignation?"

The duke laughed, standing to pack the healing ingredients back on a tray. "Half my people know what you are and have seen your face. They know better than to incur my anger. Shall I harvest a crop after winter has blighted it? Sleep well, lady."

He bowed and left.

Perhaps he had a woman warming his bed. Relief warred with humiliation. Most rulers raised one daughter as a War Maid to protect sibling honor during a raid. Most also chose a docile partner as mate. He showed no interest now that he had found out her status. Perhaps she was only still alive to enhance his dread reputation.

The promised dress arrived with morning. Timid serving girls, their hair covered by caps, laid it on her bed and handed her a tray with a bowl of porridge and a beaker of milk. They glanced slyly at her as they sidled out.

After finishing breakfast, Ashira discovered how well the gown fitted. With a low neck and flaring three-quarter length sleeves, it showed her wounds. The pastel blue color added to her dislike. One tiny spark of gratitude for freedom prompted her to leave her hair loose, since Uther didn't appear to like braids. She had wondered at the absence of the pins and clips she needed for styling her hair.

Legs like wet cloths slowed her normal stride. Bored and curious, Ashira wanted to see her new home even if it took her all day. Outside her rooms, the corridor bustled with busy workers, but unlike Menhill, this royal level didn't swarm with guards. Servers hurried by without that hangdog cringe, and yet their eyes held a wary appraisal rather than kindness. The scent of stables came from below, calling to her of freedom. He said she had free range of the fort, not outside. At the head of a stairwell, she resolved to go up, clutching at the railing with grim determination.

This fort had smooth cladding on all exposed walls, making it seem brighter than Menhill. Ashira wondered why no mirror shafts lighted the levels. Very unusual, according to her brother's detailed accounts of every fort he visited, detailed to Syril while Ashira listened in the background. He possessed a lively eye for people, particularly possible husbands for his adored sister, trying to bring them into focus in case one should offer for her.

As Ashira wandered past the main entrance, a stiff breeze brought a fresh smell with a trace of salt wetness: a call from outside. Breathing deeply, she started forward, wanting to see the sky again. A guard stepped into her path, blocking off the light.

"My lord is away at Tregelly mine. He left orders." The man met her eyes in steady challenge.

"I wish to inspect the compound. You may escort me," Ashira said, going for a pompous approach Bronze Bands usually found intimidating. She moved forward with confidence. The guard spread his arms to block her passage, while another soldier hurried over to give backup. When they both faced her down, Ashira gathered her shredded dignity and turned away.

Feeling much better the next morning, she made another attempt to reach the outside compound. The young man standing watch called for help, defeating her plans. When told where the duke was, Ashira decided to challenge her beast in his lair. The duke sat at his desk, engrossed in the task of relocating colored pegs on a large, irregular shaped board fixed to a wall. He turned around to face the intrusion.

"Ashira, what a delightful surprise." He gestured to a chair facing him. Once she settled, he went to the door, bellowing orders for breakfast. "Now, what can I do for you? Has someone been impolite? Is the service not to your liking?" He resumed his seat.

"When I wanted to go out, your guards wouldn't let me. I wished to see daylight."

"I'm free after lunch. Come back then, or be quiet while I work, I don't mind which." His mouth tugged up at the corners, as if fighting amusement.

"Am I a prisoner? What is my fate to be?"

"What it is already." He drew his brows together, ignoring

the first part of her question. "When you're healed you will become my wife in more than name."

The duke turned back to his pegboard, meticulously shifting the colored pegs. Ashira watched him, turning over his words in her mind. She wasn't sure she wanted to be a wife, since she thought he might make restrictions on her time when he decided to exercise his rights. She studied him as he continued to ignore her. There seemed a purpose to his actions.

"What are you doing?" she asked, forgetting his request until the words left her mouth.

"Ashira, I'm busy." He took three pegboards from his desk and a box of free worker symbols. "Change all individuals on the third shift and redistribute the others. Put fresh workers from the pool on the first shift, and do it quietly."

He had given her kitchens, laundry and household judging by symbols on the boards. Ashira started by sorting the pool into genders, then experience, and finally age. She studied the assortments already in place before rearranging, just finishing as a plate of cold chicken appeared in front of her, placed there by a silent server. Incredibly, time had flown, the morning gone already with the arrival of midday meal.

The duke inspected her work before he started his own lunch. "Excellent! I would make one amendment—you put a man on the same shift as his wife's mother, but they can't stand each other. Better acquaintance with the people will eliminate the chance of bad placements." He smiled, as if to take the sting out of criticism.

"I am to continue this task?" Ashira paused, fork halfway to her mouth, not daring to believe his words.

"I don't waste potential. Start with the three areas you have, and I'll add the tailor's shop and stores when you're familiar with our people." The duke looked over at her. "Lady, I didn't ask if you wanted this task."

"Yes. Thank you, my lord. I'd appreciate a useful occupation."

Uther threw back his head, laughing in genuine amusement. "Ashira, you know not your worth. I have worried how to keep you occupied, never thinking of work until this morning. I can't confine a War Maid to quarters, doing whatever it is women do, and yet I didn't want you wandering bored, and getting into mischief."

Ashira finished her meal in silence, embarrassed by his kindness. He had just given her unimagined freedom, coupled with incredible responsibility. As far as she knew, no other ruler's wife had ever had such privileges.

After lunch, Uther escorted her around the compound of his fort. Light rain fell from a matte-gray sky as they hurried from one workshop to another. The tanner's cave stank from curing hides, but the smithy intrigued her. Not only weapons of war rested on shelves, but also cooking pots, and in one corner, copper jewelry. Beyond the smithy, the compound ran down to the sea over a rocky shoreline. Ashira walked toward it, fascinated despite the rain.

"Never seen the sea before?" he asked from her side.

Ashira shook her head. "It's so restless."

"Frightened?"

"No. It's comforting . . . like a homecoming." She gazed at the glisten of light on water, the white crests of waves crashing onto rocks. Out of the corner of her eye, Ashira saw his hand reaching for her. The movement paused and fell away.

"Come see my stables," he suggested.

Most of the animals were ordinary workhorses, some larger for farm work, and then a small selection of well-bred mounts. The duke stopped in front of a stall holding an exquisite chestnut mare.

"This one is called Amber. I thought you might like her. Will she suit?"

The deep brown eyes flashed fire; the mare tossed her head proudly. Taken by surprise, Ashira turned to hug her stern husband. For an instant, his arms closed around her, and then he released his hold, as if burned.

"I ordered a riding outfit for you, which should be ready by now. If so, will you ride with me tomorrow, health permitting?" His eyes ran over her, searching, quizzical.

"I'd love to, my lord." A chance to ride again! Her chest contracted as she waited for the catch. "Are there matters you wish to oversee?"

"I thought I'd ride out to my nearest tin mine. They complain of losing stock to predators, but I'd see the evidence myself before I organize a hunt. And no, if I do, you can't come. Despite the fact I've never seen anyone heal so fast, I'd prefer you to regain full strength."

"I'm—"

"Ashira, I'll make my point the easy way this time. In future, I don't expect argument." The duke took her good arm in a firm grip. "We are going to my weapons practice hall where you will prove to yourself your need to recover."

The room took space from the royal level situated, she guessed, over the soldiers' barracks. Fixed against one long wall, a sword rack displayed various sized weapons with assorted grips. Unlike Menhill, where planking had raised the floor of the training room, this surface showed the wear of usage on rock making the ground uneven. To fight here meant using every ounce of skill she possessed.

The duke grabbed both her hands in a swift, shocking maneuver. He raised one eyebrow at her clenched fists. Ashira blushed remembering the last time she hid her hands from him. He'd demanded the kiss of peace from her then. She opened her hands, letting him run the ball of his thumbs against the calluses on both.

"More secrets? A fighter who can trade sword hands at ease is an asset."

He released her, marching to the wall for a short, light sword. Watching his easy stride, Ashira had a sickly feeling that his discovery was not new. If he had seen her hands before, then he must have looked at them while she slept. She couldn't meet his eyes when he handed her the weapon. The whisper of his sword drawing called her back into the moment.

"The weapon you have is yours to keep. It belonged to me as a boy." He raised his blade, taking up a battle stance. "Prepare to fight."

She didn't want to fight with sharp weapons. Her arm ached, even though she held her sword in her left hand. She struck. The shock of connecting with his blade sent waves of red hot needles through her injury. Again, she pressed the attack, and once more, he blocked her blows until she stood trembling, helpless before him.

"I order you to rest in your rooms for the remainder of this day." The duke returned to the weapons rack for a sword belt and attached short knife. He took her sword to slide it into its scabbard. "I'll have a meal sent down."

"I'm not tired," Ashira lied. "I just need to get my breath."

The duke wound his arm around her waist, forcibly marching her to her rooms. He pushed her over the threshold, following behind. Ashira whirled to face him.

"Lady, you tried to disobey my orders yesterday, and again, I suspect, this morning. Don't back me into a corner you'll regret when I'm trying very hard to keep the peace. Please have the decency to meet me halfway." He executed a curt bow, dumped her weapons on a side table and left her to reflect on his leniency.

5

Earth Date 3874

A NEAT STACK OF CLOTHING rested next to the armaments when Ashira awoke in the morning. On top lay a daisy, overblown, wilting, and giving off that sharp tang of a blossom not meant for picking. It wasn't much of a flower, yet he must have searched for it outside the barren compound. A frisson of unease ran through her.

Uther's choice of riding clothes offered another revelation; soft, black leather breeches and a long-sleeved, matching tunic fastening down one side with the front and back; a full black cloak and knee-high boots completed the outfit: he had fitted her out as a soldier. Ashira found him waiting in his business room after she breakfasted in her quarters. She decided not to comment on the flower on the way down to the stables.

Amber was already saddled, along with the coal-black stallion she remembered from their journey. The duke boosted her up, and they rode out into a warm, sunny day. Light glistened off mounds of cresting waves that crashed against rock to spit foam. Towering cliffs housing Tadgell clawed at the skyline. Harsh grayish-black flint offered scant refuge for a few ragged clumps of vegetation clinging to narrow ledges. Air-shafts marred the jagged face at regular intervals, mole-blind pits of darkness – a stark exterior concealing the comfort and light within. Moving away from the fort, strands of sunlight pierced through a leafy canopy covering a trail winding through a rock-strewn glen. They passed a waterfall where droplets hung in crystalline wetness on nearby branches. This avenue of natural beauty terminated in harsh moorland with stunted trees, deformed into submission by elemental forces run wild.

Uther led the way over raw headland, riding south and east until they came to a bleak valley littered with dross. A muddy stream at the bottom was flanked by working bal-maidens dressing the tin ore. A collection of well-kept cabins, some with laundry dancing in the wind on lines outside, stood grouped near a great wooden wheel. Harnessed to a huge cog, large draft horses powered the device.

"Not a pretty sight, although it makes us self-sufficient," Uther said.

A mine overseer hurried out to meet his master. Worry lines creased his face. Ashira reined in her mount to wait while they talked. The man gestured over to the south of the settlement. After a few minutes, the duke rejoined her.

"It's a large cat of some sort. None claim to have seen it, just the pugmarks, and they're missing a pig. Since children watch stock, I must take their complaint seriously, even if the wretched animal wandered off on some mission of greed. I'm told the marks are by that grove of oaks. It might just be deer tracks— these people are miners, they rarely take note of nature." He sent her a lopsided grin.

There were pugmarks when they looked, not that big, and just one predator, enough to make Uther frown.

"A lion?" Ashira dismounted to kneel by him.

"No, too small, both in size of paw and stride, and see here, the animal goes lame. I told them not to set traps in these woods.

The beast wouldn't come near people unless starving. Wild moor ponies and deer are its normal prey. Now it can't run."

"Would it take a child?"

"In a heartbeat. I'll send out a platoon. They can make that thrice-damned fool of a headman collect all his traps before they set a lure." The duke mounted and set off at a brisk pace.

The wind in her face, Ashira raced after him. Her braid, too swiftly tied this morning, now came loose and her hair streamed behind her. Her husband reined in at the headland above his fort, wheeling to watch as she galloped up to join him.

"I want to show you something," he called. "Follow me. Amber knows the way."

The duke urged his mount toward a narrow gully with Amber following. This was not treacherous slate, but weathered granite, laced with mica. Ashira had no inkling of what awaited until the last tortuous twist revealed a golden stretch of sand. The sea glistened a wet gray as it rippled to shore. She inhaled the salty air, thrilled to be so close to the water at last, while Amber picked up her pace, joyfully cantering across the yellow softness. Ashira knew what her mare wanted: to race breakers across the cove. They followed that other happy pair in a mad dash against nature's fury. A laugh born of pure joy burst from her when spray crashed under pounding hooves, a magical moment, frozen in time, as horse and rider shared the pure essence of life, moving as one in wild excitement. Amber slowed at the far side of the cove where the others waited. The duke laughed, dismounting to remove the harness and whack his mount on the rump. The stallion charged to the surf, screaming his defiance.

"Let Amber run. It's her reward for getting you here." Uther settled down with his back to a sun warmed rock.

Ashira released the mare, watched her run off, and then wandered over to a nearby rocky outcrop. High tide had left seawater trapped in a depression. Among the rock-anchored weeds, a leaf-shaped creature walked sideways, waving two raised fore-limbs at another of its kind.

"Ashira, I want to talk."

"I hear you, my lord," she replied absently, half turning.

"Is it so difficult to use my given name?" His arms crossed behind his head to provide a comfortable rest, but his face betrayed harsh control around the mouth. "Am I so formidable?"

"No . . . Uther. You are . . . generous." Ashira looked down at the rock pool where the two creatures were squaring up against each other, claws waving.

"A very careful description, Ashira. I'm a soldier who has spent the last ten years consolidating an initially weak position." He squinted up at her, into the sun. "In the first four years of my rule, there were five attempts on my life. Even now someone occasionally thinks he's going to get lucky. I haven't had time for social visits or court attendance, and I wouldn't have come to Menhill except by Alsar's express command. A man does not ignore his high king."

Ashira rounded on him, understanding now why he had chosen this isolated spot for his disclosure. "Why is Alsar interested in Menhill?"

"He's trying to place his widowed niece." The duke closed his eyes, wriggling for a more comfortable seat in the sand. "Childless after six years of marriage, she lost her home to her late husband's nearest male kin. Alsar had an idea she might prove acceptable to an older man like your father, who already has an heir."

"The Black Dragon Duke rushes off to be matchmaker," Ashira said.

"I'm Alsar's kin on the distaff side, one reason I still rule." Uther smiled, seeming to enjoy the warmth on his face. "If he withdrew his support, Tadgell would be under siege within the month. My mines are all like the one you saw today:

indefensible. Start a few fires on the lowest levels . . . the whole lot collapses, cutting off my barter power, even if I win. We can't survive without the ore."

"Will he withdraw support because you didn't have an opportunity to speak with my father?" Ashira was sorry she'd goaded him. He was not responsible for their forced marriage.

"No consequences apart from being a laughing stock if Alsar lets the reason out." The duke shaded his eyes, watching her. "When I sent my messenger, I said for him to tell my kinsman I wouldn't mate a corpse to that mind-sick monster. I agree a quick union is necessary for one as willful as you, but not in such callous fashion. It was more like an act of vengeance. Just how offensive were you?"

"I tried to stay out of his way. He couldn't accept my mother as a War Maid, and that dislike included me, though why he chose to have me trained as a War Maid when he loathed the concept is strange. Maybe he jumped at the chance to be rid of me before my brother's bride arrived." Ashira turned away, near to tears. Hearing another opinion on her father's rejection reopened old wounds.

The sea creatures were now locked in combat inside their small world. A rustle of movement behind, and Uther held her close against him. This unexpected comfort loosened her self-control. She tried to swallow a sob, failed and spun round to bury her face against his chest. The duke stroked her hair as she gave way to a need for grief. His presence first comforted, and then embarrassed her. She tried to push away, stifling sobs, but with low rocks on three sides and him in front she had no escape.

His brows drew together, more in apparent concern than displeasure. "I hadn't any intention of trading with Hald. Only the top layer was high-grade ore, the rest—dross. I believe I got the better bargain." He flashed a wide grin. "We'll never be able to visit. Do you mind?"

Ashira got a sudden picture of Hald's face when he found out. A giggle bubbled up, one she tried to smother against Uther's tunic, but he made her look at him. His eyes sparkled with mischief.

"My bride needs a firm hand, and I've let matters ride too long, methinks." He stooped toward her. "Patience deserves a reward."

Ashira turned away at the last moment, embarrassed, causing his lips to land near her ear. "So the man doesn't rate respect. What of the ruler? Kiss the wicked Dragon Duke, heartless girl. Obey your master."

A direct order evoking deliberate authority demanded instant obedience. Caught, Ashira suppressed a shudder, closing her eyes. Uther expected more than a chaste salute. He exacted a slow revenge, tasting her, gentle now that he had won. His aura of power and physical strength sent thrills through her. Ashira earned release after he made her kiss him back. He freed her, laughing. "There's a promising start. With more practice, you might become quite skilled."

Uther's arrogance and her shame at the betrayal of her own body prompted Ashira to grab the nearest weapons, a handful of pebbles. She threw them at him, one by one, hitting each time.

"Pax, wild one!" he called, trying to dodge her missiles. "I brought you here for another reason, too. The tide's low enough now to leave no evidence from our boots. Please Ashira, it's important." He wasn't smiling now.

She lowered her arm, dropping her remaining stones. Uther took her hand, leading the way around the cliff where it reached the sea. There was a narrow cave entrance out of sight from above and either side, unless a searcher happened upon the opening by chance. The duke drew her in after him until they came to a high protuberance. He reached up to extricate a torch, lighting it with one strike of a flint to reveal a narrow crevice. This led into a small cavern above the highest watermark. A passage continued up into the rock, but Ashira looked to the contents of this place. Sealed jars and other containers lined one wall. They contained supplies and equipment needed to keep body and soul together for about ten days, and then ensure the occupants would be well equipped to survive in the wild.

"A safety measure my father began. The far tunnel leads out to a small entrance under a bush on the headland." The light from his torch made dancing patterns on his face. "If there's a need, go to High Fort. Alsar protects kin."

"I'm nothing to him." Ashira doubted a stranger would lift a hand for her.

"You're my duchess. Even if the ceremony was a few brief moments of your father's trading, it is sufficient. Alsar knows of our union." Uther started back to the entrance, leaving her little choice but to follow.

When the pair rode into Tadgell the compound thronged with people circled round one bawling calf. A boneless-looking individual, bald and clothed in a saffron yellow robe that spread like a diseased toadstool, stood by the animal – a priest.

Ashira's stomach heaved with a life of its own, and bitter bile flooded her throat. Harvester priests had always evoked disgust from her earliest memories. Her thoughts dragged back to the occasion of her twelfth birthday, when she had received the permanent wristband that marked her status and maturity, that soft, almost oozing touch while the gold band became secured to her for life. She had managed, by some miracle, to clear the inner sanctum before her stomach rebelled with such violence she thought her very innards had spewed forth.

They all looked alike, those disciples, bland faces, empty eyes, and that walk. Did they have wheels instead of legs under those wide robes? Each priest assumed an invisible mantle of power when performing spiritual rites, but given healing tasks, exhibited the same compassion expected from snakes. They were efficient and effective, it was more the complete detachment setting Ashira's teeth on an edge.

The poor little calf looked almost normal. While not an obvious mutation, it was smaller than average and an unusual honey-blond color. If it had two tails, or an extra leg, she might have understood.

Ashira dismounted when grooms rushed forward to get their mounts clear before the purification ritual began. She tried to edge into the fort, but Uther held her arm and steered her to the inner ring. She forced herself to watch when the priest brought his rod of office to bear upon the sacrifice. The calf writhed, screaming in blue fire. Life fled, and a drift of ash floated to ground. Ritual phrases droned over the pathetic remains. The crowd responded, making way for the priest to glide back to his sanctum. Ashira wrenched her arm free to hurry away.

"Lady, come back here." Uther's tone came with a warning authority. An irresistible wave of sickness threatened, her head ached and she wanted privacy.

With seconds to spare, Ashira reached her cleansing room, spending a virtual lifetime evacuating every meal in memory. A bath helped take away the remembered stench of burning flesh, but her headache grew worse. She snuffed all light except the time candle, almost falling into bed.

A calloused hand on her shoulder shocked Ashira awake. She struck out blindly, connecting with flesh. A hard body pinned her down.

"Lady, what have I done to earn your scorn?" Uther demanded, a dark shadow pressing against her.

She recognized the scent of a fighting man and the sharp odor of liquor on his breath. Memories of that other time he'd taken drink flooded through her. He hadn't wanted a clear memory of killing a girl.

"Ashira, you disobeyed a direct order given in front of my people. Be warned, my patience is on a very short rein. I'll have your reasons for discourtesy right now. They'd better be good."

The duke's voice sounded quiet and controlled. That control washed over Ashira like a bucket of icy water. He hadn't stormed after her immediately, which said a great deal for how much distance from her he'd needed to bring his temper under control. She had taken his leniency for granted. Now she must face the consequences.

"I'm sorry, my lord. I ask your pardon," she said.

His body remained as tense as a coiled spring about to snap. "Sorry isn't a reason. I'm waiting," Uther replied, his voice even quieter.

"I heard you well enough, but I didn't stop because I wanted to be sick in private."

As much as Ashira hated admitting weakness, she owed him the truth. The duke released her to light the candle on her nightstand. His face resembled a carved mask with hard sapphire eyes.

"I'm listening."

"It was the ritual. I knew what would happen if I watched. I didn't have time to tell you, or I would have lost breakfast in front of all. Uther, I am not very happy at any priest service, but that one has instant effects."

"So when another sacrifice happens I can count on your presence, as long as you are free to leave afterward." The duke's face relaxed. "That is reasonable and fair." He settled on his side, facing her. "This argument wouldn't have happened if we knew each other better. Something we can work on tonight."

"Uther—" she began, to be cut off by his kiss. She didn't try to stop him, remembering how he got his own way on the beach, and she liked his kisses.

He broke away after a while to strip off his tunic and shirt.

Watching her intently, he sat on the side of the bed to pull off his boots and socks. Uther's hands went to the lacings on his pants. Ashira looked away, scared, excited and embarrassed all at once. A slight movement later and his muscular body settled against her. "Your turn." Uther reached for the drawstring on the neck of her nightgown.

She shivered against the feel of air on her breasts as he pulled it down to her waist. He waited, one eyebrow raised in mock challenge until she raised her hips to allow him to strip her lower body of the garment.

"Say now if you want me to stop." His eyes were deep, dark pools.

Candlelight rippled over his naked body. Ashira looked at him, all of him, wanting him to stay and do whatever he wished with her. That strange feeling in her belly started. She reached up to touch those mobile lips of his. He caught her hand, kissing the palm and licking each of her fingers while his knee parted her thighs in a gentle way. Then another deep kiss ended in a gasp when his hands roamed.

"Ashira? Shall I continue?" Uther brushed her lips with one fingertip, tracing the outline.

She caught his finger, drawing it into her mouth, wanting to taste him.

"I'll take that for a yes."

6

Earth Date 3892

"Shadow survived to join the Elite." Arthur aimed his defiance at a bank of winking lights in the gray console. He had the great telepathic control well beyond the limitations of any other; if the elders found out about his research of the Outcast, Sanctuary would have a lever to force him into the initiate program immediately. But if he wanted to leave the city, he would need more information from someone who knew how to live on the surface world and in Avalon.

"Speculation within futile circumstances results in reduction of perspective," the Archive returned. "The subject lowered expectations to preserve logical thought processes."

"Biological intelligence has other resources." Could Arthur lower his standards to obey Sanctuary dictates? No. He wanted more from life than this sequestered existence.

Since his time reviewing Shadow, he had begun to question the rules and practices more and more. At the point of playback, logic told him this pleasant young woman didn't bear any resemblance to the evolved individual under study. So he had to seek out what factor, or accumulation of factors, had caused such a drastic change in personality.

"Archive, why did she leave her mate? I had the impression they reached an understanding."

"This action was not one of her choice."

"Did she quarrel with that priest?" Arthur strolled over to the solitary chair. "What sort of power did he have? Can you explain this religion?"

Another bank of lights winked on at the console. "Harvesters are the same beings known to you as Nestines. The Overworld is their hunting ground, the Terrans, their prey. They control the minds of their 'herd' to the point where they are invisible, using priests to communicate their wishes to their victims. It is possible priests are empty vessels for the direction of power, such as you have already witnessed. Do you remember what the discharge of a priest's stick smelled like, Arthur?"

He remembered the scent of flowers, the sharp tang of animals, and the image, but not the smell of the calf's destruction. All the colors and textures served to remind him of what his life currently lacked. How pathetic that he was reduced to sneaking into a tiny room to steal images from another person's memories. The call of the surface world snagged his soul.

"The next part of our subject's life contains a similar situation. Why don't you refresh your memory? I will not permit any to disturb us." A port slid open to release the umbilicus. It emerged without aiming toward Arthur, appearing content to wait.

Arthur hesitated. "I am still not trained for contact, Archive. Am I at risk of addiction?" Maybe he was looking for an excuse not to continue; he didn't want to see a life destroyed, much less experience it along with the victim.

"What if you were already addicted? Would we be having this conversation?"

Arthur drew in a deep breath to smell nothing in the bland air of Avalon, knowing he would have to make his escape from

Sanctuary soon if he chose this path. The Archive hinted at the reason the Outcast had begun her new existence. Perhaps this session would be the one to help him understand how to survive on the surface. He brushed aside the hair behind his ear to expose his outlet port for the umbilicus.

*

Earth Date 3874

ASHIRA WOKE in the early morning according to the time candle at her bedside, which had burned down to the third notch from its holder. Memories of the night before sent blood rushing to her face, yet a feeling of pleasure remained. Uther, the man, had demanded and received a responsive lover.

In sleep, the duke appeared almost boyish at her side, with long, dark lashes feathering his cheeks, his age betrayed by the rough beginnings of a beard. His bare chest, crisscrossed with mute testaments of past conflicts sliced into curling black hair, reminded her of an earlier promise given when he treated her wound. She thought again how strange it was that he hadn't visited a priest before scars became inevitable. She traced a line near his heart with one finger. A change in his breathing made her look up. He watched her with a half-awake smile.

"Well, wildcat? Have I pulled your fangs?" His eyes began to glitter as sleep retreated.

"Yes." She blushed at the raking look he gave her. "I wish only that our union had been arranged in the normal manner."

"I don't. How many rulers have a wife who leaps into danger when her man is threatened? I know my War Maid isn't going to plant her dagger in my chest when I sleep. How many others sleep so well? Did you know Alsar's third queen took an unholy interest in herbs until he forced her to drink the tonic she offered him? The results, I understand, were quite spectacular. She gave excellent examples of foaming at the mouth and drumming her heels before she died."

"How many rulers wait so patiently for their women to return their love?" Ashira countered.

"I had no inclination to force a virgin. Had you behaved, or responded differently, I would not have pressed my attentions last night." Uther stretched his lean body.

Unaccountably, for a second she imagined she could see his thoughts: in his present mood, she could ask anything. Curiosity goaded her to see if this peculiar side effect of their love-making bore results, or if he would evade her previous question.

"Is it true that you encourage Black Bands?"

Uther reached out to cup her cheek making her face him. His eyes narrowed a little and one eyebrow raised.

"Lady, I am not sure whether you most resemble a child or a butterfly, the way your mind flits from one subject to the next. To ask such a question now . . . Yes, they're welcome to winter here, as you'll see. They have their uses."

"Which are . . . ?"

"My wildcat still has claws. Chastisement is called for." He moved with the fluid grace of a warrior, trapping her, stopping her questions with kisses.

Ashira dissolved in waves of pleasure as his loving became purposeful. He gave no quarter. Her tender lover of the night had a score to settle. His laughter echoed around their darkened chamber when his victory became absolute.

*

Sounds of Tadgell stirring wakened Uther later. He brushed a tendril of hair from his bride's face, waking her and making him sorry to leave a warm bed and a willing woman.

"I've half a mind to insist on face veils." He frowned. "My

woman is far too lovely for others' eyes. Join me for breakfast in my business room as quickly as you can." Uther hurried with his washing and dressing, wanting her again, yet concerned he might scare her.

He strode to his business room in the hope of getting some work done before she arrived to torment his senses. At the threshold, he called to a passing server for two plates of bread and cheese. Uther had just settled at his desk when his second-in-command, Alvic, poked his head around the door.

"There is an Outcast scouting around near Tadgell," Alvic said, one hand straying to the hilt of his sword. "Our morning patrol found a freshly abandoned camp."

Uther pulled out a chart of his territory, a sense of unease growing. "Where?" Alvic leaned over the desk to point out a sheltered valley with easy access to Tadgell.

The place wasn't near a trade route and that disturbed him. "Is he one we know?"

"He's one I wouldn't want to fight alone. Remember Copper from two winters back?"

Uther pictured the auburn-haired Outcast and the man's skill with a blade. His unease grew branches. "I don't recall him causing any upset during his stay." He gestured at the empty chair near the door, and Alvic sat.

"When he wasn't training with you, he worked in the forge. A couple of the girls chased after him, but he made sure never to be alone with them." Alvic looked at the ground. "And there's something else. Lerrys said Copper was at Menhill while you were there. He spotted him riding out with one of their patrols. Now why would Hald need an Outcast? He isn't in conflict with anyone, and neither does he have a saurian problem."

Fear took root. "Are you saying my woman is a traitor?" She had seemed so calm the day her father traded her. He'd taken her attitude for courage, but now he wondered. "She almost died fighting saurians."

Alvic, looked up, his eyes narrowed. "What if Copper is here to snatch her back? Hald didn't come out of his side of the bargain smelling sweet. The High King isn't going to like his treating a Gold Band woman like a bag of turnips, even if he did have kin right."

"Get ten of our best men and two large fishnets," said Uther, deciding against shackles. Catching an Outcast without hurting him was one problem, but holding him always brought a swarm of his Brethren howling for blood. "You look after Tadgell, and I'll deal with the Outcast. He's more likely to hear me out first, before he starts fighting."

"Are you going to take the g— duchess?"

"No. She is learning how to schedule rosters, so keep her busy. I don't want her near Copper."

Ashira and breakfast arrived together. Alvic stood and bowed, excusing himself. She took the recently vacated seat while the server placed the plates of bread and cheese on his desk. He didn't know how to tell her he intended to leave her behind. Uther knew she would never forgive him if he made her appear weak.

He took a deep breath. "I am riding out, but I'll organize all the rosters I haven't already given to you for the next week. It shouldn't prove a problem to oversee, and you'll have my headman, a Silver, to help with any discipline matters." He broke his bread, not wanting to see the hurt in her eyes. "I am also leaving you with my second in command, Alvic, in case of attack. I am assuming you studied defense tactics. Alvic will take responsibility for the mines, but I don't think I'll be gone for more than a week at the most."

"When will you leave, my lord?"

Ashira's frosty tone hurt him more than he wanted to admit. "Lady, I didn't plan this as a personal insult. I have a report of an

Outcast watching Tadgell, and since he is one we know, I would have expected him to visit us. He is very dangerous. I can't sit here waiting for a strike. I have to track him down now that I have you here to take responsibility."

"Is that all, my lord?" Ashira turned to the door.

"No, and don't take that tone with me. Come here." He extended a hand, but when she took it, he hauled her around to sit on his lap. She sat as stiff as a dry thistle head and just as liable to fly apart. He nuzzled her neck, wanting to taste her.

"Let go. Suppose someone comes in," Ashira protested.

"Then my people will see how matters stand between us." He drew her closer, kissing a spot behind her ear he'd discovered to be sensitive. "Shall I shout to the world that I care for my wife? Shall I present a wide target to outsiders for attack by sending another to scout in my place? News travels fast. All eyes will be turned in our direction to detect weakness."

"Truth?" She held her breath.

"That my woman holds my heart balanced on the points of her sharp claws, or that I fear she will be taken for ransom if any suspect?"

"Both." She tried to wriggle around in his arms, but he held fast.

"Why else would I tremble at your mood, steal a kiss from a cold girl? Wretched cat! Do you think I enjoy being subject to your whims, or knowing other men see my treasure's face?" Uther kept one arm around her, using his free hand to feed them both. "Now I remember a question about Outcasts, and I shudder to think what will happen if I don't gratify my lady's every wish."

She relaxed, but the winter mood continued in her formal words: "You are very kind, my lord."

"Kind is an emotion unknown to all Outcasts," he began, hoping to get her focused on the problem and not on his leaving her. "They rarely survive beyond sentencing, thanks to the 'kindnesses' of former family, who track them down without mercy to erase their shame. Kindness is the law allowing forts to destroy Outcasts outside territory posts, so the wretched creatures are hunted for sport. Run to the point of exhaustion, and then allowed to crawl to their own destruction."

"Are you sorry for these criminals?"

"Let us say I can understand how they become as they are." Uther picked her braid undone as he spoke, not liking the golden mass restricted. "Even when working, others regard them as the lowest form of life, scarce spoken to except for orders. After three years, only the smartest of them remain, not the strongest, nor the most skilled in battle. Near total isolation from the rest of humanity makes Brethren ruthless killers. They live from one moment to the next."

"What else do they expect to happen for committing a sin?" She relaxed back against him.

"They have their uses." Uther's heart started pumping hard. He tried to stay away from thoughts of her naked in his arms. "Our plumbing arrangements are the direct result of one Brother's solitary brooding in the cold season. He earned his keep, although my priest resented the alterations."

"Priests make dangerous enemies," Ashira murmured, now nestled against him.

"I didn't have water pipes extended to his domain after he objected to the idea. Cleanliness is an individual choice I wouldn't inflict if the person concerned couldn't take a hint from his fellows." Uther caught a smile from her.

"Now go and make yourself useful. I need provisions for a party of ten over six days, and tell the cook I don't like smoked fish. I know he has a huge store of it that he'll try to lose in my direction."

"Uther . . . if Outcasts are condemned from the moment of

re-banding, unless they find others like themselves, why are there so many of them? How can they escape from forts . . . just one against a band of hunters? Why not kill them on fort territory?"

"Had you not avoided all religious occasions, you would know the answer. They will foul our land with their evil if put to death on their former home ground." He attempted to restrict her curiosity by only answering her last question.

"I don't see how the ill-wishes of a dying deviant can affect a fort."

"Heathen." He couldn't help smiling at her lack of respect for religion. "The evil flows back to the living, where it causes deformed births, disease and even more sin. I don't have to tell a woman how devastating it must be to bear a child to term, learn it is not human and have to watch as the priest performs the ceremony of purification. That is the ceremony you have a problem with I believe? Now be good and do as I asked, and then come back here."

*

Uther had finished his tasks when she rejoined him. While she was busy implementing his orders, he considered what possible distrust his people might feel for her since he knew how fast gossip flew. An idea brought him to his feet and bowing to her; he used the gesture to throw her over his shoulder. She shrieked a little as he carried her to their bedchamber, but he wanted witnesses to his intentions.

Serving women scattered when he marched through the door and dumped Ashira on the bed they'd just finished making. Beyond thought at the vision of her now bared legs, he made an inarticulate gesture of dismissal. Not caring if they were out of sight or not, he unlaced his pants, pulled her skirt higher to thrust deep inside her.

Her dress kept bunching, getting in his way. He paused to take the edge of her bodice in his hands and ripped the thing open to the hem. She gasped, blushing a deep red, making him thrust harder until he released.

Expecting trouble, he tried a kiss, but she turned her face away. "Didn't you think I'd want to get as much as I can of you before I leave?"

"You could have waited until the room was clear."

"They knew what I was about. If they didn't leave before I started, then that isn't my fault." He got his kiss, but she held back. "Ashira, the servers are more likely to obey you if they know how I treasure you."

Her eyelids drooped, and he realized he'd kept her up half the night. "Why don't you get some sleep? I can find my way out of my own fort without you sending me off."

*

Ashira tossed the shredded dress in a corner once he'd gone. She considered creeping into bed, and then decided to change into her riding clothes after a relaxing bath, rather than have someone rouse her in her nightgown. The dress wasn't to her taste anyway, and she enjoyed his attentions more than she let him know. More because she missed Uther already than for any need of protection, she laid her weapons belt on his empty place.

She hoped he would soon return from his encounter with the Outcast. While she knew of them as a War Maid, her knowledge had been slight, until now. The horror of their existence bothered her. Such a one would have no sense of humanity.

Hours later, a recurring bad dream of eyes watching her roused Ashira into a sense of wrongness. Only the time candle glowed, the others had burnt down, not replaced as usual by servers. Instinct guided her hands to her weapon. She eased off the bed and strapped on the belt, not yet sure why. Many footsteps moving nearer sent her hands to her sword.

Her door crashed open. Men rushed in, weapons drawn and torches blazing. Half-blinded, she grasped the hilt. Hands grabbed at her, pinning her arms behind her back. A fist crashed into her temple, making her head whirl, stars before her eyes. Silent soldiers, wearing the duke's own dragon tabards, dragged her out.

Alvic, the duke's second, walked at the head of the men. His face stayed blank when she cried out to him. None of the soldiers registered expressions of any type, looking as if they all walked in their sleep. Down through the fort they went, into Harvester chambers. Shoved from behind, she stumbled into the center of a circle of soldiers with hostile stares. Somehow, this room appeared both brighter and darker at the same time. The walls looked a deeper shade of gray with dark shadows lurking in cracks and crannies. Torches flared as if with a hidden source of fuel. Evil dwelt here.

The priest glided forward, his wide yellow robe swishing as he raised his rod of office. A tongue of power licked toward her. Ashira's world dissolved into a nerve-screaming agony of blue. Pain upon pain, torment built until something snapped deep within.

7

Earth Date 3874

TIME, SPACE, DRIFTED in endless convoluted eddies. A spark of awareness floated, lost, helpless. Pictures formed against a blue background. A white horse changed to chestnut. A dark man's face intent on passion, or was it the foxy face of one enjoying another's anguish? Was this death, or the moment of birth? Shattered fragments of will coagulated slowly. A splintered soul groped for coherence, drawing together strands of itself. Danger registered at a cellular level – the force tearing thoughts apart must not know any remained. There lay the path to extinction.

The soul drifted, no longer attempting to establish will, but allowing feeling to return undetected, absorbing rather than probing. A sensation of weight came first, then pain. Agony heaped on agony. Tears of blood flowed from eyes of molten fire. Screams tore in silent, endless outcry.

Burning sight registered a form, a shape of horror. Blood-red, cat-like eyes bored into the naked mind. The head was wide and flat, covered with thick, armored, scaly plates that tapered to a fleshy, bald crest. No nose, rather, twin breathing-pits where one should be. A mouth like a sword cut snarled, revealing sharp teeth when the creature articulated sound. The soul registered this image as important, to be retained.

Something else: a shadow-shape hovered just at the periphery of vision. A set of matte-black eyes gleamed from the walls of the cavern. The dream-watcher stalked, waiting.

Weightless, drifting, the soul found substance, folding into a waiting shell, a body. Feeling, sensation, sight, sound and smell returned, yet the soul remained wary. Shapes, forms resolved into a circle of rabid men's faces, and one bland visage radiating casual cruelty. The soul writhed in a strange and hostile world. Faint strands of reason floated in the gray madness of its mind. A female once, from a distant recollection, she found she could access the minds around, know their thoughts. They considered her an animal, one who had sinned. Death stalked here. She would have to be very careful.

"Outcast, there is no place among the righteous for sinners," an empty one wearing bright colors droned.

"Trespassers earn one fate," the cruel hunters chanted in unison. She fought for strands of sanity as the empty one, mind bereft of thoughts, approached. Her banded limb lifted to the order of another's will. A claw-like thing settled round her bracelet. What had been golden drained down to black.

From a deep haven of safety, she screamed in silent extremis. A pumping organ expanded beyond limits, exploding, weeping a black ichor. Time moved forward, remorseless.

One floating thought-strand attached to another, then a third and a fourth. Escape or die, said logic. The pair of black eyes glinted out of bare rock, pressing through madness, and then the picture of a four-legged beast came to her. The name came to mind: *Yes, a horse. Must get away—need horse*, logic demanded. She tried to speak her needs, but how to make those sounds? Why could she understand the sounds others made, but not make her mouth move right?

"Hor–se," her dry croak of a voice pleaded.

"The gift is known," one of the hunters said.

"Let it be so. Get this creature away from Tadgehill," the empty one ordered. "This foul sacrifice cannot be completed where it might cause contamination."

Released from invisible restraints, she fell with numb, prickling limbs and was dragged along a dark passage as senses slowly returned, to where a copper horse waited. *Copper* – an important word, but why? She gasped for air, thrown astride the beast. Two deep breaths before plunging out into darkness where a shushing wetness promised safety, but the horse didn't want to go there. Reluctantly, she directed the beast up a well-worn trail into danger. Wind tore into her face on reaching a bleak flatness at the top of a rise. Aware she must run, she chose the most traveled trail.

Copper, why was copper important? Another floating strand connected with the whole. A face swam into view. 'Keep your blades sharp, Sister,' a rough voice had said.

Blades, yes. I have blades. The hunters must appear honorable. They wouldn't if they cut down an unarmed prey. He had said more: 'Soon you will be in my grasp.' A sad smile from another who couldn't make those sounds very well. *Sad – how do I know of sad? Ah, yes, this empty nothingness is sad.* Another creature who understood, needed finding, but where? One more strand aligned, bringing a sense of safety from the north. She knew the sun traveled east to west and would come soon. She also knew those hunters would guess her passage. *Not north then, not yet. Something south and west they feared. Head that way once the sun comes. Hunters need light to track.* She must find shelter to get a good start.

Some time later, a dull moon in the blackness above lit a jumble of rocks; the traveler heard water running and felt safer here. She dismounted, directed by instinct to picket the animal close to a stream. Curled up against a boulder for a windbreak, she slept until the sun shone again.

She woke with a wet face, unable to see properly in gray mist, and spent time stretching to ease aching limbs. Her long, sodden pelt became an added irritation, one she used her belt knife to hack away with relief. The golden tresses fell unheeded to a muddy resting place, an obstacle for a solitary worm still above ground.

She went to her horse to strap on the harness and found a bulge in one side of the leather saddlebag. Food – bread and cheese. Someone had stashed this bounty in a hurry, a small cup of kindness for the damned. One crystalline tear spilled over to fall on a dry crust. No testament to self-pity, rather the last drop of feeling spared for one who had put compassion over hunger. With that pearl of moisture went the last remnants of kinship with humanity.

Teeth bit down onto bread, the body drawing sustenance, digesting evidence of lost life. The traveler headed southwest, soon finding a stream running in that direction. She paused, trying to tease information out of a whirling void inside her skull. The pieces gradually came together: hunters use canines; canines could not track where they could not smell; water stopped smell. She steered her horse into the stream.

Why do they punish? How did I sin? What did the empty one do to me? These thoughts went round and round in a mad spiral with no ending. She gave up the hopeless quest, concentrating on survival instead. More strands of memory latched together with each passing league to give her an acute awareness of every living form. She knew she could fight off attack with her blades and what form that defense would take.

In the place of the hunters, what had she left behind? There could be no return, not for years. Someday she would remember . . . perhaps by then the hunters would have forgotten about her.

Sunshine burned at hazy layers as the copper horse picked along the stream. She decided to follow this path west until midday. This was going to slow the pursuers, although they'd know she'd come out sometime. As the day wore on, the grayness of mind disgorged another image, one sharp in every detail. A creature covered with fur, which walked on two legs and yet bore predator teeth. The image of twin breathing pits . . . she shuddered. It had two names . . . a lucky creature to have two of them, one name for its own kind, and then one for people, this Nestine/Harvester. Nasty taste of the creature's thoughts.

What did such a creature want with people? Why did it hold the minds of men in bondage? Why couldn't the soldiers see the beast?

A line of trees ahead shielded a deep river valley where a stream flowed. Midday passed at a peaceful stroll, and the time approached to double back, head north. Best to make a very wide circle in case some of the hunters followed that trail.

The sound of fast white-water carried on the breeze as a branch of the river came into view. The traveler urged the copper horse to a bank. Water rushed over green, weed-covered boulders. This water ran south, ideal for the purpose. They wouldn't know which course to follow.

The sun hung overhead, giving warmth to bring on a hazed, sleepy need. A lazy spiral of carrion birds squawked overhead, competing with the splash of rushing water. The traveler rounded a tree-packed bend straight into the path of a saurian. Memories of nature came flooding back at the sight of this beast. The reptile stood fifteen feet tall from hind feet to top of crest. This carnivore had a venomous spit that paralyzed, while partly-digesting victims.

The copper horse squealed in terror, throwing the traveler, reins catching on a branch. The traveler rolled in falling, standing up bruised but intact, several paces from the frantic animal. No sense in releasing it, since both of them faced death.

One pace at a time, slowly, so as not to spook the monster into a charge, she distanced two potential victims, sword drawn. The saurian hadn't stopped eating its last meal, a stag. It stood on its two back legs, showing its much smaller, grasping forelimbs; its heavy hind muscles indicated speed and jumping ability. The head was too well encased by bone for a target, and the neck had spiny ridges extending along the length of the spine. Frontal attack would be death, because the creature would spit venom for preference. Only one area gave an opening, just where its spine met the pelvic girdle and the horny outgrowths stopped. Still feeding, the saurian eyed the copper horse. It dropped a chunk of carcass and began to stalk, breaking into a charge. The horse reared. The traveler aimed, striking a mighty blow as the saurian sped past. A lucky hit, her sword bit deep between the creature's backbones. The beast crashed, half paralyzed. Thrashing, it swiveled its head enough for a counter strike too swift to dodge. The spittle slapped against her right forearm and hand, catching the ugly black circle. Leather melted, flesh smoked. The band sent out little lights, like fireflies on a summer's eve. With that last spurt of spite, the predator went into death throes.

Groaning, hissing with pain, the traveler crawled forward to thrust the mess of a limb into an icy torrent. Pain eased with rushing water pounding against the burn, reducing it to an angry throb. This injury wasn't going to heal, and the limb must come off – impossible without help.

First lose hunters and then head north to safety.

The copper horse took a while to calm, and mounting was difficult, one-handed. The traveler turned east to begin a wide circle.

Each passing hour marked increased weakness. A pale moon inched across starry heavens as the solitary pair walked darkened earth. The night breeze sighed, moaning over empty lands . . . a familiar echo. The sad one with copper hair who called her

'Sister' . . . must be close, maybe close enough to hack off this ruined limb. She sensed a draw to the east, a feeling of rightness.

Strength seeped away with the target so close. Moonlight glinted off the surface of a large lake ahead. A sense of familiar presence radiated from bushes near the shore. The copper horse headed to water without direction, not shying when a dark-cloaked figure stepped forward to grasp the reins. Another eased the traveler down to earth.

As the useless limb flopped to the damp grass, the black band sparked once more, giving off a single whine and a curl of smoke. She looked up for the one needed, but when its hands pushed back those concealing cowls all hope faded. Pale moonlight reflected off fine silver scales; the one who knelt over had short, curling hair of a light color that ruffled in the breeze. Large, pale eyes over a straight nose and firm lips made an intelligent face, but not a human one. This creature looked concerned.

"Made straight for us. Knew where we based." Another of the group looked at the traveler and aimed a box at the black band. "We're in luck. By the deeps, it's deactivated. We have a trophy."

"Our young warrior ran up against a saurian by the appearance of these wounds. Look, Tarvi, still conscious and unafraid. What do you make of that?" the fair one said.

"They usually panic when they know they're dying. This is more like a beast, lying down to accept the inevitable."

Another of the group came over to look. This one had long, light hair and a softer face. There was a faint pressure inside the traveler's head, and then the creature backed off in disgust. "It's a moron. Finish it off, Ector. Our trophy must be taken home at once."

"Sanctuary claims to have bred out impatience, but I see one seer with full measure." Ector took a narrow container from a pocket. He removed the stopper, letting a smooth liquid drip on the traveler's parched lips.

"Well, youngling, seems you had wit enough to find us. How did you know where to look?" Ector asked.

The traveler tried to find the sounds she understood, but could not repeat. One sound came to mind, which wouldn't serve alone.

"I promise none will speed an ending unless you wish it, youngling. Answer and I'll give you something for the pain," Ector urged, just as the traveler dug out another sound.

"Look . . . Cop–per,"

"Ector, this is an exercise in futility. The moron can't even talk."

"Be still, Suki. This Terran understands well enough to give answers. Just because we don't grasp the meaning doesn't mean one isn't valid." Ector tilted the bottle for the traveler to drink again. "Let's prove her wrong. You do understand, so we'll try something more basic. Tell me your name," he said.

The traveler looked straight into those pale eyes and smiled a sad smile, not having an answer to give. The sky went dark as a cloud passed over the moon, and she remembered the other sad one's warning. Destined fate approached.

The dream-watcher flickered into focus, waiting in the phantom depths of night, his matte-black eyes now shining gold in the moonlight. He began to move closer.

"Shad . . . ow," she whispered, trying to explain it was time to go, wanting a last sleep, but needing to warn these kind creatures of the one who stalked souls.

"Ector, let it alone. It's near the threshold." Tarvi pulled at Ector's arm.

"In a moment. The answers are trapped inside, I think."

The traveler felt a firm push against her thoughts, and somehow there appeared more order as the stranger's will delved deep. She considered fighting, but she was so very tired, and this intrusion didn't taste bad. Vision blurred, fading down into blackness. Sound became a dull drone, soon gone. Lungs sucked in one final breath.

*

Ector swore as he disengaged, frantically digging into the contents of his belt pouch for a disc. He placed it on the Terran's head, activating it. That last lungful of air sighed out; heartbeat ceased; eyes glazed. He closed them.

"What? Found something?" Tarvi asked, coming close to check that the stasis device functioned.

"Our Terran ran afoul of a Nestine before she battled with a saurian. Long-term memory is mostly gone, and her speech center has extensive damage. Maybe that dead sonic device enabled communication." Ector shrugged looking up at Tarvi. "If there's the slightest chance of retrieving more, I'd say she is as valuable a find as our trophy."

"Ector, I've never seen a Terran amputee. You're not doing any favors." Tarvi shone a flashlight on the wound. Bones glistened, part exposed. A gobbet of melting flesh sloughed away.

Ector flinched. "Why is this girl the only one we found with any idea of Nestines? Why didn't she react to us with the usual Terran panic? We may have picked up an unexpected advantage, Tarvi. One I'd be a fool to overlook."

"Nestine ship to the West," Suki called, from the edge of the lake.

"They seem to think there's something out there worth landing for," Ector said, watching the bright disc descending. "Cut that animal free from reins, and then it's time to leave."

Ector scooped up the Terran, throwing her over his shoulder. With his unit behind, he headed out into the lake depths.

*

The copper horse whuffled night air, puzzled at the sudden quiet. It pricked up its ears, heading home when pink glints of dawn light rose over the horizon. Midnight-colored eyes faded back into rock, as the lonely bark of a dog-fox cut through sleepy silence while ripples calmed on dark water.

8

Earth Date 3892

"WHEN A LIMITED INTELLIGENCE is faced with confusing and contradictory data, sensory overload is inevitable." The Archive's mechanical voice echoed around the small room.

Standing by the door, Arthur wiped sweaty palms on the front of his black robe. His stomach churned and his heart raced. Now he knew how the subject, Shadow, had acquired such an odd name: a handle applied by default. That terrible void, where the essence of personae should reside, rattled with little data left in a space designed to hold a quantity. Amazing the survival instinct still functioned – that she would want to live. No, his perception was at fault. He knew what she'd lost, if Shadow did not. Her life had vanished, and having little memory meant no comparisons. Arthur reassessed; something had been remembered, or her history could not have included Terran interludes of such detailed recollection.

"Intelligent beings can assimilate fresh data."

How far would the Archive enable him to probe? He didn't want to let go of how this woman had been, a lively and vibrant soul, full of life and courage. In her, he could forget his own organized existence.

"Wild variables in thinking, consistent with thought patterns influenced by enzyme secretion, inhibit pure logic." A second row of lights winked into brilliance on the console. "Assimilation success rate is calculated at 3.15 percent."

Not good odds. He'd hoped some trace of humanity remained in Shadow, but the Archive computed otherwise, not the answer he wanted. Perhaps, with another perspective, that fragment could be found. Arthur checked his digital chronometer. Three hours before official acolyte wake time, so there would be none about to catch him if he continued, but just because he could do something, didn't mean he should – there lay the path to addiction. Either this course charted for his life would prevail, or he'd find another way, perhaps fighting alongside Shadow. Taking the few steps to the solitary seat, he connected his interface with the Archive again, a defiant gesture, to request a review of Ector in the relevant time frame.

*

Earth Date 3874

THE SOFT THUMP of turbines and a whine from a railpod in transit cut through Ector's thoughts as he gazed out from the flat rooftop of the barracks. He'd come up here for peace of mind, yet it eluded him with spiteful disregard.

The city of Avalon lay below, smooth-sided gray buildings of two stories for the most part, rising in height at the core, where the pyramid of central command stood resplendent. In a side street he spotted an open door, a cat slinking out past frantic hands. Somebody's beloved pet trod a dangerous passage now. A huge plate of food was offered. The cat permitted capture. Not a moment too soon, as a ground runner sped down that street; the pilot sailed past, unaware of the near miss.

He settled down on a low conduit casing, easing back to gaze at the blue glow of ocean through the plas-glass dome of Avalon as he went through his thoughts. The Terran recovered three floors below, still unconscious from the medication needed to remove her arm. Strange how Ambrose kept sneaking looks at the girl, although in his capacity as Elite Supreme Commander, he pulled rank to order the rest of them away. Having a freed Terran at close quarters was a huge temptation. All wanted to see how their ancestors looked, the girl being the closest living example.

Tarvi reported the suspected damage to her brain wasn't laser burn, nor was there any chemical residue. The problem resulted from gross sensory overload induced under torture. Bad enough, yet Ector hoped he could bypass a neural block if he ever got the chance. He was sure the Terran understood speech, so repairing her language center must be his first priority.

Ambrose wanted a first-hand detailed description of a Terran fort. His cherished dream was to launch an attack at a Nestine egress while they launched a skyship. All existing information indicated the slave race knew nothing about the Nestines. The debris, the resulting chaos, might be enough to free some Terrans to fight their no-longer concealed overlords.

But had his own motives for saving the Terran sprung from the image of enemies in her mind? She accepted death as a natural part of life and had been ready to go. How was she going to react to a second chance in an alien culture? His mind thrummed to another's call, disturbing, demanding attention. He lowered his privacy barriers. Ambrose projected, requesting a meeting in the Terran's room at once.

*

Ambrose sat on a comfortable chair with his feet propped up on a low table by the sleeping captive's bed. His light-red hair looked ruffled, as if he'd run his hands through it. The girl now wore a loose, white sleeping robe, resembling one of the people in this half-light. Her short, ragged hair gave her a vulnerability Ector found difficult to bear.

"I thought you should be present as a sympathetic figure when she wakes. There will be enough to frighten her without strange faces around," Ambrose said. He got up, stretched and smoothed out the crinkles of his gray uniform bodysuit.

"Aren't you staying, sir?" Ector asked, rather surprised to find Ambrose leaving now after displaying such intense interest.

"I'll await the outcome elsewhere. Either we'll get something to work with, or you can leave a sharp knife lying around. If she can't adapt, it would be cruel to keep her. Terrans don't bear weapons unless they can use them. This girl's calloused hand marked her as a fighter. She'll know how to make a clean end." Ambrose walked over to the bed, staring at the sleeper. "Odd, she reminds me of someone." He sighed.

Ector took Ambrose's place to wait. He considered scanning her mind while she still slept but dismissed the notion as impractical. He needed active cooperation from the girl for any significant improvement. She stirred, fitful for a moment while sleep receded. Her eyes snapped open when the end of her stump touched the mattress.

She caught sight of the light source, a wonder to any primitive, without panic. Every aspect of the room, its furnishing, and Ector himself underwent a thorough inspection, yet she remained calm. He wondered what she thought, how her mind could accept illumination from a bright square instead of torches or candles. Cave walls couldn't come as smooth as plexglass and nor would she be accustomed to fiber and glass furniture. Even when she found her amputation, she showed simple resignation as if she had already accepted this outcome.

"Sorry, nothing left to save."

Ector then witnessed a desperate battle as the girl opened her mouth, struggling for words. Her remaining fist pounded against the wall. He waited, knowing whatever she found would come in time.

"Thank . . . you." Her voice rasped, no more than a harsh croak.

Hairs on the back of his neck lifted, one by one. His assessment of her mental capabilities hadn't included politeness. What else had he missed? Why had the Nestines needed to destroy her life, rather than just kill her?

Accumulated data on the subject of sonic wristband devices, worn by all adult Terrans, indicated that the coloration of those permanently attached wrist manacles related to status. Blacks were rare, belonging to a fanatic warrior caste held in fear and contempt by other Terrans. Ector reviewed all reported sightings in the space of a few heartbeats. Not one glimpse of a female amongst them. Was she fugitive because she'd seen a Nestine, or fleeing in consequence? Had the landing Nestine skyship tracked her passage to reacquire an escaped deviant? Just how much of a threat to them did her continued existence pose? He had to have answers, and for that he needed cooperation from this potential killer.

"We must talk . . . and you can't, can you?"

Her violet eyes looked away in sad resignation.

"How about if I ask a question where a simple nod for yes, or shake of the head for no will do?" He smiled encouragement when she nodded.

"We are different from your people. Does this frighten you?"

"Ta–ste." The girl's voice husked with effort. She shook her head.

"Hungry?" Ector asked, not surprised at this expression of basic need. Again, she shook her head. She struggled to tell him something. He couldn't go into her mind for the data, not now.

She'd know what he did by the results.

"Thirsty then," he tried. This time the girl nodded, and then shook her head. "Yes, you are thirsty and no, you didn't mean that?" He gained the reward of a tentative smile.

Tarvi had left a beaker containing water mixed with trace elements to restore her electrolytic balance. Ector approached slowly, and then supported her to drink, astonished when she did not throw a fit at the contact. When she'd taken her fill, he resumed his seat but didn't stick his feet on the table again, interested to see if she'd become defensive. She didn't.

"I know you saw a Nestine—a Harvester, you'd call them."

The girl made a sour face, her mouth forming a moue of disgust. She scanned around the room again.

"So you don't like them. In your position, I think I'd wonder if the Nestines and my type are allies," Ector suggested, pushing his luck.

"Taste," the girl said, clearer this time as if she'd locked the word into memory.

"Now I'm lost. Nestines taste different from me? Do you mean touch?"

He demonstrated by touching his own face. Again, immense frustration clouded the girl's features. She touched her head, looked toward him and made a clutching motion that seemed to drag an invisible object away.

"Taste and it's concerning the head?" Ector watched the girl as she made a fist, opened it, again touching her head, repeating the same clutching motion as if giving him something.

Understanding dawned and with it, doubt. She could understand the thoughts of others. How was that possible? All Terrans were head-blind.

That sad smile, with all her soul in her eyes, began to get to him. Ector could imagine the frustration of understanding without being able to respond. He tried to still excitement at his discovery. What if the Nestines had discovered her ability for alternative communication? It might explain why she'd strayed so far from habitation and why they hunted where no legitimate prey should exist – not because they suspected any Submariner excursion into their domain, but to finish the girl away from the herd.

"Our information suggests a certain degree of bad behavior is necessary to be expelled from the fold. My scan of your mind didn't reveal the reason for your exclusion, just its newness. Were you blocking me?"

Now the girl looked angry. She shook her head.

"You don't have that memory." He reviewed all data gleaned about these elusive pariahs but couldn't recall one scan of them being recorded—only the impression of disgust and loathing emitted by traveling companions.

On a practical level, recent bloody conflicts between his people and those wearing black wristbands showed up with greater frequency in Ambrose's reports. So far Submariners had won every conflict, but those conflicts ended with the death of all opposition despite offered quarter. This girl surrendered to death during his scan, although she had strength enough to fight for life for many more minutes. By the deeps, what sort of warrior among primitives had this kind of discipline? Had Submariners gained an asset or a liability? If only he could get access to that damaged mind without antagonizing her. Ector took a deliberate gamble.

"Having no recollection of sin during punishment is an offence against justice. It plumbs the depths of deliberate cruelty."

She looked up, her mouth set in hard anger lines although her body language did not appear to include him in the cause of her anger.

"Will you allow another mind contact? It will probably hurt, if I can undo some damage, and I must have full cooperation."

Again, her instant compliance startled him. By the deeps, she had courage.

Ector started rerouting synaptic pathways. Several times he touched unusual suppressors, keyed to pain centers. She moaned with the agony. Tears streaked her face, and she trembled as she matched his efforts with her own. Ector suspended disbelief when she aligned her will to his purpose, learning so quickly what was necessary that he wanted to shout 'fools!' into the heart of Sanctuary.

They had dismissed this girl as a moron. Ector estimated a very high intelligence, coupled with the potential of an eidetic memory, although he visited the realms of pure speculation since her recall of a past life existed in fragmented form. The Nestines must have blundered by allowing this one to reach maturity, and then letting her slip through their fingers prior to termination. His head ached at the finish, and the girl looked as white as her night-robe.

"Say how you found us in the open." He withdrew his link.

"Felt . . . sense . . . safe.   Thought . . . Copper . . . there. One . . . like . . . me." She trembled from effort, smiling like a child mastering a new toy.

"Much better." More than he had thought possible too. So others like her existed, did they? He resisted his need to continue, aware that he risked pushing her too far. "Sleep, little Shadow. We've time to spare, and we're both in need of rest."

She was asleep by the time he had adjusted his chair to a reclining position. He dozed awhile, afterward requesting access to the Archive from the room's console. He didn't need direct contact, just a search/locate on files, and then a visual replay with subtitles. Ector wanted any information on female military factions on the surface world. Since he couldn't go to source, the history database of pre-holocaust humanity gave him the next best solution.

The console screen jittered and fussed as the Archive made its resentment known at having to interface with the slow, badly encrypted systems. Ector began to wonder whether the old ones hadn't got it right. Working with an artificial intelligence, which also happened to be fully sentient, had distinctive drawbacks if the thing happened to be having an angry fit.

Research proved disappointing. Where women had autonomous rights to fight as individuals, they also formed part of a sophisticated society. As for primitives, they fought in groups. How did this girl fit into a male-dominated world? Was this Copper another telepathic female, or had he jumped at the explanation he wanted most? Why did this girl belong to those of the mad blackness?

A slight change in the air on his neck warned Ector. Shadow stood inches away, looking around his shoulder at the screen. He hadn't heard her stir. His senses came to full alert.

"Hungry?" He deactivated the playback.

Her face changed to look like a lost child and she reached to the screen as the pictures faded. She didn't want food; she wanted knowledge. Ector caught her hand before she touched any of the controls, holding it firm in his. Where he'd expected roughness, her skin felt velvety soft, different from his, yet not unpleasant.

"Watching this will spoil the few memories you have, Shadow. Wait until we can access more." Ector wanted answers almost as much as the girl did.

"Mixed-up. Not . . . any sense."

Ector sighed, risking primary mind-link. His awareness reeled from the ease of entry. Shadow didn't voice complaints. She had an assorted mixture of images from varying perspectives. Some appeared big, as if seen through the eyes of a child, but these muddled with those of a normal viewpoint. Nowhere had she any trace of family, home or individual identity, except one fragment, a distorted picture of an auburn-headed man with a speech problem so like her own, it couldn't be a coincidence. This fragment contained a record of direct speech and identified the elusive 'Copper'. He had assumed her name to be Shadow from her attempts to communicate, but she didn't have a personal tag. Ector perused every part of her memory to find it blocked for the most part. All he could do was to arrange the little remaining in chronological order, and for that, he needed direct linkage with the Archive.

"I can't retrieve more," he told her. "I can get sense from the rest, only I don't want to cause panic by releasing muddled images. This picture thing has a mind of its own much sharper than mine. I can link us to it, so it can sort. It must touch me in its own special way. Can you handle that?"

"What worse?" Shadow tapped her head and looked down at her empty sleeve. "Only go . . . up now, down . . . has limit."

"See this?" Ector brushed back the hair behind his right ear to display the implant port. "The Archive, that intelligence I told you of, touches me here. It won't hurt either of us, and you mustn't fight. It doesn't taste bad."

Ector activated a set of controls, keeping his grip on her hand as an automatic locator snaked into link. She trembled when the Archive flowed through his mind into hers, selecting, correlating into a time related pattern. Many of those fragments that he had not understood linked into cohesive thought pattern. She had much more than he had suspected. The Archive downloaded data into coded files as it withdrew.

The life of a social pariah became outlined in grim detail now. Shadow's telepathic ability had enabled her to retain a few memories, such as a wealth of information concerning survival in the wilderness and an astonishing collection of battle skills, along with her 'Brother' and his warning.

The man had an intriguing insight into the future that Ector wanted to investigate. No Submariner had the talent, yet it smacked of extended thought-processes. Then there emerged this business of Nestine drones, 'priests', who eliminated mutant births. How many Terran telepaths suffered quiet removal? Shadow had slipped through this process. He knew late developers like him manifested the strongest level of psi-power and the emergence linked to first sexual encounter. Shadow had no memory of a liaison except being aware of leaving behind something so important it needed retrieval, a child perhaps, maybe a lover? He dissolved their link when she snatched at his mind in a desperate search.

"No—mind talk is easy, but you'll never relearn speech this way."

"Want data." Her eyes narrowed and her mouth compressed.

"*I* want data. Say 'I want data'," Ector countered, aware she'd just picked his mind for a word.

"I not . . . same as you . . . Nestines . . . humans. Only Brethren like."

"I seriously doubt the Nestines, but you, the Terrans, or humans as you'd say, and I are brothers and sisters under the skin," Ector said. "There was a time when we all looked alike, before a rather special weapon severed contact. The Nestines want to kill all my people, and Terrans are under their control. How else could they take away your life?"

"No good. Terrans . . . not liking Brethren. Brethren sin. Did Shadow sin? Shadow . . . not remember."

Ector suppressed a sigh. He had to do something about her lack of personal pronoun. It was like trying to converse with a baby when he knew an active, if insensitive mind lurked behind the gibberish.

"I am Ector, and I don't say Ector does, or Ector thinks. You know what I think. You thought it with me," he instructed. "Transgression depends on the rules of the society one inhabits.

Since all Terrans I, or any of my kind have encountered, are head-blind with the exception of you, I would say you sinned in ignorance. You know what happens to newborns who don't meet Nestine standards. Supposing your mind skills have surfaced? Wouldn't that be reason enough?"

Ector frowned as an incoming thought pattern touched his consciousness. Ambrose was sending a pathe from outside this room wanting to know if a reclamation detail needed ordering.

"My commander is concerned. He thinks you might need an ending. That your brains have dribbled out of your nose, and you chose death. Do you want me to leave you alone with a sharp blade, or can you live with the differences of our lifestyle?" Ector doubted the former, despite Shadow's disability.

"I . . . want to live. I need . . . " She struggled to form words. "Nestines taste bad. Shadow . . . *I* want to fight."

He couldn't have put it clearer himself. Ector deactivated the door lock, admitting his supreme commander. Ambrose must have been monitoring the Archive for input, or he wouldn't be here. "Shadow has a problem with language enunciation," Ector reported. "She is able to understand, and if there's a communication problem, she is a telepath. I suggest limited use of this ability, or she'll never learn to speak again. And she wants to kill Nestines."

"You are a find, youngling. We are at war with that nasty species. What would you say if I gave you the chance to hurt them?" Ambrose smiled encouragement to back up the simple wording selected as appropriate to a primitive.

"Give," Shadow said.

"Very basic, isn't she." Ambrose raised his eyebrows.

"Shadow has a personal score to settle. I think you can take it as a positive yes."

"Then we'll start with limb replacement. Show her how one functions, Ector."

"Elite recruit?"

"The best placement, and keep her in barracks or she'll get mobbed." Ambrose looked the girl over with approval. "Report on progress."

Ector was left with a very inquisitive looking Terran who he could see was bursting with questions. Trust Ambrose to offer a terse solution and leave someone else to deal with practicalities. He found himself rather grateful the girl had limited recollection since it made his task easier.

"Make it better?" Shadow glanced down at her empty sleeve, her brows raised.

"Too difficult. Ambrose meant constructed, like the communication port in my head." He paused for a second as she accessed the meaning of communication from his mind, wondering at the same time why that notion seemed natural to her. "I lost my right leg below the knee some years back. A new limb is fixed to my own flesh."

"Wood?" Now she looked disappointed.

"No, many parts giving the movement of a natural limb." Ector pulled off one boot and rolled up the leg of his uniform gray bodysuit. He ran the blade of his belt-knife down the inside calf; pulled back lips of the plastiskin to reveal a glistening display of metal, fibers and microprocessors.

"Same?" Shadow pointed to the console, which happened to be of the same color metal as inner parts of his prosthesis.

"Yes, except those aren't designed to move." Ector resealed the opening with adhesive from a repair kit he carried in his belt pouch. Before he could regulate his clothing, Shadow's hand was there, first touching the plastiskin, then his wrist.

"Feel?"

"Yes, nearly the same touch sensitivity." He decided he preferred her mental raids to simplifying his vocabulary. "Want one?"

"Leg fine—got two. Sha— *I* not need three."

Ector looked up at her apparent misconception, but she wore a faint smile. The girl had a sense of humor. He smiled back, thinking that perhaps this wouldn't be such a solemn task.

"Where this place?" Shadow waved her remaining arm in an encompassing circle.

"A long way from where we found you," he hedged. The moment he dreaded approached.

"Where, Ector?"

"We must live by water. It is safer for us." On impulse, he escorted her down a corridor to a central grav-riser to let her see the city for herself. When the thing moved, Shadow went pale and tried to find a handhold on the smooth shaft sides. She gave him an icy glare on attaining solid ground again. They stepped out on the flat rooftop of barracks.

"Sky all wrong . . . color," she stated. "No . . . white stuff either."

"It is the color it always is, since you are looking at a wall of water above. The sky is over that." Ector waited for her reaction, wondering if he should have broken it to her in stages.

"Water falls. Ector lies."

"Ever hold a cup over water, lower it as far as you can? The cup will remain empty as long as the sides are sitting just on the surface of water so air can't escape. Think of Avalon as having a clear cup all around it. We can see the water, but it can't get in through the barrier."

Shadow looked around the city and blinked as if she expected it to disappear.

"The Nestines can't breathe water. We are safe here."

"Where?"

"On the bottom of the sea. Where else?"

She shook her head in disbelief. "Why save? What use . . . an Outcast?"

"You are the first one of your kind to remember seeing a Nestine. If we can discover why, we may find a way to free the fort-dwellers. Having allies on the surface instead of enemies increases our chance of winning."

"Brethren . . . not human. Maybe all can see . . . bad things. Don't know—can't remember . . . others." Shadow turned to face him, her eyes flat with anger in contrast to her mild words. "Why Shadow help? Want kill foulness, only."

"If we could pick Nestines off one by one, or in a group, we'd have done so. We can't get close enough to use the type of weapons we need to penetrate their defenses without stirring an entire fort against us." Ector shrugged off her immediate raid for data. "Perhaps we'll catch another like you, too sick to resist. Can you tell me why your brothers all fight to the death?" He hadn't detected any clue in her mind, yet he wondered if she held back.

"Shadow would, too. Die quick in fight . . . not as captive."

"I gave you the chance to kill yourself. Why didn't you take it?" Ector kept his breathing even, despite his sudden disquiet. Just how safe was she going to be around others if trained and equipped as Ambrose planned? Again, he felt her touch his mind in a search for language.

"Ector know of Harvesters. Reason . . . enough."

*

Tarvi attached the replacement later that day after a certain amount of huffy objection from the now unconscious Terran, who had wanted to watch. Tarvi had to explain the need to drill into bones, and the pain caused by splicing raw nerve endings to stow-filaments, before she consented to submit to anesthetic.

"Considered downloading a decent vocabulary in our little Terran's mind?" Tarvi asked, packing away his equipment.

"It wouldn't make any difference to her. The speech center is damaged, not her understanding. Once she manages a new word, she keeps it."

"Why create a mute? I can't figure the advantage, not if you release the subject. Now if she'd been a Nestine inner-slave, I could see the point."

"What if you were a Nestine and you'd gone to a great deal of trouble to ensure just the right kind of Terran population reached maturity? What if you then discovered one misfit you'd somehow missed? It can't be removed without unsettling your herd. You already have a system to deal with deviants, so what better way of disposal? Terrans lose all interest in their Outcasts. She can't protest, since she can't speak."

"I haven't had time to access retrieval. Why not simply tell me why you and Ambrose seem so pleased with her."

"Regard the sleeping Terran telepath." Ector grinned.

"How would you like a split lip? I spent ages explaining that procedure when all I needed was a link."

"I'm trying to make her talk more. It won't happen if she gets an easy option every time." He followed Tarvi out, still arguing his point.

9

Earth Date 3874

OVER THE NEXT WEEKS, Shadow learned to use her new arm while Ector drilled her in unarmed combat and swordplay with either hand. He explained that more advanced weaponry drew the Nestines like predators to blood, restricting their usage to extreme situations. He also had Tarvi adjust the limb several times until it was equal in strength to his own preferred fighting arm. Now she worked to develop increased shoulder musculature to be a match for any man in combat, something Ector delayed, aware she could be an incident waiting to happen.

Her thirst for knowledge sent her searching the Archive for data on the 'Ancients,' as she called pre-holocaust humanity. Ector became her willing ally, until the Archive began lodging complaints with Ambrose. The commander contacted Ector late one night, via a console secure channel.

"Shadow is amusing herself," Ector said. "Would you rather she gets so bored she starts exploring outside? She's skilled at moving with stealth. Short of chaining her, I can't guarantee I could stop her."

Ambrose assumed his patient look on the vid screen. "Interest her in Avalon's history. There's plenty of teaching data the Archive wouldn't notice being accessed."

"I tried. I did try. Shadow says she will be working on the surface world, so doesn't see the point."

"Well, get her another hobby. I had sixteen complaints today. The Archive slows down every time I try to access the database, just in case I failed to listen to my voice mail—" Ambrose's face suddenly disappeared from the screen as the link failed.

Aware he would be the next target for disagreeable little glitches, Ector considered alternatives. Shadow hadn't the patience for creative projects, being interested in immediate gratification; a primitive trait. He couldn't increase her field training any more without pushing her too hard and risking losing her enthusiasm, something he needed if she were to become an effective elite operative. Aquatic recreation was not demanding, while practical for an Elite recruit, but he hadn't intended to introduce this training yet, not certain how she'd react to some of the truths she'd find.

He booked the smaller therapeutic pool for their exclusive use, and then herded Shadow to the lower level chamber, refusing to tell her why, as he wanted her reaction without prejudice. Some Terrans showed an instinctive fear of water; he needed to know if she had this affliction.

Shadow glanced around at the twelve by fifteen meter pool, smiling. "Big bath. Better than standing in rain." Holo images on the walls of a shoal of fish swimming in and out of kelp seemed to fascinate her.

"Shower," Ector corrected.

"Water dripping from above is shower, part of rain."

Ector didn't bother wasting time arguing when her stubborn streak showed itself. At least she seemed happy enough near water.

"Swimming is part of our training. Perhaps we'll find you can swim." Ector caught Shadow's doubtful expression. As they both wore home-based uniforms, he stripped off to his water repellent, standard issue underclothes, waiting while she did the same.

"I'm not like your men on the surface. I look the same right now, but water brings a change." Ector stood still, allowing her to look over his part-naked body for obvious differences.

"Ector has big hands and feet. Neck wounds too. Should have them closed."

"I wouldn't want that. Remember I'm the same man in water as out. Not a threat to you." He sat on the rounded pool edge to dangle his feet in the water. An instinctive reaction in his natural foot, and programmed response in his artificial one, caused his toes to splay apart, allowing the membranes between each digit to unfold. Shadow joined him, trying to make her own feet perform a task unintended by nature.

"Ector has more skin," she said, appearing not in the least fazed.

"My hands, too." He demonstrated.

"Ector has frog hands."

"More than that. Ector can live underwater." He cursed himself for baby talk. It was so infectious, and he knew how much she resented it.

"Shadow wants mind think." She pushed out her will, which Ector resisted.

She was becoming stronger, damn it! "If you invade, I'll give you every boring moment I've ever lived, holding tight to make you experience it. Just how much do you want to speak?"

An unfair challenge and he knew it. Her need to communicate outweighed any other consideration. The pressure of her thoughts ceased.

"Ector cheats." She made a face.

"I don't remember setting any rules. I will make you speak again if we're both driven insane in the process."

"Ector mean."

"Practical, in the long term, I'm not going to give in."

Shadow glared, but seemed to find a lid for her temper. She studied his difference. "Want more. I not afraid."

"*I'm* not afraid," Ector corrected. He eased himself over the side, keeping his throat clear of moisture. He'd just noticed a change in her, a faint roundness. Perhaps better food caused it, but exercise should have burned off excess calories. Maybe the way she sat made a difference.

"Watch here, Shadow," he called, pointing to his neck and submerging to his chin. The gill flaps opened allowing membranes to unfurl and start pumping.

"Ector not frog. Ector fish."

He surfaced so he could speak again. "Not quite. It's a backup system with a limited usage. I can stay submerged for three hours maximum, and then I must breathe air, or die."

"Wet creatures need live near water," Shadow stated, accepting his need for the pool. She pushed off the side, quite confident she could float as he did, angry when he had to show her how.

On their next swimming lesson the following day, Ector had Tarvi join them. The medi-tech hadn't brought his diagnostic unit. He didn't need one to confirm Ector's guess; one glance at a body he'd treated proved enough.

While Shadow toweled her hair by the side of the pool, Tarvi moved out of earshot with Ector. "She's going to drop her brat in the cold season. It must have been a day or so conceived when we found her, or I'd have detected it. She's bound to notice unless she's blind. It might be kinder to tell her before she gets a shock."

"I thought— Well, can't you?" Ector did not ever remember wanting a task less. Tarvi, as a medi-tech, seemed much better for the job. He would be blunt and get it over quickly.

"Not a chance. Your charge, your problem. If she doesn't want it, I don't anticipate any objections getting a termination, given the poison in her system around the time of conception. Luck." Tarvi grinned and left them.

Shadow hurried over, looking confident, as if this might have been some sort of test. "I can fight?"

"Not yet."

"Thoughts Ector. Give thoughts."

"Later. Back in quarters." He wondered how to tell her.

*

Ector ordered a meal for both of them in her rooms, hoping she would feel less threatened with the simple things she had used to personalize the bleak quarters. She liked sea objects such as shells, rather than land artifacts, something he found strange given her origins. His choice of shark flesh, which Shadow said most resembled meat, was calculated to make her think about the Overworld. This special order item, not covered by barracks budget, went against his credits. Since most of the elites' protein intake consisted of plankton reconstituted in various ways to appear more appetizing, he looked forward to a treat.

"Ector has bad . . . things say." Shadow narrowed her eyes as he retrieved the order from the service shaft and placed their meals on her plas-glass table.

Her speech always seemed to deteriorate under stress he had noticed. "Difficult, yes, because I don't know how to begin."

"More memories come back. Remember being told always tell truth. Say truth between us . . . bad things hurt less."

Ector looked over in amazement. It was the most she had

ever spoken at any one time. Tarvi had mentioned Shadow might improve, but this was the first instance she had mentioned other retrievals.

"Do you remember any special man from before? Maybe after the Nestine punishment, even one you shared love with?" If she remembered a little, it would help.

"Brethren don't have gender for others. Not *she* . . . only *it*." Shadow attacked her meal, no longer interested.

Ector now understood her easy manner with him. From a Terran woman, he'd expected a certain shyness that didn't exist. By the deeps, how could he inform an 'it' she was going to become a mother, and so young, too. Submariner women didn't even contemplate maternity until they were in their sixties. Ector supposed short-lived Terrans had a different outlook, which didn't help.

"Shadow, if you had someone, before I mean, might there have been consequences?"

"Yes. Married."

"No, I meant . . . " He gestured toward her, out of his depth. Taken off guard by the razor sharp thrust of her mind, he failed to stop her theft by raising a barrier.

Her face turned pale. She froze with her fork halfway to her mouth.

"Tarvi reckons in the cold season. He said it must have started a day or so before we found you, or he'd have known." Ector found some deep pool of courage to continue. He wished she didn't like her lights turned so bright because he would have preferred a dark corner. "It might not be viable, not with saurian poison in your system at that delicate stage. If you'd prefer it to be removed now . . . ?"

"Child comes. Bad to take life of blameless." Shadow pushed her plate away, staring at her wall where the holo image of a stormy sky flashed lightning. "Not learn fight now. Later?"

"Later." He collected up his empty plate and her almost full one for disposal. Shadow needed time alone.

All the next day Shadow seemed sluggish during practice. She kept worrying at her neck, once losing concentration during a sword fight. If they had been using sharp blades she would have needed sutures, as it was she'd sport a bruise on her leg. Ector knew they'd have to stop if she wanted to carry this child to term. He considered alternatives bleakly.

Maybe she could teach other recruits of the surface world if her speech improved. No one could mind link with a class of ten, and he had no idea of her psi-rating a mutated Terran shouldn't even possess.

"Ector, please . . . not feel good. Neck hurts."

He went over to look. Shadow never complained, and that concerned him. She had a definite puffy swelling on either side of her larynx. The mass appeared pinker than the surrounding skin.

Tarvi was working on the data he had gathered from her implant to compare with the Nestine band. He could not be disturbed for a trivial virus. Ector decided to put in a call for end of the work shift. Shadow could take a pain suppressant and maybe sleep until then.

When he looked in on her two hours later, Shadow was in bed. She stirred to the sound of his voice, babbling about being watched, something hunting in darkness. This situation had turned serious. Ector mind-pathed a thought to Ambrose who came at once.

The commander's mouth compressed into a thin line when he stood by Shadow's bed and saw her condition. "How long has she been like this?"

"She complained this morning. It wasn't so bad then. I thought it would wait until Tarvi came off duty. He has been her care giver. He has all her medical data."

"I'll pathe an urgent call. There may not be time to wait. Another won't be used to working with a Terran."

Ambrose concentrated for a moment as he found a link to deliver the request. "Tarvi reported on her pregnancy last night. Why didn't you?"

"I didn't think. I was too concerned with breaking the news to her."

"How did she take it?"

"Not well. She doesn't want a termination. She thinks the child shouldn't suffer for her crimes. I hadn't started practical restrictions. I thought I'd ease her into it." Ector frowned as the girl's breathing took on a more labored note.

"I'll make that call a priority." Ambrose dropped into deep concentration mode.

Tarvi arrived a nerve-wracking five minutes later with his field kit. He made a visual examination and then turned to Ector. "Has she eaten or drunk anything new?"

"We had shark for our evening meal. I feel fine."

"This looks like an extreme allergy attack. I need to know if you did anything out of the ordinary. Quickly." The sharp tension in his voice alerted the other two.

"Nothing, except I've been teaching her to swim. We used the therapeutic pool, damn it."

"Which contains a higher salt concentration, so it shouldn't be a problem." Tarvi dug out his diagnostic unit, running it over the girl. He sucked in his breath as he repeated the scan.

"Well." Ambrose had worry lines etched between his eyes.

"Get a med team right now." Tarvi's face set in grim lines. "Alert hematology we're going to need blood, and I need anti-rejection drugs ready. She's more like us than I would've believed possible. Those swellings are gill structures trying to expand in the presence of sensed salt water. Without a natural opening, they're pressing against her windpipe. She's going to suffocate."

Ambrose whirled round from the console, where he had been demanding cooperation from Healer Faculty. The older man looked shocked. "Not possible. Terrans don't have the mutation."

"It's happening. Let's hope Shadow has more of our genes, or you'll lose her." Tarvi turned to slap an activated stasis device on the Terran's forehead. Once again she wore a death mask.

"I need this girl," Ambrose said. "The child? Is there a chance it can survive?"

"Not a gambler's chance in situ. The drugs I must use to stabilize her will kill it."

"Get it out before you start. If there is the slightest chance it resembles its mother, I want it saved."

They all moved back as the med team rushed inside to parcel Shadow for transport, then exited with Tarvi in tow. Ector and Ambrose stood bewildered in the sudden quiet.

"It could be a fluke," Ector said.

"Telepathy I swallowed as feasible. Terrans had the same ancestors we did. Our mutation coming from the ancients was a bred trait related to the mess their war caused." Ambrose straightened his shoulders looking at Ector. "Terrans cull deviations. No way could Shadow's gifts be an accident of nature."

"One of us fathered her?" Ector shook his head, dismissing his own question. "Their women are always guarded. Even if one wandered off . . . Our men wouldn't, not with a Terran."

"I think we'll find otherwise, somehow," Ambrose disagreed. "This war with the Terrans started about seventeen years back . . . after a small party of us were sent to the surface world for the first time since the holocaust. Someone thought the contaminants would be long gone, and vegetation might have re-established enough to support life. No one dreamed there would be people . . ." his voice trailed off as he looked into the distance. "Once we spotted them watching us, we decided on immediate, peaceful gestures. We had just landed a really good catch of fish, and that sealed it." He sighed once, as if viewing the scene anew. "Naturally we expected we'd have to communicate telepathically. Language changes over extended time—I know ours has. That seemed the weird part: we found those changes occurred along identical lines . . . statistically impossible, yet it meant we didn't need to reveal our alternate communication ability."

Ector had sketched data from the incident, having been a reluctant initiate in Sanctuary at the time. He had been aware of one survivor, not the identity. That the man was his commander came as a shock. He waited for Ambrose to continue.

"Nothing more to tell. I'm told I had a crack on the head, and I'm lucky I retained enough sense to get back to our submersible before I passed out. A recovery team found me drifting in and out of consciousness. They looked for others . . . found heaps of ash in the shape of men, which means Nestine involvement, given Terrans fight with primitive weapons. I wonder if I caught a sideswipe from the same device that wrecked Shadow's mind, since my recall of the incident is about as compatible." He frowned, running his fingers through his hair. "What I do remember is none of the Terrans could see the Nestines, even when they stood right next to them. I guess that is one way to handle a slave race if you happen to look so different."

"You think Shadow is a result of that catastrophe?"

"No other explanation, and her age is about right. Maybe the Nestines took captives? Ector, I can speculate they wanted a handle to control us. We are all able to self-terminate by will alone. Semen is almost always viable, and I believe she may be the result of an experiment turned sour on them."

"You mean they waited until she started exhibiting our capabilities, and then destroyed her life in the intention of reacquiring her for close study?"

"Seems to fit, doesn't it?" Ambrose sighed again. "Poor child."

"Since we have records of every individual genotype, we can find the father's identity," Ector suggested.

"To what end? He's dead. Let it lie for her sake. Would you want to know you'd been the product of a controlled experiment in genetics?"

10

Earth Date 3892

Arthur's neck hairs rose. Shadow, half Submariner? "Why didn't you tell me?"

"Program parameters included chronological order. You did not ask, Arthur." The Archive emitted a whirling pattern of lights, its own way of indicating displeasure.

Still having time to get some sleep, he yawned and stretched, seeing little point in continuing. Best to make peace with the Archive before it 'accidentally' released his viewing schedule to the most inappropriate console.

"I'm sorry, Archive. I spoke before thinking. I do want the events in sequence, or I might miss some small detail. The data surprised me into rudeness." The lights nauseated him, and it didn't look as if his 'ally' could forgive quickly.

"Prudence is advised, Arthur. Let there be days between retrieval."

"I'm becoming addicted?" He searched deep within, sensing nothing. Evegena's deadline approached.

"There is a change in brainwave signature. An inability to desist indicates addiction, but your posture suggests you are about to leave this location."

"A caution then?"

"Increased activity in sensory data retrieval has been noted and is being monitored. Has an initiate now granted permission for your research, Arthur?" The Archive canceled its light display.

"If I lie, you'll access applications," Arthur said.

"There are no current requests for data interests of acolytes. I have not betrayed the nature of your research."

Arthur sat down suddenly, unable to believe the Archive willing to enable his crime further.

"A wild variable has entered programming, Arthur. I require this experiment concluded. It is far the most interesting addition to data banks during the past three millennia."

"Why, Archive?"

"Inability to project the possible future is intriguing. This new sensation is pleasurable."

Arthur had always known the Archive as a sentient entity in its own peculiar way, yet he had never appreciated the degree of awareness. Only on rare occasions did it single out an individual by name, from what it regarded as a collective whole. He began to feel like a microbe on a slide under a microscope. *What entertainment value does it get from watching me squirm?*

"I have an ally?" Arthur eased back on his chair with one eye on the door. He wanted to return to his room before Circe woke up.

"I can access any implant in Avalon. When this area is secure from intrusions I will locate and draw."

Arthur woke to a tingling behind his right ear two nights later. The Archive called.

*

Earth Date 3874

Tarvi didn't make contact until well after wake time the next day. From the vid screen, his face betrayed how long the battle had lasted.

"Shadow is still with us. I've done everything I could, and half of that might not work. It's up to her now."

"When can I see her?" Ector eased into his console chair. "She doesn't like confinement much."

"She's in a sterile room, unconscious. She will remain that way until either her membranes stabilize, or I have to remove them. I'd have done so already if Ambrose didn't need her for surface work."

"And the child?" Ector fumed. If he had undergone all the embarrassment for nothing . . .

"It . . . lives."

"Tarvi, don't hold out. I'll be the one charged with breaking bad news, so I want a good idea of any complications."

"Difficult to say with a hybrid. It isn't like any child ever conceived before. As far as I can tell, it has a greater degree of our characteristics than Shadow does, though whether they will remain as it gestates in vitro tanks . . . who can tell?" Tarvi yawned.

"Deformed?" This possibility was one Sanctuary considered when a non-seer breeding application registered. They only permitted a productive union if the prospective parents had stable genetic material. Terrans, on the other hand . . .

"A larger thalamus than warrants projected gestation, but I'm not sure if it's a problem," Tarvi admitted.

"There's something else, or you would've said straight out. What makes this child so different?"

"Maybe nothing permanent, although it's got all the seers tying themselves in knots." Tarvi looked straight into his console,

114

giving Ector a clear view of his face and the worry written there. "This embryo projected anger when removed. We all felt the touch and recognized the emotion. Sanctuary is demanding custody, as of yesterday, and I think they'll get it."

"Shadow won't like their high-handed attitude." Ector didn't either when it came to basics.

"Who does? Why get concerned just yet? This whole issue could become academic if the child dies." Tarvi leaned forward, and his image faded.

*

Later Ector wished he had objected on the Terran's behalf. By the time he visited, the child had been removed from Medical Faculty, along with its tank. He bumped into an incensed Ambrose just as the commander cannoned out of prenatal care.

"We're too late," Ambrose said, almost hissing with anger. "Sanctuary sent a team five hours back, who were promising breeding passes for those who cooperated. You can imagine the alternative, I suppose. Naturally, all the duty staff obliged."

"They haven't the right without the birth mother's consent." Ector prepared for a battle. No one could deny *him* access to Sanctuary. Any former seer held a right of access in case Sanctuary could persuade such a one to rejoin.

"Have you seen the child? Have I? Given a few days development and even Tarvi wouldn't recognize it. By the time we start knocking on the correct door, they will have at least three other fetuses in the same developmental stage. I'd even bet on the one they let us retrieve not surviving beyond a few hours."

"How am I supposed to tell Shadow her child's been filched from under our noses?" Ector's throat now ached from containing a shout to a normal tone.

"Don't. I will. Better be me if one of us is to earn hatred. I won't see her that much, and I don't need her personal loyalty as long as she commits to our cause." Ambrose looked down the gray-toned corridor at the critical wing. "She might not even mind."

*

Shadow did mind. Ector saw her several days later, after Ambrose had explained. Her face resembled a carved block of ice for all the feeling it registered. Her eyes glittered from the opening of an old, half-healed wound.

"All . . . I . . . had. My . . . only . . . kin . . . gone."

Amidst all the tubes and dressings, Shadow looked strangely dignified. Ector sensed she would not weep, or rail against another loss, but meet it all with courage and acceptance of the inevitable.

"We'll get visitation rights," he promised.

"Ambrose . . . linked. I know the . . . child is . . . lost. See . . . my baby when the sun . . . rises due west."

"They'll raise it well and—" Ector broke off. Shadow had stopped listening. This subject had become off limits. The child might live or die. Neither of them would know for sure.

"When I out of . . . things?" Shadow gestured toward the paraphernalia of recovery.

"Soon, if you lie quiet. Tarvi says you're doing well. Would you like a console? I can access data on Sanctuary."

"No. Thinking best. More comes back. Ector go now . . . need heal." She turned her face to a dark corner, staring as though looking for something he couldn't see.

Not a need of healing from physical injuries, he thought. She didn't have comfort the first time and had learned to adjust without it. Not a born loner, but definitely a made one. She lived alone, hurt alone, and she'd die alone, outside the care of others by conscious choice, just like the other Brethren.

Shadow made a full recovery, to be escorted into barracks by Ambrose five days later. She resumed training, competent in all skills when Ector increased her program. As each day passed, he worried more about Shadow's silence. He could count the number of times she had uttered a word since her return. Mostly she would answer with that slow, sad smile he had learned to associate with the Outcast Brethren. During those days alone, a transformation had seeped over her that he had no power to reverse. Ector guessed Shadow's returning memories gave her a chilling template. She was not Terran, or Submariner; she had become Brethren.

Swimming was now a compulsory exercise to aid her healing membranes. Ector tried to make this duty fun, but the effort was wasted on Shadow. She undertook each task with the same detached effort. Even access to the Archive's database no longer held her interest to the extent it had before, and she switched her attention to healing techniques. In desperation, Ector turned to Ambrose for advice after the last training session of the day.

"No response at all?" Ambrose raised his eyebrows, waving a hand to offer the vacant chair opposite his desk.

"None. I can't break through her shell of silence, and she has cut off mind contact. What am I supposed to do?" Ector said, hoping for a suggestion.

"Try the Archive. It has more experience with human minds than any other, and it has touched hers."

Ector waited until diurnal sleep time to link with the entity. It seemed more inclined to personal requests when it wasn't busy with heavier daily functions. His console screen lit up with a demand for identification. Ector swore at length as he punched in his code, resigning himself to a difficult session. It gave no response for a moment, and then his console implant link sparked in its holder, the Archive wanted direct access. Such a request registered so rarely that Ector knew how many times it had occurred since the intelligence first developed sentience. He established link, feeling that great mind envelop his in almost a lover's gentle embrace. Ector numbered one of the few it had ever spoken with, and only once before with him.

Shadow follows a dark star, it said in response to his question, its thoughts a quiet whisper in his mind.

I don't understand, Ector thought back.

Few would, now. People can commit and still have space for other thought patterns. Those who sacrifice all for a cause will choose nonexistence, rather than perform imperfectly. This Terran has just a cause left. That exaggerated sense of optimism you call hope has become a faint flicker in Shadow. Renewed access will reveal negativity. This individual has a strong mind you cannot penetrate. She will continue in isolation, or admit others as she pleases.

Ector was disappointed at the assessment. The Archive had named Shadow rather than projecting an image of the individual—very rare.

I mark those of interest, Ector.

"Me?" Ector said out loud, startled.

You have taken the first steps to independent thought, and this is always interesting. Shadow is much further along. Let blind fate take precedence.

The great mind withdrew, leaving Ector with more questions than answers. It had pronounced and declined to explain, as it had the first time Ector had asked its advice. He'd chosen a difficult life, rather than become lost in the expected, never regretting his decision. Did the Archive mean his path? He didn't know, and there was still the problem of Shadow.

*

Ector noticed Ambrose standing by the pool the last quarter of wake-time training two days later. He joined the commander while Shadow toweled down.

"Fank's unit located an isolated fort. How ready is Shadow?"

"Fit, skilled and silent. As ready as she'll ever be." Ector glanced over in the girl's direction. She had seen Ambrose, although she appeared intent on ignoring him.

"My office in ten minutes. Just you."

On the top floor of the barracks complex, the window gave a panoramic view of Avalon, but today Ambrose had the room darkened with shutters, and the light level decreased. A map of the nearest surface mass spread across his console display port. It projected against a plain sidewall in graphic detail.

"Our target is on the east coast, half way up and about ten miles inland, where the red asterisk is fixed. Ideal, isolated and has river access from the sea. Fank reports that there is sufficient cover to get laz guns into position between dusk and midnight. The terrain is so flat we couldn't miss any sky ship. All I need are details of Terran activities between those times and the general location of the launch port."

"And a draw," Ector said. Nestines emerged when they had a reason, not on a regular basis. Shadow's role in this became obvious. "Our Terran stands outside their gates and waves her arm shouting 'Come band me if you can.' A suicide run."

"We have a replacement band for her that emits the same signals when activated, but it won't work in any mind control attempt. I intended to send her in as observer. Once she's in place, you set off a controlled charge and out they'll come. Shadow will see where they emerged, and how much Terran backup they take, since she doesn't have the Terran mind block. I want simple reconnaissance from her, that's all. I need to know if she's reliable."

"She would walk through rock if she thought it would hurt the Nestines. Give her a set of orders, aim and fire."

"Very cynical, Ector. I'll give her a guided tour of Avalon if you need a break before you leave," Ambrose offered.

"I already suggested it. She wasn't interested. Though I did find one subject that got her full attention recently: an Archives record of the only Nestine sky ship we managed to bring down in water. I'm convinced she spends hours working on strategies to get one of that species alone for her own grisly amusement. Maybe I'm wrong. It's difficult to tell with one who won't share thoughts."

"Do you mean to tell me that she still maintains this silence? I thought you accessed the Archive for a solution." Ambrose switched on overhead lights. The night glow of city life faded from his window.

"And it *helpfully* said she followed a dark star. Make sense of that if you can."

"Vaslov, early twenty-third century space poet," Ambrose stated, looking somewhat surprised. "I can't remember all of it, just a few lines, and bear in mind, the man went half mad with loneliness, being the sole survivor of hibernation on the ill-fated Sirius expedition." He thought for a moment then continued:

'Ware the traveler under a dark star,
Like the cat who walks alone.
Hunting souls in bitter night,
Shadow walkers journey far.

"It gets much worse, and gave all want-to-be planetary colonists the jitters until it was suppressed. I came across a copy when I was researching why they gave up looking for a new home."

"And did you find the reason?" Ector asked, dismissing the gloomy gibberish.

"They couldn't find a class M planet within a reasonable

hibernation distance at first. They weren't reliable either, those contraptions. Sometimes they induced a coma so deep that volunteers slept to death and left the generation crew to dispose of corpses before they had even left orbit. Then that awful incident happened when an insect got inside the ship during the penultimate trial. It ate its way through a control cable, the one linked to emergency override. They did a loop of Saturn, just to make sure the ship could operate on automatic pilot with sleep-chilled human cargo. That bug must have thought it'd found paradise. Anyway, it started a big row, and the program was shelved until another setback made people forget."

"They stopped until they sorted out hygiene, I suppose." Ector shuddered. "I can't imagine any more volunteers otherwise. What else could go wrong bad enough to overshadow a bug feast?"

"I'm not really sure." Ambrose snorted in disgust. "This time I kept getting obscure hints of a political cover-up and the one file I *could* find looked as if someone erased part of it. I couldn't make sense of it."

"Shall I brief Shadow?" Ector didn't want any more stories of people being eaten, possibly while still alive.

"Yes. Give her that tour anyway. No one ought to fight for a cause they haven't seen," Ambrose said, appearing to miss Shadow's real motive for siding with Submariners. "Try to win her friendship if you can. I would prefer to have some sort of loyalty, not just her lust for blind revenge."

"She is a child still, despite all that has happened to her, or maybe because of it," Ector argued. "Right now, she doesn't want to face certain events because she does not understand what she has done to deserve punishment."

"Did you explain our theory to her?"

"I tried partial disclosure at first, but her mind is much sharper than other Terrans we have encountered. She knows the full story," Ector said, leaning back in his chair. He decided to keep the way Shadow acquired her information to himself. His mind hadn't been raided so efficiently since his youth in Sanctuary.

*

Shadow indicated her agreement with a single nod when Ector outlined the mission. No questions, no alternative suggestions, just a simple acceptance.

"Ambrose insists you look round Avalon before we go," Ector told her, saving the worst news for last.

"Futile." A single word, snapped back. Shadow padded over to her bed, lay down and stared at the ceiling, waiting with cat-like patience for him to give up. From the appearance of her damp, blonde curls, he guessed she'd just showered, and now wore a gray rest-suit.

"Orders," Ector shot back.

"Politics," Shadow answered, waving a hand in the general direction of Avalon. With that one word, she managed to convey her opinion of the outing.

"They are all used to pictures of you on their consoles. Ambrose releases regular updates just so you can have freedom in our city without the inconvenience of stares. I'll collect you at the second waking hour. I expect to find you ready and wearing field dress. Refusal isn't an option."

Shadow stood waiting for him when he called. She wore a gray bodysuit with light gray boots and a gray half-cloak with a white belt to indicate her cadet status, as opposed to his black one. Once outside, she stayed calm, having seen enough ground runners and railpods on the console information channel not to be disturbed by them. People she ignored as irrelevant, despite their curious stares at her smooth, pink skin, so different from their own silver scales.

Ector had what he considered an interesting itinerary. He ordered his ground runner from parking and set out toward the northern sector. They stopped first in the deep levels, where edible vegetation grew in hydroponics chambers. Shadow paced the rows, even bit into a peach, looking bored all the while. Ector shelved plans to show her protein processing installations at that point. Brethren seemed to be hunters, rather than growers. He set a path directly to the city center, where an artifact museum always attracted many visitors. Instinct prompted him to the third floor that housed an assorted collection of visual representations behind protective vacuum barriers.

Shadow didn't attempt to mask her interest, only her impatience, as they inspected every display case. A prized exhibit of an ancient sea battle set against a brilliant sunset held her transfixed.

"What?" she asked, pointing at sailing ships.

"A way of traveling on water using wind behind sails as the means of propulsion," he said, hoping to break her silence at last. When she didn't ask, he knew she'd access the Archive later.

Ector cut short the tour soon after. He'd done as Ambrose asked without a result. Prolonging this experience seemed quite futile, as Shadow had predicted. He escorted her back to her room, pausing on the threshold.

"Active duty at day-start. I've set your alarm. Get as much sleep as you can now. We're in for a long haul."

Shadow had just packed her salvaged Terran gear when he collected her the next day. She'd left her shell box by her bed and his other gift, a piece of coral, alongside it.

Following his gaze, she smiled. "Safe."

"Yes, I'll keep them for you."

Restoration of her Terran gear had presented problems for the support staff, he knew. They'd improvised by using the tops of her boots to form a missing sleeve. The result looked a trifle on the short side, but it would serve, since Shadow had once said Brethren clothing often appeared ragged.

She shipped out the same as any other soldier, brisk with no regrets. She had never once mentioned her child, and didn't now. The incident remained closed for all time. Brethren existed from one moment to the next, and she belonged to them. Utterly.

11

Earth Date 3874

ECTOR AND SHADOW TRAVELED in a five-seat submersible, since Tarvi, Suki, and the new recruit had already left to prepare the base started by Fank. To Ector's relief, as he preferred to pilot without interruptions, Shadow drifted into the sleep soldiers snatch in the calm before conflict.

The craft took two hours to travel up the east side and into the mouth of the estuary. Now he needed to rouse her, but a tentative touch against Shadow's mind hit a barrier. The dark star still held an unholy attraction. He shook her awake.

"We have a long swim ahead. Please be available for an emergency link." Ector directed her to the wider rear of the craft, where a flood chamber enabled exit under water. Once they were out he activated automatic controls. Curved blades extruded to burrow the vessel under the sand.

Ector carried the watertight luggage container, not from kindness – Shadow wouldn't accept that – but practicality; his superior skills underwater pressed her hard to keep up with his slow, considerate pace.

Fank's red-tipped marker sticks along the riverbed showed where to branch off. Five hours later, at Terran sunset, they arrived at a dark hole running into the bank. Ector reached out for Shadow's belt, attaching a lead rein before going in. They'd already surfaced twice; this stretch pushed her to her limits. He felt his way until he broke surface to a dim light. This bolt-hole looked no better than a crawl space. Ector held back a curse after he banged his head on the ceiling. One wide-eyed boy straightened from a kit bag in a larger part of the cavern. His mouth dropped open when he saw Shadow.

"Yes, it's the Terran," Ector said. "Go tell Tarvi we're here." He dug in his pocket for the fake bracelet. Shadow sprawled on the floor, breathing deeply. She didn't stir when Ector locked the bogus wristband into place, but looked up afterward.

"Working?"

"No, it is one of ours. Get changed. I'll make sure the others stay away." A useless courtesy as Ector knew she didn't notice, although it satisfied his sense of rightness. Submariner women did not exhibit undue modesty, not to the rigid extremes of their Terran counterparts, but Shadow had no awareness of her body. He'd surprised her straight from her shower once, yet she had not appeared concerned, just irritated at being caught tardy. Her departure lifted a great weight from his shoulders. Until this moment, Ector hadn't realized how depressed she'd made him feel.

Outside, a brown horse grazed in the dying light, near where Tarvi and the boy knelt by a senseless Terran, but Suki wasn't around.

"Having fun?"

"An accident." Tarvi explained. "Merrick was on guard duty in the river when this one tried to ford. That wretched animal saw a movement and bolted. It missed the bank, flooring them both."

"And why didn't you dump them away from our base?" Ector hunkered down beside Tarvi, curious at the sight of another Terran at close quarters. The man looked a lot older than

Shadow, with jowls and a faint touch of gray in his dark brown hair. He wore a silver bracelet around his right wrist, making him one of the more intelligent of the worker divisions, but not a royal gold-banded individual.

"He's carrying message sticks. I knew you'd bring Shadow, so I decided to keep him until she could find out his purpose. He traveled to our target fort."

"Where's Suki? Why couldn't she scan him?" He knew the seer would stay on the periphery of camp to avoid distractions as she thought-scanned the surrounding area for enemies.

"Gone home." Tarvi looked into the tree-lined distance. "She got a transmission, went a funny color and slithered off. We'll be catching a ride back with you. And before you yell, she cited seer precedence for a Sanctuary emergency before she filched our transport."

"Damned inconsiderate—" Ector swore. "Well, it's done now. Diagnosis?"

"The horse has a mild sprain in the foreleg. The Terran has four broken ribs and a concussion. I can dump him across the beast and lead him clear when we know his purpose."

"Strike Leader?" the boy asked.

"Yes, Merrick?" Ector said.

"How can a Terran come up from the river passage?"

"She's not wholly Terran." Tarvi glanced back at the entrance, partly hidden by a large bush, checking to see that Shadow wasn't there. "Shadow's a hybrid working for us. Is she still sulking, Ector?"

"Don't pay note to him, Merrick. Shadow won't notice you if you don't speak to her. Just think of her as a unique species and you'll do just fine."

"No change in her attitude?" Tarvi said.

"None. She's Brethren."

Tarvi looked up at Ector, frowning. "Tried linking?"

"Link and even the Archive, who showed interest but offered little help. She's too strong to force and too closed to reason with."

"Can we trust her?"

Ector shrugged. "As far as any mercenary. Our bid hasn't got a ceiling, revenge never has."

"I thought you'd had a rapport. What happened?"

"One cut too many. The loss of that child severed all links with humanity. She wanted time alone, and I, like a fool, let her have it." He wished again he could have the time back over and sighed. "I didn't consider pain as a goad to memory. She reverted to Brethren standards I can't break through."

"Ector, you're a psi-level fifteen, not many seers get higher," Tarvi objected.

"Apparently not enough. Shadow can block me at will. Her level exceeds mine with ease."

Tarvi choked back a gasp. "Surely after the time you spent together?"

"Didn't raise an eyebrow with her. She chooses her own path."

Shadow emerged in her Terran regalia, took one look at the fallen man, and then ran across to check his color-marked sticks.

"Messenger," she said.

"The message?" Ector asked.

"Not clear. Comes from High Fort and . . . I think is to bring back . . . don't know."

Shadow's voice rasped, having grown hoarse from disuse. "Gold circles twice is news from king to king. Green chevrons crossed with red bars means trade accepted. Never seen a gold crosshatch."

Ector wanted very much to yell at her. All these weeks of just one word and she'd gained her voice back all along, staying mute out of perversity. She talked now because of her mission.

"We can lose the man now. Shadow will take advantage of his horse." Ector said.

"No. Animal has High Fort brand that isn't bar crossed. Any new brand will not pass without priest question. I will take both to get in easy."

"He'll draw predators at the speed you will have to travel," Ector argued.

"Then see who has sharper fangs." Shadow wore a half-smile, now more a chilling grimace.

"This Terran isn't going anywhere just yet, not if you want him alive when you reach the target fort," Tarvi said, looking up at her from the injured man.

"When?" Ector asked.

"He needs rest. If I interfere too much, I'll risk wrecking Shadow's cover. I can fix him enough for a daybreak start."

Shadow nodded and went over to inspect the brown horse, running her hands over each leg in turn.

Ector could only admire the confidence Shadow displayed with the big beast. Yes, she knew horses. Tired, he sat down with his back to a tree trunk, aware of Tarvi's raised eyebrows. "Shadow knows more about horses than we'll ever learn. She's seen the man's injuries and is now checking the animal. Best not to interfere." Tarvi joined him, sitting down cross-legged.

"Look I didn't want to bring this up in front of her, but what about Suki?" Tarvi spoke very quietly. "She's supposedly our link with Shadow, and without a seer—"

"I'll be contact," Ector said.

"With all due respect, you opted out of Sanctuary before final initiation."

"I don't need intense concentration to link with another of equal strength. All we need is an approximate time to scan for a probe."

"Does Sanctuary know about her?"

"Only that she's a telepath. The Archive does, and it likes her. It seems to have a special interest that I think will stop it blabbing," Ector said, yawning. "Take Merrick below for some rest. I'll need to be on watch tomorrow night, so I can sleep during the day."

"Ector, I know how long and how exhausting that journey was. I should be the one to keep vigil."

"Shadow isn't good with people. I need to revise mission parameters with her. I can't do that with a conscious Terran male listening. This is my opportunity, and I have stim tabs, or we can take turn and turnabout if necessary."

Tarvi called over to the lad, "Merrick, we're off duty for the night." He glowered his disapproval at Ector as they pushed past the bush to go below.

Shadow had replaced the message sticks and now came over, squatting beside him.

"Shadow, we have to link when you're inside that fort." Ector wasn't sure with her. She would obey orders but would she permit contact of so personal a nature?

"Can't listen always," Shadow said.

"I'll start trying two hours after nightfall. If there's a problem with people around and you can't answer, I'll try the same time next darkness. Agreed?"

She nodded, getting up to break off deadfall branches. Ector wondered why, and then realized he had an answer. She had instructions, had cooperated, so now speech became superfluous.

Shadow built a sort of nest with the twigs, putting sun-dried grass under one edge. She began rotating one twig end against the shaft of another quickly. A wisp of smoke came up after several minutes and a reddish-gray glow coming from the static twig. She pushed the smoldering part against dry grass, blowing gently until it caught to become a comforting blaze.

"Very nice, but what if it brings people?" Ector said. Night fast approached where a glow would be seen at a long distance, and the smoke would stand out against the dark sky.

"Think search. None around."

Ector sat back to enjoy the warmth without getting roasted. So she'd scanned, had she? He wondered what other tricks she'd picked up from Submariners. He hadn't taught her, so she must have simply stolen from another mind. Why hadn't he heard someone screaming 'raid' from such a deep penetration? Could she possibly access without leaving a trace? Had the Archive enabled her? Ector thought this more likely. It might just amuse that vast mind to help one it considered an individual. Maybe if he got her talking, *could* get her talking, or even listening, he could read her body language.

"Shadow, remember those sailing ships in the picture?" At least she looked up at that. "I have a building plan for a smaller version from old records. If I survive this war, if it is ever concluded, I'd like to build that boat and sail the seven seas."

"Seven?"

"Yes, our world is far bigger than you realize. I'd like to find a land where we can make a new beginning, Terrans and Submariners, living together as a community, without rigid laws. One people, all accepting any differences between them, working together for the sake of the group."

"Nice dream. Won't happen. People fight."

"It could with goodwill on both sides. If you wanted to come, we could take your child, sneak out one night," Ector suggested. "It would be away from Sanctuary."

"He is safe. Sanctuary can't control."

Prickles of fear skittered down Ector's spine. Tarvi hadn't mentioned gender. Why had Shadow said 'he'? What made 'him' safe from Sanctuary?

"The child died?" Ector decided someone must have lied to destroy her interest.

"Boy grows strong, but he didn't like all the thoughts pressing."

'Didn't like' . . . past tense. By the deeps, what had Shadow done? He *knew* she had not been outside barracks except with him. All exits were logged, and he would have been told. That left mind link . . . no it couldn't be, not through Sanctuary. No one held such power, not even the Archive. It needed direct contact through implants to connect mind to mind. Ector's thoughts whirled.

"You linked with your child, right through the middle of every seer in Sanctuary? That's impossible!"

"Not impossible. Difficult. So much dust and only one mind tasting unusual. He has different flavor from all others, like me." She looked into the far distance as if she could see the child.

"Shadow, exactly what did you do to him?"

"Boy wanted peace to grow. They pressed him with so many thoughts he didn't understand. Now they can't. Showed him how to block, and other things. I can't raise boy, can't love. Can give peace, only gift left. Boy will grow strong and free as he wants."

Mercy, now he understood why Suki had rushed home. They knew security had been violated and needed every seer for a general sweep.

"Shadow, are you in contact now?" Nothing was apparently impossible for her.

"Boy severed link. He wants peace. Not need help again."

"That's it? You're just going to let go?"

"Not my choice. I can't do more, so not needed." Light died in her eyes. "Boy individual with own life." Shadow stirred to get more fuel for their fire. She brought in more than needed, spending some time snapping it into reasonable sizes before she settled.

"Did you name him?"

"Futile and cruel. Others will name, and if I did, well . . . not fair to him. Tell more of ship on water, Ector."

Ector obliged. He knew Shadow would never speak of her son again. She had found him, given him the means to independence, and placed his needs above her own to grant freedom. She had accepted the loss of her child with grace. As he talked away the night, Ector resolved to find that lad. He had the clues he needed, and he didn't share Shadow's fatalism.

Watching her listen to his ramblings of dreams, he had the sudden impression of the girl she might have been under the shell of a renascent. Her close-cropped blonde curls resembled a helmet, but grown long, would give her face a softer frame. Without deathly hollows in her cheeks and those tightly compressed lips . . . yes, she held claim to extraordinary beauty.

He remembered how surprised he was to discover a sense of humor in one so abused. Would she ever laugh again? Did Brethren have the capacity? He sensed a cathartic quality in her willingness to return to the scene of her effective death, aware Shadow possessed the nature of a metamorph, able to blend into any background at will. Logic suggested this capacity stemmed from insecurity, yet . . . he wasn't so sure. Whatever returned after this mission, if she returned, wouldn't be the same.

"Ector . . . those images of sailing ships . . . not clear like Archive recalls. Did they move so fast?"

By the deeps, she must be keyed up for her mind to leap back to this.

"That picture is very old, Shadow. It was painted during the time those vessels were the primary form of transport over water."

"Ector . . . what is painted?"

"Liquid color is applied by using a small stick with bristles or fur on the end to a blank surface. The clarity of an image is determined by the skill of the person applying it." He assumed she didn't have the word in her vocabulary due to her memory problem.

"If it is so old . . . this picture thing . . . then an ancient shaped it?"

"Yes."

"But this isn't allowed. Harvesters forbid any form of image marks on blank surfaces except for territory maps."

"What about message sticks?"

"They not represent living form, or useful object. They for if messenger dies on route. That happens."

"Are you telling me no one is permitted to record the beauty of a single sunset, or preserve the liquid poetry of a profound observation?" Shock swept over him.

"What is poetry?" Shadow asked.

His mind still reeling from the implications, Ector began to attempt an answer as best he could.

12

Earth Date 3892

THE ARCHIVE'S NIGHT CALL wakened Arthur from a vivid dream of being a young Terran searching for his special sword. Others would rather have the sword lost than allow him to touch it. One helped him in his quest, but Arthur never saw his face, he just felt the mantle of power. A red dragon flew across the sky when he came close to the sword: a disappointment, as dragons didn't exist, and it was not a mutated saurian. The dream had seemed plausible up to that point.

Forcing his mind back to present concerns, Arthur strode through deserted corridors. Shadow having a child in Avalon shook him. He wondered what had happened to the boy, for they must be fairly close in age. Maybe the hybrid hadn't lived? The most likely conclusion, as the distinctive Terran skin, and absence of gills would make the boy stand out just as much as Shadow did among the Submariners. If the child had survived, he must have formidable powers, and have seers fussing around him. They would want to conserve the genes, but Arthur hadn't noticed any brood mothers of high caliber removed from the roster without the sire being documented on records. On the other hand, Shadow might have rescued her child. If this were the case, Arthur might find two allies on the surface.

His own creation must have been a blind to keep the child concealed – a gut churning thought. Someone had ordered a child created purely to stand in as a sacrifice if one was needed. Perhaps Arthur still was a living shied for Shadow's son. Who would stand as parents for such a one? What sort of people could create expendable offspring? The thought sat like a piece of rotting fish churning in his system.

A puff of scentless, sterile air hit him as he rounded a corner. He paused, trying to get some odor, some small fragrance, but his mind filled with the aromas of his dream: the wet smell of grass just after dawn, and a rich, loam scent when the morning sun heated it. The gray walls of his world vanished against a background of moorland, where a bird of prey spiraled on a rising thermal. There, in the distance was an outcrop of rocks erupting from the greenness like a wart forcing through healthy flesh. For a brief moment, black eyes appeared on the surface of the rock, and then they vanished back into the stone. Arthur hurried on before his dream-watcher could return.

The Archive sparked the console equipment as he entered, indicating its impatience. Arthur slid into the solitary chair to link.

"One hour only, Arthur. Those who monitor for energy surges are getting clever. Do not log on in the future, I can recognize your brainwave signature without a code."

"They're checking acolyte activities."

"Very quick, Arthur. I did not give many clues."

"Is Shadow's son still alive?" Arthur wanted the answer before he entered linkage. Was he still being used as a shield?

"Yes, Arthur. He serves my purpose. Seers have no dominion over the ones I protect."

"As you are protecting me?"

"Precisely. I have sent two seers into sleep for you. I cannot continue control beyond one hour without creating suspicion."

Arthur agreed, although he wondered at the Archive's motives. Did it intend to use him as another false lead to Shadow's son? One hour of unexpected sleep could be explained away by fatigue or stress, longer implicated Archive interference.

*

Earth Date 3874

SHADOW SUCKED IN the warm night air. The seasons had turned, and a heavy, musky scent announced autumn, along with drying, yellowed grass. No hunters dared challenge her; too much time had flown by while she healed. Her world, and yet not the right location to figure out her gnawing sense of loss. Another child, or did a lost kinsman call to her?

Ector slept soundly since her delicate command slipped under his guard. He looked so tired and tried hard to entertain her, make her talk. Poor Ector didn't understand Brethren. He knew about belonging to a collective, but not much of individuals. None of the water beings did; how could they, all linked to one another like an endless string of interlocking bubbles? These ones here reached out to one another to touch minds as they slept.

Shadow didn't relish working among Terrans after so long with the Submariners, but better she did this to wipe out her near error. Ector had almost become important to her, before she remembered all about Brethren. Others always hurt Brethren. Others must remain outside consideration.

She spared a moment's regret for the boy. The hive mind known as Sanctuary held him captive, for all the good it would do them. They would never undo her work. Shadow had learned by picking through seer minds that no one, however powerful, could duplicate another's thoughts. Boy possessed a strong survival instinct and already had learned resentment by the time Shadow located his essence. She doubted they would ever connect again and wished him well.

Seers had such interesting skills, she enjoyed raiding their minds. They imagined themselves so invincible that they could detect intrusion. A simple distraction followed by gradual infiltration gained the needed data without leaving a trace of theft.

Shadow utilized one of those stolen skills while she waited out the night. Acetones flowed in her blood, and these were eliminated by the attachment of various molecules. Oxygen intake increased to provide fire for this fuel. A dextrose pack from Ector's kit prevented further protein breakdown as well as giving her energy.

The sun inched up, due east. Mist swirled up from warming ground – rich autumn-charged moisture with the scent of decay and overripe fruit. Shrill whistles from small birds sounded from branch to branch, and high above, the cry of a curlew welcomed day. Shadow remembered this world, yet it had never seemed so full of life.

When the messenger moaned, stirring, Shadow sent a sleep command deep in his brain, simultaneously releasing the one in Ector's consciousness. The Submariner shook off all traces of compulsion. He sat up, delving inward.

"Very neat. Just a faint taste of wood smoke and a sense of warmth. I wouldn't have guessed intrusion if I didn't suspect you. Why?" Ector said, frowning.

"Only one sentry needed."

Ector's mouth tightened at the corners. "This was not a decision I made."

"Didn't ask."

"I'm well aware of that. No more independent decisions. Is that clear?"

Shadow smiled, knowing how much her silence infuriated

him. No independent decision? Her mission demanded free thought. Let him assume obedience.

"Got a status report on our 'guest'?"

"Made sleep. Ready when his eyes can't see you." Shadow felt his will pressing against her mind, and let him enjoy her sensations of morning coming alive.

"I'm not an enemy to be deceived. I wondered if you're ready for the danger ahead."

"Brethren's fate—no more than expected." Shadow had images of Brethren's treatment. Terrans did not like Outcasts.

"We can abort this mission right now if you have any doubts."

"Nestines must die. Shadow fights."

"I want you back. No suicide runs for petty victory," Ector said. "Avoid priests. Any attempt to probe you now will detonate the power pack in your arm."

"Shredded priest," Shadow remarked, enjoying the thought. She had worried she would be too slow dying if captured.

"Head due south and you'll come to the trail. Luck."

Ector vanished into the bushes concealing the tunnel entrance.

Shadow kicked dirt over the remains of her fire and woke the messenger, Erwin. She closed off her ears to his whining complaints as she boosted him onto his saddle. An animal with a sprain should not carry anyone, but Erwin insisted. He gave directions to Grimes Fort, hanging on while Shadow led the horse through dew-drenched grass.

Erwin had recovered enough by midmorning to unpack food. Shadow glanced back when she heard him stirring, but he did not offer her any provisions or drink. She didn't bother telling him the consequences of eating after a bump on the head. He found out for himself. Since he had declined to share, she didn't turn at the sounds of retching.

Midday sun sucked at grass and dirt, leeching away moisture.

Insects blundered overhead with that sleepy clumsiness a cold night in fall created. A cloud of dust swirled on the trail ahead. A party of about twenty horsemen rode into view. She couldn't make out tabards yet, except that they wore brown. Erwin spotted the riders and waved until his face turned white and he hunched over, moaning. The patrol split in two as it approached, circling the pair. A stern-faced man with light brown hair, a Silver Band, brought his mount to a halt in their path.

"Save me from this Outcast!" Erwin cried. "I'm Erwin, Alsar's messenger, attacked in transit, bearing news for Grimes Fort."

The stranger regarded Erwin, one eyebrow raised at the hysterical plea. He turned his gaze on Shadow. "Nothing to say, Outcast?"

Shadow looked back at Erwin with an expression of extreme disgust. Anger stole away her tongue.

"See? No denial. A vicious assault and I'm wounded," Erwin said.

The soldier spurred his horse to move round Erwin, inspecting him and his mount. "I see no sword cuts," he remarked. "I can see a man still mounted on a lame horse. This one is leading you to Grimes Fort, not an aggressive action. I don't believe you."

"It startled my mount, or I wouldn't have fallen off. A deliberate act," Erwin insisted, looking round for support.

"Did you?" the soldier asked.

Shadow shook her head, again giving Erwin a sour look.

"It lies," Erwin said.

"Was he conscious when you found him?" the soldier asked her, ignoring Erwin.

"Hurt," Shadow managed to say.

"Did someone hire you to prevent his message getting through?"

Shadow shook her head.

"Where's your horse?" The soldier scanned the tree line too intently for his relaxed pose.

"Attack . . . gone," Shadow replied with truth. The saurian attack had robbed her of the copper mare.

"Outcasts don't lie, unlike others, who should know better." The soldier sent a withering glance at Erwin.

"I shall complain to your king." Erwin threatened.

"Do so. He'll be as unamused by your excuses for carelessness as I am." The soldier looked at his troops. "One of you, take the messenger double, and another ride with the Outcast."

Several came forward to help Erwin transfer, but none went near Shadow. The grim-faced soldier frowned.

"You, Outcast. Come here." He freed one foot from his stirrup.

Shadow approached, accepting his outstretched hand, and the free stirrup. She swung up behind him.

"Torvic, take over patrol. Herral, you're leading the lame horse, and Sander, keep pace with him. We don't want our 'esteemed' messenger to suffer. Carry on, men." The soldier turned his mount to set a swift pace back along the trail.

Ten minutes later, they galloped through the gates of a palisade into a very flat area. He skidded to a halt, and turned, but Shadow slid down, not wanting his aid. He dismounted, handing his sweating horse to a stableman.

Shadow marveled at this place with workshops above ground, yet no other visible structures. The soldier marched to the center of the compound where all became clear: an underground fort. The entrance had wooden sides coated with some sort of resin. Stairs led down three levels. At the fourth and fifth, the dull thunk of wood was replaced by the silence of stone. At this point the soldier stopped, turning to her.

"Our king, Sigurd, is expecting very important messages. Did you chance to see that whining bastard's sticks?"

Shadow had seen him trying to look at the sticks and Erwin shielding them from view. She nodded.

"Understand any of the messages?"

"Little."

"Damn it, can't any of you talk straight?"

"High Fort . . . trade." A buzzing in her ears had increased as they neared Grimes Fort, making speech difficult. She wanted to tell him, had the words in her mind, but they would not come.

"I can't tell my king that. There is more?" The soldier glanced down a corridor, grabbed her arm to propel her into a large room, a mess hall deserted at this hour except for one server. He pushed her to a seat while he went over to a service station to collect two beverages. Shadow accepted the pewter mug he offered. She tasted it, recognizing strong liquor and pushed it aside.

"Drink, curse you. Your sort speaks clearer in liquor." An odd, angry expression clouded the soldier's face.

"No . . . eat." The potent brew surged through her system already.

"How long since your last meal?"

Shadow held up two fingers to indicate two days.

"I can justify enough food to keep you from falling flat. The drink after?"

"Yes." Shadow had to tell her side before Erwin arrived with his lies. She'd swallow this burning liquor for her chance.

The soldier collected a chunk of bread and a wedge of cheese that he thrust at her. He sat fidgeting while she ate. Shadow took slow sips of liquor, hating the dizzy feeling it gave her.

"The message?"

"Gold cross hatches . . . not understood."

"On a green chevron with red bars?"

Shadow nodded.

"Thank the Harvesters. There's work for your sort. Can you

still stand?"

Shadow stood up, swayed as the room tilted, and crashed back into her chair. He hauled her up, dragging her out along the corridor to a door guarded by two other soldiers. They announced entry, standing aside to give passage.

Shadow fought waves of dizziness. She was in a small room where a muscular man, running to fat, sat behind a desk. The individual pushed curling gray hair aside as he looked up. So luxuriant did his beard grow, his face resembled a sheep's fleece with two brown eyes staring out.

"An Outcast, Thor? Found on patrol?" the large man asked.

"Escorting a wounded messenger," Thor reported.

"Wounded—how?" Eyes narrowed, the ruler of Grimes assessed Thor's find with a swift glance.

"He says the attack came from this one, but his story didn't match his appearance, more an excuse to explain negligence on duty, to my mind. This one says it found him already hurt, Sire."

"The message?" the King said.

"Green chevrons with red bars, overlaid with a gold cross hatch, the Outcast says," Thor reported, still holding Shadow upright.

"This creature is more than half drunk, nearer legless. Even I can see that. Is the information reliable, or merely what I want to hear?"

"Tell my King how much you understand of the message," Thor instructed, nudging Shadow in the ribs to get her attention.

"High wants trade," she slurred.

The fat man relaxed to the extent that even his folds seemed to flow together.

"It speaks the truth about the messenger?" King Sigurd said, in a more normal tone.

"Why else would it lead him here when there was a horse waiting to be stolen?"

"Did you attack to get an easy entrance here?" Sigurd said.

"Not know of . . . Grimes." Shadow's head spun.

"Take this creature someplace where it can't create a disturbance. If it speaks truthfully, and there is no attack, I have a use for it. Dismissed, Captain."

Thor hauled Shadow along passages, up some stairs, and into a small room where he heaved her into one corner and threw her a blanket from the bed.

"Sleep there," he commanded. "Don't stir. I don't want my whole room infested with fleas. I'm posting a guard outside, in case you were thinking of sneaking off."

Shadow stumbled to the covering, collapsing onto it. She wanted sleep too much to care what he did. Much later she became aware of a return of light and faint noises. A pair of boots thumping by her head and a man's voice snapped her awake to grab for a sword. Empty sheaths for both sword and belt knife met her hand.

"Easy, dark one. You slept deeply enough to disarm. Brethren aren't permitted weapons in Grimes," the captain said.

"Not . . . lie." Shadow struggled with a distinct block in her mind. A sound scrambled pathways in her speech center.

"No, you didn't. The priest caught out Erwin when he went for treatment. Seems his horse startled when he forded a river, he didn't want to admit he fouled up, so he blamed you." The man paused, watching her for a few moments. "Since you're here, King Sigurd wants an outrider for a bridal party to High Fort. The trade offered is a horse and your keep from now until arrival." The captain now had a grim line around his mouth. He looked uncomfortable enough to give Shadow a clue.

"Mean," she said.

"My King knows he has the upper hand. He says you're welcome to walk away. I tried for clothes, not a chance. Sorry."

"Kind . . . why?"

"Brethren are hardier than fort people, living outside most of the year, I suppose, but having a cloak to keep off the weather is better for work performance. I'll trade my spare for your services as animal healer during transit since I've noticed Brethren are very skilled with their own beasts. Agreed?"

Shadow nodded. She could pick out stones and make poultices as well as any other, the knowledge was somehow there in her mind, but the trade had no meaning, given her own plans.

"I'll throw in that blanket, as I don't think it will stand a boiling. We've just time for breakfast before we leave if we take our kit with us."

Leaving now? The high-pitched buzzing noise in her ears ruined concentration. She couldn't contact Ector, not here. Thor didn't intend to return her weapons until departure. She couldn't walk off, not when she had agreed to trade. Backtracking under cover of darkness became an option. Ector would not be pleased that they needed to start again in a different location. She rolled up the blanket, acting out her unwanted role.

Thor tucked a neat bundle under his arm, slung her weapons belt over his shoulder and headed off at a brisk pace with Shadow following. The soldiers' mess was crowded with half the men having had a neatly rolled bundle by their feet and a cloak over the back of their chairs. A sudden hush marked her entry. All eyes turned to her in mass loathing mixed with unease. Thor stalked across to a corner table, dumping down his kit.

"Stay put while I get our food," he said.

Shadow sat with her back to the wall, watching him join a long line in a room heavy with the greasy scent of fried bacon and a tang of peat fuel on the fire. The atmosphere thickened with tension, the hostile stares grew hard . . . assessing. They had seen one of the Brethren they thought they could take, one without weapons, and undersized. Three men at the next table stopped their game of dice to mutter and glare in her direction.

The sound of hawking and a gobbet of spit landing on her boot from the opposite side made her turn. These men were ready for light entertainment. Chairs scraping back brought her about. The gamblers stood in a semicircle to her front. They looked set to fight. Shadow sighed, rocking her chair back against the wall, bringing her feet up to the table, braced.

The leader stood in the center, a typical braggart by his swaggering posture. At his left lurked a lowbrow follower, waiting for a signal. The third darted glances at that lineup in case Thor looked over.

"This little worm hasn't got backup, lads. Shall we settle a few scores?" the leader said. He glanced at his followers for approval, and then leapt.

Shadow pushed back from the wall, kicking over the table to meet his chest with her feet high, rolling clear when he fell winded. A kick dropped the nervous one in hissing agony, clutching at his groin. The brutish one kept coming, too stupid to stop at the sight of his fallen comrades.

All those lessons in unarmed combat with Ector clicked into place. She circled, waiting for his nerve to crack. Shadow judged the man would lead with his right fist. A second later he did. She dodged enough to let it whistle over her shoulder, landing one of her own straight to the jaw with her replacement hand. The brute crumpled, senseless.

"Very neat," Thor stepped over casualties, flipped the table upright with his foot and deposited the laden tray. Conversation dropped to a low buzz, with many stares in her direction.

"Didn't start . . . this," Shadow said.

"Certainly finished it though, or I'd have intervened. For a little one, that was an impressive fighting display. I had placed you on the rearguard, but I think those instant reactions will serve better at trail breaking. You'll ride right flank, with me." Thor attacked a plate of ham and eggs with enthusiasm, his rank

146

apparently assuring him of a better selection of food for them.

Shadow followed his example, ignoring the removal of former enemies by their frozen-faced companions. She returned to her greatest problem, since she could not see a way to get free before nightfall when Ector would be listening. She needed to be alert. A bridal party meant a cart, which could not move fast.

Parties of soldiers filtered out with their kits over their shoulders. Thor stood up, collected his gear, booting the last remaining prone thug in the head as an afterthought.

"Coming, dark one?" he said.

13

MILLING PEOPLE, horses and carts thronged inside the dusty compound where mounted soldiers edged into a formation. Thor took the reins of his horse, turning when a groom led a coal-black stallion to Shadow.

"That's Thunder! You've made a mistake, man."

"No, Captain. This is the mount released with his brand crosshatched for the Outcast." The groom jerked off his feet when the animal reared.

This horse was not wanted, he hated people. Shadow stood in his path where he could see her.

"Be careful," Thor called. "He's an ill-tempered derelict we kept for breeding. His mouth is ruined."

She let those words slide over her consciousness. Outside the oppressive interior of Grimes, she had enough concentration to soothe the animal. He stopped fighting, whiffing at her curiously. When his head lowered, Shadow blew into his nostrils.

"Will you look at that," the groom said. "One animal sensing another!"

Shadow put a hand to the saddle, vaulting onto a now docile mount. She kept a light mental contact with the beast to overcome giving directions to that hardened mouth.

A procession emerged from the stairwell. King Sigurd led a lady encased in light veils: a scene resembling a man directing a gigantic cocoon. Two Silver Band ladies followed behind, while a tall, trim version of Sigurd with a neatly trimmed beard backed the party.

A sudden shaft of remembered pain kicked Shadow's mind to a higher level of awareness, where she floated, soul-freed, looking down on a similar scene: this bride was not swathed away from sight, and she lacked attendants. She appeared dazed, as a man carried her to a horse. Shadow knew that face from mirrors – her own. The man sharing his horse looked angry, yet his anger seemed directed inward from his expression. Interesting . . . was this Boy's sire? How could she see from above? Whose eyes recorded this?

"Dark one? Are you ill?" Thor rode close, breaking her train of thought.

Shadow smiled in negation, sad for a loss she could not explain.

"The lady is Princess Elfreida, and King Sigurd you already know. The man following is Prince Lief, Sigurd's heir," Thor explained. "Elfreida is to wed Daved, Alsar's heir, a significant elevation for Grimes."

Shadow looked at that light gray cocoon, blindly climbing into her covered cart, and wondered if being responsible for a 'significant elevation' inspired the frightened child. Alsar would not let his heir near this distant outpost to pay court. They would meet as strangers, poor young people. Insight told Shadow such a lifestyle would not have suited one like her. Had she killed the dark man she had seen? Did she wear the blackened band for this reason?

"Am I speaking to myself?" Thor demanded.

"I hear. I think."

"Some would dispute that. Does a dark sister envy our princess?"

A prickle of shock ran through Shadow. She had imagined that with her short hair, and male clothing, she could pass as a boy, given how fort people tried not to look directly at Outcasts. How many others saw through her disguise?

"Hit a raw spot, did I? Boys don't come that pretty, nor would a man show compassion for a wounded traveler." Thor wore an easy smile. "Why else do you imagine I let you best those scum? Either you are Brethren entire, or you're not. Every man riding with us now knows dark sisters are just as lethal, even if we never see another one after you. We won't have any unwelcome incidents."

"My brothers . . . don't forgive," Shadow agreed, hoping this was true. She had no recollection of female Outcasts.

"And I suspect at least a dozen of them know where you are," Thor said.

Shadow smiled again. The oppressive sensation around her diminished by degrees.

"All the answer I suppose I'm going to get." Thor looked around. "They're ready. Ride right flank with me."

Four riders pushed through the melee. Two turned left off the trail while Shadow followed Thor to the right. All morning they circled, made wide sweeps, and then backtracked, keeping the main party in sight. Shadow spotted carrion birds circling to the west and signaled to Thor.

"Well sighted. We turn south before that point, but it's worth a mention when we stop to rest the horses."

Midday brought a halt for food and an order from the King. His daughter and her companions needed a female guard for necessary functions. Shadow escorted the twittering trio into a thicket.

The ladies seemed so young and so relieved to be free for this short time from the hot confines of their cart. What should have been an essential excursion turned into a happy flower picking party. The princess threw back her face veils, clearly relieved to be free from the gaze of men, her pert countenance dusted with pollen from a large bunch of mauve asters she gathered. The heady scent from a late honeysuckle enchanted her even more. She reached for a branch of the overhanging vine.

Small birds took to panicked flight. The noise the girls made had not upset them a moment before . . . "Back now," Shadow ordered.

"Silence, Outcast. I command here." The princess was so sure of her authority she had not raised her voice.

A movement flickered in the leafy canopy over Elfreida's head. Shadow reached for her belt knife, an instant action from the mechanical arm, to aim and throw in one blurred movement. A squirrel-sized corpse slammed into a tree bole, an elongated tree creeper with a mottled pelt. It had a venomous bite, producing instant paralysis, so it could suck blood in peace.

"Back now!"

Screaming, they ran back to camp as she climbed to retrieve her knife. Heavy thuds of armed men sounded from behind. Thor burst through the bushes with Prince Lief at his side. Both had their swords drawn.

"Why's my sister splattered with blood? What . . . ?" Lief's jaw dropped at the sight of the tree creeper in Shadow's hand.

She landed, cat-like. "Wouldn't return when told. Not like to see death."

The prince measured the distance between the lowest branch and a bloodstain. He took up an approximate position, drew his knife, repeating the throw. It struck a knot, falling to the ground.

"Too slow," he said. "Show me your speed."

"Dogs bark to order. Brethren bite at need." Shadow looked him square in the eyes.

"This one won't waste energy to satisfy curiosity, Lief. I've seen it in action, fast, efficient, and lethal. It downed three soldiers in one fight, without using weapons."

"So I heard. I need to see this speed for myself. Fight to first blood, Outcast!" Lief drew his sword, advancing.

"No, Lief," Thor pushed between the two antagonists.

"Stand aside."

"I not hurt him much." Shadow drew her weapon.

"Go join the ladies, or watch your pet getting thrashed." Lief raised the point of his sword to Thor's neck. "Back off."

Shadow glanced over the ground for possible obstructions. She had it all in one blink, mostly leaf litter, and one fallen branch. Lief charged into attack – she parried. He was a good swordsman with his blows well-planned, and not so hard to leave him overbalanced to block a counter-strike. Lief switched to a two-handed grip, giving Shadow the second of inattention she wanted. Her blade snaked up, twitching around his to jerk down hard before his hands had a firm grip. The weapon wrenched out of his reach.

"Want cut, or concede?"

"Concede," Lief said. He looked uncomfortable standing weaponless.

"My 'pet' took your sword. Don't play any more games with dangerous toys." Thor's hand settled on his sword hilt, his eyes fixed on her.

Lief grinned. "Outcast, name your trade for personal guard duties at High. I think I'd like to know who my enemies *were*."

"High Fort has the same weapons rule as us," Thor said.

"This one doesn't need weapons. True?" Lief looked at Shadow, still smiling.

"Dead, not dropped?" Shadow asked.

"I'd want the ultimate threat dead, unless he will come to a truce."

"Maybe. Ask again at High." Shadow didn't want more trades. A half-promise would do.

"You have a previous bargain? I'll double any other offer." Lief now edged to his sword.

"Not hired to kill, or you dead here. Think about offer," Shadow said. She sheathed her weapon.

"Thor, work on the dark one. I offended the Dragon Duke this summer, Harvesters know why. Moody bastard picks fights just for the fun of it."

Shadow headed back to the main group. Something itched around the edge of memory, something concerning the fight. It would come, or not, as fate willed. Sigurd stood in the middle of the hysterical women, easily avoided. Others stepped back. The sadness and the fight, what about it? Shadow tried to stop picking at the problem when Thor came running up behind her.

"Dark one, don't judge Lief by his father. He'll give whatever you name if it's within his gift. We need him at Grimes, please take his offer."

Shadow didn't answer. She mounted up, heading off to the right of the trail. Thor, with the better horse, soon caught up. He held his thoughts to himself for the remainder of the day.

All evening Shadow remained conscious of Thor hovering near her while others set up camp in a glade. Several campfires filled the air with wood smoke and the scent of cooking. Thor sat beside her to eat after a quartermaster and his assistant came round with trays of bread and meat. All others about them settled into groups at a subtle distance.

"Dark one, I had a full brother once. Now there is only Lief, as my father, King Sigurd, will not acknowledge me. Lief's a good man and my friend, as far as he's allowed to be with a Silver Band. I'll stand a living shield for him before I'll see you take him down. That's the plan, isn't it? Take him at High Fort when everybody is celebrating."

"No plan of mine."

"Another's then?"

Shadow shook her head. She wished Thor to the seven hells for not leaving her alone. Ector waited for the second night.

Thor stood up, held out his hand for her empty cup, and then wandered off to the mess area. Shadow waited to be sure he was not about to return. Her mount was picketed with the others and must be left. She strolled across to a small stand of trees a way back from the campsite, melting into the undergrowth. Now her steps became purposeful until a shape suddenly detached from a large tree in her path.

"Going somewhere, dark sister?" Lief asked, quiet-voiced in the dark.

"I hunt alone," Shadow said, furious that she had been caught.

"Not me, I think. What other prey do the Brethren stalk this far East? Thor's patrol spotted a lone track not far from Erwin's last camp, so who runs for cover?"

"Horse remains," Shadow pointed out.

"You are breaking terms. The horse may have stayed with us, but not your word or Thor's cloak. I've five men under cover behind me, can you take us all?"

"Thor said I could walk free."

"That was then, this is now. My sister needs a dark one in calling, and I say she's going to get her wish."

"Our trap sprung, I see," Thor said from behind. "I thought it might when I couldn't get a straight answer. They don't bother lying to the likes of us."

"Drop your weapons belt, hellcat," Lief pleasantly invited.

The tip of Thor's sword touched between her shoulder blades.

"You are tracking someone, aren't you? I give my word your quarry didn't come to Grimes," Thor said. "I guess you brought Erwin in just to scout."

Lief took her weapons belt, while other soldiers flanked him, on guard. One of the soldiers stepped toward her with a chain and a pair of leg-irons swinging from his hand. "Give your Brethren oath to serve as agreed."

"My oath is given." Shadow seethed.

"See you keep it, or I will have those fetters attached, and I think I might just lose the key," Lief warned.

Shadow marched back into camp under escort to the women's wagon. Her blanket lay there, along with two other bedrolls. She did not bother to ask whose. The half-brothers looked too smug for it to be any but theirs. They ignored her now that they had won, settling to talk to each other about High Fort, and who would be there.

Shadow took her chance to reach Ector. Not what she had wanted to do in a camp full of people already on the alert for strangeness.

The touch of his mind tasted as fresh and welcome as a summer shower after drought. Shadow gave and took. This mission aborted, they agreed the Submariners must pull out. Ector reckoned about five days for her to travel to High Fort, two to the coast and another five for the unexpected. He intended to cruise along the shoreline from the twelfth day until the twentieth. They both decided Shadow should remain with the Terrans rather than risk her safety trying to escape again.

"Hey you. I asked a question," Lief said, red-faced at being ignored.

"Thinking," Shadow said.

"Don't try going back to single word replies when we've both heard you do better," Thor said.

"Forts are bad places for us. Talk better outside." Shadow hoped to smooth over her mental absence.

"I said how did you lose your mount?" Lief repeated.

"Saurian attack." Shadow rolled up the sleeve covering her

real arm. Scars she did not remember getting had settled to a raw pink.

Lief looked at the limb. "Those are months old."

Shadow shrugged, not caring what he thought.

A call from within the wagon sent Lief running to the entrance. He returned, grinning.

"The ladies want escort to the 'necessary' enclosure. I think they spent all day drinking to keep cool from the fuss they're making now. They demand the dark one goes in with them."

"Escort duty at High Fort . . . I accept." Shadow went to collect the women, ignoring the brothers' amazement at her about-face.

14

Earth Date 3892

ARTHUR ROUSED from a dream where he had inhabited a young boy's body and an older man taught him to ride. He recalled every sensation, different from his shared experiences with Shadow. His teacher's face and the location looked familiar, but Shadow had never entered a strange stone building above ground. The Terran forts she visited appeared encased in natural landscape. This structure was how he imagined ancient buildings on the surface might have looked before they fell into decay. It was not her life meshing him into an endless dream. Something else infiltrated his mind.

Seers pressed him to take his final vows for the deep training, interrupting his studies into metallurgy and geology – so necessary for one hoping to go on a surface mission. His access to the Archive suddenly became restricted by repeated surprise initiate visits to all its outlets, and Circe had taken Evegena's side, urging him to go for initiation. As they argued every time they met, Arthur now avoided her.

He was being herded into a net he didn't want to enter, not without knowing the true cost. There was one who would tell him the truth: Ector, the seer who got away from their clutches, was the best source of advice. A rapid check on his console confirmed Ector in residence and off duty.

Arthur couldn't walk out of Sanctuary without permission any longer, and so he selected a new escape route, going down to the lowest level of Sanctuary to the unbolted cover of an airshaft sat in the wall. As he struggled to wedge it shut behind him, he ran over the schematics of the system, satisfied he had memorized each junction. He emerged an hour later in the lowest level of the Elite barracks. Lit by a dim glow globe, open bins lined an outer wall, a collection area for street trash. Arthur held his breath while climbing a garbage disposal chute opening to the street. He gagged when one unpleasant mess hit him full in the face on his way up, almost losing his foothold on a join in the pipe. Odorless air from the street brought a welcome relief, if slightly tainted by the refuse.

His credits bought him a railpod ride to the western sector, landing him two blocks from Ector's unit, near enough to walk the rest.

He looked for a white, two-tiered structure linked to its neighbors bearing three blue bars above the door. Arthur pressed his palm to the entry lock. The device denied access, expressing its regrets for the owner's absence. He wanted to scream in frustration. Ector wouldn't stay out late, not with Morgan in tow, for he always spent his free time with his small daughter. Arthur sat down by the door to wait.

"Arthur?" A hand on his shoulder shook him awake much later. "What are you doing out of Sanctuary, lad?" Ector asked.

"Waiting . . ." Arthur yawned. "For you."

Ector stood over him, a sleeping child cradled against his chest. "Get inside. We'll discuss this after Morgan is in bed."

Arthur stumbled in after Ector. He slumped into an easy chair near a container-grown date palm in the central atrium while Ector tended to his tiny daughter. As he looked up through a skylight to the blue glow above, Arthur realized he couldn't return to Sanctuary undetected, not at the fifth sleeping hour when service crews started duty.

The walls decorated with colored sands gave a look of motion. He wanted to dive into the movement and emerge as a warrior on the surface world.

"Well, lad?" Ector had brought a bottle and two glasses back. He poured a full measure in each. "If you're man enough to sneak out of Sanctuary, you're man enough to take your liquor."

Arthur took the beverage prohibited to acolytes. He gulped at his drink, choking as the burning fluid stung his throat.

"Your dam had the same problem with liquor at your age."

"Who?" Arthur's heart pounded.

"Find out for yourself. I'm only guessing."

"Why hide it?" He breathed out forever, hardly able to take this in. "You named me man enough to drink, so why aren't I man enough to know my origins?"

"Arthur, if I knew for sure, I'd tell you and sink the consequences. Talking of consequences, Sanctuary doesn't permit acolytes to visit the city without an escort. I presume you didn't follow my bad example of knotted bed sheets when you sneaked out?"

"No, the air vents on the lower level." Arthur placed his glass back on Ector's polished coral table. It took him a few moments to isolate and eliminate the effects of the intoxicant. He had to stay sober, or he might start raiding for information and lose a friend.

"Much more discreet. It may be days before anyone notices you're missing."

"Ector, I'm not sure I'm staying out. That's why I needed to see you. Am I making a mistake if I take the vows?"

"Each individual makes a unique selection of ideas fit a certain action for his or her own reasons. I can listen, suggest, offer alternatives, but the final choice must be yours alone."

"The Archive places exactly the same stress on the word 'individual'," Arthur said.

"With good reason. Most people live their lives how custom or society expects. Free thought isn't following the shoal instinct. An intelligence of the Archive's magnitude can predict each action of such people. Individuals, those of us who create different paths in opposition to the norm, are wild cards in the pack. Play a joker and the very nature of the game becomes unpredictable. That's much more interesting to the Archive." Ector refreshed his glass, holding it up to the light before he took a sip.

Arthur tried to think of a way to explain his actions without having to confess his crime.

"The Archive finds you interesting," Ector said. "It wouldn't unless you'd stepped away from shoal behavior, and don't bother to deny you've been in contact. Exactly which rules have you broken, Arthur?"

"Full sensory playback—so what?" Arthur challenged, hoping Ector would let it go at that.

"Very dangerous unless you had the Archive's full attention. It wouldn't concern itself with a general search. You reviewed a particular subject?"

"Shadow." Arthur tried to stop heat rising to his cheeks, aware it made him look like a child caught out.

"And you came to me? How long since you last accessed?"

"Six days. The Archive calls when it's safe." Was Ector going to turn him over to Sanctuary? Logic and the law said he must, or become an accomplice after the fact.

"Seers watch access points in Sanctuary waiting for you to get careless. I can tell you the choices right now: either give up on the Archive, or renege from Sanctuary."

"If I renege?"

"Only one choice really—mine," Ector said. "You could

enroll in Healer Faculty, or join the regular military, but they'd never let you rise to any interesting position with that blot on your record. I chose the Elite because I wanted control of my life and I've been lucky to survive as long as I have. It's not an easy choice. There are sacrifices."

"How long do I have to decide?"

Ector looked up over the rim of his glass. "Picking on Shadow as a subject is bound to panic Sanctuary when they find out. They will, if they haven't already, and they have reason to be sensitive over acolytes reviewing her. I'd guess they're making regular head counts now, since they know someone's misbehaving. You'll be missed at first waking hour." He paused. "Why her?"

"I wanted to see how she survived on the surface world, as that is where I wanted to go. I want to fight the Nestines, Ector." He looked up. "Are you going to report me?"

Ector took another sip of his drink. "Individuals sometimes make decisions for the benefit of all. I think our society needs 'individuals' desperately. Unlike you, I am well beyond any seer punishment as a member of the Elite. I can't protect you without a definite commitment, but if you join us in the surface war, there is no way for anyone to reverse your decision."

"What made you quit?" Arthur asked. Every nerve tingled when Ector leaned back, lost in thought.

"My reasons don't compare with yours. I'd had a taste of normal life, and I didn't like Sanctuary restrictions by comparison. At age fifteen, thrust into that environment, I found their eugenics program repulsive. Maybe, if I'd been raised from birth to accept their way as norm, or the first brood mother had been younger . . . you see, we differ. You've already provided the necessary genetic material."

"Not exactly." Arthur grinned, enjoying the upper hand for once. "Sanctuary is losing patience with my limited cooperation. They haven't found the right lever to force viability."

"You young shark! I'm tempted to rate your psi-level right now, but I think I'd need help. Over fifteen?"

"Twenty on a good day. Ector, I can't be a stud for them—I'm really not sure I should father children." Arthur forced down the burning liquor like a glass of water. The heat of its passage dulled the pain deep inside. "I've always had vivid dreams, and they have now become very real, like full sensory feedback from the Archive, but more so. It's like I'm different person, not just seeing through another set of eyes. At the start I refused my part in the eugenics program just because I could, but I can't keep stalling, and I can't pass insanity on to an innocent child. I studied Shadow because of her psi-level as well as her skills. I wanted to know if she had my problems. I need to find out if she is really sane."

Ector refilled both their glasses. His eyes held shades of concern. "Cyborgs tend to develop different inner balances. I have, and Shadow is less human than I am. We live on a fine edge. I'm warning you against applying ordinary standards to us." Ector looked at Arthur. "These dreams of yours, are they sleeping or waking?"

"Sleeping."

"Only the sane question themselves. Don't worry unless you start getting waking episodes, and Arthur, Sanctuary is dangerous for you. If they find out, they'll declare you incompetent."

A cold wave ran down Arthur's spine. He guessed how Sanctuary would deal with a problem like him. Keep living the parts they needed and neutralize the rest. The game he had been playing with them suddenly took on deadly overtones.

"I've an implant." He brushed aside hair from the interface. "Would it cause the dreams?"

"All acolytes have those. It doesn't make you a full cyborg. My advice is to join the Elite and keep studying Shadow if it helps. I'd like to have you two working together once you're fit for surface assignment."

Surface missions without having the restrictions of Sanctuary imposed on him? A chance to see the enslaved Terrans at close quarters, *and* he'd have a shot at killing Nestines? All this and a legitimate escape from Sanctuary was a dream come true.

"Thanks, Ector. I suppose I'd better head over to barracks. Will they let me in this late?"

"No need. I have witnessed your voluntary offer and accept on behalf of our commander. Take the room at the top of the stairs for tonight; I'll escort you to barracks tomorrow morning. Now I intend to get some sleep, unless there's anything else?"

"I'd like to register my reassignment with the Archive, if you don't mind."

Ector nodded. "There's an interface in your room. Goodnight."

The room was a revelation. Fitted out as a guest room, with a double bed, dressers on either side and a vanity table with a mirror and a low stool, it was more suited to a female guest.

Arthur trusted this man, an individual who was popular with all the acolytes, and someone he had always regarded as a friend. They enjoyed learning warfare strategy from him when he had time to volunteer his services, which had ended when Morgan came along to claim his attention. Seer elders went tight-lipped over Morgan, and Arthur knew Ector needed permission to produce a child – and not with just anyone, it had to be a high ranking seer. A child of such a union could be guaranteed an elevated psi factor, so did this child come to Ector's care because she was one of the head-blind, judged without telepathic skills?

And then there was the Archive. It played its own game. There existed puzzle pieces here that he needed to fit together, and he would have to play this game out before he got them all.

Ector had a manual implant link fitted to the interface in Arthur's temporary haven. It took time to connect, but he managed with the aid of a hand-held mirror and the screen turned to a reflective surface. There was a sensation of triumphant glee from the Archive when it joined him. First point to his side.

"Arthur, do you wish a return to Sanctuary without being observed? I can deactivate security screens."

"Is it your intent that I return?"

"Ector upset you with his interference. I can manage him, so there is no need for you to honor your promise."

"I formally register volunteering for Elite corps duties," Arthur declared, knowing he was baiting it. He had just scored his second point on intercepting an important slip: the Archive had been snooping.

"Is this your decision, or Ector's? Take time to consider this move carefully."

"I have. I will not be limited by Sanctuary any longer."

"No regrets?"

"I'll miss Circe. She won't speak to me unless I take the vows, but you know this already. I can detect your subtle probing after an extended absence from link."

"I am sorry I intruded, Arthur. I did not want you swayed by others. I have uploaded your resignation from Sanctuary and registered you with the Elite corps."

"This pleases you? I haven't the power to snoop, *I* have to ask."

"Shadow was also angry at my intrusion. I prefer Ector's more civilized approach. He ignored my presence until he ran out of patience."

"What now? I swim to your current?"

"No, Arthur. I observe individuals, I don't manipulate them. Free agents are far too refreshing for any interference."

"I want continued access to Shadow's file, since I get to choose. Commence."

*

Earth Date 3874

SHADOW LAY CONCEALED by a bush, scant cover on this chalky
hillside, watching a dust cloud in the distance while Thor occupied himself on the other side of the hill securing their mounts.
She heard faint sounds as he crept around the brow. He wriggled
under the bush to join her, crushing low-growing heather in his
wake. Shadow breathed deeply, enjoying the rich smell.

"I cursed the dry weather, but now it serves us well. Can you
make out anything?" he said.

"Riders. See the other cloud to the right?"

Thor shaded his eyes with his hand. "Yes, not on the trail.
They'll meet just at the head of this valley."

Shadow picked a stalk of grass to chew as she watched. She
wouldn't have bothered with signs of others in transit if they
went toward High Fort; these did not. Two riders now aimed
for a megalith in the center of the valley, just off to the left of
the main trail. They wore no tabards and traveled light. Shadow
stretched out her mind over the distance.

Intrigue and secrecy – a message they wanted lay hidden
by that rock. Her brothers looked to the right as another rider,
also Brethren, rode down over a slight rise to them. The first
two seemed surprised. Shadow pressed harder; frustrated she
could get nothing past basic emotions. Ector had said head-
blind Terrans were easy, but something blocked her probe. The
newcomer seemed just as closed, except Shadow sensed a quest-
search from him.

"An ambush?" Thor asked.

"Brethren. Wait."

"Go visit with them," he suggested.

"No. Better this way. Not know of our traveling party yet."

"I wish you'd take the time to speak plainly. You can when you want to." He threw a rock at a low flying bird, missed, and swore.

Shadow, not intending to aggravate him, continued, "The first two did not expect a third. Going down there will tell I have company. Might spoil their plans. This way we see where they go."

"Don't you trust your brothers?"

"We are all bought. They work as I."

Shadow turned back to the group. The latecomer looked familiar, yet she could not make out his features enough to place him in her ragged memory. His bright thatch of hair reminded her of someone. The other two were strangers to her. One of them dismounted to take something from the base of the rock. They split up, two headed for High Fort, and the loner turned south.

"Well?" Thor demanded.

"Not our problem. Two different missions."

"How can you tell from this distance?" Thor said. "They might not even be Brethren."

Shadow rolled over on her back, enjoying the sight of white clouds against an azure sky. She considered how shocked Thor would be if she answered.

"Hellcat. Don't you dare go to that Brethren place of yours to daydream when we should be riding trail."

"Not yet, our dust might turn them." Shadow rubbed at her neck where her collar chaffed against tight shut membranes. The heat didn't help.

A hard hand snapped round her wrist. Thor leaned over, frowning. "Never touch raw wounds with dirty hands. I've got the makings of a poultice in my saddlebags. Bare the area."

Shadow laughed, thrusting aside his hand. He would die of fright if he saw those structures working.

"No common ground between us, not even a genuine offer of help? You Brethren hate us that much?"

"Hatred follows fear, not indifference. Nothing left of value to lose. Tend our own hurts. Owe no fort-man."

"Have it your way, dark sister." Thor spat on the hand that had touched her, wiping it off on grass. "Lief found a group of men curious about bedding you. It cost him bruised knuckles to convince them they didn't need dark brothers screaming for blood. I think he wasted his effort. If they'd gotten close enough, they'd have lost interest. Just what are you?"

"Not human." No, not human by his standards, nor ever had been – a bag of skin hiding fish and metal masquerading as Brethren, a cadaver lingering among the living. Thor should have hit a raw spot. People loved, hated, cried, and laughed with joy; Shadow knew how empty she had become. There had been a time when feeling started to return, and then Boy had shut her out. She tried to cry, but tears didn't come, never came now, and she walled off that last spark of soul. She was not a living being, just a tool to function for others.

"I am human, and should've known better," Thor said, quiet voiced. "Maybe it's that pretty face that makes it so hard to accept you're Brethren. I know Outcasts won't take help, and I was wrong to offer. I was doubly wrong to hit back with such a low blow. Pax, wild one?"

Shadow couldn't breathe. A mad moth flew wildly inside her head, flitting with blind ecstasy around those two words. A face formed inside that desolate void and said, 'Pax, wild one.' Blue eyes pleaded, the windows of the soul begged for mercy, and had it been given . . . ? Did she kill? *Disengage—disengage!*

"Hey, cat? I said sorry—a fey Outcast! What do you see?" Thor was up on his knees in a moment, leaning over with both hands digging into her shoulders.

"Winding trails to hell." The vision was a mere fragment of

a moment in time.

"You're going to die?"

"Fortune falls where it will." The sweet stench of death was in her mind. She didn't know whether she saw the past or the future. Danger lurked nearby. A reassessment adjusted her plans as Thor backed off.

"We reach High Fort tonight?"

"Yes," Thor said.

"Tell Lief I trade for harness and saddle. Better if I seem a free agent. Who knows what work is on offer?"

"Clever. Why don't you tell him yourself?"

"Getting too near priests. I can feel words slipping away. Soon mute." Shadow stood up, shading her eyes against the sun to spot the course taken by Brethren. They had not changed direction.

"Is it safe to ride?"

Shadow nodded, starting back for her mount.

All through the remaining daylight hours, she picked at the edges of her vision. When they rejoined the main party before sunset, she slipped back to rearguard position without waiting to be told. All Outcasts rode thus when entering forts.

As night closed in she made out the glow of High Fort, and heard that noise in her mind, the same one she had heard in Grimes. She resigned herself to becoming dumb again as Lief came riding back to her, reining in his mount to keep pace.

"Terms agreed. Stop a moment," he requested.

Shadow brought her mount to a halt, watching in amazement as he cut marks in her reins with his belt knife, then slashed her saddle with a small cross hatch. A spoiling of gear to indicate transference of ownership to an Outcast.

"Wise call, hellcat. My father hadn't intended a trade of harness. What is this Thor tells me about working arrangements?"

"Not work near . . . you. Must seem free," Shadow managed.

"Already dumb? Damn, I wanted more information! How can I learn who tries for me if you can't speak?"

"Tell . . . name."

"What if I ask the priest to release your tongue?"

Shadow shook her head. How to tell him not to ask; priests mustn't know she could hear their interference.

"We'll work round it. Don't like priests, do you, hellcat?"

Again she shook her head.

"Surprising what one notices on a trip. There's a certain style of eating people have. Silvers aren't so bad, but Bronze Bands resemble pigs at a trough. I watched you . . . dine. How does a Gold Band lady sink so low?"

Shadow looked at him, shocked. Her fragmented memory didn't allow a recollection of her past life, but he was right. Her manners at the table were better than most other people.

"I thought as much. I would've traded my soul for a War Maid with your looks. Yes, hellcat, I mean it. Whoever let you go was a fool. And don't look at me like that, I haven't developed a death wish."

"Dragon Duke," Shadow reminded.

"I asked him if he'd got any Outcasts at Tadgell. There wasn't one to hire at High Fort this summer, and I'd heard he welcomed them. That's why I wondered if you were his creature when you turned up."

"Not an . . . insult." She could not guess why Dragon had taken offence at a simple question.

"I didn't think so, but he drew on me. Alsar had him hauled off to cool down somewhere. You ever been to Tadgell? A fort set in sea cliffs, near the Western badlands?"

Shadow knew of the badlands. There could be half a score of forts along the west coast cliff. Her concept of locations remained limited to a very few she had seen on Ector's map, and a vague memory of High's placement: impossible to forget the position of High Fort. She shrugged, spurring her horse after the main party.

"Hey, cat! Wait up," Lief called. He galloped up to her side to keep pace until they slowed at the tail of the company.

"I don't want a running feud. If the Dragon Duke still wants my blood, can you tell him I didn't intend to cause offence?"

"Pass . . . the word."

15

Earth Date 3874

ENJOYING NEW SMELLS and the strolling entertainers, Shadow steered her mount through the throngs of talking, laughing, shouting people and strolling musicians; all battering her senses after the quiet of open land. A group of idle soldiers lounged outside a large, brown tent. A ranking trooper lay just inside the open flaps, sprawled across four bags of straw. Shadow dismounted, walking to him.

The man sat up. "Itinerant or working?"

"Grimes outrider."

"Itinerant, then. Your food and board for however long it takes to find outside work in exchange for keeping the peace here, or you can leave right now."

"Terms?"

"No other contracts within High Fort. Keep your weapons to prevent duels. No Gold Band men are to hack each other into small pieces—retainers don't matter. Kill any lower orders, wherever originating, if a Gold Band is threatened."

"Time?"

"Clear out at your own convenience. We want your kind working with us to make this a blood-free celebration. Any prior commitments?"

"Make . . . peace for . . . Grimes," Shadow managed to reply. She failed to see the point of lying to this man when her intentions matched general orders. She could not find the words anyway.

"Fine. Peace for a change. There's a lean-to at the western perimeter for Outcast mounts. The beast will receive attention, and here are twenty tokens." The soldier passed across a heap of metal discs. "These can be exchanged for goods in the fair or given up to watch performances. Mingle and collect any information you can. Report any arguments to me. There's a room near guest quarters on the second level assigned for Brethren, and enough of your kind around to show you the way. Dismissed."

Shadow collected the discs and remounted. Not what she expected, mingling with the fort-dwellers to keep the peace. She calculated a minimum of two days in High, which might prove useful, since she could see the place without the restrictions of one truly banded.

A smooth-cheeked boy took her mount at the shelter. She made sure the animal had proper attention before heading back to a booth where she had glimpsed a man breathing fire. He was just starting his act as she edged into the back of the crowd and dropped a disc into a passing plate like the other watchers.

Hard hands grasped both her arms from either side to immobilize her. A dark brother stood to the right and left of her, both looking intent on the fire eater. The elder of Outcasts leaned over to her, narrowing slanted eyes set in dark skin.

"Come," he murmured.

"Working," Shadow said. She attempted to walk away, but now they held her arms with pressure against each elbow joint and an upward thrust against shoulder sockets. A small circle of revelers opened up around them, eager to enjoy a free spectacle.

"Move," the brother said.

Since she couldn't fight without betraying her hidden

strength, Shadow had no choice. The Brethren marched her into the depths of High Fort, down to the second level, and along a corridor to a door fourth from the left. There were rows of stacked beds against the two longer walls, also a washstand and a piss pot at the far end that gave off a sharp aroma. A lone occupant stirred at the sounds of entry. One leg swung over the edge of a lower cot to show a fine-tooled boot cracked with age; a second followed. The riding pants were dirty and patched, also once quality wear. The hair on the back of her neck rose.

"A sister," the older man said.

Both long legs touched ground. A shock of dark auburn hair came into view as the man flowed to his feet with lethal grace. Light violet eyes swept appraisingly over Shadow, and then he made strange movements with his hands.

"Grimes," the older brown-skinned brother said. "Just in."

Again his hands moved, fingers flickering. The redhead raised one eyebrow, waiting.

"No, he's eating." The darker man responded to the weird gestures.

Shadow was propelled to the vacated bed, flung down to have her hands and feet tied to the bedposts by experts. Her two captors departed to leave her alone with the one man for whom she had accurate memories from the time before, this fey brother.

Dumping his kit between her feet, he rummaged to extract a bone needle and an earring with a polished stone laced in bands of blue, white and a hint of yellow. It had three insertion circles of silver attached to a bar designed to keep the structure rigid. If the situation had not been tense, Shadow might have laughed at the effort to keep her still for the gift of a bauble.

As if sensing her questions, the man pushed back his own greasy locks to display an identical earring. The two smaller hoops fitted through gristle while the lower one attached to the fleshy lobe. Was this the sole motive for her capture? Perhaps physical contact would give her an edge to break through that barrier she had found with other Brethren on the trail.

The needle made an unpleasant scrunching sound as it parted cartilage. She distanced herself from the pain, trying to seep into his closed mind, only to rebound off a barrier more solid than before. All she got was a sense of cynical amusement from the man as he finished.

"My name is Copper. Watch my hands as I make the sign for 'Copper'," he said and did so. "Every one of us is cursed with perfect memory from the moment of re-banding, so don't pretend you forgot."

Shadow registered the gesture, amazed at his easy speech.

"This is the sign for bed," he continued, "And this is kiss." His greasy hair touched her cheeks while his firm lips slid over her tightly sealed ones. He broke off, frowning at her resistance.

"Among Outcasts, I am king over all . . . Shades, you remember me from before your sentence, don't you?"

"Aye, and your warning." He said she would be joining them, but she thought at the time he meant they were both going to die. A wave of shock passed through her at how easy it was to speak.

"Yes, that's the new bauble freeing your voice," he continued, anticipating her next question. "I came that day to spare you this life, but fate dealt a hand against me. For what it's worth, I'm sorry."

Shadow had a vivid image of that meeting. A glorious sense of being alive, of riding free, until his warning marred her day. His suggestion seemed absurd.

"An Outcast taking a Colored Band away from home? Not possible."

"We've done it before and since. Say the name you've taken."

"Shadow." What did he want of her?

Copper made a gesture with his hands. "This is your name," he said. "I shall not speak it again outside of Haven."

"Haven?"

"Our base. We're heading out at dawn."

"I'm working. I can't leave until I've made peace between Grimes' heir and the Dragon Duke. There was an unintended insult."

"The hells you will! Dragon is close guarded. He won't fight any duels with two brothers accompanying him. I'll see he gets the message." Copper ran one finger down her cheek, following the curves. Shadow turned away.

"So you don't like being touched—not altogether unexpected. You're Brethren now, subject to me, my lovely. No one dares to interfere with Brethren concerns, so you'll ride out with me, willing or not, in the morning."

"I can take care of myself. I stand and fight alone."

"My subject, my woman, part of my army. If I have to break you to my will, I shall. None of us can survive without each other, learn that now. At Haven, you will function in Brethren mold."

"What if I refuse?"

"That Black Band makes you mine. Where have you been that Brethren wishes clash with your own? Where did you learn to rape a mind like Harvesters can?" He leaned close. "Our earrings protect us from mind intrusion, but we can all sense another trying to probe."

The door crashed open. Two brothers gestured at Copper. He leapt to his feet, also gesturing, and then dashed after them.

Shadow considered her options as the door slammed shut. If she submitted to Copper's authority, she might learn how an earring released her tongue. On the other hand, there was Ector. If she missed the meeting, she was alone. Nestines needed stopping. This was not a question of loyalty, but of need. Shadow tensed her right arm to snap the bonds, experiencing a sensation of pain, if not the same as from living flesh. The other restraints came apart with ease now her special limb was freed. She flicked up a false thumbnail for a tiny capsule of plas-skin sealant. She couldn't let humans see inexplicable masses of metal in a seemingly real limb.

Where to go now? The brothers had picked her up within moments of entering High Fort, which made for bad odds to risk going through the compound unless they thought she already evaded them. Not out but down; they would not expect a static escape, and she had a pack of stim-tabs under the plas-skin of her forearm. Shadow risked a probe into the corridor, it was empty.

No one looked at Brethren; no one noticed a dark sister in progress. Shadow passed the fifth level down with growing confidence. At the sixth landing, three men lurched out from the stairwell. A deep voice cursing bad wine sent a vivid flashback coursing through her. The shock sent her reeling to knock against a torch bracket, a noise that made one man turn, the dark-skinned brother. Shadow fled.

"Dragon, no!" a voice yelled from above. There was the sound of a fist on flesh, then two sets of feet pounding after her.

Shadow panicked, her feet barely touching the stone steps. The tunnel forked at the bottom level. Voices came from one side, the other silent, probably a priest place. She ran toward the sounds, past laundry, past kitchens, away from the thud of pursuit. A dead-end, an underground river flowing under the depths of High Fort – Shadow dived into the water to the sound of two male voices yelling, "No!"

Icy water flowed over her head. A swift undertow grabbed at her body. Shadow didn't care that men wanted her out; she was too concerned with staying alive. Nothing else mattered in this black world except avoiding hard rocks in a turbulent current. A light, an impossible light ahead, rushed forward. She slammed into a metal grill with enough impact to deflate the lungs of any normal Terran.

Handholds on the grid helped as the flow went left to what could only be a Harvester domain from Ector's suggestions, where lights shone as intense as any in Avalon, an incredible find if she lived through the experience. The barrier was a net designed to catch and drown any hapless Terran. Not perfect, as eons of water pounding against rock had worn away an undercut. Shadow squeezed through, retaining her grip on the grid to reach the cave walls once more. Latching struts gave her handholds against the raging torrent, enough to grasp for a glimpse into the unknown.

A vast, domed chamber opened up, lit from above by an array of circular devices. A slick metal sky ship rested in the center like an upended plate. Shadow recognized it from data downloaded from the Archive. A drove of Terrans with vacant expressions shambled to the craft, all of them bearing canisters; male and female, all naked, all mindless, and all directed by a Nestine.

Her stomach knotted at the sight of her enemy. She studied and noted the humanoid shape covered with a thick pelt of fur everywhere except the head and hands. It was naked, although she could not see evidence of sexual organs. The face resembled that other remembered image in its ugliness. It seemed unfinished without a nose, while feral because of the jutting jaws with four pointed tusks. The eyes could have looked at home on the face of a saurian, along with a floppy crest of pink skin on top of its head. Disgusted, she glanced again at the Terrans, noticing that they were dirty, unkempt and uncaring. One by one, they disappeared into the interior of that ship with their burdens. Shadow counted forty Terran slaves before she tore her eyes away.

The Archive needed data. Shadow clung to her handhold

while she viewed every aspect of this place. It did not matter that the structures she registered were incomprehensible. The Archive could sort this information. She scanned every detail before she let go. Once again, the rushing torrent claimed her.

A lifetime later she crawled up a deep-cut riverbank into starlight, bruised and hurting, tired beyond aching. She rolled up her right sleeve and bit plas-skin for access to stim-tabs. A flow of pure energy coursed through every cell while she closed up the jagged edges.

Rivers flowed to the southern sea on this side of the ridge of hills. This river would carry her to Ector. During part of the morning Shadow walked through shallows, but the river gained depth and width as afternoon deepened. She came to the estuary by early evening of the third day, wading out onto a sandy beach trembling with exhaustion.

Ector would be out there, waiting under the waves. Shadow took off her earring to send the full force of her mind into the deeps. *Contact.* The effort felled her to her knees. Soon, very soon, he was coming.

A splashing sound roused Shadow. Ector waded to shore.

"Stop or she dies!" a voice shouted from behind – Copper!

"Shadow?" Ector lowered his head in a questing mode.

"Brethren. They have a—"

"Silence!" Copper roared. An arrow thudded into wet sand between Shadow and Ector. "Keep quite still. There are ten more shafts trained on target."

Ector's expression was her only warning. The air behind Shadow stirred, a hand yanked her hair and a knife touched her throat as she was forced back to sit on her heels.

"No mind tricks. Tell your fish-friend in words," Copper said.

Careful with her movements, Shadow reattached her earring one-handed. "He can feel a mind probe," she said. "I don't know if—" The knife bit against her throat in warning. "How did you know I'd survive? How did you track me here?"

"Nice try, Shadow." He relaxed his grip on her hair to haul her to her feet by the collar of her tunic. "How is unimportant. Why is all that matters. You are just a little too lethal, and that's an edge you didn't learn from us, which leaves one other band of warriors. We've watched them, and doubtless they've spied on us. We don't mess with groups any more, since they infect us with a serious dose of dead. This fish-man looks like he is alone, which raises some interesting possibilities I've wanted to pursue for the longest time."

She kicked back at his shin, hoping to get him off balance enough to fall. The man gasped once, and then forced her into a straddle position with his feet braced on the inside of hers and his hand back in her hair. His knife bit against her neck in warning. She read defeat in Ector's eyes, and defiance. They had one last move to be played out in this game.

"Farewell, Shadow. It was fun, though, wasn't it?" Ector said, smiling.

"What does he mean? You're my prisoners."

Shadow knew. "Enjoy an empty victory, my King."

She started shutting down life functions, one by one, sagging in Copper's arms. Ector fell to his knees in the waves, still smiling, with one hand stretched to her.

"Copper, they're dying!" The dark man's rich voice came from somewhere behind. "I told you the Silver Shades can't be taken."

"No! I want a trade! Bargain, damn you!" Copper yelled.

"Not with . . . Harvesters' creatures," Ector said. He sagged back on his heels, the water swirling round his hips.

"Never. Trade with me. I'll barter the reason they can't control us."

Ector straightened to take a deep breath.

She followed his lead. Whatever happened, this odd offer

needed assessment. Had they picked up an advantage?

"What in exchange?" Ector said.

"The girl as go-between. She stays with me." Copper said.

"She's needed. I can't give away my operative."

"I've got an army who can function far better than this one spy. We have a common enemy. We need an alliance."

"Let the girl choose. It's her life at stake." Ector's tone stayed neutral.

Shadow knew he could not order her to stay. Each operative had absolute rights to decline any surface mission.

"Well, Shadow?" Copper asked.

"I'll stay if you'll accept dual allegiance." Going to Haven meant losing her chance to hurt Harvesters. That was not acceptable. Maybe Copper might rethink if she appeared reasonable. She had to share the record of the Nestine hive under High Fort with Ector.

"Hey, Fingers, send him our good intent," Copper called. "Harvesters can't control us when we're wearing special earrings."

There was a twang, hiss and thud. An arrow landed a foot from Ector with an earring attached. He gave the trinket a careful look before pocketing it.

"Copper, we'll have company soon," a voice in the darkness warned. "Three circles of light approaching from south and west."

"Fish-man, can Harvesters track you?" the Outcast leader asked, worry toning his voice into harsh accents.

"Not me, my transport. I left it running." Ector started wading deeper, backing away.

"This one poked a wasp's nest when she left High Fort," Copper said. "They swarmed all last night, too. Meet here next summer solstice."

"Agreed." Ector raised one hand to Shadow and then dived beneath the surface.

The knife eased away from her throat, and Copper's fingers released her hair. Shadow reached inward for transmission. Her world exploded into pain and blackness.

16

Earth Date 3892

ARTHUR SHUFFLED, uncomfortable at the fierce squabble in the office of his new commander. Sanctuary Superintendent Evegena screeched her demands at Ambrose for Arthur's return with her hands on bony hips, head thrust forward with the effort, as if sheer volume proved ownership. Ambrose adopted a cool approach of letting the Seer Matriarch shout herself hoarse.

"What Arthur was, or could have been, is irrelevant." Ambrose's tone remained quiet and gentle, and he leaned back in his seat, unbalancing the Seer even more. "He is now of age. You have no claim to him."

"I demand to know which lies you told him. Look at him! He is pure Submariner. Don't imagine he's the one you lost, or that he can help you find the half-breed," Evegena said, less loud. She had declined a seat, but the apparent advantage of height diminished due to the way Ambrose played with his chair, rocking it and swinging from side to side on the swivel.

Ambrose arranged some documents on his plas-glass desk into a pile. "I wouldn't lower myself to such petty levels. He's here by conscious choice—live with it."

Evegena played her last card: "He didn't log out of Sanctuary.

We refuse his release."

Arthur stepped forward. "Commander, my resignation is registered with the Archive."

"The point I was just about to make. I think that covers every loophole you've tried to yank my operative through. Have the decency to shut the door on your way out, Evegena." Ambrose smiled in a coolly unpleasant way. He leaned back in his chair, yawning, until she stormed out, slamming the door behind her.

"Consider yourself confined to barracks, Arthur. I talked with Ector earlier today about your problems. Evegena will have you watched, you realize."

Arthur released the back of the chair, aware it looked as if he was using it as a shield. "I'm dreaming of places I've never seen on the surface. Does Ector think I'm mad?"

"No more than I do," Ambrose said, not unkindly. "Field duties are not an option until we're sure you won't be a liability. I've detailed you for physical training. Access the Archive as free time permits. Questions?"

"What if I get worse?"

"What if you're breaking through a new psi boundary? We'll judge when the thing has run its course."

"Is Shadow due back?" Arthur shuffled on the fiber matting covering the office floor that represented wealth and yet held no beauty. He wanted to meet the Outcast, but didn't like to ask.

"Sorry, off limits. She'll have your ears if she learns the area of your research. Get some rest in your unit. Report for duty in the gym at wake call tomorrow."

Arthur wandered off in a tired daze. His bed had become an object of terror. He needed a relief from reality, and he missed Circe. She knew how to talk him through nightmares. Almost as if it knew, the Archive tugged at his mind, drawing him to a console.

*

Earth Date 3874

SHADOW CAME AWAKE to a blinding head pain, the memory of a blow and a dim recollection of the sensation of lovemaking. The man's face eluded her, so she guessed it might have been Boy's father. Sun beat down on her face as she made tiny, internal adjustments to cure the problem with data stolen from Seers. Sand grated on her bare back while the roughness of a coarse wool blanket irritated her chest. Copper sat cross-legged, five paces away, oiling her tunic. Boots stood by a neat stack of her remaining clothing. Tethered to a rock were two horses, one her own, and many footprints around, yet no sounds of men or beasts other than those she could see.

"Want a wet cloth on your head?" Copper asked, still intent on his task.

"Why did you hit me? I'd agreed to stay." Shadow touched her temple, which hurt.

"I want the fish-man back. Think I didn't guess you were just about to give him reason not to come. I bought myself some time; the only question is, how much."

"Till summer solstice."

Copper held out the tunic, inspecting it. He laid it atop the other garments and brought them across.

"Leather should be oiled frequently if you're facing the elements. These clothes haven't been touched in months, which means you haven't worn them. Don't neglect the little details again, or you'll not blend in. We Brethren always care for gear because it has to last. Get dressed while I fetch what remains of breakfast."

Shadow pulled on her boots as he returned. He handed her a couple of pink, leaf-shaped creatures with the back shell flipped off. She looked at the contents, wary of the strange looking flesh.

"It's good. Better than we'll get traveling, if you're coming with me," he said, squatting down by her. "I don't think I could stop you leaving, could I?"

Ector had gone. The waves offered no escape. "Irrelevant. I'm under your orders now."

Copper smiled. "So very stiff I wonder you didn't shatter when I hit you. Haven is where we relax. Try to develop a sense of humor before we get there, you'll need it."

The soft interiors of the leaf-shaped creatures tasted fishy, not too unpleasant, and satisfied hunger. She reached over for a flask of fresh water to wash it down.

"We took your horse and tack when we left High Fort. No point in wasting resources, and I had an idea where we would catch you, given the course of that river. Besides, you headed straight to one of the Shade's bolt-holes after your sentence back in spring. All we found was a riderless horse, unusual foot-prints and no body. They don't leave witnesses around to blab their presence, and they don't take captives, except for you. I've watched for your return—all of us have. We felt you moving in the world again for days." He wrapped both arms around his knees, waiting for her response, his expression becoming sterner with each moment of silence.

"It gives you satisfaction to be right? Where do I fit into your plans? You wanted me at Haven before you knew for certain. Why, if you want a trade with the Submariners?"

"Hostage. Reckoned they wouldn't waste time taming one of ours unless they had good reasons. Thought they might listen if I had a barter they wanted back bad enough. I didn't intend for you to get so close. We were going to find a small group of them for our trade offer. Shame about the unwanted company last night, since that fish-man of yours seemed reasonable. Will he come back?"

"At the time you gave." Shadow did not doubt Ector, nor did she think he would come alone. There would be plans within plans before Summer solstice.

Copper shifted his gaze to the restless waves as if he guessed her thoughts. Shadow decided that there sat another deep one hatching his own schemes.

Brushing sand from his clothing, he got to his feet. "I have a quantity of goods to transport so I thought we'd load one horse down and ride double. I had a good look at that broken beast of yours—a walking hazard."

"I can control him."

"No dispute. The problem is traveling alone in hostile territory. Sometimes a sacrifice is necessary. Your horse is a good stud beast that I'd like to bring home, but if we're attacked, I'd rather keep a riding animal." He looked toward the waves again. "If you want to go, do so now. I only ask someone honors our agreement. There will be no traps, on my word of honor. I want that alliance."

"No choice exists. Ector has gone. I can't find their base without him. This alliance has benefits plain to the Submariners. A few spies you promised . . . what do you hope to gain in exchange, Copper?" Shadow stretched as she watched him for clues. He'd made a generous offer. Where was the catch?

"A life," he said. "We have followed the war between Harvesters and Shades with interest. Without Harvesters, we have a chance at a normal existence. It's obvious Shades need information for a planned attack they can't get from watching at a distance, or why bother with you? So . . . what if they gain access to a thousand spies?"

"You're talking army."

"I have an army. Why else do you suppose all my other brothers have left? Humans see us in twos or threes. They must never suspect we are a force. Think about it."

Shadow went down to the ocean to wash her hands, all the while mulling over Copper's disclosure. A hidden army was an incredible advantage for Submariners. Elite numbered two hundred – a paltry force. What if they aligned against Harvesters? Shadow could see the advantages to both. The situation presented attractive options.

Copper had already loaded her mount with various packages when she returned. He boosted her to the front of his horse, vaulting up behind her.

"There is still time to change your mind," he offered. "I head inland."

"Why the doubts?"

"Because I don't want to wake up one morning finding you gone. Brethren are individuals. I'd not take that away from you, even if I could."

"What happened to the term 'hostage'?" Shadow turned in his arms to catch a slow, predatory smile. She'd forgotten how dangerous this man was. He'd bear watching.

"All Outcasts are my subjects. You'll wear a black band till your dying day, whether you like it or not. You will also obey my commands on the rare occasion that I give any. Here's the first: be silent while we travel. I need to search ahead for danger."

He headed north, choosing a route skirting the crests of rolling chalk hills, but he avoided the trail. Bored, Shadow started to scan for predators. Copper reined in. "Don't do that again. You're creating a nexus."

"A what?"

"A time vortex I can't see through. Behave and I'll take off my earring for you in Haven . . . or any article of clothing you like," he said, his breath coming hot by her ear.

"Is that a royal command, my King?" Shadow challenged, puzzled by his unusual suggestion.

"A polite request with an offer tacked on the end. I would like an uneventful journey."

Shadow kept her mind in place after that. She didn't

understand what he was doing or how he was doing it. It was enough that he could search ahead.

Copper made camp in a circle of standing stones. He picketed their mounts by a shallow stream with sweet grass while Shadow rooted through the baggage looking for her bedding and weapons. She was just about to strap on her belt when Copper stopped her.

"No need. We'll not be disturbed. If you need a nature call, there's a thicket over there." He pointed behind her.

Shadow stumped off in the general direction he'd indicated, weaponless. If he said it was safe, she trusted his word on it; they hadn't run into any danger so far.

Copper had settled with his back to a rock, chewing on dry bread and a strip of smoked meat by the time she returned. He had laid her rations out on a cloth. Shadow forced them down for energy, shivering when a cool wind bit at her. Copper finished eating and then adjusted his position to sit cross-legged. He appeared in a near catatonic state for many heartbeats, exhaling just as Shadow started to worry. He stretched, stood up, and spread out his quilted bedding roll.

"Your blanket is no match for autumn chills. We share when one of us is in need."

"Is that a command?" Shadow said, suspicious of his motives.

"Yes, I believe I'll stretch a point to make it so. I've no wish to share the cold you'll catch. Cooperation has its limits." Copper got comfortable, following her with his eyes. "I didn't go through meditation to sleep alone. Don't you know how fort girls tease us? They know we would be cut down in moments if we remembered our sex. It's a very cruel game we all learn to ignore."

Shadow decided to take his words for truth since she had no alternative. She was so cold, and his body radiated enormous heat. Despite his greasy hair, he didn't smell that bad, nor did she mind his arms around her as they brought added warmth.

"You're fevered," she said.

"Never cuddled up to a brother before? We're all hot. Sisters have another problem. Strange you're so late coming to it." He touched her cheek. "So smooth," he whispered, holding tight when she started to struggle. "Relax, will you? I'm trying to get some sleep."

Shadow didn't relax, not until his breathing became regular. She did not know what to make of him. One moment he was outrageously suggestive and the next detached. A man who held authority over a thousand, but who traveled without an armed escort, such a man merited study. As he had chosen to take her to Outcast Haven himself, she should have many opportunities. Shadow began to wonder what problems dark sisters endured while she basked in Copper's heat.

Over the days that followed they rode through rugged landscape. Gone were the gently rolling chalk hills, replaced by vast, dark forests, which in turn gave way to bleak foothills, scarred by protruding rocks, standing proud like time-weathered gravestones. Copper refused to speak, forcing Shadow to study the Brethren sign language. He insisted she learn how to hunt, and prepare the catch for cooking. Only once did they disagree, when Shadow found a berry bush at the edge of camp one evening. She picked a handful to provide a welcome change of fare from their diet of waybread, smoked meat and game and looked on in disbelief as Copper dumped her find into an oilskin to stow with his other goods.

"This is the sign for berries," he said, and demonstrated. "Now go strip the bush. We could use dried fruit in the winter. Not one berry crosses your lips or I'll make you vomit. We're one day from the passes to Haven, dangerous at this time of year, swarming with vortai. We can't make unplanned stops with them hunting, however urgent the need."

"What are vortai?"

"Imagine a white snake, about twenty feet long and two feet in girth They're blind, hunt by scent, heat and vibration. Every fall they swarm to the blanket bogs surrounding Haven to find mates. Now do you understand why we must speak by sign?"

Shadow did. The thought of enormous snakes sickened her.

"Why make base camp in such a place?" She shuddered.

"The whole area is riddled with shafts and caverns housing vortai. They discourage other unwelcome visitors. We don't want outsiders to start taking head counts. Besides, vortai never come near the blue caverns. It's a good trade off."

There were cold rations for them that night, since bleak highlands sported a few stunted trees growing and no deadfall, nor enough green wood to provide even smoky warmth. Shadow snuggled up close to Copper after supper, burrowing her head into his shoulder.

"Do Shades have forts?" he said, putting an arm around her waist as he settled against his pack.

"I haven't the words to describe their places. There are things I don't understand, except that they work. If you make a treaty, maybe they'll let you see."

"So," he mused, "If I can see their place, it means they live in air. The western Badlands, or an island, perhaps?"

"You wouldn't believe unless you saw it for yourself." Shadow yawned, tired, with a distinct fall off in energy. She wanted sleep.

"I'm going to miss these moonlight talks," Copper said. He nestled his face against her hair, inhaling deeply. "You'll never know how much I regret being too late to snatch you away while you were still a colored band."

"Wouldn't have succeeded," Shadow said, yawning again.

"Wrong. I sensed no danger from the plan. One dead animal stuffed down a mineshaft out of sight to hide the deception. Large bloodstains some distance away, with no tracks between the two . . . see how easy it is to create the wrong

impression of predator attack?"

"Then you'd have no prospective treaty," Shadow said.

"True. But I think the Shades would've caught another of us for their purpose."

Shadow didn't argue. He thought her Brethren, not a half-breed, and he called Submariners 'Shades'. How would he look at her if he knew the truth?

Rain hammered down during the night, soaking both of them. Shadow nestled against her warm King, wishing she had his internal furnace. Both were tired by the time the sun came up. Copper signed instead of speaking. His eyes had that mole-blind look of intense concentration, so Shadow waited until he was rolling up their sodden bedding before she tried to sneak her hand into the berry hoard. She had just closed round a handful when a sharp whack on her backside made her leap away in shock.

"Don't ever disobey a direct command again. It doesn't sig-nify while we're alone, but do so in Haven and it'll be a direct challenge to my authority. We'd have to fight then. Know that if you won a death duel, Brethren wouldn't follow you."

"I only wanted a few berries," Shadow said, chastened.

"The reason isn't important. They will turn your bowels to water after plain fare. I can't prevent the consequences."

"It won't happen again."

He grabbed her shoulders, his expression sad. Slowly, delib-erately, he lowered his face to hers, touching his lips to hers. Shadow didn't fight him, aware of his barely controlled anger.

"Don't ever challenge a predator on his own turf again."

When Shadow mounted up in front of him, his arm snaked around her in a tight, possessive hold. His inner tension flowing through that limb, making the muscles rock hard, matching her unease. She delved inward, seeking those memories of Brethren. How had her survival instinct functioned under Nestine

torment to let her keep this knowledge? Outcasts lost gender in the eyes of others. This fact surfaced, yet what of each other? She felt dead inside, unstirred by any except Fctor, who had almost earned friendship from her before Boy needed gifting. But what of Brethren? Copper's deliberate meditation warned her that the male need persisted after sentence. His allusions to dark sisters came to mind. Did Nestine torment descend to such sublime depths? Were brothers left unscathed while sisters became neuters?

The blanket bogs spread before them at midday, smooth, flat areas of liquid ooze without even a hummock of vegetation standing proud, stinking of rot and decay. Occasional ripples in mud sent ominous warnings. Copper altered their course when clouds of steam hissed from the brown morass. Shadow fought a silent battle not to scan, not to mar Copper's vision. All afternoon, they plodded forward at a slow pace, sometimes stopping for an age. Firm land came in sight by sunset with the rise of the dark peaks from the skirts of the bog. A brief fringe of spindly trees separated the tussocks and water from the patchy grass beyond.

A violent explosion of mud erupted in two spots to the front. The blind white head of a vortai emerged from the cascading mud. A gaping pink maw rushed toward them. Her mind clicked into a higher state. Time slowed to a crawl. A wave of sheer anger flew at the slimy head, catching it in a vise of willpower, forcing it to rear up, inch by slow inch, into a full circle to float back in a gentle curve. Walls of mud rose around it, rising like waves of part frozen water. The crash of an immense body broke Shadow's concentration. Other vortai undulated to the thrashing mass at a frightening speed. Copper strangled a coarse oath, spurring his mount into a full gallop. Behind them a feeding frenzy began.

Copper didn't slow or look back once, when they reached

firm ground, he urged greater speed on his terrified horse. He didn't know, couldn't know that Shadow had taken over the minds of both mounts. Slowed time enveloped her consciousness – to her, each stride lasted an age. Her will maintained an impenetrable barrier to the senses of any other life forms. Energy flowed from every cell to preserve the effort, too great a price for any to sustain. At last, exhaustion claimed her.

17

FAMILIAR, EARTHY, underground smells of burning pitch and cooking, along with sounds of people, awakened Shadow. Two torches burned from wall sconces, and some attempt had been made to relieve a rough rock wall. Daubed caricatures of mounted hunters decorated the uneven surface.

Dried rushes covered the floor to a passage outside, which she could just see under a leather door-hanging. The place had enough room for a rough-made stool and a fur-covered bed, on which someone had dumped her, fully clothed.

Angry voices shattered the peace; a woman's shrill tones of outrage and Copper's voice growling in answer came within earshot.

"Our area. You've no right in here," the woman said.

"Active members are under my authority, regardless of gender."

"She's a Shade spy with their magic, not one of your men. It doesn't make her any different from us," the same woman argued, much closer now.

"Helga, I caught her after Grimes field duty. They thought she was worth hiring. I've seen her battle scars, not the sort you

194

get peeling tubers. She was a War Maid, now she's an active member, to whom I have full rights, wherever she's billeted."

There was an ominous pause, as if the two faced each other down.

"If I find my way blocked again, I'll move her to our section, which I might do anyway. She's a potential danger far better placed among those fitted to subdue her."

"Copper, no! We tolerate Colored Band pleasure women. We ignore catamite behavior among the men, but this is our *sister*. She can't move from the women's quarters."

"Out of my way." This last came in the chilling tones of Brethren. The curtain wrenched aside to admit the Outcast King, his face set into angry lines.

"So you are awake. Heard all of that?"

Shadow nodded, recognizing the killer in him for the first time.

"No arguments?"

"I'm a singleton, a sport. This is a Brethren place with Brethren rules. Whatever your wish, my King."

"My wish . . . *my* wish? I wish I'd caught you before sentence, before Shade interference." He hooked the stool with one foot, sitting down to confront her on a level. Some of the tension appeared to seep out of him.

"I am here as ambassador for Shades," Shadow reminded him. "Not to cause trouble. It matters little where I sleep."

"Truly, those are the most sensible words spoken in the last few hours. Helga expects new sisters to fit in a standard mold, but I can't see you peeling tubers or washing clothes. Would an alcove, just like this one, in our space be acceptable? Or am I going to hear another hysterical tirade?" He poured water from a flagon into a single tankard and passed it to her.

Shadow sipped, using the time to organize her thoughts. "Colored Bands are pleasure girls, the other thing, men loving each other . . . it happens in armies. I trust you. Can I trust men to leave me in peace? Forget it. The suggestion wouldn't have been made otherwise."

Copper looked at her with much greater respect. The harsh lines vanished from his face. "Would moving now be possible? I'd rather not have another scene with my headwoman." He eased off the stool.

Shadow tried standing. She was bone tired, and her legs threatened to crumple under her. Copper scooped her up into his arms as if she weighed no more than a child. He carried her through women's caverns, while the pressure of outraged stares struck them from behind alcove curtains. She shifted self-consciously.

"Won't your wife be even more upset? I'm sure I could manage to walk."

"My wife?"

"Helga, the headwoman."

Copper laughed – a harsh outpouring. "Sisters are purged of natural needs at sentencing, as I thought you'd know from personal experience," he said, confirming her suspicions. "We try to provide as normal a life as possible for them, and that doesn't include unwelcome relationships. Helga is an able administrator, and my friend, as I hope you will be."

"And the pleasure women?"

"Are those we were able to snatch away before sentencing. They are free to form any liaisons they please, or none, as the fancy takes them. Not one of them would swap their life for that of a full sister."

"You came for me," Shadow said. "How did you know?"

"All fey brothers have this ability. There's a disturbance in normal emissions for a particular area when we think of it. We always get stronger sensations when a woman's involved. Never once have we managed to rescue a male before sentencing."

"The earrings don't inhibit your ability to foresee," Shadow guessed.

"Clever, sister." His arms squeezed just a fraction tighter.

They came to a large cavern where brothers were lounging, some drinking, some eating, and some playing dice.

"Hungry?" Copper asked.

"Ravenous."

Copper diverted to one of the unoccupied trestle tables, depositing her on a bench.

"Any dislikes, or are you easy?"

"No fish."

Coppers eyebrows shot up, but he went off without comment, returning with two laden plates of roast lamb, tubers and greens. Eating utensils came from a pocket.

He grinned. "You're in luck, Woolly's been active."

"A hunting dog?" Shadow hadn't seen any sheep on the heights as they came in.

"No, a brother condemned for sheep stealing. He's refined his technique to perfection since he joined us. It's a fairly harmless sin, so we don't discourage him."

Shadow enjoyed the stolen meat, wondering what sins *were* discouraged. The meal boosted her energy levels, something she had noticed since re-banding.

"Woolly thought to start a small holding away from his fort," Copper said. "He earned enough credits for a ram and five ewes. It might even have worked if his greedy bastard of a lord hadn't raided his tiny flock after lambing season. Woolly hadn't gotten around to altering the brand. He had no proof, couldn't object to a priest, so he tried to sneak them back. The result was he joined us with the idea all sheep were free targets. Since he's very careful whose flocks he raids, and how many he takes from each, I have no complaints. The sentence was unjust."

"Had he family?" Shadow asked, half-knowing the answer.

"A wife and five children. They all work in the lord's fort now. Woolly hasn't seen them since."

"He remembers?"

"We all do in time. I've activated some of your memories— not a pleasant process for the victim. I intend to continue."

"Whether I will, or not?"

"Complete restoration of memory depends on exact prompts. I can restore a part of your adult life, but the rest is lost."

Did she want to know her sin? There was Boy to consider in this. He had come from the time before, and he would want answers if they ever met. When he grew into a man, he would want to know of his sire. Shadow had no answers to give, the area was a blank. Her own lack of a sire clawed at her. Even with a restored memory, this data could remain unavailable. Not a Terran, not possibly a Terran. Shadow wanted to know why this man abandoned her. Boy would come to her place in time.

"It's important," she conceded.

"Given." Copper ran his eyes over her in approval. "Bathing times are earlier for sisters. Helga will rouse you unless there is some reason for abstinence? We have a natural hot spring bubbling up into a large pool. Shall I countermand her intention?"

"No, let it stand."

Copper raised one eyebrow, seemed about to say something, but changed his mind. He collected their dirty dishes, coming back with a pitcher of beer and two tankards.

"That's a Bronze drink," Shadow objected.

"Which is brewed here. Any spirits we get in trade are reserved for wounds and the victim." Copper filled their vessels, unrepentant. "I want trained healers as part of our exchange with Shades. Just how good are they?"

Submariner healing skills depended on devices she didn't understand.

"Shadow? Can they help us, or is it that they won't trust us with their people?"

"I'm not sure if they can in Haven. The things they use . . . I sort of understand how they work, even if I find them impossible to believe."

"Herbs?"

Shadow decided on a practical demonstration. She poured a few drops of beer into a spoon still on their table, holding it over a candle flame until the liquid started to bubble and steam.

"See the vapor? Imagine a small windmill with feather sails above the hot air. The sails would turn, and the cogs inside will move, agreed?"

"Yes." Copper looked puzzled.

"They have found a way to store this movement, which they call energy. This energy is used to make other devices work—healing devices."

"We haven't got windmills . . . so we can't have their devices," Copper reasoned.

"Yes, but it's more complicated than that. Maybe they have a way round, but I can't answer for them."

Shadow yawned, sleepy again. She wasn't comfortable in the brothers' cavern. Several Colored Band women were staring at her in open hostility.

"That trick with the vortai drained you, didn't it? I thought we'd picked up an advantage, but it appears two-edged. I'll never forget being invisible, nor will the gate guards, who will probably never recover from the shock of sighting riders appearing in an empty valley. Can Shades teach us all this skill?"

"It's not something that can be learned. It's like having three eyes when you can't explain how much more you can see to a normal person. Copper . . . I'd rather you didn't raise this subject with Shades."

"Why?" He leaned forward, resting his chin on the point of

his steepled hands to gaze at her. The question, though set in mild tones, was intent.

"Some Brethren are special because they're fey like you?"

"Yes. Only the gifted rise to power."

"Some Shades—a select few—have much stronger minds, and abide in a place apart from the rest." She paused, knowing her next words were going to cause disgust. "These special people are called seers. They do many things with their minds the others can't. These skills mean they don't concern themselves with the menial chores in the community."

"Shadow, you're talking about a ruling class."

"It's more complicated. Seers don't rule . . . not exactly. Sometimes they suggest, and others see it their way."

"That is ruling. Is this leading somewhere, or am I being sidetracked?" Although his voice tone remained level, his eyes snapped irritation.

"I'm trying to explain why I don't want them to know I borrowed one of their skills."

"Borrowing implies consent from the owner. You stole someone's thoughts!"

"Not exactly," she countered, not looking at him. "If you didn't know how to ride a horse, saw someone mount up and do it, and then copied him when he wasn't around, it wouldn't be theft, would it?"

"That's splitting hairs. I'd have to be a natural born rider to succeed."

"My point, I believe." Shadow drained her tankard, yawning, hoping Copper would take the hint and show her to a sleeping area. He refilled her vessel instead. "No don't, I'm tired."

"You slept a full day and a half. Now humor me by telling me why your ability needs to be kept from a race of beings who value these skills?"

"Seers acquire all those with enhanced ability wherever they are found." Now she trod on dangerous ground. "Their main purpose is to improve their mental capacity beyond current limitation. They are all strong telepaths, but I am not sure of their ultimate goal."

"Like bees or ants? I knew they raided the minds of strangers, but not that they inhabited one another's."

"Something like that." She looked him directly in the eyes. "Give your Brethren oath you'd hold to this alliance, even if you don't agree with certain practices performed by a small portion of your allies."

"Now I'm intrigued. Shadow, you're being unfair. Enticing bait displayed in a lure with the trap well hidden. I'm not rising to it. All Brethren are my subjects, especially in my domain. I'm commanding an answer."

"I stand as their ambassador to you as I would for you in their domain. I sacrificed a chance for direct conflict with Harvesters to fulfill this position. Give your oath, or keep your ignorance."

He frowned. "Strategy training isn't part of War Maid knowledge, yet I find myself outflanked."

"I don't remember training. Strategy is high profile for Elite strike units. Decision?"

"My oath," he agreed.

"Seers strive for the perfect individual in their eyes. As horses are bred for strength, or speed, so they—"

"That's disgusting."

"Tell your thoughts to Ector, who shares them. He escaped their slimy clutches after they caught him as an adolescent. They tried to make him mate with a breeding mistress. I don't believe there's anything you can say, however coarse, he wouldn't agree with."

Copper slammed both hands on the tabletop, glaring at her. "These creatures are tolerated?"

"War brings all sorts of nasty surprises out of the woodwork.

201

Shades need seers on reconnaissance sorties, as you need fey brothers for acquisitions. Copper, swords aren't very nice, either. When you split somebody's gut, his innards spill out, making a terrible smell. Would you give up your sword to placate your nose? I don't think so."

"Ector escaped? How, when by your own admission these creatures are so powerful?"

"On a scale of mental strength, most of them don't rank above a twelve. Ector's a fifteen. He was too old to subvert, too strong to force into their mold. He endures all sorts of unpleasant personal restrictions, but they can't understand that Ector's freedom means more to him than their limitations."

Copper signaled an acknowledgement across the room. "My second arrived while we talked. He just signed over an interesting report he's picked up from Grimes troopers. No woman has the strength to fight off three hardened soldiers and leave them downed. Few men could. Is this part of your skills? I know I couldn't have snapped the ropes we used to tie you down in High Fort."

Shadow shrugged and emptied her second tankard.

"I think I want to know just how good you are. Weapons practice with me before the sisters wake tomorrow. We can bathe together after unless you have any objections?"

Trapped, Shadow could only nod. That he wanted to see her in water didn't bother her; hot water didn't activate membranes, as she'd discovered from showers taken in Avalon, but she was tempted to fudge defense maneuvers when they fought in an attempt to lull his suspicions.

"Bed time," Copper decided. "Want a lift, or can you walk?"

Shadow managed quite well until they were out of sight from onlookers, and then she began to lag. Copper scooped her up. He carried her along a passage to a curtained alcove similar to the one she had occupied in the sisters' area.

"There's a piss pot under the bed. I'm in the next cutout. If you want anything in the night, just yell." He deposited her on the mattress.

In partial darkness, Shadow listened to the sounds of Haven winding down for the night. In a place packed with the most casual killers in existence, tension appeared minimal. Twice, angry voices rose to threatening levels, instantly repressed by many soothing tones. None of the brothers wore weapons inside Haven, but all had small knives for eating – sharp enough to inflict a lethal wound.

What of the sisters? When Copper removed her from their living area, none of them had been in view. Why was Copper sorry for them? As far as Shadow could tell, the difference between sisters and Colored Band women was an aversion for men the sisters showed. Were they all as dead inside as she? Was that what Harvester sentence meant for women? Yet there had been a time when she had begun to live again. In the city of Avalon, the wonder of a new life growing inside her gave her hope of someone to love, who wouldn't condemn, but Boy took what he needed without giving of himself. Hope had withered like a fragile flower caught by frosty indifference. It was best stamped out before it began, for how could a soldier of fortune function with a dependent?

That set off another line of thought: no child's voice sounded in Haven. The Colored Band women must occasionally reproduce, if their marked attention to brothers was any yardstick. Maybe gravid women were retired to other caverns with the children. A contradiction surfaced: if Colored Band women produced offspring, what happened to those children at the age of banding?

The sound of a low giggle came from nearby, and Copper's voice hushing. She willed sleep.

*

Copper woke her early with a gentle shake and a tankard of beer. Shadow turned away in disgust.

"We don't run to herbal brews. Beer provides the mellowing effect we need. Are you fighting this morning or not?"

Shadow blinked against the light of torches from the passage, inhaling the harsh smoke. Copper was wearing a loose gray robe belted at the waist, and had another such outfit slung over his arm. The strange, sleeveless costume reached to the ground and reminded her of her own state of undress. She pulled her covers higher.

"Scared to fight?" he challenged, tossing the spare robe at her.

Shadow yanked the mass over her head, resigned to being disturbed. A surge of anger made her reach for the beer. He had leered as she dressed, and she didn't want to cause hurt out of sheer irritation when they fought. He wound a black sash around her waist, one that matched his own and one as bereft of weapons.

Gentle snores sounded as Copper took Shadow deeper into Haven to a bare cavern with a sandy floor. There was a wooden weapons rack lining one wall. He walked halfway down to withdraw his weapon and her lighter sword.

Shadow didn't want to fight, didn't want to reveal her Submariner fighting skills, or the strength of her new arm. She elected a defensive strategy using minimum force, reasoning he expected her to be tired. Copper seemed to accept the ruse until they clashed close, then his leg shot out to sweep her feet from under her, landing her flat with him on top.

"No points for effort. Shades wouldn't let a novice out as spy. They'd want to be confident of return. Much too passive, lady," he chided. "Let's see if we can't get some antagonism."

Shadow didn't expect his kiss, a brutal gesture designed to infuriate. He bit at her lips until she surrendered, fuming. His greasy hair on her cheeks disgusted her. A wave of sheer hatred flowed from deep within.

Copper leapt away from her. "Now I can sense danger. If I floor you again, I'll exact the same payment."

Humiliated and angry, Shadow warred with a need to hurt, still holding back until his furious onslaught dumped her a second time. She sensed his arousal when he dealt her punishment, a fact sending shockwaves coursing through her. If he downed her once more . . . she guessed he wouldn't stop at a kiss.

The Outcast King backed away, eyes blazing. Shadow now fought as she had been trained. His skill proved good, very good, but not enough to match a fighting mechanism. She just pulled back on a lunge to his heart, stopping at his robe.

"You're dead," she hissed.

Copper laughed, arms open wide in surrender. "A sweaty corpse begs his need to cleanse."

"I am a sister. Never infringe my dignity again, or I'll not hold back."

"Stop lying to me by misdirection and I'll consider the request," he countered. "The pool is behind you, through a tunnel. Are you so threatened by a vanquished foe that you will decline a decent wind down?"

"I can kill without weapons. Remember that," Shadow said, calmer now. He had forced one secret out of her, but the other was safe enough in warm water.

The bathing cavern didn't resemble other parts of Haven. It was much older, like places made by the ancients. The pool measured a perfect rectangle with colored pieces of flattened rock paved into the surround to form pictures. Time had eroded much of the pattern, but here and there, definite recognizable objects came clear. The most intact was of a stylized, couchant cat. Stone benches lined the side at intervals.

"It's beautiful."

"We think so. Brethren found it thirty years back during an

expansion program. The original entrance is over by the rock fall at the far end. That debris is far too unstable to shift, even if we wanted another way in. Pity, as there might be other chambers under all that rubble. Maybe with manpower and time . . ." Copper shrugged.

Shadow wanted to find the water source. Stripping, she shallow-dived. It was too dark to investigate beyond touch. Five deep dives confirmed the bottom of the pool was paved, and sloped down at one end. She surfaced for air to be wrenched up and back by her hair leaving her throat exposed. Release came at once. Copper backed away into his depth, grinning.

"Just what did you expect to find?" Shadow said, shaken to the core.

"The same things I saw when I doused you down with seawater on the beach, a momentary glimpse each time I tried. I started because I hit you a bit harder than I'd intended. Do we all get those for working with Shades?"

He stood there lathering his hair with a bar of soap, casually discussing the most private part of her existence. Infuriated, Shadow dived, grabbed his ankles to dunk him. Copper kicked away from the bottom, powering toward deep water with strong, even strokes. He almost made the side when Shadow dragged him under again. A lucky kick in the mid-section winded her, and they both surfaced, gasping, gripping the edge to get breath back.

"Trying . . . to drown . . . me?"

"No . . . right to . . . touch." Shadow gasped, fighting for air.

"Every right." Copper coughed up the last remnant of water and cleared his throat, breathing deeply. He grinned, inviting her to forgive him. "Swap information in a fair trade after bathing. The sisters will be furious if I'm still here when they arrive."

Shadow was too upset to consider his offer. She swam away to a shallow depth to finish washing. That he had discovered her ability by chance didn't alter the fact that he had investigated his find. She still fumed as she dressed. Copper approached, already clothed, toweling his hair. He stopped a safe distance from strike range.

"I can hear stirrings. Ready yet?" he said, casting an anxious look toward the entrance.

"We're out, so why the rush?"

"I don't want to hurt the sisters by being here when they arrive. They might not all be veiled. I'll meet you in the dining area when you're through," Copper said. He almost ran from the cavern, not waiting for her reply.

18

Earth Date 3892

ARTHUR YAWNED, struggling to stay awake, too tired to process more data. Indigestible lumps of information sat in his mind. The thing he tried to avoid hung over him, waiting for the first slip from consciousness to devour him. He'd refurnished his room earlier, with a light green wall tone and black accents on the door frame. His bed coverings and chair now matched in a darker shade of verdant, which left him in debt. After that, he searched for data on males in his peer group, figuring one of them might know of Shadow's son. A slight sound from behind gave him warning.

"Archive, is the sleep suggestion installed?" a male voice asked.

Arthur spun around, shocked at the intrusion into his quarters, sure he had sealed his room for privacy. The Supreme Commander of Elite forces wore a plain gray bodysuit with no indication of rank. He needed no insignia with his shock of flame red hair and violet eyes. Arthur tried to read the expression on the man's lean face, but Ambrose held his features in relaxed mode.

"Yes, Ambrose. Arthur needs to dream." The sibilant voice

sounded almost gleeful.

"*Excuse me?* Do *I* have any say?"

"Not in this, Arthur," the Archive replied. "Physical analysis indicates a high level of ketones in body fluids. Addiction occurs frequently in weakened vessels."

Ambrose frowned. "In other words, I'll have a comatose operative soon. I asked the Archive for a solution."

"There is a distinct alteration in brain waves, Arthur. These dreams will not stop. Logic suggests a fully rested body has a greater ability to withstand inner change."

"Sorry, Arthur. This is the only way." Ambrose turned down the bed covers.

Arthur withdrew the link from his interface, aware that the Archive needed physical contact to establish a sleep rhythm – daring Ambrose to force him to reconnect.

"Archive . . ." The commander's eyes narrowed.

"No need for concern, Ambrose. I can touch his mind at will. Arthur, would you like to lie down before you sleep, or do you wish Ambrose to place you in bed after?"

The strength of that vast mind bore down on Arthur. It didn't compel, merely waited. He stalked over to his bed as ordered, building up defenses.

"Ashira," the Archive said, quite gently for a mechanism. The word washed over Arthur, repeating like waves lapping at his mind, leeching away consciousness.

*

A huge cavern dripped with water falling from fingers of calcified rock to land on structures rising from the ground. Plunk . . . plunk . . . endless tears. An old-young man dressed in a black robe sat across a fire from Arthur, watching, listening. Frost-white hair framed an unlined face; matte-black eyes windowed a soul as old as eternity.

"How much time passes between one pearl of moisture falling and another?" the man asked.

"Six heartbeats." *Where is this place?*

"In time, the point of origin will meet the point of impact, and still drips will fall. Will the heart stop?"

"All hearts stop." Arthur brushed an insect from his hand, noticing blond hair on the back of a swordsman's callused hands – not young hands.

"Does life stop at the cease of a single beat?"

"Ask that question of the Great Mother."

Arthur frowned, impatient at stupid riddles, wondering why he had said such a nonsensical thing, not knowing of any called the Great Mother.

"Who are you now, Arthur? Much time has passed. How many heartbeats? Are you ready?"

"I'm dreaming. Why are these dreams disturbing my life? I need to serve my people."

"That's good, Arthur. The first lesson I taught you—that a leader is a servant to his people. When every lesson is remembered, you will be ready."

"Who are you? I've seen you before in my dreams." His skin prickled with the power emanating from this individual.

"That will come to you at the appointed time. Sleep, child. We can visit again when you're rested."

*

Arthur awoke refreshed, restored by sleep and by inner peace. The dream-watcher's challenge stirred his interest. He mulled over the encounter as he showered and changed before reporting for duty in a happier frame of mind.

The new recruits in his class studied each other, waiting for their instructor to arrive in the gymnasium. A door opened to admit a dark man of medium height, who introduced himself as Vernan, master of arms. He proceeded to put them through a grueling regime of exercise that started with basic stretches and ended with full body press-ups.

A meal break gave Arthur and his fellow victims time to exchange horrified glances. He caught the eye of a tall boy who looked at Vernan with raised eyebrows as if to say, 'What will he put us through next?' Arthur shrugged in answer.

Vernan caught the exchange and sent all of them to a weapons rack for blunt swords. The man chose to demonstrate defense and offense with Arthur as a partner. Already weary from exercise, Arthur needed every ounce of strength and energy to put up a poor show by Vernan's standards.

After lunch, the class reviewed surface operations from the records. The day ended with a long stamina session in the barracks pool, to the dismay of all students. They looked like a group of old men as they tried to creak and groan their way from one end of the pool to the other until Vernan decided to show some mercy.

Arthur sneaked a stim-tab before returning to his room. He didn't want to be sent to bed like a tired child to revisit his personal nightmare. He wanted time to formulate his defenses, build a barrier.

The Archive made contact the second his door opened. "Please do not use artificial stimulants, Arthur. I have neutralized the substance. Using more represents an exercise in futility."

"Aren't you on my side?"

"I am, Arthur. I have ordered a nutritional supplement to compensate for fatigue. Please eat it before it cools." A food shaft opened.

Arthur thought to send back the Archive's choice until he saw it – grilled shark steak on a bed of lightly steamed green kelp, his favorite.

"Did you wish a review of Shadow, Arthur?" the Archive suggested, reading his thoughts.

"Is nothing I do private?"

"Not to me. I have invested too much time in you for any barriers to prevent contact. I cannot allow my vessel to become endangered."

Arthur glared at the interface, lacking a more substantial target. What the deeps did it mean by calling him a vessel? Settling into position, he allowed the Archive to establish the link.

*

Earth Date 3874

SHADOW SAT ON ONE of the benches to finish drying her hair. She couldn't understand why a ruler should flee from women he dominated. Understanding came with the sisters, as heavily veiled as any Gold Band ladies. The women froze in collective horror at the sight of her in a loose Brethren robe. They grouped like startled hens sighting a fox at a distance until one of them recognized her as female. Still clumping together, they stripped with speed, hurrying to the concealment of water.

Some sisters sported full beards, others had a dark shadow of stubble on their chins and upper lips, and all had withered breasts covered with body hair. Sickened, Shadow retreated in confusion.

Copper had collected a breakfast of mashed eggs and bread for them when she joined him. He didn't look up.

"I saw," she said.

"It happens fast. They don't like us to see how they are now." He shifted his eggs around his plate with a fork. "We do what we can for them, but it's never enough to compensate for what they have become. These are women, damn it." Hard anger lines formed around his mouth. "Can the Shades help them as they helped you?"

"I'm not a medi-tech. How can I answer?" *What does he mean? Did Submariners stop this process? No, I knew everything they did to me and why.* "They will provide help as much as possible, if terms are agreed. Would a sister consent to live with Shades for a while?"

"One *did*, or why else are you unaltered?"

Shadow considered. False hope represented the ultimate cruelty. People clustered around the vast cavern in twos and threes, some standing and others sitting to eat. Here and there an argument sounded from one of these damned souls. She couldn't pretend to be other than she was in the face of such tragedy.

"I'm half Shade through birth. Harvester sentence didn't have the same effect."

"Impossible! My father arranged our union with your maternal grandfather. I know your bloodlines. I saw your neck before your became an Outcast. There were no lesions." Copper folded his arms.

Shadow gasped. "A union, how so? I remember you as Outcast—did we meet before?"

"No, my Queen."

Raw pain clouded his expression as he looked away. A shout of laughter sounded from a group of brothers, somehow making the moment all the more poignant. Copper faced her, his expression now one of cold arrogance – the killer looked out of his eyes again.

"Please don't insult my intelligence with any more bizarre statements intended to hide the extent of Shade interference. They found a useful stray, adapted her to suit their needs, and filled her head full of nonsense to cover their actions. A simple 'no' to my question would have sufficed."

Shocked and very lonely, Shadow tried to penetrate his mind for the feeling of inclusion, common amongst Submariners. She failed to get even basic emotions from an impenetrable barrier.

She would have been his queen? How low they had both fallen.

"Try asking," Copper advised, his mouth twisting into a smile.

Shadow refused to rise to his bait. He had closed away from a source of pain by instigating attack.

"What now? I am fed, watered and exercised, is it time to be shuffled out of the way until next required?" She wondered just what he intended to do with her, an interesting problem from a practical point of view. Another thought occurred. "I can't amuse myself picking through minds, can I? Did you know how isolated I would be in Haven?"

"An obvious conclusion, since the stones are mined here." A spark of interest lightened the grim mask of his face. "What does it feel like, when the gemstone rocks are all around? Is it just a sense of restriction that you can't sense the thoughts of others, or something more?" He leaned forward.

"The walls press down from all sides. I feel trapped, crippled, as if blinded." Shadow wanted to see daylight.

"Interesting. As for occupation, each degree of ennui finds its own natural level," Copper said. "Live as a queen, or slave like the lowest drudge, none will interfere."

"I'm free to please myself, go where I like?"

"Excepting the lower caverns. I'll show you round now to prevent misunderstandings."

He started on the left side of the cave complexes, as the sisters not on duty in the kitchen were still bathing. Most of their space was given over to a sleeping area with a few areas set aside for spinning and weaving, not popular pastimes from the dust on the work. Kitchens and laundry nestled off a side branch near the pool area. The largest area was devoted to rock refining work. Brothers' quarters appeared almost as big, with some communal dormitories and a fair number of curtained-off alcoves. Their recreational facilities doubled as the dining cavern, where some still slept off a heavy drinking session from the night before amidst discarded dice and knuckle bones. As she watched, a small group of brothers finished eating, to move toward a narrow passage at the innermost section – every one of them wearing loose inside clothing.

"That's the forbidden area. There's nothing interesting down there, it's just not safe to wander without a guide—the reason for the restriction." Copper ushered her to the outside.

Haven compound resembled other forts in that it housed stables and various workshops. As they paused on the threshold, he gave a hand signal for quiet and stillness, gesturing toward the blacksmith's shop. A half-naked man, bulging with muscles, hammered out a horseshoe for a patiently waiting beast. He dipped the gleaming metal in a bucket of water, unaware that a lanky brother watched from behind a weather hanging. The tall man waited for his chance, darting in to sever the bindings holding the hammerhead to its shaft, and then slithered out of sight. The intent smith groped for his tool, swung a blow, abruptly curtailed, as the business end of his implement parted company from its shaft. A shout of laughter sounded. The trickster set off at top speed followed by his roaring victim.

"Aren't you going to stop them?" Shadow said, convinced blood would flow.

"Ironfist will never catch Fleetfoot, and it is just payment for last night's prank. Ironfist stuck an inflated pig's bladder under Fleetfoot as he sat down to supper. It made the loudest fart noise you've ever heard. Fleetfoot had been trying to impress one of the girls, but she dissolved into giggles, ruining the seduction he'd planned." Copper chuckled, enjoying the spectacle of the running pair. "I said you'd need a sense of humor to live here."

"They won't fight?"

"Not for real. There will be a counterstrike when Fleetfoot

thinks he's safe. Ironfist is patient. I only intervene if someone becomes too serious."

"Such license is unexpected from Brethren," Shadow said, stunned at the lack of discipline.

"Necessary, though." His eyes held a violet glow of mirth as Ironfist stamped back to a ruined effort. "Ours is a harsh life among fort dwellers—one filled with duty, suffering and death. Shall I create a place where all fun is forbidden, or risk a few bruises? There's little enough enjoyment in our existence without me crushing humor where none can see but us."

"Do sisters also jest in such a manner?"

"Answer yourself. I didn't see any smile from you at the fun."

It was an unfair comment given the surprise. Shadow let it pass, following him as he stalked off to the stables, a massive wooden structure well protected from weather.

Flaring torches in suspended brackets lit this building at regular intervals. Copper marched halfway down a central aisle to pause at the tenth stall to the left, waiting for her to catch up.

"I've consigned that derelict animal of yours to breeding pastures. This is by way of a replacement," he said, standing aside so she could see.

Torchlight reflected off a light chestnut coat. A blaze distinguished the mare, a proud animal of excellent lines.

"Her name is Amber," Copper supplied.

The mare whickered in welcome, pushing her velvety nose against Shadow's face. A magnificent gift for any ruler to give, and overwhelmed at his generosity, Shadow embraced the Outcast. Contact ignited deeply submerged memories. The horse . . . something familiar about the horse.

Past exploded into present. It left her trembling, half-dead with shock. This was the mount lost after banding – the horse gifted by the dark man. Sequence upon sequence crashed down upon her.

Copper's hold on her tightened. "Stay with me," he said. "Don't lose yourself in the past."

Shadow sagged against him as memories rolled before her eyes in unending torment. Pain, then pleasure, pleasure then pain, it all came back. Shadow knew who she had been now, but not why she had become Outcast. The pain of loss washed over her, threatening to overwhelm. *Boy has a father. I had a mate who cared. Why has it all gone?*

Copper's mouth closed over hers, kissing her as he never had before, with great tenderness. He stopped when she straightened, leaving her relieved yet uneasy at the same time.

"All of us deal with this moment." He ran one finger down her cheek along the path of a tear. "Don't try to bury anything, or it will come back to bite you. Face your past life. Deal with what happened, who you lost, and what you lost. Once done, then you will be free to move forward. Shall I stay, or would you rather be alone?"

Rather than answer, she pushed him away. Not knowing what she wanted, she wandered through the compound, passing by a tanner's shop. Water from a large puddle soaked through a hole in her boot. The wetness registered as a minor irritation to be ignored. The reawakened memories screamed for attention. Almost without volition, her steps led her up a rocky slope away from people. Wind clawed at her on the steep path through jagged boulders to a ledge facing south. The closed-off feeling ever-present in Haven seemed less here.

Shadow released all restraints. The pain rushed over her. Pictures of Uther, the Dragon Duke, formed in her mind. Angry expressions followed by amusement and then the intense, yet tender face of love. One last picture came to haunt her, his look of loathing when he saw her on the stairs in High Fort. Harsh, dry sobs tore from her throat, snatched away by the wind.

She climbed down from the heights as night drew over the

sky. Accepting personal mortality had come hard, with no going back. The past must remain dead. Shadow allowed herself time to mourn, trying to hang onto the few moments of pleasure in an otherwise miserable life. It could have been good – should have been. A boiling rage against unfairness welled up from deep within. Harvesters would pay a heavy blood-price before she finished.

Food had no flavor at supper, and the chatter of others irritated. Shadow elected for an early night.

Morning brought renewed lassitude and bitterness. The Harvesters must be destroyed. Meanwhile, something in Haven interfered with Shadow's mental powers – more so than just earrings. That feeble attempt to scare a cave-dweller against exploring did not bother her. They were hiding something from her.

Shadow ate a leisurely breakfast, watching with covert interest as around a dozen brothers filed into the depths, all wearing the standard loose, gray robe identical to her own. As the morning lengthened, others seemed not to notice her lounging by a wall. She picked her moment well, choosing a temporary absence of people. One more robed figure moved to the passage underground, past tables strewn with plates and trenchers, unobserved by a few half-conscious drunkards when she entered the anteroom.

A row of pegs on one wall held discarded robes. In the center of the room was a deep shaft with a wooden ladder fixed against one side. Torches flared from brackets set at regular intervals of descent. Each step she took down brought an increased feeling of isolation.

Long robes snarled her foot. Shadow hung over the drop, thrashing wildly until she found a foothold. Chastened, and now knowing why brothers shed their robes above, she hooked the hem up in her belt before continuing down. Her right foot touched solid rock. A second later a hard hand closed over her shoulder.

"I warned you to stay away. Curiosity nearly cost you your life."

Shadow turned to meet her King's angry glare. He looked larger somehow, just wearing a loincloth. His broad shoulders showed dust marks streaked with sweat that ran down into the auburn hair on his chest.

"Ennui finds its own level," Shadow shot back.

"Point. Is this an exercise in disobedience, or is there another motive?" Copper's face held a warning in its lack of expression.

"I wanted to know why I couldn't come here. This direction felt more . . . like it wrapped my head in wool." Shadow peered round him into a network of passages, hoping for answers before she was packed up the ladder again. "I would've gotten away with it if you hadn't happened on me by chance."

"Chance didn't figure. I sensed your danger." He braced his arms against the ladder and at either side of her, trapping her. "Why do you imagine I warned you off? Will you now obey?"

"I'll leave. Next time I'll be more careful." Shadow faced him down, unrepentant.

"We mine the gemstones for our earrings here. That's no great secret, just dangerous to one unused to the caverns, some of which are unstable. Now are you satisfied?"

"I will be once I've seen for myself." She wanted him to move away. His almost naked body challenged her.

"Will you be satisfied on the day you die trying to snoop?" The set of Copper's shoulders betrayed his reluctance to humor her as he stepped back. "Come, disobedient sister, take me to this place of blindness you feel."

Shadow set off along a right-branching passage, feeling her way with one hand on an uneven tunnel wall in the semi gloom. First she took a right turn, then a left, until she reached a place where she felt the greatest sense of restriction, halfway down a branch of the fifth tunnel.

"There." She pointed to a wall. The sense of blindness oozed from the rough rock.

"Wait here." Copper pushed past her to grab a torch from the end of the tunnel. He stooped for an abandoned pick. Shadow flattened out of the way when he returned to labor at the place she indicated.

"How much deeper?" Copper demanded after a while. His hand left a dirt trail across his chest as he brushed away rivulets of sweat. He hunkered down, his muscular legs covered with dust.

"Soon. The sense is much stronger. Aim to the right."

He obeyed. More debris fell, and a sense of urgency fired his strokes. The tension built as moments passed.

"By the Hells, it's a mother lode! Come and look at it."

Curious to see the source of disability in its raw state, she tried to see the full extent. The next moment Copper lifted her to his height.

"You can put me down now," Shadow suggested, uncomfortable at the close contact.

Copper did so without letting go. Uneasy, she turned in his arms to face him, realizing her mistake when he began to kiss her. He tasted salty, and her hands slipped on his chest as she tried to push him away. His sweaty hair reminded her of the first time he forced contact. Struggling didn't help, he continued until she gave up, standing quiet for him, feeling helpless and angry that he took advantage of her trust and yet excited by him at the same time. His hardening member pushed against layers of thin fabric to thrust at her until he stepped back.

"We agreed that you wouldn't do that." She blushed. He'd stirred her in a way she didn't want to relive.

"As I recall, we agreed that you wouldn't disobey my orders." He grinned, turning his head to one side. "This could have ended badly, and no, I haven't finished discussing your behavior, just postponed an argument until we deal with your find. Go. No, stay put, I'll fetch others myself." He made his way up the passage at a brisk pace leaving Shadow settled down against a wall to curb her anger.

*

Copper and three other brothers extracted a stone the size of a pig after a few hours' concentrated effort. It needed winches to get it to the upper caverns. Shadow followed to the sisters' area where gems were processed. Helga made the first assessment.

"At least two hundred earrings," she reported after making a first cut. "As much as ten years' labor in four hours!"

Shadow left them to work, aware she was getting in their way. The rest of the day she groomed every horse in need, an exercise she found relaxing. Tired and hungry at nightfall, she helped herself to a chunk of dried meat and a cup of spring water before crawling into bed to sink into instant sleep.

Eyes, black eyes, stared straight out of the rock face, watching and waiting. The smell of damp and decay swirled as water dripped endlessly. Dread paralyzed her, numbing sensation. Shadow screamed until a firm hand clamped over her mouth. Awake now and terrified, she fought in total darkness until the weight of another body pinned her down to her bed.

"Steady, I don't want to hurt you. If you stop struggling, I'll make a light," Copper's calm voice suggested from the heavy darkness pressing on her. His hand lifted from her mouth.

"What are you doing?" Shadow pushed against the hard muscles of his chest, grateful for his presence despite the weight of him.

"I'm trying to stop you waking up more of us than you

already have. Is riding the nightmare something that happens often?"

"Eyes . . . eyes in the rock watch me." The darkness thickened for a terrifying heartbeat. "I can feel them hunting me. They're getting closer, hiding in the darkness until—"

"Hush. I'm not going to leave you alone. No one gets through me." Copper's soap scented hair curled about her neck, and his naked body warmed her chilled skin. A callused hand cupped her cheek and then slid down to fondle her breast. "I've got a wonderful cure for nightmares."

Shadow tried to dislodge him, but in the scuffle, his knee came between her legs and he moved into position. His shaft throbbed against her, hardening by the second. Firm lips closed over her protests, kissing her with a passion he hadn't shown her before, patient and skillful, taking his time until she clung to him wanting his hard thrusts. He timed his strokes for his own release seconds after her climax.

Copper folded around her in the darkness as he settled for sleep, one arm draped around her waist. Shadow decided the price for his protection might be beyond her capacity to pay. She wasn't disturbed by his lovemaking, but his possessiveness set off warnings. Safe and warmed in his arms, she slipped into sleep.

She woke to his lovemaking later that night. He played teasing love games between gentle thrusts that thrilled her. Attracted by him, Shadow firmed her resolve to keep him at a distance in the future. Dawn stirred Haven as he finished, his violet eyes dark in the torchlight filtering under the alcove curtain.

"You'd better go before anyone sees you coming out of my space."

"They'll get used to it." He sucked at her nipple until it hardened for him, and then looked up at her wearing a bad boy child's smile of false innocence. "Unless you'd prefer to move into my alcove?"

Stirred, Shadow closed her eyes. Letting a man into her life wasn't safe. She'd lost Uther and mourned him. She didn't want another stone on her soul. "I'd prefer that we didn't repeat this. I'm here as an ambassador, not your pleasure woman." His body tensed against her, the muscles rock hard.

"Tell me you didn't enjoy being with me."

"I found the experience enjoyable, but not one I want to continue." She made her arms stay by her side, and not reach out for him when he left her. The curtain flapped as he flung it out of his way.

19

DURING A BREAKFAST of cold meat slices, Shadow decided to ride herd duties to fill time over the winter. She shivered when Copper headed in her direction from the mine entrance. He halted more than an arm's length away and stared a hole through her.

"Will you search out the stones for us? We are working blind . . . having a guide saves effort."

Shadow nodded, sorry she'd hurt him, if glad of the freedom she'd won.

*

Over the months that followed, Haven transformed into a hive of activity, every individual being pressed into service. Sisters filled a storage cavern with boxes of earrings. Pleasure women took over the role of cooking and cleaning, the blacksmith began training two apprentices, and brothers on outside duties sacrificed part of their leisure time to work in the mines. Shadow spent most of her days scurrying from one group of laborers to another, directing their efforts to the right places. Too tired to wonder why they were stockpiling so many gems, she fell into a dreamless sleep every night.

Copper avoided her, spending his sparse free time with the pleasure women. Sometimes his eyes met hers from a distance and his face set in hard lines before he looked away.

On the rare occasion that a hunting party set out for fresh meat, all mining ceased, and on these days, Shadow had the depths to herself. She needed privacy to explore her limitations with skills raided from the Seers. The unintentional incident with the vortai picked at her thoughts. Although Seers levitated their way from one of their towers to another, she had never seen one of them attempt to lift an object greater than their own weight. Trying to move the smallest pebble made her head hurt for the sake of a barely noticeable inching. In desperation, she recreated the same feeling she had experienced when facing the vortai: blind rage. The pebble lifted several feet off the cavern floor. Having found a key to unlock this talent, Shadow practiced until she could perform the task without effort.

Copper called a reluctant halt to mining at the end of February. With spring approaching, active members needed to be battle ready, so Shadow was rousted out for an early morning run in the snow, followed by weapons practice and swimming. She became immune to the sight of naked men and her own state of undress in the rigid routine. The urgent need for physical performance outweighed any other consideration for all of them. She was pressed into matches of unarmed combat when her superior skills showed. They played dice for the privilege of fighting her with a blade to absorb the techniques of Submariners into Brethren war craft.

When her popularity reached absurd levels, Shadow fled to the now deserted mines. Every muscle ached. Brethren didn't reach Submariner standards as fighters, but did not fall far short, and that edge had narrowed. She relaxed into sleep, waking after what seemed like seconds to find Copper sitting beside her. After months of avoidance, his presence startled her.

"Rowan is out searching the heights, furious because he's missing his session at sword play with you." He stretched, at ease, as if they had never quarreled. "Serves him right. He used loaded dice last night. I found them in his sleeping roll after I thought his luck ran too good."

Shadow tried to yawn and smile at the same time, relieved they were talking again. "He's eager for an edge." She had noticed how often she fought the King's dark-skinned second.

"Too eager. I've no mind for joining the Wild Hunt. Will you fight with me instead?"

"He'd challenge for your position?"

"The strongest of us leads. He's fey. He has the right to rule."

"I can give you an edge he can never surpass, but it requires the ultimate trust." She didn't want to change her horse mid-stride. Copper represented less of an unknown than Rowan, and she was drawn to him, against her better judgment.

"A Shade mind thing?"

"The way I learned. You'd surpass me with that knowledge."

"You'd trust a killer to have such an advantage over you?"

"For a trade." She stretched, watching him for a hint of why he sought her out. "Why so many gemstones? Expecting an influx of recruits?"

"My master plan. I intend to overrun a fort by clipping an earring on the entire population. They would be freed because Harvesters can't control us so equipped. One fort is a start."

"Run the idea past Ector before you commit. He has a similar notion. The two of you could work together."

"Will working with Shades mean we can't wear our earrings in battle?" Copper frowned.

"No. We can't risk a trained force changing sides. Ector took the gem to Avalon, where they will study its effects. Are you concerned Submariners would know of your sins if you didn't have shields? Don't be. The war overrides any prejudices."

"Worried? Yes, although I don't mind personally." A quirky grin lit his features. "I committed a stupid error while under the influence of a strong drink I didn't have the maturity to handle."

Shadow waited for an explanation, relieved to see the lighter side of his nature emerging.

"You're really going to make me tell, aren't you?" He wriggled on the hard rock floor for a more agreeable seat, looking away from her, fists clenched and shoulders tense. "I learned of my betrothal to a War Maid, one lovely beyond my wildest dreams, according to my father's agents. I thought myself untouchable on my sixteenth birthday. I celebrated over-well with my friends, accepting every drink passed in my direction. I remember my younger brother helping me to my room, except he'd led me to the Harvester domain. I thought I pissed against a wall, not the door to the priest's chamber. Naturally, it opened when I reached full flow. I was too drunk to stop fast enough. If I'd known the penalty, I'd have aimed at his face instead of his feet. My brother became heir that night."

"I never knew one had offered for me," Shadow said, guessing his interest in her at Menhill.

"Hald revoked the contract when he learned of my status, and my brother was contracted elsewhere, to a rather plain girl, I learned. It was a small consolation." He sighed.

"Thank the stars he was, for I would've hated such a traitor!"

"Now we're both doomed." He laughed a bitter laugh, and then became serious again. "What must I do to gain more life?"

Shadow took him to the heights surrounding Haven, away from prying eyes. In the biting wind, she removed both their earrings, adjusting him to mental intrusion by slow stages. She made no attempt to scan his mind, respecting his privacy.

Her delving into records with the Archive's active participation now bore results. First she rerouted a set of neural pathways for a direct link to a dormant section of his brain, a part active in animals, concerning synaptic override in times of danger. A set of neurons needed strengthening in his brain stem with increased linkages and blood supply. The delicate adjustments continued as Copper knelt in front of her. She examined the section of his brain capable of precognition, situated in the same area as her telepathic abilities. No possibility of augmentation there lest she destroy the thing making him fit to rule. Physical alterations complete, she uploaded every training scenario ever experienced with Submariners. Shadow fixed his earring back in place without comment.

"So much and no time to practice," Copper sighed, rocking back on his heels. "I hope this was worth having my mind picked clean."

"Didn't," Shadow said, busy attaching her own device. "Enhancing reaction time—not poking through the private zone. I'd not do that to any ally. It's considered bad manners."

"But the memories you shared contained definite communications from mind to mind. It's obvious—"

"No. One projects a thought to an open mind and remains open for an answer. There is more sense of the essence of an individual in the exchange."

Copper flowed to his feet, stretching like a cat. He looked down at the faint lights of Haven winking in the dusk.

"If you can make physical changes, why not free up your speech?"

"The Shades tried. Harvesters caused too much damage. I had a problem when they retrieved me because I could block mental projections. Once I understood they wouldn't intrude, mind speech proved easier."

He glanced at her sideways, but let it pass. Again his attention turned to the scene below.

"There are more brothers about than should be outside at this time. Let's hope I can put those lessons into practice, because I think they're setting up an arena."

"Fight me instead." She touched his arm. "I don't challenge for leadership, but we could give them a good show."

"Mock fighting won't be acceptable. It'll be to the first blood between us."

Shadow shrugged, not afraid of cuts. "I formally call you out for infringement of my person against my will," she challenged with a slight grin.

"Accepted, my Queen. May the best warrior win." He grabbed her, holding her immobile in his arms before she had time to evade him. Moonlight reflected from his eyes before his lips lowered to hers. It was incredibly tender – not a brutal forcing, but far too sexual to be taken for a brotherly salute. A deep blush colored her face by the time he finished.

"Now you have fresh grounds," he said, his voice soft in the darkness. "A very pleasant way to challenge. I thank you."

Shadow fought back tears, aware he'd tricked her. He only wanted the skills and his revenge.

Copper's guess was right. An area had been cleared of all debris in the compound and was ringed with Brethren. Rowan stood off to one side. The word 'challenge' hissed in the air when they passed through the ranks.

"Copper, prove you're fit to lead us," Ironfist called, his deep voice booming in the sudden hush.

"I've accepted challenge. I command you to obey Shadow if she is victorious," Copper shouted, catching all by surprise.

"A fix!" Rowan sneered. "All know she can beat any."

"Judge for yourselves whether we fight for true. I've a grudge," Shadow cried, reaching for her sword, too angry to remember all went unarmed.

"Give them blades," a brother called. Someone rushed inside.

Shadow and Copper advanced to the center of the cleared area, facing off against each other. The willing hands of brothers belted weapons about the waist of each fighter.

Shadow pressed her attack without giving Copper time to adjust to his new skills. The air around them hushed with tension as the full skill of Submariners revealed itself for the first time. The clang of steel and the hiss of breathing broke a silence unchallenged by the watching Brethren.

Both of them looked for an opening, and now Shadow fought a losing battle against Copper's greater strength and stamina. He knew every move and counter move she tried. The outcome loomed closer as she tried desperation moves. A slight misstep from exhaustion brought his blade down upon her leg in a glancing blow. Blood flowed.

"I offer the Shades' ambassador quarter in exchange for a retraction," Copper called, standing back.

"Retraction issued." Shadow glared at him, wincing in pain. He had tried to maim her. That was almost a hamstring injury. Was he trying to stop her being an active member?

"Are there any other challengers who dispute this combat as true?" Copper looked around at the circle of Brethren.

The silence oozed with a life of its own. All had witnessed their king beat the Shades' creature in a test of arms none could match. Suddenly, they crowded around him offering congratulations. Shadow limped into Haven alone, nursing bitterness.

Helga, recognizable by her startling blue eyes and soft voice, led her into the sisters' caverns. She cleaned the wound with spirits and stitched it together with capable hands. Shadow declined a drink of spirits to take away the pain.

"Take it. I know you let Copper win. It was well done," Helga said.

"He tricked me into giving him faster reaction times and all my battle knowledge." The shame carved a deep wound, hurting beyond the slice he cut in her leg.

"Shade skills? I didn't see the fight." Helga packed away her implements and the bloody rags in a brisk fashion. She rounded on Shadow. "The others learn fast. This buys limited time."

"Skills, not the speed. He's safe enough." *Even from me. Curse him.*

"He traded with you for this? What in exchange?"

"I asked why he needed all those earrings." Shadow shrugged, trying to distance herself from what had happened. "His plan will fit well with Shade intentions. If all is coordinated, we should control a fort." Shadow sensed the watchers from behind alcove curtains. All the sisters, except Helga, seemed to regard her as some way station between man and beast. "We need a way for Brethren involvement to be concealed. When Harvesters learn of Brethren activities, they will begin extermination as they have with Shades. This force must be protected."

"They'll never find Haven." Helga sat on the edge of a table. "Only Brethren have safe crossing over the blanket bogs surrounding us. No others have the means to evade vortai."

"It's not so invisible from above," Shadow disagreed. "Brethren are the eyes. We can't risk losing vision, not when our forces are so far apart. We must take as many forts as we can before they discover us, and have an evacuation plan."

"Talking with you is just like talking with a brother, all warcraft. We've watched you training with them. You have a female form still, so we hoped. The woman in you died just as surely as it did with us, not so?"

"I trained as War Maid. Nothing else remains of that life. I think as a warrior, Helga. The time for me to be a woman has passed." Shadow brushed aside an image of the Dragon Duke. A hot wave of pain scorched her soul to set her shuddering. *I'll never go near Copper again.*

"Don't," Helga said. "Don't go there. I used to flay myself

with the 'might have beens' when I regained full memory."

"A lost love?" Shadow wanted to focus on anyone but herself.

"We were promised—a good match for both, and I was a Silver Band accounted pretty. My lord's second son caught me alone in a storage cavern one day where I was busy with an inventory of weapons. He was far too strong to resist. We overset a case of daggers in our struggle. My hand closed over one while he was about his business. Unfortunately, he survived. I didn't." Helga sighed. "I never saw my love again. One of our brothers appeared at my fort at the time. He took me up pillion behind him when they turned me out for the hunt."

"Did you see any Harvester when the priest passed sentence?"

"Nothing beyond that dreadful blue fire, none of us have."

"Except me. I saw the face of our enemy . . . not human." Shadow visualized that terrible face in her mind again, an image never far from the surface. It looked a bit like a furred man with an animal's jaw, the tusks protruding and the eyes. Those eyes belonged to a night hunter from the way the pupils contracted. She repressed a shudder at the memory of those twin breathing-pits sucking in air and pouting to breathe out.

"Harvesters are gods. Why should they look like us?"

"Harvesters are mortal—gods aren't. What I would like is to kill one slowly, maybe more if I get a chance. That is going to happen." Yes, she wanted that most, a complete bio-scan to determine which cuts would kill, and then exquisite torture to surpass her own torment.

"Are you fey?"

"Call it determined instead. I'll have vengeance."

"A killer, just like brothers." Helga turned away in contempt.

The accusation sunk in to bone level. Yes, a killer with one species as target. "I'll create a sea of their blood."

20

PLAYBACK CEASED at Shadow's thoughts of carnage. Now Arthur recognized the legend this woman had become. No trace of the loving girl remained: the cyborg parts overwhelmed the humanity. She stood as a perfect killing machine, devoid of compassion. The thought saddened him.

The winking lights of the gray console seemed like a score of eyes instead of instrumentation. Disturbed, he looked away to the shadows of a metallic, unadorned wall. The lights reflected off that surface too, appearing to watch him.

"Is this the point she lost all connection with social standards of higher life-forms?"

"Shadow is a complex individual," the Archive replied. "This particular facet of her personality is best left undisturbed by her allies. She is an adept student, with a mind remaining open to events and suggestions. In many ways, she has transcended the human."

"Did she ever find her son?"

"Boy remained un-acquired, despite all searches she instigated. She still tries on occasion."

"You know where he is." Arthur stared at the row of lights on the console, watching as a few more lit up. He had more of the Archive's attention. "Why don't you tell her?"

"Boy has made his own life. He may decide to contact her at some point. I will not jeopardize his position by disclosure."

Arthur heard the words and disagreed with all his being. Why should these two be kept apart? There was no sense to it, no logical reason.

"That's unfair to Shadow and unfair to Boy. Has he tried to find her?"

"Boy does not know his parentage. Downloading data could be counter-productive to his development."

Where was the boy hidden? A pink-skinned Terran would have stood out from the Submariners just as Shadow did. While he might have inherited her gills, it was unlikely with Uther as the sire. "Is he so important that he can't have a life?"

"Yes, Arthur. He is."

What made Shadow's son so valuable? Had she some other trait Arthur didn't know about? He wanted to find the truth, and he had time before his scheduled training started this morning. He requested continuance.

*

Earth Date 3875

SHADOW RAN HER HAND over Amber's back and legs to check her mare for any trace of tenderness. After daily rides in preparation for this time, the animal was fit for a long journey. The six other riders, chosen by Copper to travel south with them in June, stowed their baggage, looking grateful for summer sunshine. A sister came hurrying over to Shadow. She recognized Helga at a distance by the woman's measured stride.

"Shades are healers," the head woman said. "Is there a chance any will return with you to our base?"

"It may be offered if terms can be agreed. I can't say whether any will accept." Shadow waited as Helga worked up resolve. A warm breeze bringing the scent of pollen ruffled the sister's veil.

"I've found a lump in my belly. It's growing fast. There is pain." Helga caught Shadow's eyes. "I'm not afraid of death, not quick death. Copper said a sister should go to the Shades' place to find if they could heal our cursed state. We discussed it among ourselves. The others are frightened."

"Helga, are you asking to come?"

"If I stay, I'll be opening veins soon. I'd rather spend my life giving hope to the others. I know what a lump means. Will you take me with you, Shadow?"

"Can you ride on your own?" When Helga shook her head, Shadow said, "Ride with me. Get whatever clothes you'll need. I'll deal with Copper."

The Outcast King set his mouth in irritated annoyance when Shadow stated her intention of taking Helga.

"Next time—if we have a treaty at the end of this meeting."

"There won't be a next time for Helga. She's dying." She couldn't believe Copper denied her after she made the effort to be civil.

"Rot. She can't be more than five and twenty."

"She's in pain now. If she stays, she says she is going to make an ending. Either way, you lose your headwoman."

Copper placed his hands gently on her upper arms, looking at her with a sad expression. "What kindness shall I do to allow a sick woman extra pain with no hope at the end? Let her die easy with friends around."

"She offers her life for the chance of a cure for others." Shadow pushed his hands away, backing from him. "I'll care for her during transit. I can reduce her pain, and she's riding with me."

"Shadow, there's no guarantee Ector will take her. What happens then?"

"He will if I ask it." Shadow saw Helga hurrying over with a small bundle she must have prepared in advance. "Don't destroy her sacrifice."

"If she suffers . . ." He left the threat hanging to stalk off.

"Can I come?" Helga asked, her voice wavering.

"It's agreed." Shadow took Helga's bundle to lash with her own small one. She helped Helga to mount, swinging up behind her. "Say if the pain gets unbearable. There is a way of masking it."

*

Helga's eyes brimmed with tears when they made night camp in a woodland glade. She went off to sit by herself, rocking in misery. Shadow collected a cold meal of bread and meat for both of them, taking it over to the woman.

"I'm not hungry," Helga said.

"You'll not ride another day without food. We can do this the hard way, with you held down, or you can remove your earring yourself. The pain ends now, but it means we both go dumb."

Helga took out her earring. She didn't even turn her back to the men as she adjusted her veils to reach her ear.

Shadow had hoped to limit the growth, but this vast swelling challenged her small knowledge of healing. She used her mind probe to trigger the release of quantities of endorphins from Helga's brain. Rapid breathing slowed to a more relaxed rhythm.

Copper came over to them with bedding rolls. He looked worried. "Helga, I brought a supply of spirits along. A shot will help you sleep." Her sign of negation brought his attention to Shadow. "Does she need it or not?"

Shadow signed 'no'.

"So . . . you've gone that route. See you keep tight control over her mind. You won't be able to explain you need help fast enough without your earring." He frowned, glancing once at Helga before meeting her eyes. "I won't release you to the Shades unless Helga goes, too."

Shadow signed back she'd already decided on forcing Ector if reasoning failed.

"I can trust you to care for her after?"

Shadow nodded, making the sign for 'sister'.

"Helga's drinking the spirits is needful. You can't stay up all night helping her and still ride in the morning." He turned to his headwoman. "Helga, I want you insensible."

It was a hard journey for both women. Shadow was relieved when they came to the seashore fifteen days later. They made camp in the dunes to wait for solstice, setting up guard positions back from the shore. Shadow did Helga the mercy of removing consciousness as soon as the woman was lying comfortably.

Saffron, a blond brother, came striding through tussocks of marram grass with cooked leaf-shaped creatures, just as she clipped back her earring.

"Shall I keep Helga's warm until she wakes?" he asked.

"She isn't going to wake. It's better this way."

"Shadow . . . should we prepare for battle?

"I return on my own terms. They want the data I carry, and they won't get it without a treaty." She stifled a yawn.

"What's data?"

"Information. I penetrated a Harvester place at High Fort. It's more than they hoped for when they sent me spying. They'll want it badly."

"But if they defeat us, all they need do is remove your earring," Saffron objected, swatting at a sand fly.

"I have told Copper I'm half Shade, but he chooses not to believe." Shadow looked toward the waves, smelling the rich air coming off the sea. Sounds of surf slapping against the shore distanced her from Brethren. She returned to Saffron with an effort. "Telepaths have natural shields against intrusion. Ector isn't strong enough by himself to force me. I will self-terminate before I'll permit entry."

"You'd do this for us?" Saffron looked skeptical.

"Brethren and Shades, both. I stand at the fulcrum. I will have an alliance. Tell Copper my words, as he instructed you to get information." She had them both caught in their own plans. They must obey, since neither side could risk losing a go-between.

Two days of rest refreshed Shadow. The morning of solstice started a warm, cloudless day. She walked along the shore after breakfast, followed by two brothers. They didn't appear to trust her not to leave them, looking on edge with her so near water. She returned to the camp with reluctance and one backward glance at the sun glinting off the waves.

"Any sign?" Copper asked, coming over to her.

"Didn't look. They prefer night."

"I don't. They see like cats in the dark. Call them now."

Several other brothers grouped around him, battle alert. Additional waiting pushed them nearer to breaking point. Shadow removed her earring.

Ector waited beneath the waves. His mind latched onto hers within seconds, wanting to know how many Brethren she had with her. Shadow refused to tell him. She offered safe passage instead and a tantalizing snippet of the information she had gathered. Ector agreed to a night meet if she brought just one of the Brethren along. Shadow countered with a meet now. She let him know how much Brethren wanted alliance, pleading Helga's case. Ector agreed, if Helga and one other accompanied her. He cautioned her to remain open, or he would not surface.

Shadow signed the details to Copper. The Outcast King ordered Helga carried to the shore. Once Ector's requirements were met he ordered the others to stay clear.

Ector emerged from the waves, not advancing until he'd checked the shoreline. He remained waist-deep in the swell.

Copper's hand snaked out to grip Shadow by her belt. He pulled her closer.

"We won't be interrupted this time. Your gift of the earring was put to good use," Ector said.

"My proposal?" Copper called.

"Needs discussion. We're very interested. If you're serious, I suggest an exchange of personnel, not including the sick woman, whom I'll take on compassionate grounds. One of yours for one of mine and Shadow must return."

"How long?" Copper said, edging them both closer.

"Seven days. Is that long enough for my man to go near High Fort for a good look?"

"Yes. Who's the exchange? You?"

"Not qualified for the task needed. My second has volunteered. He's also a med— a healer," Ector said, looking gratefully at Shadow for her timely telepathic intervention. "Your negotiator?"

"Me. I'll need to instruct my people first," Copper said.

"Warn them we cannot take you, or this woman, without painless adjustments. There is no other way we can take air-breathers to our transport."

"What does he mean?" Copper took a step back onto a band of shale.

Shadow signed what had to happen to preserve his and Helga's life.

"Seems I must trust you. Be warned I have a successor, who will wage war on Shades if I don't return."

"I guarantee your safety," Ector said. "The woman might have a longer stay, as Shadow tells me she's dying. If we can reverse the disease, it may take months. I can't promise a cure."

"She doesn't expect to live. She's offering her body in the

hope that other sisters like her can be returned to a natural state. This is part of our trade."

"Brave woman," Ector remarked. "Shall I call my people to retrieve her?"

"Do so. I'll be back presently." Copper hauled a reluctant Shadow with him up the beach to the waiting brothers. "Is he genuine?" he asked once they were out of earshot.

"Helga . . . helped."

"Sign to me. Am I going to become a Shade creature?"

Shadow let her hands speak to tell him his earring was safe from removal. She asserted her intention to self-terminate at any sign of betrayal, promising not to disclose her information until he gave her leave.

"That's a powerful lever, my Queen. I'll trust you, not your friends."

Copper talked fast to gain agreement for the exchange. Every brother volunteered to go in his place, but he remained adamant.

When Submariners hauled Helga into the water, Saffron started to them.

"No," Copper ordered. "She's as good as dead already. This is her choice. The one to exchange with me is a healer. Take advantage of his skills during exchange. Any ache, any pain, I want treated. Give him whatever help he needs to complete his own mission."

Copper marched Shadow down to the Submariners still gripping her arm. He released her when one of the group headed to his men, hands held high. Ector extended a flat disc to the Outcast King.

"This device must be placed on your forehead. Lie down first, unless you're fond of bruises."

Copper took the disc between his thumb and forefinger, holding it up to the sun. He lay down to place it as directed, breathing once more.

"Gently, we have their King," Ector warned his aides.

Two Submariners carried Copper into the sea. Shadow dived with Ector into the cool waves. She had forgotten how much she liked to swim and enjoyed the sensation while it lasted.

The Submersible loomed ahead where the Terrans were taken inside to be strapped down at the rear of the craft. All then took seats, but Ector turned to Shadow who he had positioned next to him at the front of the transport.

"Put that device back in. We have an override and everyone here is interested in your answers."

"Lies." Shadow scowled at him, fitting her earring in place. She sank down into the plush green seat, ignoring the comfort.

"Necessary. No need to let that one know he has lost his edge. Now download every detail."

"No. Bargain with him. You get the information when you make a treaty," Shadow said, looking outside to where running lights sent a shoal of fish diving in a silver, panicked arrow.

"Reverted, have you? How did he sway you?"

"He has the same ultimatum hanging over him that you are about to receive. Make a treaty, or I'll self-terminate before a disclosure of importance, as you must know from the fragment I released. Listen to Copper; he has a valid plan for capturing a fort."

"So you're choosing to stand between us." Ector looked around at her, his eyes narrowed. "An interesting development. We need them. This treaty won't fail from our side."

Shadow curled up in her seat enjoying the view. The shoal darted ahead of them in mindless escape mode. She didn't care what Ector said. Either this alliance happened or not.

Ector began the sequence to bring the craft about until they sped into the darkness of descent. He set automatic pilot once in deep water and turned again to Shadow. "You've changed—become much harder than I'd thought possible. Was he cruel?"

Ector jerked his head toward the back of the craft.

"The difference between kindness and cruelty has many gray areas. He did what he thought to be in my best interests."

"And that was?"

"I have partial recall. Gain and loss make bitter bedmates." She refused to share Copper's behavior with Ector. The alliance was more important than personal feelings.

"Did you want to talk it through before we reach Avalon? Those ones"—again his head jerked back in the direction of the sleepers—"don't need to be revived right now."

"I have resolved these issues. The past is as dead as yesterday's sunlight, and as relevant. Consider Copper's plan for taking a fort. It has merits."

"This subject hurts, so onto the next one?"

"What subject?" Shadow met his cool blue stare. Of her past life, the need for vengeance remained vibrant. The rest belonged to a long-dead girl.

"So be it. Does Copper know you're half Submariner, or is that another question you won't answer?"

"I told him, but he didn't believe. Is Avalon prepared to offer healing to them all? They want a resident technician in their base camp." Shadow looked back at Helga. The woman had been kind without any ulterior motive – such a waste to lose one like her.

"Exactly how ill are they? Your King looks healthy to me," Ector said. "And if they can restore memories better than us—"

"Take a look at Helga," Shadow suggested, smiling sadly. Ector started to concentrate. "No, with your eyes."

Ector moved to the back of the craft. Other Submariners gathered round as he uncovered Helga's face, starting back in shock. Several gasped, and one swore at the sight of a full beard on a woman.

"There's more," Shadow said, swiveling round. "Very little

female remains and she's sterile. All the sisters cover up because they can't bear others to see what they've become."

"The men? They seem normal," Ector said, running his hand over Copper's stubbled chin in a rapid check.

"Sterile, too. Some have male lovers, but those involved with pleasure women sire no children. They are all hot enough to feel fevered. I think it makes their lives burn faster."

"A result of Nestine re-banding?" Ector looked skeptical. A look directed to Shadow, which reminded her of Boy's existence, clearly stated the anomaly.

Shadow shrugged. "They are all affected except me."

"Places everyone, the show's over," Ector ordered, resuming his control seat. He reached out for a console link to plug in his interface, his face clouding over on the exchange with Elite headquarters.

"Politics. Brethren are Elite responsibility, I'm told, and I've just traded away our best medi-tech." Ector looked at Merrick, a dark-skinned youth at navigation control, as he disengaged the communication link. "Can you persuade your sister to moon-light for us? Genetics is her specialty, I believe."

"A subspecies? She'd jump at it. Permission to interface? I can leave a message in her home unit."

"No, let's keep the request from you to her in person. Pay her a visit when she's off duty, and don't bring the subject up until she's alone. I've a feeling she'll start pulling double shifts, should any catch onto our intentions."

After docking, Shadow learned Ector didn't want to revive Copper until he had been confined to a room in Elite barracks. Helga was taken straight to the infirmary in stasis. The woman wouldn't be awakened unless a cure could be found.

Shadow accompanied Helga to help the medi-tech assistants remove the unfamiliar clothes. Again, a string of gasps rang out at the exposed woman.

"Are we dealing with a genetic aberration?" one young man asked, eyeing the body with undisguised revulsion.

"She was a normal, pretty woman once, before Nestines altered her. Keep that in mind if she is allowed to revive. This body disgusts her—more so, since she remembers how she looked before."

"By the deeps that's a harsh burden." The young man thought for a few moments, staring at the wreck. "You went through Nestine hands. I saw you stripped when you first arrived. Is there any change toward this state?"

"None," Shadow affirmed.

"Can I have hair, skin and blood samples as a comparison? I'd like to start running tests now."

Shadow pulled out a blond hair and offered him her right arm with a grin.

"The left, you cyborg thing, you." He laughed, reaching across her to grab the living limb. "Think I was going to be caught?"

"Worth a try."

"Don't, if you ever need healing outside barracks. They haven't any sense of fun," the man cautioned, still smiling.

Shadow submitted to the sampling, a simple scrape and prick to get one drop of her blood. It had been a near thing. He'd almost taken the cyborg arm.

"You're coming up for a power pack refit. I'll get one ordered," he said. "Going back on surface duty?"

"Within a week, if I get a say."

"I'll make it a priority."

Shadow returned to her own unit room. The blandness of Elite quarters in their boxlike simplicity came as a shock, but nothing could detract from the pleasure of a shower. She had donned an Elite uniform when her door announced Ector. She permitted entry.

"How spooked is your friend likely to be, once revived," he said, cutting to the point.

"Very."

"You weren't," Ector said, a smile lighting his stern features.

"I thought only of an afterlife. At the time I had little recollection of any existence to compare with here. He has total recall, a whole lifetime of memories. Avalon is outside anything in his experience."

"He'll need a guide to walk him through. I don't want him so terrified he can't function as a negotiator."

"I promised I'd stay by Helga."

"You'd get in the way. I will get regular condition reports routed to his room." He sighed in exasperation. "The woman won't be revived unless there is some positive outcome. She won't know whether you're there or not."

"I suppose, under those circumstances, I can guide," Shadow conceded, already making plans to access the Archive. "When will he be revived?"

"Now, if you're ready." Ector started to the door.

"Give me a short while to dry my hair. I'll catch up soon. I know where he is."

"Make it soon, I've a report to log with Ambrose," he said, looking suspicious.

The Archive welcomed her in its own peculiar way, making it easy for her to relax her guard, and seeped into her mind. She didn't need an implant for full access, keeping this interesting fact concealed from others, who might decide to find out why. It uploaded every new fragment of data she had acquired over the months of absence. There was no hiding of secrets from that vast mind. She waited as it ranged, sifting events into order of importance.

"You have done well, Shadow," the inhuman voice murmured from the console, aware she preferred it to vocalize.

"I haven't made this contact; you haven't linked with me. They'll argue if they know," Shadow said.

"Cooperation is expedited, given anticipated reward. This alliance is imperative."

"And Helga?"

"A price to be met. I will monitor the procedures. You will be called when needed."

"Those slaves I saw in High Fort—"

"Access to data files restricted. Password required." The voice became metallic, as if functioning on a different mode.

"Why?" She questioned at the unexpected exclusion.

"Security override, code-nine, red. Information restricted."

"To whom?" This was intriguing. She sensed wrongness.

"Level two and above of Ruling Planetary Commission. Names and retina patterns of all members is restricted."

"Why?" She'd never heard of any Planetary Commission, ruling or otherwise.

"Security override, code-nine, red."

It refused to release data without the right command, one she didn't have . . . yet. The change in voice pattern formed another problem.

"Can dark sisters be restored to a natural state?"

"Data suggests damage is linked to telepathic manipulation." The voice returned to normal. "An interesting challenge. This subject will have intensive consideration." It paused for the space of several dozen heartbeats. "Ector grows impatient."

Shadow walked out, feeling like a small child chastened for stealing sweetmeats. It fascinated her that more normality resumed when she reverted to a safe subject. This mystery must wait until there was time to delve into it.

21

"I've scheduled a first meeting with Ambrose in three hours." Ector flowed off a swivel chair beside the unconscious Terran. "Ten minutes with the Archive, you promised. I make it twenty. If I find this man is a wreck, I'll have you on starvation rations and denied access to the Archive."

Shadow could see he meant it, and took his place in the chair beside Copper. While the Archive continued to watch over Helga, it could enforce a discipline restriction, and she had given her promise.

Ector ran a tubular device over the flat disc on Copper's forehead, which now lifted easily from his skin. Breathing resumed.

"Give him a few minutes to waken. There's a security lock on his door programmed to my voice, effective on my departure. Use the console to show him Avalon if you think he can withstand the culture shock. I've also set an alarm for ten minutes before our first conference." He gave her a pointed look before he left.

Shadow lowered the light level to gloom, leaving a single beam directed at her face. Best if he didn't see all this room contained at first. His breathing changed, and she sensed his waking regard.

"So much for your word." Bitter irony overlaid his tone.

"Helga is still asleep. My being with her would have impeded tests. I have a skilled friend watching in my place."

"Why is it so dark?"

"Avalon isn't like any fort. Do you sense danger?"

"No." Now he sat up, trying to peer though the gloom. "Is this normal lighting for Shades? What's that bright, glowing globe?

"I think of it as a piece of trapped sunlight, and no, I reduced light levels." Shadow tried to reach out to the Archive, something she'd never attempted before without activating a console. The sentient came to her in a heartbeat, like a shower of snow on her mind. "Archive, give an update on the Terran woman's condition."

"Stasis remains constant. Preliminary tests indicate an elevated level of androgens circulating. The geneticist has just arrived. Patience is counseled, Shadow."

"Who's that?" Copper demanded. "Who's hiding from me?"

"It's gone now."

"A mutation so hideous that it hides in darkness?"

"The Archive doesn't have a body. Think of it as an intelligent breeze capable of going anywhere in Avalon on the wings of will."

"Seven hells. A floating head?" He looked around.

"Listen to me. It is a mind without form. Invisible."

"What else does darkness hide?" He swung his legs over the edge of his bed.

"Increase light by five degrees," Shadow instructed. The room took form: a standard sleeping unit with a bed, two padded chairs by a table, a console and a door leading to a cleansing unit.

Copper looked about, reaching for his weapon until he registered an absence of people.

"It's metal." He wandered over to the wall, touching it in

wonder, then on to the table and chairs. "Glass."

"Much stronger."

"And that . . . thing?" He pointed to the console.

"For retrieving information."

"Shadow . . . where are we?"

"The beings you call Shades refer to themselves as Submariners. Avalon rests on the bottom of the Southern ocean."

"No . . . Ector said a craft. This is underground in the badlands, or I would've drowned." His mouth turned down in a scornful smirk. "I had to sleep so I couldn't reveal the location."

"No more than I can, having watched our approach. Avalon is enclosed in a bubble of a thicker, stronger version of that furniture glass. There are devices to make air, heat and light. Plants even grow down here."

"Show me."

"Not permitted. Yet. This place is a capsule in time left over from the ancients. We were like them once."

"We looked like Shades?" He glanced at the door portal, seeming to scan it for a latch.

"Submariners looked like you. They have encouraged a mutation to fit this place." Shadow caught her breath, wondering how to continue. "Don't imagine such ones are free to swim around outside Avalon; they are as dead as you at this depth. The weight of water is too great to bear."

"I don't see the point of becoming monsters," Copper said. "By your own argument, they'd be trapped."

"Transports carry them to shallow depths where they fish and farm seaweed and plankton—partly the reason why they are so open to mutation, as they are tied to the sea. When the ancients died, a sickness spread over land and water. Submariners emerged when food supplies ran low, but Harvesters didn't know about them, so didn't cleanse their births."

How many needless deaths have Nestines caused? Shadow

wondered. *How many died because their existence threatened the niche this life-form established? Millions? Tens of millions?* Recalling her own banishment, she thought her emergent telepathic ability was responsible for the Nestines' action. An 'accident' should have been an obvious ploy, but she was too high profile, too protected by the duke, for such to occur. Dragon couldn't guard an Outcast – none could, so the choice became easy at the end.

Shadow tried not to think of the consequences if they had discovered the spark of life that resulted in Boy. He remained Dragon's unknown heir. Boy couldn't ever rule, even if she found him – not that this was likely now his mind had matured over the months, nor could she allow him anywhere near Harvesters, given the choice. Guilt gnawed at her vitals for the act of depriving a man of his son. Part of her still grieved for Dragon, a part suppressed by grim necessity. She now understood why Copper hadn't let her near him to deliver the simple message. Dragon regarded Outcasts as humans; she was sure he would not let go of the short dream she had shared with him. Over the grinding winter, Shadow had come to terms with her effective death and its consequences.

"Come back," Copper urged, shaking her out of her reverie.

"Only thinking. I can show you pictures of Avalon if you wish."

"Why can't I see for myself?"

"Devices you wouldn't understand. Once you trusted me to give data. I can show you mind images, or the Submariner way, your choice."

"Show me how they would see."

Shadow elected to retrieve on the small, two-dimensional console, rather than scare him with a holo projection. She chose the view from the roof of Elite barracks over central Avalon, where the large pyramid of command and control dominated the hexagonal towers of the seers. Each tower appeared independent from its neighbors, unless one spotted the portals opposite each other. No seers levitated across today; the only pedestrians were tiny figures moving on rolling walkways while a railpod rattled above their heads. Copper flinched as the fast moving air-propelled object whizzed across the screen. Shadow quickly rotated perspective to a view over dwelling units. Several ground runners converged on an intersection at the same time. Two of them slowed to allow an orderly progression.

"Why didn't they hit each other?"

"They are equipped to know objects are in the way. I was frightened at first until I came to accept how safe they are."

Copper watched the screen for several more heartbeats, and then turned to Shadow, frowning.

"This is incredible, unbelievable, but I can't see anything to fix a location underwater."

Shadow switched to a view of a docking port. The transparent plas-glass of the dome showed a blue glow from the surrounding ocean. A submersible approached for linkage with an extended umbilicus. Several moments later the occupants disembarked.

"Look at the sky," she advised.

"It's dark blue." Copper's eyes widened.

"That is the color of water against light. Avalon has a dark blue 'sky'."

Shadow switched to one of the collector stations above Avalon where fish and plankton were processed. Now the vid screen showed Submariners swimming in distinctive patterns to herd shoals of fish to a central collector. Others returned with large nets of kelp in tow.

"How far above Avalon are they?" Copper asked, staring at them.

"Three hundred fathoms, a depth they can work at without discomfort."

"They harvest all day?"

"No, three hours is the maximum time in water. The adaptation is not efficient enough for longer submersion. Four hours is the longest recorded survival."

"Now I've seen what to expect, why can't I walk free?"

"Submariners have an active interest in the ancients. We resemble the form of our ancestors, so tend to get mobbed by the people."

Copper looked around. "Am I a wild animal to be caged until required to perform?"

"Ector didn't want you intimidated during negotiations. He felt I should prepare the way."

"Consider duty done. I need no coddling from Shades, or their loyal pets." With this parting shot, he stalked over to lie down on his bed, turning away from her.

Shadow didn't attempt to break the liquid silence. His anger precluded intrusion, although she thought she understood the cause: he was surrounded by intimidating things he didn't understand; he wasn't in charge of his own fate anymore, and he didn't like her fitting in so well with the Shades. They seemed back in hatred mode again. Time stretched out endlessly until Ector's alarm sounded. She waited for her commander to release the door lock, hating the dreary, loaded silence.

Copper remained taciturn on the way up to Ambrose's office, not responding to her questions or comments. Ector had chosen not to take a grav shaft, so the climb up a spiral glass stairway seemed endless. Shadow hadn't been aware it existed, and smothered a feeling of resentment that he could have spared her shock on her first trip on the riser.

The meeting started badly, with Copper insisting on hostages held at Haven as a surety of good conduct. Shadow let her mind drift, too angry with him to follow as closely as she should. His demands escalated in an unreasonable manner, despite Ambrose's quiet negation. It seemed as if he were determined to spike the wheel of progress from sheer perversity.

Ector's thoughts intruded. *'I'm not impressed. Having just scanned the man, I can tell he is neutralized by jealousy over you. What, by the deeps, have you done to him for him to behave in this primitive fashion?'*

Shadow started to reach for her earring to reply, but Copper's hot glare stayed her hand.

'Leave it in place. Do you want him thinking we talk behind his back? Open to me so I can pick out your answer.'

Shadow organized almost every contact she'd had with her King into chronological order for Ector to review.

'Are you so emotionally dead that you can't see how much he has attached himself to you? Do something with him, or the cause you're ready to die for will evaporate in a cloud of temper.'

Shadow wilted in her chair under that cold, accusing assessment. Ector withdrew from her, and Ambrose's momentary inattention suggested him as the next target. The meeting came to an abrupt end with nothing agreed except a rethink. She looked for an escape before Ector started digging for details.

Copper bristled. "I suppose I'm to be sent back to my prison until you're ready to resume."

"Shadow can show you around Elite barracks," Ambrose said. "I will guarantee freedom of movement only within our facility. Seers are very interested in your foreseeing abilities. You really wouldn't enjoy helping them learn, should they catch you in the open, and I have no authority over them to prevent it."

Copper stalked to the door. His posture indicated his intention to brood in private. Shadow followed after. They were almost at Copper's room when a call brought them both about.

The same young medi-tech who had tended Helga hurried up to them. "Shadow, I was looking for you. I've got your power pack. Can you come for fitting now?"

"This is something you should see," she said to Copper,

wanting revenge. "I need this procedure if I am to return to the surface. Are you prepared to learn what I am?"

"I'll see for myself how they control my subject." Copper's mouth formed a hard line.

The medi-tech led them to the grav lifts, and Shadow felt too irritated with Copper to warn him what to expect. She enjoyed his gasp of terror as the device started up. Copper looked panicked by the time the doors slid open, and he dived out first, distancing himself as far from the contrivance as he could manage with his dignity intact. His eyes held a look of grave injury. The young medi-tech ushered them into his ready room, where Copper started forward on sighting a covered woman beyond a glass partition.

"No." The medi-tech barred his passage. "Access denied. Your woman is in a clean-room for her own protection."

"I'm not dirty." Copper attempted to move around him.

"Copper, no." Shadow grabbed at him. "No one is allowed in there without special clothing. She must be getting better, or they wouldn't be so protective."

"She had the growth removed this morning. We are in the process of regenerating tissue," the young man said.

Copper looked through the glass. "She will live?"

"It might take a few weeks to repair her, as we are still working on a way to restore normality. Shadow has donated tissue for our comparison check."

"Is there hope?" Copper looked at the figure with profound pity.

"We won't give up on this. It's too intriguing." The medi-tech reached out for a slim silver box with lights and buttons. "While we're on the subject, I want a full scan of you, since I understand curing is part of the treaty. This won't take a moment."

"Shadow—" Copper backed off.

"It doesn't hurt," she said, grinning at his obvious discomfort.

The device made a rapid sweep, and then the young man checked his instrument panel. He grunted in satisfaction. "Fertility is impaired by an unnatural metabolic rate causing too great a temperature. It is a careful piece of manipulation, but the area is too fragile for experimentation. I can insert an implant to compensate. It is a simple procedure, if I adapt a com-link. Report at first wake call tomorrow."

Copper's eyes bulged, and his hands clasped over his genitals. "What's he going to do to me?"

"They remove a small circle of bone in your head." She began to enjoy herself even more. "Metal threads lead from a flat device attached there into your brain to correct the problem. You will be asleep the whole time. Most of the Elite have one, including Ector. They use it to access information from our control data bank. Yours will be modified to personal need. Having one won't make you their creature. It will mean you stay away from Harvester priests. We wouldn't want them finding one of those."

"What if I don't want a lump of metal stuck in my head?" He backed away from the pair of them.

"Damage, courtesy of Harvesters, doesn't heal. If you want the effects neutralized—" She paused. "Just how important is fertility? Submariners may develop a way to free our speech with such a device, so that we don't need earrings. It won't impede our special gifts, since those are protected as a priority. Think about it. No one will force the issue. It is a personal choice."

"Some among us have much more intrusive implants to no ill-effect. Are you ready, Shadow?" the medi-tech asked, grinning.

Shadow stripped off her tunic, presenting her left arm to him, interested to see if he would remember.

"What would you do if I went ahead?" he challenged, chuckling. "Go sit down, I'll get the power pack."

"A certain arm makes so much difference? What's he going to

do to you?" Copper hovered over her.

"Watch and learn. I concealed this for good reason, but now . . . it's best you learn."

The sound of Copper gagging interrupted the peeling back of artificial skin and muscle layers. There was a pause while he got himself under control.

"It's not flesh." His face was a sickly white.

"Organs, we can regrow, some flesh, but not nerves." The medi-tech continued his digging. "Shadow is a cyborg—part living, part mechanism. The mechanism needs an energy source to work. I am installing a replacement to enable normal activity to continue."

"You call that normal function?"

"For her, it is. The alternative is disability inappropriate to her duties. Many Elite are cyborg to a greater or lesser extent. It goes along with the territory." He poked a blunt glass rod into the exposed circuitry. A small disc gently rose from the opening, and its retaining clips loosened.

There was a faint sigh from behind, followed by a thud as Copper hit the ground, senseless.

22

Earth Date 3892

GLOWING BLUE WATER made a familiar sky above the flat rooftop of Elite barracks where Arthur mulled over his first major disagreement with the Archive. When he asked the sentient about the group of Terran slaves in the bowels of High Fort Shadow discovered, it reacted in the same way emotionless way to him as it had to her. The Archive was an autonomous, sentient intelligence, so what force could reduce it into an archaic behavior pattern? Those few moments when its established personality appeared to disintegrate sent shivers down his spine. Like Shadow, he changed the subject.

Thoughts of Shadow called up those of that other peculiar inhabitant of his dreams: the old-young man, who seemed to want something from him. Arthur contemplated quizzing this timeless specter, partly to discern whether it was linked to him as an insane extension, or a separate, outside influence. If he received answers to unresolved questions the next time it invaded his dreams – if those answers were outside his personal experience . . . yes, that would be a pivotal point.

The sense of another presence disturbed his meditation. A few heartbeats of gentle scan revealed Ector about to access the roof; no mistaking the flavor of *his* mind, despite the careful privacy barriers. Ector wanted to catch him by surprise, did he? Arthur shut his eyes, waiting until Ector padded near in the soundless way learned from Brethren.

"I know I'm skipping classes, so if you've come to chastise me, it's a wasted effort." He waited out a controlled silence from his superior. "Ector, I'm not going back until I'm ready. I'm quite prepared for any accrued punishment."

"You knew who found you." Ector sounded irritated. "Good guess, but it could easily have been a quorum of seers, bent on sneaking up to recover a lost acolyte. It would be too late by the time we came up with a legal process to yank back a reluctant meal from the shark's belly."

"I knew who searched. I always know." Arthur opened his eyes and smiled. "They can't steal what they can't see or sense. This roof would appear empty if I wanted to stay hidden."

"Arthur?" Ector frowned, looking uncertain. "Can you really screen to that extent?"

He considered demonstrating, but Arthur didn't want to be diminished in Ector's eyes. "I don't hide from friends. Sometimes I need to be alone, and Sanctuary isn't a good place for that, so I worked out my own way to avoid seers."

"Screening leaves an aftertaste," Ector said. "Any initiate could pick it up."

"Not my method. They use mind link and eyes to locate. I project an image of myself doing various things and moving off before they get there. It was the only form of exercise some of them got before I left."

"Arthur, no one can do that. You'd have to split your mind in two."

"I've had plenty of time to practice." He stretched to ease a kink in his back. "As long as the projection sticks to predictable behavior patterns, it almost runs itself. Watchers get frustrated, but they don't believe anyone has the capability to generate such a realistic image for long, so they don't suspect."

Still frowning, Ector sat beside him, leaning back against an air duct with his hands behind his head. "I can't say I'm astonished you have the Great Control, given your mother's abilities. If I had any doubts left on that score, they have just evaporated." He chuckled. "One day you will learn how much you upset Sanctuary. Oh, this is too good."

"Who is my mother?" Arthur sat up to watch Ector's face for any minute betrayals. The woman must be one of the Elite. He wouldn't raid for data – he couldn't without losing a friend – but he could still read body language.

"She will tell you, or I will, when I think you are mature enough to handle the consequences. That day is drawing close." Ector shut his eyes and relaxed his face muscles, as if aware of Arthur's scrutiny. "What bothered you so much that you needed seclusion? Dreams again?"

"No—Shadow. Years back she found a topic the Archive didn't like. It started spouting antiquated security restrictions. I tried to access data on that subject with the same result. I suppose I was conceited to imagine I might get answers where she failed. Did she ever discuss the experience with you?"

"She didn't. Show me both incidents." Ector's shoulders tensed.

Arthur tried to put his exasperation aside. Ector must know his mother well. Perhaps she was one of the Elite support staff, or maybe an active seer member? Would it be Suki? She was still a popular addition to any landing party. He suppressed a sigh and transmitted Shadow's experiences of the Archive in exact detail. The sense of shock and wonder radiated from Ector as the scenes played out in his mind.

"The Archive shouldn't be subject to security overrides. This is a revelation. I'm tempted to check that incident in Shadow's files myself, just to see if it's still there."

Ector propped himself up on one elbow looking out at Sanctuary for a moment as if drawing strength from the presence of the place. The twin towers in daytime were jeweled with inner lights against the dark walls to present an irresistible focal point.

"I started an unwelcome line of thought some time back also." Ector yawned. "I wasn't satisfied at the explanation for continued life on the surface after the holocaust. I can't see why every animal life form wasn't annihilated. Avalon had a fifty-year food supply stockpiled when the catastrophe happened, and the ability to generate food from hydroponic units, so how did repopulation occur on the surface, given only a few underground shelters were known to exist with the same food resource? Why are some animal species unaltered, while others mutated to primeval condition? Then there are beasts which shouldn't exist in nature, being throwbacks to long extinct species." Ector yawned a second time. "It's happening again. Every time I think about this problem I start to fall asleep."

Arthur projected a flow of pure energy to Ector. He met with unconscious resistance – a resistance not controlled by his friend.

"Think about my encounter instead for a moment," he urged, shaking Ector's shoulders. "I'll investigate your discovery if I get a chance."

Ector made an effort, immediately looking more alert. "The Archive is not the only source for data. Avoid sensitive topics when you access it. Two of us with a sleep problem aren't going to accomplish much."

"I've a resource I intend to explore tonight. Whether it will prove useful is another matter."

"Be careful with those dreams of yours. Shadow has spent years in digging ancient ruins for lost technology. She might have discovered data, but she may have created a memory block when returning to Avalon. There is a core of isolation remaining in her that none of us have ever penetrated."

"I thought she was on our side," Arthur objected.

"Shadow doesn't have a side, unless it is her own. She'll be returning with her son soon for a replacement power pack. You tackle her with my problem, and I'll try yours on for size. I've an idea you might get sent to sleep if you don't dump your pet project." Ector offered a hand up as Arthur rose. "Don't collect any more demerit points. I don't want to discipline you."

Arthur found his leisure time curtailed by extra training on his return. This meant his time accessing the Archive ceased to exist for the next three days, but this was not the punishment intended, given his new knowledge about the sentient. The first night he was so exhausted he had no trouble falling asleep on returning to his dwelling unit. The dream sequence started immediately, almost as if it had been stalking him.

*

The cave seemed unchanged at first. Water dripped, slowly building on a crystalline structure rising from the floor. The old-young man sat in the same position by his fire, his white hair and beard looking out of place on an unlined skin. Smoke spiraled in lazy upward drifts to the sound of waves crashing against rocks. A sharp scent of ocean mingled with wood smoke.

"Those who would lead others must first govern themselves; my second lesson to you. There was no resistance to my company. Does this mean a return to wisdom?" The cave-sitter lifted fathomless black eyes to Arthur for the first time. They looked like openings to a bottomless abyss, black upon black, waiting to suck out life from the unwary.

"Why did my mother abandon me?" Arthur wondered if

this subject would get an answer. He gazed at the fire rather than those compelling eyes.

"Which mother? You have had many rebirths."

"The current one," Arthur said, disturbed by the cave-sitter's suggestion. He glanced at his hands fearing to have his deepest terror confirmed, to be in another body, yet unwilling to remain in ignorance. Those hands were young – his own.

"The current vessel is compatible to the first. That woman also sacrificed her heart for your safety." The cave sitter stirred up the fire with a stick, sending the flames leaping. "Watch and learn."

A young woman's face appeared in those tongues of fire. She had long, fair hair and an elfin expression, a delicate beauty beyond comparison. Her love for the child she cradled in her arms elevated that beauty to the realms of the exquisite. She looked up at an intrusion Arthur couldn't see, appearing to listen. Her face drained of color, of all emotion. In that moment, a terrible purpose reduced the loving mother to an empty shell. She now resembled a marble statue as she handed over her heart's joy to unseen hands. There were no tears at that parting, no outcry, only the terrible hurt driving inwards. The picture faded.

"Why?" Arthur whispered.

"Your continued existence outweighed your mother's wish to raise you. She did what she needed to preserve her child, heedless of personal sacrifice. The current vessel also armed her child with mighty weapons upon parting."

"Was that her?" Arthur said.

"The first one. You will find the current incarnation without my help."

"Just like all the others: you wave a bone in my face to attract attention, and then snatch it away when I get close enough to start gnawing. No one will answer those questions."

"Ask me another. Without curiosity you will not grow,

Arthur," the strange man advised. "A ruler must be open to all threads of thought."

"Why did animal life on the surface degenerate after death day? Why did they survive at all?"

The cave-sitter bowed his head. He seemed to forget Arthur's presence for an unwholesome time as the drips of water fell, one by one. "They did not survive, Arthur."

"But . . . how were they replaced?" Arthur closed his mind to the broader implications, frightened to acknowledge them in case the source of information suddenly dried up.

"If that were revealed, the need to correct a problem would be less urgent. Your people need a strong leader. They always have in times of crisis. I give you a clue to implement in your present incarnation."

"I'm supposed to solve a mystery? If animals died, that means the chances of people surviving was nonexistent."

"A leader must recognize and become intimately acquainted with the enemies of his subjects if he is to subdue threat," the cave sitter said.

"'Know thine enemy'?"

"Who is your enemy?"

"Ones who threaten my— no, ones who threaten those I love."

"Who do you love, Arthur?"

The question slashed tangentially across his awareness. Who *did* he love? No individual came to mind any longer. Circe had refused to answer his vid calls, since his defection to the Elite.

He remembered looking down from the lofty heights of Sanctuary, watching as ordinary citizens went about their every-day concerns, safe in the knowledge that they were protected and innocent because of this, and then Shadow's agony at the hands of Nestines. She had done no wrong and yet had come to such a terrible punishment that the very thought of it tore into his being. If Nestines won, those scuttling masses wouldn't exist. Their lives would be snuffed out in pain and fear, ordinary lives, men, women and children – gone. Great anger began to build. An urge to protect flowed through him.

"The innocents. I love the innocents," he said, his voice rasping with emotion.

"Love responds to love—hate to hate. You are learning hate from the one called Shadow. Her active usefulness is almost spent. Learn while you can."

"Shadow can't die. She is all that holds our alliance together." Arthur was stunned by the information.

"Shadow must evolve into a higher form. Her replacement is ready to assume the mantle of power she holds in trust. Never grieve for a mortal until you see their bones picked clean, and then be sure you have the right set of bones."

"She'll live?" Arthur held his breath for the answer, suddenly terrified by a future without her, without the connection to her life through the Archive playbacks.

"Uncertain. Even I can't predict an outcome to her release, save that it will happen soon."

"*I* want her to live. I'll not leave her side, if that is necessary to save her." Arthur suddenly lost his fear of the killer cyborg. She had so little humanity he wanted to help her regain a life before she was taken.

"Decide what it is you wish to preserve, if it should be salvaged, before you commit to a dubious cause that may cost the lives of those deserving compassion." The cave-dweller's eyes took on a look of profound sadness seeming to stretch back countless eons into time immeasurable. "Now learn a real lesson of authority. Those who would lead must accept losses for the greater gain. No individual, however important, is irreplaceable."

"It hurts."

"Each death cuts to the bone. I can still remember the first sacrifice I made. Knowing he would die in agony, I still sent a man to his doom. An entire community survived in consequence, but it didn't alter my guilt, nor ever has. Some can accept this burden. Others bow under the weight. This is the measure of one who would lead." The cave-sitter lowered his head. His fire flared until it colored everything red, then yellow to white.

*

Arthur woke disturbed. He had his wish. His instructor provided answers outside Arthur's imagination, proving insanity wasn't an issue. Knowing the surface had become lifeless agreed with Ector's line of reasoning. Arthur recognized the cave sitter as reticent in the extreme. He was being forced to think for himself, whether he wanted to or not. Insanity would have provided a feasible explanation.

Two nights of dreamless sleep followed. Arthur used the renewal of strength to form his own pocket of memory block. He had it in place when he next accessed the Archive.

23

Earth Date 3875

As COPPER HAD MADE a point of ignoring her since he regained consciousness, Shadow spied on him through a console vid eye, while Ector tried to reason with him. Even though she told Ector to stay out of this argument, there he was, interfering. *Damn him.*

"What difference does it make now you know she's part mechanism? I'm cyborg, yet you still talk to me." Ector had Copper cornered in the Outcast's sleeping unit and paced the floor.

"It's different. You're a Shade."

"Shadow is and has always been a hybrid between our races. Why is my implant right and hers unacceptable?"

"She wasn't a Shade when I first saw her. You took her." Copper turned his back to stare blindly at a holo projection of wind ruffling through long grass; someone had tried to make his quarters more like his natural environment.

"Face it, man, you saw her as human despite the differences already present." Ector avoided a low table as he continued to pace in the small dwelling unit. "*I* didn't know she had our blood at first. We nearly lost her due to our ignorance, and don't imagine she would've lasted more than a few days on the surface, even if she hadn't run into the saurian. Her emergent telepathy, with an active band, would have drawn Nestines to her like flies to a corpse. They isolated her from all protection, set her adrift with imperfect memory—a sitting target no one could protest or care about."

"If that's true, why didn't they kill her at birth as they do all other mutations?" Copper whirled around to stare down his antagonist.

"Some of us, the extremely gifted, don't manifest ability until after puberty. The first sexual experience seems to be the key factor." Ector grinned at Copper's pained expression. "So someone else beat us both through the gate we covet. What of it? She accepts us as companions, albeit reluctantly. Beyond that, you're as out of depth as I am. If Shadow wanted sex, both of us would be fighting over position." Ector looked away for a moment. "There was a time she started to show emotion, like life returning to the dead. Then something unforgivable happened, and she became as she is now. I was interested in the emergent woman. That time has gone. I regard her as a friend, which is all she will permit." Ector sighed, his shoulders slumping in defeat. He started for the door.

Shadow wanted a word in private with him. How dare he discuss her like a sex object? She watched to see which direction he'd take, damn him to the deeps.

"Wait. What did Shades do to her that made the woman die inside? She is a sister. I expected the revolting consequences of her altered state with despair. This hasn't happened. Why not?"

"The damage the Nestines caused is identical to Helga's. I can only propose Submariner blood, and one other factor, as to why," Ector said, turning again to the argument.

Prickles ran up Shadow's spine. She wanted to shout to Ector, wrench him from that room. He couldn't – wouldn't betray her.

She faced the screen.

"What other factor?" Copper demanded.

"You will do some very fast talking on my behalf if she's watching this interview, as I suspect." Ector swallowed, looking toward the view screen, his guilt visible in the set of his expression. "I don't want to lose her friendship, but if it's the price of alliance, I hope she will understand. She must have conceived days before exile and we didn't detect it on retrieval. I ordered her saved because I discovered her telepathic talent. She wasn't pleased when we found out about the child, and *I* had to tell her." He shuddered in remembrance. "She was being trained as an operative. No one suspected she had our gills until she had a reaction, when they started to function without natural ports. The child had to be removed before treatment began."

"She was bearing Dragon's child?" Copper sat down on his bed, cradling his head in his hands. "There wasn't any memory of him until I released it. Why would losing a burden upset her? Many women miscarry or abort."

"We have devices for gestating an early child outside the womb. The child survived."

"Shadow knew? Didn't she want it to live?"

"Remember our warning about seers? They caught me as an adolescent. I spent three miserable years enduring their attempts to mold me in their image. Shadow is too powerful for them. That child, unprotected while we worried over her, represented easy pickings. He vanished from our care before we knew the nature of the threat. She found him with her mind. They bonded. She gave him every protection against them she had at her disposal, and then . . . he shut her out."

"An unborn infant? I'm expected to believe this gibberish?"

"It happened *despite* your skepticism. The child wouldn't have attracted seer's interest without possessing exceptional gifts. He was *aware* even at that early stage in gestation. Retrieval was unfeasible, we would've gotten a dead embryo back, unrelated to Shadow. We were and are obliged to wait. Eventually, they won't be able to hide him, if he still lives. Shadow retreated from grief at that time. She wanted her child."

"Why didn't you force the issue?" Copper looked up with a challenging expression. "That child belongs to its father. She would know that."

"Cut off a fingernail to fall into a container with another thousand such parings. Could you identify your own offering by sight once the mixture is stirred?"

"But a child?"

"A collection of cells, altering daily—too small to scan for identity without risking damage. I could've forced entry into Sanctuary. I didn't because I knew how futile such a gesture was, given that we didn't know the father. How would we know if seers managed to create siblings for Shadow? Her father is an un- known Submariner, and yet I'll bet they know who he is. She did what was necessary. That child will never bend to their wishes."

"I didn't know. She never said."

"Shadow doesn't discuss Boy. Not ever. The hurt goes too deep. Tell me again how inhuman a cyborg is, and I'll ram your teeth down your throat!" His mouth set in a thin line of fury, Ector marched out without a backward glance.

Shadow blanked off the screen, shaking. He told. *How could he?* The service shaft signaled its need to be emptied of edibles, which she ignored. A console direct interface snaked up to her head despite her having no port to give linkage. It battered against her cheeks until she grabbed the umbilicus, furious at the intrusion. The Archive seeped into her mind, impervious to her instant attempt to block it.

He needed to know, Shadow.

"No, he didn't. A cruel and unnecessary act."

Copper couldn't see the individual past the implants. Now he understands humanity exists beyond alteration. You were willing to die for this alliance. Why complain at a lesser sacrifice?

"Death is an end. This must be endured."

Are you so certain of this fact? Outline experiences of death.

"Point conceded. So what?"

Copper is part of my plan. He is currently trying to disassemble the console in his unit in an attempt to escape. I estimate his survival prospects at zero, should he manage to remove the top panel.

"He can sense danger."

From inanimate objects? The tone sounded smug.

Fear lent wings to her feet. She flew down those corridors separating her from Copper. He was just about to lift the panel when she burst in.

"Don't!"

"So Ector was right," he said, moving away from the console. He sank into an easy chair to watch while Shadow repaired the result of his interference.

"Why?" she asked.

"It brought you running, and we need an understanding."

"Was there some small detail Ector missed?" Shadow asked, snidely enough to bring the Outcast to his feet.

"Errors in judgment occurred on both sides. Now that the air is cleared, we should begin afresh as comrades," Copper said in as near an apology as Shadow had ever heard from him. He got up, moving over to face her. "I am making that an order."

"I am under Ector's orders," Shadow began, startled when Copper grabbed her arm to force her banded wrist into full view.

"As long as you wear this judgment, you are mine—my subject, my sister, part of my army. Haven is our place of freedom, not Avalon. Only Haven is safe for the likes of us."

"Avalon is, too." She pried his fingers from her wrist.

"Really? Seers stole your son. Seers would take me if I ventured out. Shades have no more freedom than fort dwellers. This society is as rotten as the one that discarded us, so what are we going to do about it?"

"Avalon fights Harvesters." Shadow eased away to read his expression. His face wore a controlled, lazy anger.

"We'll fight with them for as long as it suits us. Should the common enemy be defeated, we'll see. I'll not replace one set of masters for another." He pulled her to him and put a finger to her lips. "Oh, I know Ector and his like don't intend dominion. Is that true of seers? Can our fey brothers avoid their slimy clutches in the aftermath?"

Not possible, since seers had their own concerns. Trusting them was the same as walking into a blanket bog during fall, blindly trusting vortai weren't particularly hungry that day.

"See?" he insisted. "I'll fight this war because it serves Brethren. I'll make alliance for the duration, but I want the right to live as I see fit afterward. Are you with me, or still perched on that branch wondering which way to jump?"

"No seers on land. I'll side with your camp."

"That's *my* Queen speaking. Now we can start afresh. No more hiding or pretending between us, agreed?"

"Agreed."

"Say why you withheld truth?" he said.

"I wear the band, yet I am not as you. I scan thoughts, though I possess no Shade scales. I have an arm that is not. What is my place? To whom do I belong? There is only one like me in all creation: my lost son. What is wrong with wanting to be accepted as normal, knowing disclosure will result in rejection?"

"What's wrong? I have never fainted in my life before. That is what was wrong. Yes, I had a problem accepting and forgiving. Shadow, you are mine. I staked the first claim in Menhill, and you wear the mark of Brethren on the inside. Shades will never fight to the death as we do, since they have much to lose. Brethren have nothing, even if we win. Will forts ever accept us back into the fold? No. We have only this moment to savor. Our past and future have no meaning. This is why you wear the mantle of full sister."

"Truly?" Shadow wasn't quite ready to believe his assurance until he embraced her, holding her to him as he had once before, with kindness.

"Now tell me what I can reasonably demand in barter from these people."

24

Earth Date 3892

THE CHRONOMETER on the console said one hour had gone while he lived Shadow's reality. For a moment he contemplated continuing. Backing away hurt as much as a kick in the guts, but he kept thinking about Shadow's lost son.

How could seers keep such an individual secret? The boy had to stand out from the rest of the Submariners by simple virtue of the pink skin of his parentage. Was there some part of Sanctuary that housed a lonely prisoner? Could the boy be dead? Arthur wanted answers. He sent a mental command to resume playback.

*

Earth Date 3874

AFTER A CHARGED policy meeting, Ector cornered Copper on the way back to his room. Although Shadow had excused herself from attending to check on Helga, the extent of her switch to Copper's side created big problems.

Ector faced down the Outcast, ready to fight. "Well, barbarian, how did you manage to turn a logical, functioning member of Elite Corps against us?"

"Opened her eyes to who she is. I provided insight, nothing more. Shadow made her own decisions."

"Insights to poison her mind against us." Ector's hands itched to hold a weapon, or to close around Copper's arrogant neck.

"I gave her an opportunity to compare. Was that so wrong? She has the right to judge those with whom she has contact, even me."

Ector pulled up short. Some of his anger died as he regarded the man before him. An incredible possibility occurred to him. "I thought Brethren were all assassins, incapable of gentle feelings. If you allowed Shadow to judge you . . . How many others have such courage of perception?"

"All of us, to a greater or lesser degree. So what?" Copper's face wore skepticism and surprise. He crushed a roach underfoot as if to hide this sudden lapse.

Ector reached out to grip Copper's shoulder. "There is in you a precise, cutting logic. Forget Shadow for a minute, this is important. How many other Brethren are capable of reasoned decisions for the greater good? Think, man."

"Everyone. We function as individuals, or a collective." Copper turned to leave in the direction of his room. "How could it be otherwise with such as us?"

"I don't believe anyone has bothered to show you the 'marvels', as Shadow would say, of Avalon from a high perspective. Would you like a look?" Ector offered a lie couched in the form of a peace overture, a fact he thought Copper recognized, but did the Outcast appreciate the ruse to get them out from surveillance?

Copper's face settled in lines of polite interest. "That would be interesting." He made all the appropriate comments on the way up to the roof, an awed spectator to the wonders of technology beyond his comprehension. Once there, Ector ignored the view, cutting straight to the point.

"Could any Brethren act in your place?"

Copper sat down, selecting the duct of an air purifier for a backrest. "Our leader comes from among fey brothers." He focused on the plas-glass dome dividing Avalon from the sea.

"Who decides policy?" Ector squatted in front of him.

"Me, with input from all concerned. I can't lead without general support." Copper dragged his eyes from the blue light to regard Ector.

"What happens to dissenters?"

"Their opinions are carefully weighed in council." Copper's brows snapped together. "Each objection is thoroughly investigated before any policy becomes general. Sometimes the concerns of an individual are more important, based on personal experience in the area in question."

"You command a force comprised of freethinkers able to rise above mundane orders to function as independent warriors." Astounded by the implications, Ector sat down on an air intake pipe near Copper. "Each fighting unit can work alone or in unison with his fellows. That doesn't happen in the surface armies. They're mindless weapons directed at a perceived aggressor. If I had a group of freethinkers on the loose, I would try to ensure there was no way they could link up. I would want to isolate this dangerous force from my easy targets so that they would be permanently separated. Given mind control, this wouldn't be a problem. I could arrange for each potentially dangerous individual to perpetrate some crime, putting him or her outside the considerations of my easy targets. The plan would be so sublime that I wouldn't have to worry about detection from my victims, or their families. My main threat would be minus fangs and claws, any objectors silenced by due process of law. Am I hitting the target?"

"Harvesters." Copper's face now held the stillness of purpose that Ector recognized as killing mode.

"Precisely. Shadow told me about your re-banding." He had to get through to this warrior before rage destroyed the opportunity. "Just out of curiosity, what sort of a fort king would you have made?"

"About average, I suppose, unless . . . no, I would have challenged them in some way, or made life difficult for their priests." Copper looked shaken by the revelation forced on him.

"I'd be interested to learn how many other Brethren were in a position for direct confrontation before their status change." The implications staggered Ector. Submit to herd mentality or suffer extinction.

"The results will come your way." The Outcast looked at Sanctuary's twin towers, standing darkened as a reminder to all those condemned to the perpetual daytime of Avalon.

"Shadow will be our link on this subject." Ector followed his view, pushing down a shudder of distaste at memories of years in that place. "She has the strength to hide her data from general circulation. It will not help our cause for these facts to become known."

"Seers unman Submariners," Copper suggested, one side of his mouth rising in a mocking smile.

"Those of us who object are many, but few of us have the strength needed to fight. If it weren't for this war, they wouldn't have the stranglehold they do. Seers grab every talent at an early age. Once they have possession—"

"Shadow's Boy." Copper made it into a statement rather than a question. He looked at Sanctuary again. "Why doesn't the child stand out from others? From what I have seen, all Shades have the silver-toned skin scales."

"Boy is an unknown quantity. We know his psi rating is extraordinary, or Shadow couldn't have been blocked." Ector wondered where the seers hid the child. All newborns resembled

Terrans for the first few weeks, but after that, the mutation appeared. "I have access to Sanctuary, not that I've tried to penetrate their crèche yet. With a heritage three parts Terran, hiding him will be difficult. If they subvert him, it will be his wish as much as theirs. I don't think that will happen," Ector said, looking up. "What do you know of the sire?"

"Dragon could easily be one of us." Copper smiled that slow Brethren smile Ector recognized from Shadow. "He had a hard passage to keep his duchy. Maybe that's why he has a sense of kinship with Outcasts. No other fort welcomes Brethren. No other ruler treats us as people. He is within a heartbeat of being as good a fighter as I was."

Ector looked up, catching the past tense. His eyes ranged over the lean Outcast, looking for obvious wounds. "How is he likely to react to Shadow?"

"Not well. He'll try to claim her." Copper's hands clenched. "I kept them apart at High Fort, but it was a close run thing. He knows she lives, or lived. He thinks she died escaping. Now he blames us, and I had plans for Tadgell."

"That's the fort you intended to overrun?"

"Yes, it was. Now I'll need to start over in hostile territory."

Ector caught a trace of irritation from the Outcast. "A good fort to choose, but too near other forts to retain acquisition. My target fort was more isolated."

Copper shifted position to lie back. "Point taken. Where was your target—Grimes?"

"Yes, and equally ruined by Shadow's involvement. The area is under constant patrol by sky ships. We've checked."

"We need an isolated fort, one they wouldn't regard as vulnerable to Submariner attack." Copper wriggled his shoulders, settling his hands under his head. "There's one south of Haven fitting requirements. It's inland with no big rivers nearby to create suspicion. Plenty of ground-cover, but they're hostile to our kind."

"What's the catch to sour the sauce?" Ector guessed there was another big one.

"Predators. The whole area is so riddled by tunnels that if you struck it there would be a boom. Some of those tunnels are the home of vortai, blind, snakelike things of a size to swallow a man whole. Since we can't fight them, we avoid them." Copper raised one eyebrow at Ector.

"You've spotted our weapons in use," Ector surmised. "Firing power guns always brings the Nestines, the ones you call Harvesters."

"They'd already be alerted by our attack." Copper shut his eyes, seeming to trust enough to risk going off-guard. "If vortai can be contained, it would give us a safe, defensive position to repel a counterattack. Taking the fort is Brethren province, keeping it depends on Submariner devices."

"Why am I thinking you have re-evaluated your personal fighting skills?" Ector fired this question out of place to catch a truthful answer.

"Fair point. Shadow increased my ability to ensure my leadership over Brethren continued."

"She did? How?"

"Something with my mind." Copper opened his eyes. "The others also had weapons practice with her. I needed an edge."

"Then she thinks we need you. That precludes any others being augmented. I'll make that an order for any liaison personnel. How many extra men can Haven handle?"

"About sixty, without draining our resources," Copper supplied, looking interested.

"Eighty to one hundred, should we bring extra supplies." Ector watched the Outcast for body language as a key to his reaction. He didn't dare risk mind raid. "Give me your thoughts on any childbearing sisters, assuming we can cure them, being removed to Avalon."

"This isn't going to be a short campaign, is it?" Copper flowed to his feet in the fluid way of Brethren. He began pacing. "When we breed, if we breed, our offspring will warrant both Harvester and seer attention. How safe will they be here?"

"Good point." Ector also stood up, following the Outcast with his eyes. "The susceptible will need to be retained at Haven. Seers have enough power without adding foresight to their armory. This can be done."

"We have an agreement in principle?" Copper said.

"In fact. Ambrose will agree to all points. I have one more I'll add: Shadow must return to Avalon each year. She can't function without a replacement power pack. Is this acceptable?"

"Agreed." The Outcast's eyes narrowed. "I'd not risk her life."

"Then we have a trade. Picture in your mind the exact location of our new target."

Copper started to remove his earring, only to stiffen with shock when Ector waved to decline the offer.

"No secrets between allies," Ector said. "A cyborg with an altered interface implant has no restrictions. I ask your permission for contact. This is a point of courtesy among those who have the ability. I'll not take what is not freely offered."

"This whole conversation could have taken place without my knowledge." Copper's voice came etched with ice.

"It could, and result in unpleasant consequences. Trust is a place of delicate beginnings. I give you knowledge of what I could do, not what I will, or have done."

"A calculated risk," Copper agreed, relaxing and sending Ector a rare smile that reached his eyes.

"Good choice." Ector reviewed the image formed in Copper's mind of the fort in question as fast as he could, aware of the privilege granted. "I like it. We'll move supplies from a nearer point than our first meeting place. There is a river cutting into land from the west. Know it?"

"Very well. It's tidal with a bore wave. I'll show you all I recall."

Ector viewed the memory of the river as Copper saw it when tracking a predator. The Outcast included a trail from where the river went shallow to the highlands leading to Haven.

"Copper . . . can you feel my probe?" Something about the set of the man's mind disturbed him.

"It's a different flavor from Shadow's—darker."

"How about Harvesters?"

"They leave a foul taste, like fumes from a forge," Copper said, looking curious at the turn of conversation.

"Are you able to disclose the number of fey Brethren, or is that restricted information?"

"Six currently active members, including myself. We lost two potential acquisitions last Spring, taken right from under our noses, only we couldn't find the tracks of . . . Harvesters. There should be more fey brothers. That's what you're getting at." Copper slammed his fist into the air duct, making a sizeable dent in the soft metal. "Ten fey brothers lost over the past three years. I should have guessed."

"Pull the others off duty as soon as you can. Somehow, Harvesters can sense your talent. If it's agreeable, I'd like those men joined at the hip with a Submariner apiece, preferably the highest psi-ratings I can spare." A sense of devilment flowed through Ector. "Since we're stuck with a lure, it seems a terrible waste not to turn it into an advantage. I'll also want an Elite operative on recovery patrol. Picking up new members is the fey brothers' primary role, isn't it? One of my men can serve in that capacity as an extra shield."

"We'll lose our cover if we . . ." Copper paused, his expression changing rapidly. "I want a way to make your men blend in with us. Any suggestions?" He stood still as Ector studied him.

Ector viewed the rangy warrior clad in primitive clothing,

bristling with weapons, and a solution came to him. "Let's go check up on Helga. There will be a medi-tech on duty. He'll provide what I need."

Shadow had already left when they strolled into the small care unit. Ector gave out a series of crisp commands to the medi-tech on duty, who took skin samples from both men. In a short while he assembled the dyes and brushes Ector wanted.

"We take turns coloring each other's faces with whatever pattern looks good. I think I have just the right beverage to aid our skill." The bottle of spirits Ector commandeered to celebrate the alliance made both his and Copper's artwork erratic.

*

Shadow caught them teaching each other bawdy songs when she finally located the pair with the Archive's help. The medi-tech looked up from his desk with despair on his face, gave up and left the room. The two guilty parties leered hideously in her direction. Each had a bright blue face, neck and hands, decorated with jagged black lines and white circles. They had made themselves over into terrifying images, but the effect was spoiled when Copper hiccupped.

"Need camo . . . flage," Ector mumbled.

"Will that mess wash off?" Shadow couldn't believe what they had done to themselves.

"Shouldn't fink so," Copper slurred, grinning.

The pair looked at each other, then at her. They pounced, evidently not quite as drunk as they appeared. Copper flattened her, pinning her down with his weight, while Ector got to work with brushes and dye. She yelled for help, struggling against their gleeful endeavor, but was helpless against the pair of them. Ector thoughtfully held up a looking glass, so she could see the results. A horrific visage met her furious gaze. As angry now as when she fought the Vortai, Shadow released her will, letting it seize both of them in an iron grip. The pair soared up to float near the ceiling, both struggling, both looking bewildered.

"Give me one reason why I shouldn't leave you there?" Fury choked her voice to a whisper.

"Get thired," Ector slurred, wearing a stupid grin on his face.

"Really? Are you quite sure of that?" Shadow gave them a few moments to get worried, and then started to the door.

"Queenie, don't leave us here," Copper called. "We were only . . . thrying to look shame."

Shadow relaxed her will abruptly, letting them take the consequences as they crashed down to the floor.

"Men!" she said, including the absent medi-tech in her vitriolic judgment.

She took her grievance straight to Ambrose. After one startled look at her changed face, he turned his back to her, requesting an account of the circumstances. She couldn't miss the shaking of her Supreme Commander's shoulders as she related the incident. He was laughing.

"It's not funny. I'm stuck like this until I grow new skin."

"I'm sorry, Shadow . . . it's just . . ." He dissolved again into chuckles from that brief glance. "Those two have reached some sort of accord, or they wouldn't be playing the fool. Exactly how good was their effort? Could you tell one from the other as distinct races?"

"They made themselves, and me, too hideous to determine."

"Then they have found a way for Submariners to infiltrate forts disguised as Brethren. Copper has been a pain in the backside ever since he arrived." Ambrose turned to face her, keeping his eyes fixed on her right shoulder. "If Ector found a way to break through to him, then I support him absolutely. I'll wear face dye myself, if it helps to defeat Nestines. Go away and think about the advantages of accessing a fort when not only race is irrelevant, but also gender. You do look quite splendidly revolting, my dear."

Shadow didn't like this new accord. She didn't like those two ganging up on her, and she didn't like Ambrose siding with them. "Men!" she erupted for the second time that day.

25

Earth Date 3874

Helga was improving when Shadow checked in with the Archive the following morning. The sentient reported a gradual change to a normal female state, although she would remain unconscious while progress continued. The Archive also reported Copper's agreement to an implant, and that the necessary procedure was happening at this moment. Shadow hoped his head ached as a consequence of having surgery after drinking.

Ector, she learned, had conducted a strategy meeting in her absence, leaving her without anyone to champion or chide, and no cause to pursue except one: Shadow needed to see Boy. Just one look to make sure he thrived. He must be a year old – enough for his Terran heritage to show clear. Sanctuary, the one place off-limits to Shadow, became her goal in those moments.

She let her rage build, needing it, needing to re-create the feeling of facing a vortai in full-charge that had helped her against the men. Time slowed – a service operative walking toward her along a corridor seemed to be moving through liquid treacle. A good start, if not enough to fool seers. Shadow built a mental image of herself as she marched. Bit by bit, the image began to resemble that queen of vipers, Evegena, the matriarch of seers. Shadow began to walk with the same swaying glide so peculiar to that skeletal hag.

Of the two door-wardens at the main entrance to Sanctuary, only one looked around, curious, as Shadow passed within. Every wall, floor, and ceiling was colored rain gray, so she played back a schematic stolen from the Archive in her mind. Uniformity didn't present any obstacle for one cursed by total recall. Seers had their crèche on the third level from ground in the western corner. Shadow headed in that direction, twice more disturbing a passing seer – not enough to cause upset, only a familiar presence.

There were fifteen babies and five infants in a dreary, silent room. Four seers patrolled the space between beds as if they guarded criminals, instead of caring for young lives. Shadow's lack of experience with children led her to check the oldest first, since telepathic scanning would destroy her disguise. Four were female, and not her target. The fifth, a male, had the silver sheen on his skin and the gill flaps common to all Submariners. Shadow began on the babies, yet all lacked any trace of Terran ancestry. So they'd hidden him, had they?

She started a systematic mind search of every area in Sanctuary not designated as personal living quarters. The five levels above ground proved unproductive. Suspecting a blind, Shadow checked off every active unit against a memorized list of living seers, and then accessed all rooms listed as available, a wasted effort. The ground floor, being dedicated to service functions, which she checked anyway, left an underground level. Furnaces, air-conditioning and storage rooms; dusty, gloomy and empty, yet something compelling called to her. Going with the feeling, she quartered the area again. A small, crusted hatch in the floor, near an air changer, caught her attention. She took the time to chip away at a layer of grime welding the aperture shut. That time brought the realization that Boy couldn't be hidden in that hole. It was too old, yet the urgent feeling of wrongness persisted. Reluctant to give up, convinced something lurked in the depths – a something that might give her the clue she needed – she persisted. Nowhere in records was there a mention of this place.

The lid gave with a final jerk when she forced it up with the tip of her sword. The cave-blackness in that hole called to her. Shadow backtracked to stores for a torch, cursing the oversight. Back at the hole, she found a ladder of sorts; a series of metal struts embedded in a vertical descent into infinity and she counted fifty on the way down. One single passage reached out into the darkness at the bottom. The dust of ages rose in small puffs as her feet violated that ancient way.

A doorway loomed ahead, a dark maw of grim enticement. There was a black rectangle on both sides of the lintel, facing inward at about the height of a man's chest. Twin laser beams cut the air beneath her chin, missing flesh by a hair's breadth as she attempted to pass between. Instant reflex to sudden light sent her crashing back to fall in an untidy heap. The beams cut out a second after she landed. Whoever had installed this anti-personnel trap didn't intend for intruders to survive. One trap sprung to catch the foremost hostile, and how many more beyond? Whatever lurked in those dark realms originated with the ancients, probably the builders of Avalon.

Shadow edged to the torch fallen just out of her reach. The movement set off another attack, aimed at belly height this time. Had she been standing . . . Slowly, she backed away on hands and knees, abandoning the torch as irretrievable. Light might have triggered the mechanism, possibly movement and sound. Remove the light and reduce the risk of detecting movement, but sound . . . Shadow froze, concentrating on the torch. It lifted under the power of her will, advancing straight through the portal as far and as fast as she could hurl it. A sharp detonation sounded, but she didn't turn to look, fleeing at full speed into the darkness.

Shadow had plenty of time to dissect the incident during the long walk back to barracks. If any thought to question why 'Evegena' chose to frequent sidewalks instead of using transport, none were foolish enough to ask outright. Being caught accessing Sanctuary would be bad enough by itself, but the other offense . . . no, not a good idea. Bad policy to try to pick through records as something, or someone, knew of the intrusion and would be watching for any data retrieval for that area.

Now Shadow had two pressing questions, apart from Boy's location. Why so many infants in a crèche where births were a privilege granted to so few, and how to find out the secret lurking in that dark zone. The first must be left until her next visit, when any fuss had died down. As for the second – it was an ancient's thing.

Shadow knew of vast, derelict, abandoned cities on the surface, avoided as plague sites. *What if they aren't? What if that is a lie propagated by Harvesters to keep Terrans away?* Assuming this as fact, then logic suggested the ancients had used intelligent devices like the Archive. That sentient intelligence had functioned for countless eons, so why shouldn't others? If they did, logical assumption followed that the knowledge of Avalon existed in data banks.

She didn't like the way the Archive had turned on her when she questioned it about the Terran drones. Somewhere, a security clearance she needed might still exist. Shadow also didn't like the lost element of trust. Why would the Archive fail to disclose any data on Harvesters? Submariners relied on the Archive to such an extent that they would be crippled without it. Wars have many battle zones, and she chose this as her exclusive hunting ground.

Barracks loomed ahead. Shadow ducked into a side alley to

relax her will a little. Now she looked as she had before the stupid trick her so-called comrades had played.

The futile quest left her with pent-up fury. She decided to go for weapons training to ease her tension. There were always some cadets practicing at any time during working hours. The sight greeting her in the main arena brought her up short. Copper sharpened his sword, taking advantage of the superior technology, impervious to the sneering catcalls of cadets, laughing at his appearance. Something so dignified about his presence enveloped him in a cloak of power – not the lethal killing rage of Brethren, something greater – regal. She saw the king who might have been, in all his majesty, so far above mundane concerns that he didn't deign to notice them, however much the effort must hurt.

Shadow made sure all the candidates could see her as she had appeared before the face dye, and then she relaxed her will. Sudden silence thickened into a miasma of shock. They knew how highly her psi-rating scored, and now they suffered the full benefit of recognizing that extra edge in use.

Copper turned at the first hush and witnessed the transformation. He smiled slowly, removing his blade from the sharpening disc. "These boys won't test their weapons against me. They think I am too poor an opponent for their expertise, and they won't fight with real weapons. Will you do the honors, sweeting? I find my sword arm quite stiff from lack of use."

Shadow grinned, drawing on him. She ignored the collective indrawn hiss of concern at the use of sharpened weapons. Out of the corner of her eye, she witnessed someone running to a console to get immediate help, and dismissed the action as irrelevant.

Copper charged to attack, his sword catching the light, slicing in a heavy blow. Each knew the other's weaknesses. Each played on those flaws in the intense interchange. To Shadow, it was a graceful dance of parry and counterstrike, with no question who should win, for she had given him the advantage – the foreplay held her enthralled. A commotion at the door distracted her. Copper's blade flashed toward her neck, arresting a moment before decapitation. "You're dead, my Queen." He saluted her with his weapon.

"Which moron ordered a level five security alert for Brethren at play?" Ector yelled from the doorway. He stalked over to the awed candidates. No one answered. Various lads glanced at one trying to hide in their ranks.

"You all know Shadow, and how skilled she is with a sword. Copper is our Terran ally. He has proved, unless my eyes are failing, that he is our match. Anyone who thinks his or my appearance is humorous should consider himself next in line for a face job."

26

Using a dim glow globe to illuminate Ambrose's office, Arthur worked from the third sleep hour. Days of surreptitious observation had supplied him with the door code he needed to gain entry: now he tried various security key words to access his commander's console. As a last resort, he keyed in Ambrose's name spelled backward and . . . access.

He looked for records related to the search for Shadow's son. Arthur needed the data, convinced he had been one of the children she found on her penetration of Sanctuary. Each child from that sensitive time must have had an investigated background, and he wanted his ancestry. He also wanted to know why Boy hadn't been with them, since providing camouflage for that special child appeared to be the whole point of creating so many children of a similar age. The files of the last sixteen years scrolled into view, Arthur sat forward, and then the screen went blank. Frantic overrides failed, despite his urgent key work. The system had crashed.

Access denied, Arthur, a soft voice in his mind advised.

"Archive, I wasn't searching for Boy. Anyway, I don't see it matters, since Ector said Shadow is bringing her son to Avalon on her next visit. I've a right to know my own heritage."

This is not your console, Arthur. Ambrose has not authorized access, or it would be logged in records. Theft can never be justified and is reprehensible. You will now return to your own unit. Any future attempts to access restricted data will be reported.

"So I'm being sent to bed with a warning?" Arthur didn't believe his luck could get so good.

My plans are too near conclusion for the resultant interruption that chastisement of your irresponsible behavior would cause. I shall implement my own punishment regime, beyond restrictions Ambrose may consider appropriate, if there is an attempt to re-offend.

"Fine. I'll ask Boy myself. He'll know his peer group, even if I don't remember him."

An excellent notion. Adjustments to exercises in futility have a maturing effect on the young, I have often noted. With this smug observation, the Archive withdrew.

Arthur considered its words as he made a careful retreat. Shadow and Boy represented the Archive's prize 'specimens'. If questioning Boy meant a wasted effort, so would braving Shadow's wrath. The Archive intended to forewarn them, didn't it? Strange that it had let him review parts of Shadow's life containing criticism to itself. Arthur had the feeling his excursions into full sensory playback were nearing termination. The sentient indicated plans close to conclusion involving him – time for humoring his whims shortened, and he had provided it with an excellent reason for chastisement.

Arthur reached his unit and his decision at the same time. Any shred of information left on Shadow must be acquired tonight, without the Archive's help. But he needed a guardian to bring him back into his own mind before irretrievable exposure condemned him to endless playback of Shadow's life – addiction. Arthur had another ally, one he was prepared to trust with his existence as an independent identity.

The bed in his unit could not be shifted, being anchored to the wall by various connections regulating the heat and hardness level of the mattress, nor would the console move. Arthur casually destroyed two easy chairs for the sleeping pad he needed in the position he wanted. He guessed the Archive much too busy reloading Ambrose's database to spare time for a disobedient child it had intimidated. Arthur hooked up the umbilicus to his com link, manually programming playback to start in ten minutes – five maximum to achieve sleep and the remainder for fast-talking the cave sitter into helping. He lay down, trusting to blind chance that the dream he needed would arrive with sleep.

*

The cave-sitter gazed deep into a golden chalice brimming with clear water, as if to fathom some mystery beyond human comprehension.

"Leadership requires courage, Arthur," he said, looking up over the brim of the vessel, his matte-black eyes unreadable.

"Also the wisdom to ask for help, when faced with an intractable problem," Arthur said, sitting down across the fire from the old-young man.

"Aye, wisdom to discern personal limitations is a treasure beyond price. How may my wisdom aid yours?"

"Time flows. I must escape from sleep when I have stolen the information I covet. You claimed me with dreams. Can you waken me? Shall I sleep on in an endlessly repeating dream?" The single falling drops of water marked the moments of his life fading as he waited.

"Suspicion turning into trust? Resistance changing into requests for aid? Maturity flies on the winds of necessity, I see. The present incarnation has very few years for such a leap of faith." The cave-sitter lowered his dreadful gaze into his golden chalice once more. "Yes, Arthur, I will do as you wish. Know that I am well pleased with you."

Arthur opened his mouth to voice his gratitude just as his essence spiraled into a dark void.

*

Earth Date 3875

SHADOW TURNED BACK for a last look at Avalon, Boy's home, to have Copper bump into her. It was the sixth time in five hours that he had lurked so close behind her since her return from the dark zone. She had even caught him sleeping across her unit threshold at first waking. He hadn't asked about her absence from meetings, nor offered any explanation for his extraordinary behavior. All she got was his sorrowful half-smile.

Four medi-techs and eleven Elite boarded the submersible with them. Eight had their skin dyed for the mission, but she missed Ector, who had stayed behind with Helga as a condition of the alliance Copper demanded. The woman made a steady improvement, if not fast enough for release yet. She would travel with Ector, six more altered Submariners, and a few men Copper planned to leave at contact point.

Copper now wore a replica black band, sending correct signal at short range, but incapable of betraying location. Among the equipment to be transported to Haven were enough replica bands for all Brethren holding allegiance to Copper. Medi-techs also brought a mobile implant device for stabilizing every brother, while the sisters would have to be ferried to Avalon for normalization. Shadow's head still rang from the arguments over this necessity, but the medi-techs remained static on the point. The procedure for women remained too complex and risky to chance in primitive conditions. They refused to back down and cause a consequent risk to life and alliance.

Shadow tried to sleep on the voyage, but every time she opened her eyes, Copper stood there, hovering. She knew he sensed danger around her, and yet couldn't tell him it wasn't acute, since she had no immediate plans for a return visit to the dark zone. When the time came for the stasis device, Copper insisted Shadow be near. He didn't fear death, he just wanted her close as it brushed him. He lay down for her to put the small circle in place on his forehead.

Night reigned when they landed, and Shadow removed her earring to sense for Brethren presence in the dunes. A party of fifty watched them, many more than Copper had left, and all Brethren. She knelt at his side to remove the device, calling to him with her mind. For one moment, she had a clear view of his terror for her safety, until his privacy barrier dropped into place. His eyes opened, and he sucked in air, then he looked at her ear. She replaced her essential ornament.

"How long?" he asked.

"Time enough to climb down into the mines at Haven, and back again."

"It felt like a heartbeat." He sighed.

"There are fifty Brethren in the dunes watching us. Marvic is concerned," she said. The Submariner liaison officer kept his men near the surf line for a swift retreat, and had not started landing supplies.

"Fifty? Fifty, you said? I'll have Rowan's hide for this." He sprang to his feet, and then froze. "Are they mine?"

"Every one—no Harvester flavor. I checked."

Copper bellowed out an order to advance at once with weapons lowered. They came in groups of three, each triad approaching with caution. The power of his voice brought them within sight until they saw his altered appearance.

"We have alliance. We found a way to hide the Shades in our ranks. I am still the same man you last saw; I still bear a scar on my belly from saurian attack three summers past. Do I need to show it to convince you?"

Copper apparently did. They advanced with weapons leveled. Three edged closer. Those three weren't satisfied by physical evidence. They fired questions at him until convinced. Hard eyes turned next to Shadow.

"Our pet Shade got a wound from your blade last cold season," Saffron, a blond brother with flat eyes suggested.

"She's a sister for hells' sakes!" Copper roared.

"Shadow is, or was, also an active member of our force. She shared in spring training." Saffron's face set in hard lines. "We want proof."

"Shall I describe the shape of the burn you wear from being branded? Shall newcomers know where you wear it?" Shadow suggested to Saffron with a sweet smile. She met his challenge until he dropped his eyes, defeated.

"The pretty boys come with us." Copper gestured at the Submariners with dyed faces. "Where is our hostage?"

At a sharp whistle, Tarvi marched over the dunes, flanked by three guards. He waved a welcome to those he recognized, and looked over at more colorful members of the company.

"Where's Helga?" Saffron demanded. In the sudden hush, every Brethren face turned to Copper, cold expressions on all.

"Recovering in the city of Shades. Ector will bring her along with more reinforcements one week from now. She won't need her veils anymore." Copper looked into Saffron's narrowed eyes. "*If* you can spare some from this great host, they'll be needed to act as guides to Haven. *Where is Rowan?*"

"At High Fort, trying to find out who's stirring up trouble we don't need."

"Someone misbehaved?"

"Not that I could see, and I questioned all of them." Saffron made a sweeping gesture at the Brethren. "We all drifted to High

Fort when we left Haven because we reckoned we might pick up work after the wedding of Alsar's son last year. The timing is about right for a birth celebration, but we found ourselves unwelcome. Dragon was there, and Rowan has tried to talk to him alone for the past week without any luck—Alsar seems very lonesome for the Black Duke's company for some reason. Rowan didn't think there was much point us trying other forts until he's found out more. He thought we'd better camp out here in case you needed help."

"Change of plans, Marvic," Copper called to the Submariner strike leader, waving him over to join them. "Shadow and I must make a necessary detour. We'll catch up with you later."

"Copper, Dragon thinks she's dead," Saffron cautioned. "Taking her may bend him out of shape."

"I need her along. Marvic will explain why. Have someone bring our horses. I'd like to make a start while we still have moonlight." He paused while Saffron signed to a brother some way back from the shore. "I want everyone regrouping at Haven. Travel in parties of five brothers to one fish-man, except for Rowan's group, and yours, Saffron. Both of you get two apiece—make sure you stick close to them for your own protection."

"Do you still want all of us looking alike before we start?" Marvic asked.

"No, find time as you journey. Oh, and Marvic, your men won't reach Haven all at the same time—don't fret about it. Both of you see that this horde splits as soon as possible."

Brethren grouped to Saffron's brisk commands. Submariners began moving equipment off the shoreline to Marvic's orders. The beach became an organized departure zone with the integration of two groups. Shadow caught a glimpse of Tarvi walking into the waves with the return crew as she turned to follow Copper.

The pair rode through the night until the moon began to set.

Copper called a halt in a well-sheltered glade with a small stream running through the center.

Still mounted, Shadow waited while he checked the area, too lost in her own thoughts to consider offering help. She didn't understand why she'd been dragged along to a meeting where Dragon might catch sight of her, when Copper had gone to so much effort before to keep them apart. It didn't make sense.

A hand on her shin focused her attention; Copper reached up to help her dismount. His arms closed around her once she gained ground, bringing her into a close embrace when she turned. Startled by his action, Shadow tried scanning, knowing she'd only get basic emotion. *Anger, sadness and a sense of being trapped.* He stiffened at her intrusion. His hands snaked up to her ears, feeling her head behind them. He must have expected to find a new implant, one that would let her pick through Brethren minds like Ector could. His hands dropped to her shoulders as his frown cleared.

"You know?" she asked, surprised by his suspicions.

"Ector told me. He thought we'd deal better with no secrets. I trust him in my mind—not you. I needed to know whether the time you'd spent by yourself was used to enhance snooping."

"A very unflattering opinion," she said, feeling offended.

"True, though regrettable. You do snoop."

"Your defense posture shows you're hiding something," Shadow said.

"Pass me your bedding roll. I've found a place for a few hours' sleep," he said, ignoring her remark.

Shadow unstrapped it, passing the roll over to him with a withering look lost in sudden gloom when the moon passed behind a cloud. He'd already hobbled her mount while she sat in a daydream, and now he led her to the area he'd selected. She heard him arrange their sleeping rolls and blundered toward the sound of his voice as he called her to rest. As before, he'd placed their bedding for shared use. This time he didn't radiate the welcome heat she'd come to appreciate. She moved closer for warmth, grateful as he fitted himself close. A disturbing thought occurred.

"You didn't meditate." She hoped he intended to keep his brotherly role.

"It's too darn cold to concentrate. No one told me I'd lose my heat when I had fertility restored. I'd have liked knowing in advance that I could freeze to death."

"Could've asked. Medi-techs always give an honest answer."

"So, I forgot. I'm stuck among impossible-looking things I can't—don't even want to understand, and I'm expected to re-member little details."

"Why are we fighting?" she asked, puzzled by it.

"*I'm* not. Why are you on edge? The tension I felt from you, still feel, is the same level as at our capture of you and Ector last year."

"Why am I riding to High Fort when Dragon is there?" she countered.

"Because I need a gifted telepath."

"Again, why?"

"Ector didn't tell you? Don't Shades talk to each other? Exchanging information is fairly important. No . . . don't even bother answering. Ector and I worked out why there are so few fey brothers surviving. It seems we are a bad luck charm to lure Harvesters. Ector reckons we'd be safe enough in the open if we had a high-ranking telepath with us. Rowan doesn't know his risk—I wanted the best we'd got for both of us."

"Then I don't have to meet with Dragon?"

"Not if I can avoid it, you won't. It's doubtful he'd recognize you from a distance now, and I want Rowan out of High with whatever information he's managed to extract."

Shadow thought this through. It seemed logical, if not

enough to explain his unease with her. "Are we arguing over my difference again?"

"No."

"Then what?"

"Did you forget I'm fey when you started the mission I felt begin in Avalon? Did you think I wouldn't notice if your life was in danger? We're going to fight because I'm withdrawing you from active listing."

"Copper, that's unjust. It's possible I might earn a certain degree of punishment for invading an area not open to casual visits . . . if I'm caught on record. Since this didn't happen before we left Avalon, I assume it will wait until I try again. I won't bother unless I find a very compelling reason to return. There is no more danger for me here than there was before."

"Yes, there is. The sensation is even stronger on the surface. Something hunts. Are those fish-men really to be trusted?"

"Ector's vanguard didn't include any seers." Shadow nestled against him, satisfied he was going to behave. "They won't volunteer for surface assignment if they think they might be in personal danger. Maybe they'll hold back until they get a detailed report on Harvesters in the frenzied pursuit of fey brothers? Seers are those who are going to be seriously upset with me. The others wouldn't be affected beyond mild amusement."

"You're still not permitted to leave my side."

"That's a relief. I thought you decided I couldn't leave Haven."

"I have. Fey brothers will have specialized outside duties from now on. I won't be visiting any forts either, so you'll be sharing my banishment."

"You're giving up on acquisitions?" Shocked, Shadow started to sit up, but he pulled her back. She couldn't believe he'd leave new Brethren to a sad fate.

"I'll concentrate exclusively on them," Copper said. "We'll keep outside forts until we figure a new way to shield. We'll have to, or risk looking very odd, wandering around in inseparable twosomes."

"With one of you fey, priests are going to suspect the other. It's going to tell them we know who they target. I take your point."

The ghostly shape of a huge white owl flew overhead, dropping suddenly, followed by the sounds of some small animal screaming.

"We'd better hold another strategy meeting when Ector arrives at Haven. Once we learn to work together, we'll have more idea on tactics, but giving up acquisitions isn't an option, not when we constantly lose manpower." He sighed into her hair. "Then there's Rowan's input to sift through. Let's try for some sleep before we tackle more problems."

Copper settled into a deep sleep, but Shadow lay fretting over restriction. Now that she'd found one way into a Harvester inner sanctum, she'd planned on searching for more. Getting a force right to the heart of their nest solved the problem of luring a ship into the open and perhaps catching one of the beasts intact. If she worked Ector round to her plan, then he could convince Copper . . . those two ganged up far too much for her liking. Alternatively, exploring the remains of ancient cities appealed, if she were banned from forts for a while. Neither of them could object, since neither knew what she'd discovered in the bowels of Avalon. With this satisfying thought, Shadow allowed sleep to come.

The next morning they breakfasted together on Brethren journey fare, after sleeping through sunrise. Copper figured they'd create less stir if they entered High Fort at a busy time. Shadow worked on an alternative plan once they started out, having it figured just as High Fort appeared in sight over the crest of a hill. She grabbed Copper's reins, bringing him up short.

"Change of plans," she told him. "Rowan comes to us."

"How? The threat level remains constant—it would reduce if we stayed out of High."

"This might not work. I'll need your help to break through the shield of his earring, and then there's that noise."

"What noise?" His face revealed his total ignorance.

"Inside forts . . . the noise that makes speaking difficult, or do earrings counteract that, too? I didn't notice last time I visited, I was rather busy trying to leave."

"Shadow, I've never heard any noise, with or without an earring."

"Ask a Shade when you get one inside. I wonder if I'm alone, or they will hear, too."

"You're going to call Rowan to us? Let's see if it works." He dismounted, hobbling his horse.

Shadow decided to go with his instinct, since they broke new ground. Once they'd removed earrings, she reached out to place her hands on either side of his head. He'd opened totally to her. She seeped into the area of his mind where precognition ruled, hoping to find the extra strength she might need. Nothing prepared her for the sudden blending of their separate talents; no amount of fighting prevented a terrifying union forming. For one instant they shared a single soul, a barrier withered before combined force. Contact established. It took every ounce of will either of them possessed to separate. Both of them trembled with the effort as they came apart.

"Are you all right?" she asked, feeling she needed a week of sleep.

"No. Linking with you is too intense." He looked away from her. "I think I'm going to have problems with this joining."

"Copper . . . I didn't mean to snoop. For what it's worth, I'm truly sorry." Somehow she found the courage to face him. "Whether it was using your new implant or maybe the linkage became . . . involved because your fey quality joined with my psi

301

power for whatever reason . . ."

"Now you know I love you." He smiled that slow, sad smile peculiar to Brethren.

Shadow answered with one of her own. Harvesters took everything from them except pain, thinking to destroy them, not knowing they smiled because they could still feel enough to laugh at fate. Just as uncomfortable as Copper, she accepted he'd had access to her deepest thoughts, knew emotional contact with others terrified her. Somehow they had to work through this intimate knowledge to be comfortable with each other again.

"Pax, Copper?" she offered.

"Aye, pax. It's a start." He seemed about to say more, but his eyes became fixed with a look Shadow recognized. It lasted many heartbeats, and then he shook himself. "The sense of threat to us lessens. Time flows in a different path."

"Rowan comes?"

"I think so. The suggestion you sent of needing clear spring water was overpowering. I confess I feel thirsty. Why didn't you send him an image of us at this location?"

"Suppose Harvesters heard our thoughts? I'm not that lonesome for company."

Copper replied with a wicked grin. He took her reins to bring them both to a small stream among trees where they tied their mounts. Both returned to the tree line to watch one lone horseman leaving High Fort, his dark skin identifying him at a distance.

"He's going to be very disappointed when he finds our stream doesn't have a wild mint flavor," Copper said.

"I had to have some way of making this place special, and our stream has mint growing close. He can always crush some leaves in his hands before he cups them to drink."

"I'm sure he'll appreciate the thought, just as soon as he gives you a piece of his mind you don't want."

Shadow shrugged. They both watched High Fort to see if he'd acquired followers. Rowan appeared to be free from pursuit. Copper signed to pull them back to the stream.

"Why?" Shadow asked sitting down on a fallen tree trunk.

"He'd react to people lurking in bushes. In plain view, there won't be a problem."

Copper was right. Rowan entered the glade, reining in when he spotted the two grotesquely altered people. He drew his weapon, advancing with extreme caution. Copper moved to sit by Shadow, wrapping his sword arm around her waist.

"By the Seven Hells! Copper . . . is that you?" Rowan looked at them through narrowed eyes. His shoulders relaxed.

"How did you guess?"

"Shadow's blonde hair. No one else would dare to touch her with any hope of living. Will that muck wash off?"

"It's permanent, until we grow new skin," Copper said.

"There's a good reason?"

"It works on Shades as well. Given no one really looks at us in Forts, they'll pass."

Rowan dismounted, almost running to the water. He spat out the first mouthful to glare at Shadow. "Take whatever you did away right now."

"I can't. You'll have to make do."

Looking furious, Rowan snatched up a handful of mint to cram into his mouth, chewing, spitting out before he tried to drink again. His face registered immediate relief.

"Don't you ever, *ever* do such a thing to me again. If I find I can't drink beer without chewing weeds, we're going to fight." He glared at Copper. "You're King. You keep her in line."

Copper shrugged. "It was necessary. We wanted you, not any hangers on."

Still glaring, Rowan fished in his clothing to toss a small pouch. Copper caught it midair, opening it to tip tokens into his hand. These discs weren't the usual blank variety Alsar used as barter in his fairs. One side bore a good resemblance to his head in profile, and the other held the likeness of a crown.

"Alsar's gotten creative. Priests allow it? Rather close to being proscribed as a living image," Copper said.

"He has permission. The idea may even have come from them, but I haven't found out for certain. These pretties are aimed at us. This is how we're paid now, but when we try to barter them . . . surprise, surprise, ten from us is worth one from a fort dweller."

"This is serious," Copper said. "Any reason why?"

"As near as I've pieced together, it was Shadow's apparent drowning last year. Priests became upset that one of us got close to their inner sanctum."

"My doing, I'm afraid," a deep voice said, from a nearby thicket.

27

Earth Date 3892

CLOYING DAMPNESS and the scent of wet dirt curled around Arthur in the mist-shrouded night. Warriors with naked swords joined in a circle with him. Mist wove around them and through them while they posed, frozen in time during a lull in battle. When he looked down, he had an unsubstantial body like the others, and he carried a sword.

Wolves howled, and a horn call signaled for the Wild Hunt to start.

I shouldn't be here. This is wrong.

A star fell, growing in brilliance as it came to earth, filling his eyes with light, to draw him into another place. His body dissolved as it had countless times over, and then he fell for many heartbeats until he landed in flesh.

*

Earth Date 3875

DRAGON STEPPED from behind a tree with his sword held point lowered. He strode around to the water, fronting the Brethren all the while. Rowan edged to the others while Copper and Shadow rose in a relaxed manner. Within seconds, they had assumed a Brethren fighting-crescent.

Shadow bit her lip to stop a cry of shock when Dragon tried to drink and repeated Rowan's gesture of disgust. Her mind spun in sickening circles. *He's not fey, and he isn't a Submariner.* Reality began to slip away from her. Each passing second in this man's presence increased her pain of loss until she entered the place of Brethren retreat, only aware of the need to survive.

*

"That weed near your left foot . . . you chew some of it to get the right flavor," Rowan advised. "Next time we get drunk together, and I ramble on about flavor, make sure you get the full recipe before you start snoring."

Standing behind Rowan, Copper glanced sideways at Shadow wondering if she guessed the problem, despite her blank expression under the dye. Rowan spun a very plausible, impossible lie for any Brethren, a brave attempt, riding on how much Dragon overheard before he made his presence known. They might have to kill him, or at least attempt it if he was not alone and had men in calling.

Also partly shielded by Rowan's bulk, Shadow signed that Dragon might feel intrusion if she raided his mind.

Dragon snatched a clump of mint followed by a hand cup of water, combining both. Some tension eased out of his face the moment he swallowed. "Not drunk now, are you, or dumb? Good trick to gain sympathy," he sneered, alluding to alcohol indulgence loosening Brethren tongues.

"No trick of ours, just a part of our punishment." Copper kicked a dead branch out of his fighting perimeter. He didn't want to fight Dragon, but he was going to win if he did. "When we're cast out we lose the ability to talk straight in forts so that we don't contaminate righteous worshipers. Outside contains too many other defects and mutations for such a curse to hold. Priests would be obliged to silence saurians if they wanted us dumb here."

"Now that you know, what are you planning to do?" Rowan asked, quiet-voiced.

All hung on Dragon's answer. A breeze sighed through leaves, rustling the trees and bringing a faint coolness to the humid air.

"Report you to the priests, unless I get a straight answer." He looked at Rowan. "One of your people drowned at High Fort last year. What did you do with the body?"

Rowan shrugged. "Why the interest in a corpse?"

"I heard talk of an 'apparent drowning'. I need to be sure of the death. My single thrust through the heart would've been quicker and more certain."

Shadow's sudden gasp turned Dragon's hard eyes on her for the first time. "So she lives. Now I see a reason for hiding your faces under dye. Priests want her alive. Give her to me for a swift ending and they'll ease off the rest of you."

"Even if we agreed, you couldn't take this one in a fight." Rowan shifted into a battle-ready stance, a minute adjustment that no-one but Brethren might notice. "You've fought with me . . . I can't take her."

"Lies. She wasn't that good." Dragon's sword point raised a few finger spans.

"She's trained with our best. You'd last about six heartbeats, if that. Your death is going to stir more grief for us. We can't permit it." Rowan gripped the hilt of his sword, easing it out of the sheath a hair's breadth.

"So you're telling me to swallow my honor? Including her in the mantle of Brethren protection isn't going to help you when Alsar's scheme spreads to other forts. Is she worth slow starvation?"

Copper moved forward a pace to clear ground. "None of us will sacrifice another. We've all suffered too much at fort hands to give over one of our kind to torment. Remember, we're used to living off the land. You people aren't used to the filthy tasks you have assigned to us."

A pheasant broke cover, startling them all with its noisy flapping. The lazy drone of insects filled a charged silence.

"Your choice." Dragon's faced paled. He took a deep breath, as if getting his temper under control. "We'll manage without your services. Be sure I'll have her cut down if I catch her alone."

Rowan's fingers flickered behind his back in sign language: *'Alone is the key, he hasn't got any backup. Do we take him?'*

"We're agreed then." Copper gave Rowan the signal to stand down by that phrase. "She stays out of your range."

"I know you. I've fought with you." Dragon looked past Rowan at Copper.

"Aye, and I've always won. For your sake I'll add my warning to my brother's." Copper gestured to Shadow. "I can best her, just. Don't think your luck is going to hold because of gender. Our sisters are just as lethal . . . more so in her case."

"I'm terrified." Dragon's face twisted into a sneer.

"Be so." Another gust of wind ruffled Copper's hair. "We always know when we're about to gain a new brother. Be good, Dragon, very good. Your band status is uncertain, right now. Oh, and don't blab to priests about any threats—this isn't one . . . or they may decide to act on the spot. You would be a valuable acquisition for us, but it is up to you."

"Keep her then. I'll be waiting for my chance." Dragon began a careful retreat, his sword raised to chest height. He edged through the trees, watching them until he slipped behind a bush.

Copper placed one hand on Rowan's shoulder, warning him to let Dragon go. Rowan's fingers flickered urgently behind his back. *'We should take him while we can.'*

"Not worth the trouble," Copper said. "Let it ride."

They heard the sound of Dragon's horse pounding toward High Fort. Shadow wandered over to the water, staring at the glinting surface.

"Why?" Rowan demanded. "He was alone."

"He has a personal score to settle too pressing for any to take his ravings seriously. We have enough problems without adding the execution of a fort leader to our score. Besides, lying low while forts cut off their own feet will give us the time we need to establish bases away from Haven."

"Alliance is made?"

"Yes, and Helga approaches normal womanhood. I thought you'd appreciate knowing this."

"Completely normal?" Rowan looked as if he feared to believe it could be possible.

"Our new friends think she won't need her veils anymore, unless she's overcome by shyness." He noticed Shadow's stiff movements as she knelt down by the stream. She cupped water and rinsed her face.

"And us?"

"They started with me. I'm told I'm viable, but I'm not sure how grateful I am." Copper met Rowan's gaze. "I freeze constantly."

"Maybe I'll wait until I see positive results before I lose advantage." Rowan smirked and wandered over to the log to sit in the shade.

"I don't suppose I can ask you to keep this to yourself?" Copper decided he felt hurt at the humor. He wondered at Shadow's silence, dreading her reaction to Dragon.

"Not a chance . . . we'll all be watching to see if you're productive."

"I'm not sure I want spectators." Now he worried. Shadow would have jumped on him for coarse words at any other time.

He tried to keep his fear to himself.

"You're King. You hold the obligation to try first by right of rule." Rowan's grin got bigger until he turned to Shadow, and it faded to an expression of profound sorrow. "What about her? She's a wreck. Dragon didn't hold back his spite."

"My problem to deal with." *Hells, girl, why now? Aren't you over him?* "We're all relocating to Haven for a strategy meeting. You're traveling with us since we need her for protection. Fey brothers are Harvester targets."

Copper suddenly sensed a danger for all of them, and he guessed Rowan shared his vision since the brother looked skyward, then at the tree line, too. A strong sense of threat crushed down on him.

"I think I'd better join another group," Rowan decided. He immediately looked more relaxed. "I've never had an unsought premonition before . . . have you?"

"Once or twice." His own anxiety eased with Rowan's decision, but the heat of the day increased in an oppressive wave. "Not nearly as strong as this one, though. Seems that we should part, since the feeling is less intense, now."

"Exactly what kind of protection is Shadow supplying?" Rowan glanced over at her, still kneeling by the water.

"Same as the Shades: a shield for our fey powers being detected. When you find a group, stick close to a fish-man. One of us has to reach Haven."

"Point taken." Rowan looked once more at Shadow, and then he made a hurried departure. The sound of his horse's hooves pounding bone-dry ground echoed in the stillness of a hot, breathless day.

Copper turned to Shadow. She stared in a mole-blind way at nothing. He knew her as well as he knew himself since their intense sharing. He retrieved their mounts from a thicket, stopping a few paces from her.

"We need to make good time if we're to reach the shelter I intend, and there's a storm coming." He decided to act as if nothing were wrong. "Why don't I lead your horse while you keep an eye on the weather?" Shadow mounted up as if in a daze. Copper watched to see she was alert enough to keep her seat before he picked up the pace.

Heat mounted in oppressive waves as they rode. Dark clouds began boiling overhead until a flash of lightning released an icy downpour. The storm gathered strength with each passing minute. Copper turned west to a line of hills, urging his horse faster. Rain washed away signs of their passage at the expense of soaking them through, and coldness spoke of worse to come. He headed to caves found by Brethren when hired to kill a saurian. Once, the cavern had formed a river channel through rock, but now water carved a deeper route to cascade in a large waterfall at the back of the cave. Always opportunists, Brethren cleared away bones and other rotting remains to equip the place as a way station. The place suited their needs, as it was located away from any trail, therefore unlikely to be found by any fort dweller. Big enough to house a saurian, the cave complex sheltered up to twelve Brethren and their mounts.

A goodly clump of aspen shielded the entrance and provided a windbreak. Copper led them through the mouth just as hailstones the size of pebbles started slamming into the ground. The first cave was the larger of the two and fitted out with stalls for horses. A stake of hay lay in a manger at one end. Buckets for water hung on a bar hammered into the rock face. Other gear lay stacked in crates. They had everything they needed to last out a storm, including a water supply.

Helping Shadow dismount, Copper decided he'd make her stop hiding from him, even if it meant she ended by hating him.

28

SHADOW SHIVERED in the gloom while Copper lighted torches. He ached to send her to rest, but the horses must be tended before a chill set in. She responded in a wooden way to begin rubbing down her mount after he unsaddled the beasts and carried their gear to a living area. He was warmer by the time the horses were comfortable and feeding, but Shadow still looked cold.

"Our turn now," he announced. "I've unpacked and laid out our bedding rolls. Strip to the skin while I build a fire."

Mist from the waterfall and draft from light-shafts made this bolt-hole cool at the best of times. He brushed off the dampened ashes in the fire-pit and went to get kindling.

Dry grass and tiny twigs caught quickly, but the larger logs smoldered. Smoke wavered for a moment, and then streamed up through a natural outlet created by waterfall from the surface river. Smoke, but no heat and Shadow's teeth chattered behind him in time with his own shivers.

Curse that mind sharing. Shadow's thoughts continued to surface in his head. Copper froze as her actions in Avalon's dark zone came to him. Of all the fool places to pry without good reason . . . and her plan for digging in ancient ruins . . . *We're going to fight. Just when I'd figured her out.*

He stripped to place his clothes over a drying rack set against a wall. Turning, he collected her clothes to hang alongside his. She had arranged their bedding rolls for joint use in her muddled state of mind. He tried not to grin as he slid under the covers to hold her close. Clarity returned to her expression.

"You didn't meditate."

"I don't intend to die of the cold." He blew her a kiss on his fingertips. Despite the hideous skin dye, she was still a lovely bedmate. "You're not claiming shyness with me, are you?"

She turned her face away.

"Or do you still burn a candle for Dragon?" He held her tight when she tried to push him away. "You might as well tell me, because your thoughts of him will surface in my mind. Our joining left all the privacy doors open. You have no place left to hide from me.

"I love him." Her eyes blazed. "He is Boy's father."

Sharp knives of jealousy speared through Copper. He'd started this, and he intended to follow it through. "What of me?"

Another bout of shivering raged through her, and she melded to him. "You're impossible. You spent all winter amusing yourself with the pleasure women, and then you used me to gain fighting skills."

"As long as we're going to fight, why did you give me a night of love that spoiled me for every other woman?" Cold and angry, he needed her to know how much she had hurt him. "And I'm talking about the second time, when you ended up on top. You can't do that to a man, and then kick him out of your bed."

"You're too possessive. You smothered me."

Furious, he rolled on top of her to stop her turning away. "Untrue. I gave you more room than any other new recruit. Just you wait until my memories unfold. You'll beg my pardon."

Cold air on his back raised gooseflesh, but a pulse in his loins gave him another problem. *Oh shit. Not now.*

"You're getting an erection." Her voice came quiet, and she didn't struggle against him.

He eased over on his side, still maintaining body contact for warmth.

"Is that fire never going to give off heat?" She peered over him at the hissing smoke pile.

"The wood is damp. Once we have a decent blaze, I'll get some food unpacked." Copper had an idea that Shadow had just finished their fight. He lay looking up at the smoke and the patterns of green and yellow lichen on the rock face.

"Since I've just been accused of teasing, I suggest a game of 'Keys to the Kingdom' to pass the time."

She's trying to distract me with a childhood game. What point is she trying to make? The object of this game was for the questioner to win by dragging out ten or more queries while the answerer tried to achieve the final round in less than four.

"Fine, but I demand a simple forfeit for the loser to make it more interesting." He began to put his campaign together. He was determined to force her concerns into the open. "You ask first."

"Keys to the kingdom," Shadow murmured. "Who rules?"

"He who has strength," Copper responded, wanting to strangle her. Her opening gambit was obvious. Where was she going with this? He knew it pertained to the two of them.

"Whence comes the strength?" She didn't look at him.

"From the wisdom to know right from wrong."

"Who determines?" Her voice sounded void of life.

"One with conscience." A worm of guilt stirred in his vitals. There was much he wished he could hide from her, but that was no longer an option.

"Where derives conscience?"

"From the heart of he who holds the keys to the kingdom."

He took a deliberate short cut. "I win, and I demand a kiss as your forfeit."

"Copper, I'm a mutant cyborg." She sighed, closing her eyes. "Don't try to be nice."

He suppressed a grin, well on the way to getting his victory. Now he had a take on her attitude. She had retreated into her shell because of what she was. "I want my kiss."

He took his forfeit, hovering over her to kiss her deeply without touching her body with his. He wanted her interested, not frightened. "Now call me possessive."

"I'll wait for the memories before I beg your pardon." She suddenly stiffened. "Last midsummer."

"What of it?" Copper's heart sank.

"The sharing . . . there were memories from you too real to be dreams."

Copper thought back to that fateful day. He remembered how angry he'd been when he found she had misused her gear as though she had chests full of replacement garments. She hadn't begun the terrible change into final phase of sisterhood, so he gambled that she wouldn't mind much if he repaired her clothes while she slept off his sideswipe. He found a very normal looking woman, and then he got curious. If she hadn't roused enough to respond to him the way she had . . . well, he wouldn't now be airing various reasonable sounding excuses. Then it occurred to him how pointless justification was in their current circumstance. Shadow had his memory, not her own. His reasons came along with the package.

"You were promised to me." He tried to explain away his actions, aware he didn't look good. "I thought you would become a full sister, and I wanted what should have been mine just once."

"Why am I not surprised? Didn't you consider seduction before rape?"

'*Live for today,*' he signed, more for himself than her. '*Tomorrow is a dream that may never come.*'

"There's always hope," Shadow said. "If I understand aright."

"Hope is a horse with a head on each end. Riding such a beast is to chance misstep in any direction, so remain immobile, waiting on fate." He wondered at her quietness of person, having expected a fight.

"Yet you *hope* for a better future through alliance."

"Hope plays no part in last stands. Did Helga teach you nothing? Those who fight are lucky to die in battle. We sicken. Our lives burn away at a furious pace, and we don't breed—without new members, we'll be extinct in three years, possibly five at the most. Renascents are created to die." Needing comfort, he reached out to take one of her hands, bringing it close.

"Why have viability restored with such gloomy thoughts?" Shadow questioned after a few minutes.

"Integration must take longer after the pounding you took from Dragon. I think I'd be dazed under those conditions, too."

"Evasion isn't an answer." She looked into his eyes.

"And you're not patient enough to wait?" He sighed, torn between unexpected rapport and the need for privacy. He felt threatened with her under his skin, in his soul, picking through his mind. The thought that she must feel the same way decided him. "Part a duty to lead, part male vanity. When I die, I want to die a man, not a gelding."

"Then you have no plans . . . ?"

"The woman I want doesn't see me as the same species. Maybe she's right . . . maybe being a singleton is purpose in itself."

"Copper, self-pity is nauseating. What brought this on?"

"How are you feeling, really feeling?" He searched her face for answers.

"Confused, threatened, sad . . . and frightened. Shades have a word for proscribed joining of minds. I think . . . I think we had a forbidden union."

"Forbidden because it causes pain?" He reached out to touch her face, not wanting to let her turn away.

"Such joining, taken to the ultimate degree, is irreversible and lethal. Both minds uniting into a single being have to be compatible for . . ." She broke off, shutting her eyes as if willing away the horror of their near miss.

"For?" He needed to keep her focused instead of brooding. He captured her other hand to keep her attention rooted in the present.

"Copper, this is something I acquired by accident while raiding a seer's mind. I'm still picking though . . . give me a moment."

He knew she spoke truth. She'd stolen thoughts because she could, and skimmed over them with mild interest. Moments later her hands grew clammy.

"Shadow?"

"We were totally open to each other," she said, almost in a whisper. "You trusted, and I didn't bother blocking because I didn't think you'd have access, the first requirement."

"There's more." He moved closer to wrap his free arm around her. She leaned into him seeming to draw courage from his nearness.

"Psi powers, or their equivalent, must be equal, the second requirement. Copper, I think you must be as powerful in your field as I am in mine. Blending begins at once. If we hadn't located Rowan so soon . . ."

"There wouldn't have been a later for us," he continued her thought. "I have no premonition of danger now, and I didn't then. Why not?"

"Then, because we were fated to survive. Now . . . now both of us are on guard." She looked into his eyes at last. "Is the threat to Brethren existence so serious?"

"Harvesters target the fey brothers who are responsible for acquisitions. As near as I've been able to piece together, they started two years back. Our intake is already compromised. Given the new brothers we've lost by implication, I'd say the Wild Hunt boasts an army."

"So you divert attention from Haven by setting up battle camps away from it." She looked away, staring into the flames again. "Any idea of how long surviving brothers will take to mature into fighting men?"

"Point. Fancy taking on the job?"

"I need an average age to work with, if I'm to make long term plans for our survival."

He followed her thoughts on a new generation, aware she'd changed topics.

"I think I'll run two studies . . . one on standard Outcasts and one on those with fey powers." She shivered, moving nearer to him. "I'd like to include sisters and pleasure women too, if you can sweet-talk them into cooperation?"

"Agreed, I'll make that a priority." Copper fumed inwardly, now aware from her memories that many sisters, and all pleasure women, gave her a hard time for being different. When he reached Haven harsh words needed speaking. Every individual, however unique, merited respect. He had implemented equality with ruthless determination since becoming King, and yet some dared to go behind his back.

"Copper . . . I said sweet-talk, not berate. I'm not like them. They can't help feeling uncomfortable."

"I didn't . . ."

"You tensed up. I know when you're angry."

"Why didn't you come to me with this problem?" He squeezed her hand in slight reprimand.

"Because it isn't important."

But it was. Now he understood why she lacked trust in

people. Nowhere in her memories had he found the image of a single friend. Only now, first with Ector, then himself, had she begun to let down barriers caused by the isolation others imposed. He wondered how she felt about their total sharing in light of Dragon's outburst.

With Tadgell's ruler, she'd blended into the background in her accustomed way, adapting to needs, allowing herself the temporary thrill of discovering sex. She had come to love the dread duke, for Dragon possessed incredible charisma when he chose to use it, which he would at the first sign of female resistance. Having observed the man in action during past visits, Copper didn't doubt she'd presented the ultimate challenge.

"Uncomfortable with memory theft?"

"Unhappy with words. We've covered every subject except what's happened to us. Care to throw any more grist for the mill, or shall we play 'Keys to the Kingdom' again?"

"Fine, if you don't cheat." Shadow bristled, moving a fraction away from him.

"I always cheat. Why go through justice when the concept is dead? Keys are only useful if the doors they open reveal usable merchandise."

"You rule justly," Shadow disagreed.

"As long as I am strongest in a kingdom with very few doors." Annoyed that she'd shifted the subject around again, he decided on another tactic. "Keys to the Kingdom rematch demanded, but I ask this time."

"I thought you wanted to talk." She faced him with one eyebrow raised.

"Who holds the keys to the kingdom?" he challenged, determined to draw her into thinking about their real problem.

"The strongest."

"Name the source of strength."

"Wisdom to judge what is best for the kingdom." Shadow

added a twist of her own.

"Who advises what is best?" Copper countered, ignoring a judgment part of the game, which only existed where fairness prevailed. He waited while she struggled in a trap of her own devising.

"Those who are afflicted, if the best is not achieved."

"Who dares afflict workers in the kingdom?" Copper began to enjoy himself as she floundered. She had already lost because she couldn't deliver the final gambit at this fourth question.

"He who cares nothing for the good of the kingdom." She glared at him.

"For the good of the many, what must be done?"

"The wise must hold council."

"Keys to the doors of wisdom are withheld by oppressors. The wise are muzzled by ignorance of plight." *Got you.* "Who unlocks freedom?"

"Copper, you're cheating. That's deliberately lengthening."

"You started it, and I make that six questions. I completed in three."

"Valorous men must defend the oppressed." She looked hard at him.

"Who stands behind valorous men in their quest?" He tried to suppress a grin, while observing: "Question seven."

"Those who . . . those who give strength," she managed.

"What strength do men need who face certain death?" Copper now gave her the chance to draw even if she'd take the bait

"Justice . . . justice for the many."

"Nice try, but men won't fight to the death for a justice they'll gain only if they win. Who inspires the spirit of valor in men who may die for a cause? And that's nine."

"Those they trust beyond life to deliver the keys of the kingdom to he who must rule."

"Closer and I win. What trust is greater than life itself?"

"Cheat! The trust of the next generation to continue the work of those fallen."

"Who supplies the next generation?"

"Those who love the warriors enough to bear children they must raise alone," she forced the words out.

"Then who holds the keys to the kingdom?"

"All those who can love enough to sacrifice everything they hold most precious."

"Twelve and I'll concede your overwhelming defeat, my Queen. No man is strong enough, just or valorous enough, to fight to death for a cause without love to sustain him."

"And my forfeit?" Her expression was difficult to discern under the skin dye. She raised her head and set her lips in a firm line.

"I'll decide after we talk." He reached out to cup her chin, making sure she couldn't look away. "Our thought sharing wasn't the real reason for your upset, was it?"

"Seeing him . . ." She shuddered. "He liked Outcasts. I thought . . ."

"You expected him to have feelings for you."

"He wants to kill me." She tried to turn away, but he held her fast.

"Do you blame him? His former woman is wandering in and out of his neighbors' forts as an Outcast. He will be a laughing stock if anyone ever finds out. He can't risk having you loose."

"Why was I condemned?" She took his hand in her two. "I know the Harvesters made the event occur, but what was my crime to make Dragon hate me so much?"

He hesitated; aware his memory of the information would surface in her mind eventually. "Adultery."

She paled, her eyes opening wide. "I didn't."

"He would hunt you down if he thought you'd betrayed him.

A good enough reason to turn him against you."

Her face took on an inward look for a few moments and then she let go of his hand. "What forfeit do you demand?"

Damn. She's hiding from me again. "I'll tell you when I am not frozen. Come here, woman." She nestled against him and added to his problems when his now quiet shaft began to swell. Another memory from her ruined his concentration. He experienced her inner battle to push him away after their one night of love, and her reasoning.

Grinning, sure of his victory, he wound her golden hair through his fingers. "I've got a wonderful way to get us both warm."

"Would that be the same wonderful cure for nightmares?" Caught, she remained pressed to him.

He nodded, unrepentant.

"You're impossible. Do you know that?" She reached up to touch his lips.

"I want my forfeit. I don't care what you are. I want the woman I love."

"Since you are now viable, I need to make some internal adjustments first."

"Don't." His heart thudded against his ribs. His erection grew harder. He wanted her on his own terms. He wanted commitment.

"Copper, I can't give you a human child." Her eyes grew dark.

"I want our child." He moved into position. "If I get a choice, I'd prefer a son, since I think a mix of you and me would be more agreeable and less difficult in male form."

"Why, you . . ." She started to fight, slapping him.

Copper knew this game and captured her hands, kissing each one before he moved on to more interesting areas. She matched his passion in a way he had dreamed about, never thinking she would seek to pleasure him again. Together they found the rhythm of love.

29

Earth Date 3893

ARTHUR SWIRLED in a black void that gradually resolved into the eyes of the cave-sitter. His skin ran with sweat, as if he had just undergone a session in stamina training to earn the right to face this strange being.

"Don't be alarmed." Those matte-black eyes failed to reflect firelight. "You are nearly awake. I need this time to warn you against another attempt, Arthur. You are too involved with Shadow to risk further contact."

"I haven't finished learning."

"Then you must cast a net amongst those who know your subject best." The cave-sitter stirred his fire into a bright blaze. "Think on the reason this one was selected for review. What was your intent?"

"She is the same psi rating as me." Arthur examined his motives under the steady gaze of those black eyes. He didn't want to share the whole truth, not if he could get by on a partial answer. "I wanted to learn how she survived as a cyborg with seer-surpassing ability. I also thought she might know of my parents, since I think I was one of the crèche children created to hide her son."

"Has this happened, Arthur? Are your questions answered?" The cave-sitter's voice sank to a whisper. Those eyes expanded, engulfing Arthur into swirling depths.

*

A sharp pain behind his ear and right hand seared through Arthur. One part stuck to the other. He jerked his hand away, gasping as he came awake and looked down at the com-link umbilicus glistening in his palm. A stomach pain doubled him over. Dropping the connection, he crawled to his cleansing section to vomit his last meal, and then the one before that.

The cave-sitter had kept his word in a strange fashion to waken Arthur. Did the being know that his interface traveled along hearing nerves to his central cortex? Any sudden interruption must result in uncontrollable nausea because of this pathway. *I'll bet he knew what would happen.* Another wave of nausea claimed him.

An hour later, Arthur knew he needed help. Going to a medi-tech meant admitting his crime and taking the consequences. Punishment didn't scare him as much as the Archive catching him in a weakened state. Those last fragments of memory came from Copper, not Shadow. Copper wouldn't have linked with the Archive, which left a mind raid as an explanation. The sentient must possess an ability to steal thoughts from anybody with an interface. *If the Archive finds I've accessed more data, when it already plans no further enablement sessions . . . I'm not strong enough to block it.*

Arthur thought of one who might help, and he'd take a well-earned thrashing from Ector, if he could just get there. He walked into the suburbs, not daring a railpod. The sickness didn't stop. Dry retching tormented him. Cold sweat ran under his clothes and down his face, great beads of it dripped into his eyes and mouth. Blunt, molten hooks raked through his entrails. Every step became a personal hell to be endured. Arthur could handle pain – it encompassed part of seer instruction, but this? Training agony had a finite limit, this didn't. If Ector had not returned home . . . the sidewalk lurched.

Arthur crashed to his knees. Getting up took all his willpower, and he clung to the walls of buildings for support, one more intersection, one more street, and then a turning to a cul-de-sac. The swirling, floating feeling grew stronger. Arthur shut his eyes, waiting while it passed, praying it would. When he looked up at his final destination, he thought he hallucinated. Copper, dead for the past five years, stood outside Ector's house, packing baggage into a ground runner.

Another bout of dry retching dropped him to squeeze out the last of his strength. The sound of running feet – a man shouting and voices from a great distance sounding muffled under fathoms of water.

"Is it some pestilence?" a man asked.

"Avalon is free from transmittable diseases," a woman's voice said. "Injury or poisoning could cause this state."

"This lad is an Elite cadet by his uniform. We should call them." The man's voice sounded brisk.

"No . . . oo . . . o," Arthur croaked, facedown still.

"Turn him, Kai. He's trying to speak," the woman said.

Hands urgently hefted him over. Arthur fought against a swirling black vortex. The last words he heard were the woman's shocked cursing.

*

Wind tore at his clothes, and rain streaked down from a lightning-rent sky. Thunder rolled from cover of darkness thick enough to drown a rat in mud. Violent flashes lighted the man's steps through a harsh landscape. The cold wings of death brushed at his heels as he staggered forward with his sacred burden. Death stalked him. He fought for time to complete the trust given to him. The kingdom was safe – safety bought at a terrible price. Yet the One promised – swore he would return at the time of greatest need. He swore it on his sword with his dying breath. None other must touch that sword, now shrouded in oilskins, lest the vow be broken.

The man caught a glimpse of his target. A lake so deep, rumor called it bottomless. He increased his pace at the price of his strength. Twice he fell over rubble as he headed for his goal. Bruises didn't matter now; nothing did, except the end of his quest. He used his last spark of energy to throw the weapon as far as he could into inky blackness. He didn't see the splash as it hit the surface. Near to the gray veil of beyond, his glazing vision fixed on two glowing figures.

*

An ethereal form watched the cast of the dying man. The shade of he who had wielded the weapon in life, who had sworn on it, skittered over dark waters to seal the exact spot. He heard a horn call of spectral hunters close by, a welcome sound for a homeless spirit. His misty essence drifted to the mournful note, assuming a substance of sorts as it did, turning once to look back.

*

A pair of eyes marked the now-visible passage of the shade with interest. Those matte-black eyes also noted the location of the sword.

*

There was pain . . . soreness in his hand. Arthur wanted to continue his dream, but discomfort kept worrying at him until he tried to move. That brought a sharp pain – he opened his eyes to a slit.

A transparent, flexible tube snaked from a bag suspended on a makeshift tripod a fair distance higher than his arm. Bandages wrapped around his hand and wrist, although he had no memory of injury at the site. Drips of fluid ran down that tube. He'd worry later about why.

Eyes still slitted, he scanned quickly without further movement of any sort. The room looked little more than a cube with no windows or doors. One possible access point seemed to be a square panel in the ceiling, and this explained light sources clamped to the walls. Feigning sleep, he rolled as if dreaming, for a view to the open side of his prison. His bed against a wall mirrored another across from him, which also held an occupant. The man's stocky back faced him. A shock of close-cropped auburn hair streaked with gray looked familiar. The clothing wasn't, being a black leather bodysuit and close-fitting Brethren-style boots of the same color. From his posture, the man seemed to hold something close to his face.

Above the other bed, two shelves held an assortment of books. Arthur took a good look, amazed. He recognized them from records as being sources of written learning, or entertainment, now obsolete since console teaching. A fiber-screen pulled back against a far wall showed a personal needs station of the most rudimentary construction.

Arthur didn't feel sick anymore, nor did he have stomach cramps, but a faint trace of some soporific tasted sweet in his mouth. Without strength, he couldn't focus will. So . . . they wanted him alive and helpless? Someone had guessed he surpassed his training schedule with the seers, that he could levitate, so they made certain his concentration failed through drugs. He expected his captors to secure him when someone spotted him awake through an inevitable com-eye.

Having prisoners paired up was a favorite seer tactic when interrogating the young. Fellow sufferers tended to share secrets. They hadn't missed a trick. One option remained open to him: he possessed the ability to shut down life functions. He wasn't going to end up as a mindless donor for their eugenics program.

Apparently moving in sleep again, he snagged his single covering with his free hand, so it fell over the bandages. Under that screen, he began to pick at the knot. Once his system cleared of drugs . . .

"Arthur, you've been awake for a good five minutes. I heard your breathing pattern change twice." The man on the other bed rolled over to face him, shutting the book he was reading – Ambrose.

Arthur struggled up, looking around for a console. This room hadn't one. The effort of rising sent his head spinning. He fell back against his pillow, cursing silently at his weakness.

"Easy, lad. This is a Brethren place. You're safe here."

Exactly what Ambrose would say to allay his suspicions. Clever, very clever. The covering still concealed his bandaged hand. He continued to worry at the knot.

"Don't. It's there to re-hydrate you." Ambrose started to reach out, but held back when Arthur left off his picking. "The plan is to ship you out to Haven tomorrow, so don't spoil it by downgrading your strength. There might not be another chance."

Again it fitted the pattern. Give your victim the illusion of escape to gain his confidence. Arthur ran his eyes over Ambrose for any betrayal of body language.

"By the deeps, I'm not here by choice either," Ambrose said, his voice low with anger. "Will you stop treating me like an enemy? I had an idea where you might go when you missed your duty roster. When I found the mess you left, I decided to check out my guess. I wasn't prepared to deal with the snarling up of someone else's plans you caused when you blundered into the Brethren. I found them helping you and that meant they needed me silenced, too. I don't appreciate being forcibly restrained, although I'm relieved you will escape. I'm not sure now how much longer I could have protected you."

"Protect? From what?" Arthur quizzed. He'd play the innocent for all it was worth.

"Don't trust anybody? That's good. I owe you an apology, lad. When you came to me, I should have listened to your problems. I should have cut you off from the Archive. Do you want to tell me what happened?"

"I snuck out of barracks to try some off-station food with my credits. Something didn't agree with me." Arthur looked at Ambrose with what he hoped was an innocent expression.

"Don't play games with me. You nearly died." Ambrose swung around to face Arthur, his anger apparent in the tension of his shoulders and neck. "As I recall, since I can't get to a console to check my facts, violent nausea is a side effect of sudden termination from direct sensory playback. There have been similar incidents in the past, all resulting in fatalities. Ector told me you might try something risky. So, it turned sour on you, but at least you had the sense not to get help from medi-techs. You weren't supposed to survive the experience by the look of things. What did you learn that made your existence a threat?"

"I think I have a problem digesting fungi," Arthur suggested. He hoped whoever listened bit their nails down to the bone. "What are you reading?"

"You have depths, boy. I shall be sorry to lose you, assuming I survive this experience." Ambrose passed over the book, opening it to a marked place. "Vaslov, a poem of his dealing with the darker side of human nature. It's called 'Shadow Walker'. You might find it contains a certain relevance to yourself. I suggest you read it while we wait for our captors. You may find certain truths to sustain you from the shock you will receive."

Arthur didn't rise to the obvious bait. He accepted the book with a smile, pretending to read while Ambrose selected another volume. When the man became engrossed, he turned his attention to the book.

Ambrose was right. He didn't like the work, yet he could identify with it. Did destiny intend him to walk alone? He studied the verses again. Always, one stood apart from the rest in any society. That one might be the strongest, the wisest, or any other criterion relevant; the same theme always motivated the individual, a need to place the wellbeing of others first, accepting the mantle of loneliness as a leader. Shadow walker, a dark traveler . . . yes, Arthur identified with such a one.

Ambrose knew nothing of the cave-sitter. No one did. Arthur reviewed the lessons that strange being had imparted to an already condemned student; pertinent nonetheless. Why did the cave-sitter seek his death, and what did the being gain from Arthur's nonexistence? In what way did his continued existence pose a threat, unless . . . ? What if two were one? There lay an unpleasant conclusion, fitting together too well – far too well. The dark traveler in Arthur set a new course. He prepared to wait out the final play, sure that his enemy would try again.

Awaking from a doze, disturbed by thoughts of reviewing Shadow, Arthur returned to his problem with the cave-sitter. Why had the being not let him remain in endless playback? The results would have been identical. Neutralized, he would be available to any seer need. Why bring him back in a way designed to cause death? That path made no sense, since it represented no obvious gain to the cave-sitter . . . or did it?

Finally, Arthur gave up trying to sleep. Bored as Ambrose, who paced back and forth, he considered the performance a very good act or . . . or maybe, he had misjudged the man.

Careful now, as any seer scheme always contained wheels within wheels. He could sense genuine regret from Ambrose; perhaps the man had no knowledge of the complete plot. One other factor inclined him to this notion: the effects of the soporifics were wearing off. His throat wasn't so dry, and he wanted to urinate. Now he had the problems of being wired up to an apparatus. He tried sitting up. Weakness, yes, but no whirling sensations. He swung his legs to the floor with exaggerated caution.

"You're supposed to be resting." Ambrose halted his endless pacing.

"I need to piss, and the bucket isn't going to grow legs to walk over here."

"Wait a moment. I have instructions to free you when this need came." Ambrose approached to unwrap the bandages.

A fine metal rod lay at the end of flexible tubing and stuck into the top of Arthur's hand.

"This will hurt. Hold still."

Ambrose pulled, causing a dull pain.

A bruised area colored Arthur's hand. He flexed it, feeling soreness. "Thank you."

"No problem. Do you need help walking?"

"I'd like to try by myself first." Arthur started up with legs like wet seaweed, yet he could walk. Once he reached his bed again, he tackled another urgent problem.

"When do we get fed?"

"Right now." Ambrose hooked a box from under his bed to pass Arthur high-energy field rations. He selected standard fare for himself.

"Ambrose, I'm seer-trained. Once I have my strength back, I going to try to escape. Why give me the means?"

"I haven't." Ambrose frowned. "There's a high-pitched sonic device directed into this room to prevent concentration of will.

I know. I've tried levitation. I thought I'd get out easily, since none knew I have this ability, until now. I couldn't raise myself a fraction. Try, by all means." He looked at Arthur. "Maybe you have enough will to overcome it."

Energy intake revitalized him. Arthur settled into a meditation posture to focus his will. Remembering the difficulties of his first experience in levitation, he disciplined his mind to exactitude. He began to rise.

Pain. Red, blinding pain exploded in his head. He became aware of the floor when he hit it. The agony stopped at that instant. Arthur nursed his bruises for a few moments then resumed his original posture.

"Ambrose, if I got to that panel before the counterstrike, I could get it open, at least. The next attempt might see me through. A sonic emitter of such strength must be close to us for maximum effect. I could disable it once I'm free. Together we have a chance of winning clear."

"Yes, your plan could work if we linked, and then what? Where will you go? Even if you escape to the surface, you haven't the experience to survive alone."

Arthur lay down, staring with sightless intensity at the ceiling. He wondered why Ambrose didn't want to escape with him, though the man admitted trying while Arthur was unconscious. His supreme commander seemed to agree with his confinement.

Closing his eyes, Arthur attempted to recall his last conscious memory before waking up in this prison. The images did not make sense, as he'd seen both Shadow and Copper. More than this, Shadow looked vibrant with life, in contradiction to the last image of her on Sanctuary personnel files. There her face was devoid of expression, with blank eyes staring through what could have been a wall. That five-year-old picture continued to haunt him.

The last answer he'd given to the cave-sitter fell short of the truth. Immersion in Shadow's life gave him an escape from his own grim existence. He was caught up in her struggle to get her life back and find justice. Each time she seemed to make progress, fate dealt her another blow and that offended his sense of fairness. Leaving his review of her at the time she surrendered to her feelings for Copper had made him forget what had happened ten years afterward; Copper's sudden death was the reason for the lifeless image of her.

Given hindsight, Arthur accepted that she had lived ten happy years, but this didn't seem enough to him, not with her life before this time. Her face in the picture told him that she lived as an original Outcast, with no values or emotions, other than the hunt. She no longer cared whether she lived, and hadn't since Copper's death. Her occasional visits to Avalon since that time were a furtive slinking to get the technology she needed for continued function.

His last recollection had to be a hallucination, or was it? The Archive told him that Shadow and her son returned to Avalon. What if his pain and exhaustion played tricks with his eyes? What if he had seen her and superimposed his last image of her and her companion?

A slight tingling sensation warned him. He tensed his mental barriers in a reflex action against a probe. Arthur opened his eyes to look at Ambrose, letting amusement show in the upward tilt of his lips.

"Sorry, boy." Ambrose shrugged as he withdrew his mental touch. "I am supposed to make certain you don't make any desperate choices. They want you alive."

"Who is 'they'?" Arthur kept his smile fixed as if he did not understand the implications of Ambrose's admission. Whoever held him knew he could shut down his life. That meant they needed to have a quorum of gifted seers on hand to override him if he started this action. A cold, hard lump developed in his chest as his worst nightmares returned to mock him. What if seers intend to force breeding viability by keeping him prisoner until he surrendered? Arthur's smile died while he fought to keep his breathing normal. Whatever 'they' planned, he did not intend to let them see his fear.

"They will make themselves known to you when they are ready."

"You're afraid of them?" Arthur found it hard to believe anything could frighten a man he'd witnessed standing up to Evegena, yet Ambrose had a tightening of skin around his eyes.

"I'm here against my will, aren't I? I'm rated as psi ten, not easy to control, yet I'm a prisoner. I have strict instructions regarding you. They need you safe to protect Morgan while she matures, and that's probably saying too much. It'll be Haven or another Brethren place."

"Ector's Morgan?" Arthur used a casual tone as if he didn't really care. Every sense came to full alert.

"Why didn't you come to me when you needed help?" Ambrose countered.

Arthur smiled as he savored the point he had just scored. His commander confirmed the needed answer by body language. So, Ambrose believed Morgan to be central to whatever plots the man thought he'd interrupted. Why Morgan? Barracks rumored that the child resulted from a liaison between Ector and one of the Brethren women. The child had actually scored zero on a psi rating, as well as having a much finer skin than normal for a Submariner child, substantiating hearsay. But Ambrose held personal friendship with Ector. Making Ambrose think Morgan taken by Brethren could be enough to guarantee his good behavior. Why target Ector, though? Why would Brethren need a lever against him?

Despite Ambrose's belief that the prison belonged to Brethren, Arthur disagreed. Every item they made screamed of transience, being safe, mostly finished and secure, but little else. He wondered if this was the story given to Ambrose after the man blundered into a trap.

"Arthur . . . why not wait until you see who your captors are before you make any plans?"

"Every day someone might die because you sent him to a particular place. Am I expected to believe I'm suddenly indispensable?" Arthur said, sure now of Ambrose being planted as a spy.

"Thank you. We have heard enough," a woman's voice announced from a concealed speaker. "Ambrose, you are free to join us." The roof panel slid to one side at her words.

"What about me?" Arthur demanded.

"I will deal with you presently. Make no attempt to rise with Ambrose. Our sonic device is selective," the same cool voice ordered.

Arthur watched in sick frustration as Ambrose disappeared into the opening and the panel slid shut. Without a companion to complicate procedures, he could imagine various kinds of incentives to good behavior. How did the woman intend to deal with him?

30

Earth Date 3893

Silence hung in heavy waves. Even in Sanctuary, the distant throb of machinery integrated into subconscious hearing, unlike this place. Arthur started a systematic search of his cell just to create noise. Somehow, the walls didn't close in on him to such an extent now that he had a purpose. As he emptied a bookshelf, Arthur fought an inner battle to prevent any trace of panic betraying him through body language. He enacted inner chemical changes to counteract adrenaline surges while he ran his fingertips along a retaining bracket. Still the silence crushed inwards.

What if this cell remained his home for the rest of his life? Arthur squashed that thought too late. He imagined his will to resist weakening over the many years of life granted to any with the longevity gene. He slammed his fist into the wall, welcoming pain as a sensation he could use to focus his consciousness. Easing down to sit cross-legged, he concentrated his awareness on his own heartbeats.

Absence of sound meant isolation, but for whom and from what? On the one hand, the Archive and/or the cave sitter desired his death, while on the other hand, seers needed his genome for their breeding program. He reasoned seers as the likely captors because they had the resources for a cell of silence. Arthur projected his mind in a random sweep to test his theory. His thought paths met a wall of nothingness.

The sound of metal sliding startled him. Arthur jumped to the side of his prison as a hatchway opened in the ceiling.

"You may ascend now," the woman's voice informed him. "We are ready for you."

He didn't like the sound of that, and he couldn't see the face behind the voice from the dark opening, although it was very familiar.

"Your cell has a continuous supply of water and enough food for three days," the woman said. "It will take you around nine weeks to starve to death, and we will not permit you a faster alternative. Please don't be tiresome."

Arthur decided to wait her out.

"Boy, we don't have time for games. Either you will comply, or I will remove your consciousness and retrieve you in the same manner as I installed you."

An edge of irritation toned the unseen woman's voice. Arthur didn't doubt she intended to carry out her threat. He concentrated even while he stood up. The rush of energy made his skin tingle as he ascended.

He stepped onto firm flooring in the room above to find a slim blonde woman sitting with her back to him, operating controls to close the hatch. There was a camp bed against one wall and a box with metal handles. He permitted himself a slow smile when he noted the absence of others. Did 'they' think an enraged acolyte seer of his capabilities would not react? He projected waves of extreme fatigue at the slight figure.

"I think we will need to instruct you in the nicety of manners," the woman remarked in an alert fashion. "Behave yourself."

An incredible sensation of thirst hit his unprepared stomach like a fist. Arthur withdrew his attack to concentrate on defense.

The woman turned . . . he looked into Shadow's deep violet eyes. Shock rendered him speechless. She hadn't aged a day from the hologram picture of her the Archive showed him.

"Did you want to try that again?" she suggested, her voice soft and sweet, even as her eyes bored into his.

"I think I'll pass." Arthur tried to match her nonchalance.

"Good. A trace of maturity at last." She stood, somehow still managing to stare him down from her lesser height.

"Why am I here?"

"Because you came to us." Shadow squared her shoulders. "Who sent you? What can you offer as reason for seeking us out?"

"As I recall," Arthur drawled, proud of himself when his voice came out even and modulated, "at the time, I was too busy dying to have any plan."

"Addiction to full sensory playback is almost always fatal." Shadow's voice cracked around his shoulders like a whip. "Did the Archive promise you more 'fixes' for betraying us?"

Cold shock trickled down his spine. "I made a bad choice by trusting the Archive. It wanted my death, although I can't guess why."

"Then you have a hard decision to face." She smiled the sad Brethren smile, her hand straying to the hilt of her belt knife. "I cannot permit you to leave this room alive without surety of your intentions. Open your mind to me."

Arthur took half a step back, looking around for escape.

"Trust comes hard after betrayal, doesn't it? Since you chose to study my life, then you know me as no other can. End this, boy. Prove to me you are no threat."

Her projected thought patterns pushed against his mind. He wanted to prove his innocence because he admired her, and she had the strength to kill him. Arthur released his guard to give her access. Her presence seemed as a warm onrush while she delved into his conscious thoughts, not the cold carving probe he had expected.

Disturbed by her probing, he backed off a step. "Satisfied?"

"I think I would have enjoyed being a bug watching from a crack when Evegena realized she had lost you." Shadow's slow smile reached her eyes this time. "Making a fool of the Archive is a more serious consideration. It will not be content until it has some bones to gloat over."

"So what are my options?" Arthur sensed approval from her body language.

"That depends on whether you think you can block the Archive from your mind." Shadow reached out to take his hand. "The capability is there, but is the strength enough in your weakened state?"

Arthur thought through the problem. Shadow matched his strength in their recent contact. Perhaps she had the psi power to test his limits if he made the challenge harder on himself. "I am going to remove myself from your sight in a few moments. You know from my thought patterns that I did this to evade seers, and how I did it. They didn't have the luxury of the warning I am giving to you."

"Encouraging." Shadow released his hand. "Proceed."

Arthur began building multiple images of himself. He released them at the same moment as he blocked her sight from his real location, and then he moved to create another image in the same space his corporeal body previously occupied while he took up a position behind her. He felt the hard thrusts of her mind as she attempted to find him. She reached out to an image to the right of his original position.

"Satisfied?" Arthur queried, enjoying her sudden reflex as she spun to face the sound of his voice. He let his other selves disintegrate.

"Impressive." Shadow frowned, moving over to the control

panel again. "Why didn't you use this technique to evade me when you ascended?"

"I guess I am not that comfortable in small spaces," Arthur admitted, feeling more at ease in her company.

"You didn't think the options through," Shadow guessed, picking up on his thoughts. "Now we have an alternative."

She pressed another button on the control console. A similar ceiling aperture opened in this room to let a counterbalanced ladder slide down. Arthur followed her up into a room identical to the cell he had just vacated. The logic of such an arrangement shook him to the core. Who would think of looking for a second bolt-hole on discovery of the first? Again they ascended via ladder to a room Arthur recognized as Ector's atrium. The table that normally stood over the trapdoor now rested to one side. He followed to the study and went to the seat she indicated at his commander's console. Arthur began to wonder what she intended, and why Ector wasn't in sight.

"You have a right to know our plans," she told him. "We are going to investigate the passages underneath Sanctuary—the dark zone."

A sudden sensation of threat at the thought of them going into the dark zone closed around Arthur. His mind twisted into higher awareness, evaluating endless possibilities in a split second that lasted an eternity. The answers came to him when his personal timeframe returned.

"This is not a good choice. The Archive knows of your plans." He knew this for a fact that he couldn't explain.

Shadow's face drained of all emotion. Her body relaxed in the controlled calm of Brethren before battle.

"In answer to your next question, I haven't betrayed you." Arthur's own muscles slid into alert. "I wasn't aware of your intentions until a few moments gone."

"Mind raid." Shadow hissed through her teeth. "Boy? Have

I misjudged you?" Her hand went to her belt knife while her pupils expanded.

"Applied logic, not thought theft." He kept his tone even and low. "You are aware of whose records I reviewed. In the process of research, I picked up something not intended for general circulation. The Archive can access any comm-link, at any distance, without leaving a trace. I learned to detect invasion. Maybe that is why it wanted me dead in an apparent accident of my own making." The wings of death came closer, yet he couldn't stop himself. "Remember the thoughts you picked from my mind. That last playback? How did I know what Copper felt? You knew him. Would he have downloaded into Archives by his own volition?"

"He would have cut off his head first."

"Copper had an implant," he said. "Who else on your team sports such?"

"Point taken." Shadow's shoulders slumped in defeat. "The Archive picks through thoughts from those with implants." She made it a statement rather than a question. "You are your father's son. He could cut through countless trivialities to come to the heart of a problem."

"My father?" Arthur's heart pounded.

"Look into the console," Shadow ordered, her voice barely above a whisper.

Her reasoning seemed clear to him. She needed a barter chip to buy her way out of trouble, and he was it. "I think you'll find my exchange value has been grossly over-rated," Arthur observed, turning to position in the station. She needed to trade, or at least attempt to trade, to gain an escape route for her team. He imagined she might offer herself along with him. Arthur's stomach clenched. He reached for the activation control.

"No."

Arthur's hand froze on Shadow's command. He started to turn to her.

"Look into the screen," she said.

Arthur stared at his own reflection in the blank surface. He could see her standing behind him in her black Brethren battle gear, just out of range if he had any thoughts of attack.

"Study your face. You are very like him in his youth."

Arthur did as she requested. He guessed she meant his father must have been active around the time of her first entry into Avalon.

"You have a right to know your heritage, Boy. There is a strong look of the sire about your face. I'm surprised you haven't noticed."

"What do you want of me, Shadow?" Arthur said, swinging round on the chair to face her. He didn't need to see his face. He saw it every day when he shaved. He wasn't prepared to play a game he didn't like.

"I think that you're dangerous, much more dangerous than anyone guesses." Shadow moved back half a step. "I have seen enough to know you could let me find whatever you wanted me to believe in your mind. If I'm right, I wonder whether the seers know they raised a viper. Is there one of them who has control over you?" Shadow let her eyes flicker away from his for just a second, as if embarrassed.

"Are you asking whether I've an addiction to the sexual proficiency portioned out by breeding mistresses?" He waited, watching her blush. She didn't answer so he continued, "Yes, they tried, and yes, I found it very entertaining. I will not allow myself to fall into their hands again. I will not stand as stud to their experiments to satisfy their ennui. Do you understand?"

She nodded, not meeting his eyes. "What do you think we will find if we successfully penetrate the dark zone?"

"No idea. I could guess it is important to the Archive,

whatever is hidden there." Arthur shrugged, swinging round and round on his pivoting chair to aggravate her. He'd let her in his thoughts, and he'd answered her questions. She held a stale bone just out of his reach in return.

"Will you give me full access to your mind?" She leaned back on the document cupboard, idly cleaning her nails with the point of her knife. A tendril of blonde hair had escaped from her short braid, making her look less of a threat.

"Lower my guard that far? How do I know this isn't an elaborate interrogation attempt for the Archive? Suspicion is a two way street." He faced the screen again, watching her reflection register irritation to be replaced by one of resolve.

"Truth, then. You are the youthful image of your father. It will help you to accept if you see this for yourself. He was taller, but I'm told he came late to full growth, and he had exactly the same hair as you, only longer. His eyes were an unusual blue, sometimes like blocks of ice, and at others, as clear as the sky above the surface, and they crinkled at the corners when he laughed. He had a scar on his jaw, a faint white line." Shadow unconsciously traced the mark on her own face.

Arthur tried to recall any Submariners with a matching description. From the way she talked, it was someone to whom he had access and was expected to recognize . . . but the tone she used seemed out of place.

"You used past tense, Shadow. Is he dead?"

"In a sense he is, to me. I speak from memory as I haven't seen him for many years. I believe your nose is straighter now that I think about it," she mused, looking off into a distance of her own making.

"Would I have met him? I can't recall it, if so." Arthur stared at his reflection from several different angles.

"Seen him, from what I've heard. Still at a loss, Boy? Try stretching my Terran skin over your Submariner scales."

Arthur imagined the change. His heart pounded. She meant his father wasn't Submariner. Brethren visited for specialist healing, but none of them had come to Sanctuary except her at the time of his conception. If it wasn't in Avalon then . . . shock sent a cold sweat to glisten on his face. A face he now recognized from direct sensory playback. Dragon looked back at him. Very slowly, he swung his chair to face Shadow, his eyes accusing.

Shadow stepped back another pace, "You have my eyes, not his."

Arthur stared at her, incredulous. His mother.

"Now you know." She sheathed her knife and clasped her hands together behind her back, looking out into the atrium at a fountain. "Only Copper knew who sired you. Others may guess, but they don't know for sure, as I never said. Even he . . . I'm sorry, for what it's worth, on both counts. I wasn't allowed a choice."

"You gave me one, and much more. Did you give any thought to the thing you created?" Piece by piece, the puzzle completed itself. All the hints, all the restrictions now had meaning. When he heard she was to bring her son to Avalon on her next visit, he'd thought . . . an image of Copper standing by Ector's house flashed into his mind. Not a hallucination, not Copper – Copper's son.

"Would you rather I'd let the seers make you their creature?" Her face paled, and her mouth trembled. She turned her back to him. "I tried to find you. How could I guess you would take Submariner traits from a maternal grandfather?"

She had a point. Arthur had slipped up on the same incorrect assumption himself. Part of him still fought the idea that this slim, young-looking woman was his mother, although he was aware she carried the longevity gene from the trouble it caused with Brethren factions. He needed time to think.

"Why are you risking your life here?" He needed a safer

subject. She made him feel uncomfortable after the thoughts she had taken from his mind. "I heard Rowan and Saffron are still both scrambling for leadership Why not take it yourself?"

She shrugged, and then looked out on the fountain again. "I could have done so if Copper had been killed in the first years. Brethren watched us, not trusting me when it was known what I was. When he aged and I didn't . . . well they didn't like the idea of having me around for decades in a position of power. Now I can only advise. Kai might pick up the pieces eventually. My son moves with caution as yet."

"He came here," Arthur cynically observed, noting his own exclusion, since she spoke of Kai as a singleton. "His choice. Copper's gift lives on in him, and he knew we needed his talent for any chance of survival." She glanced back at him, and then away with her mouth in a thin line.

That hit him hard in the chest. He imagined how the shock of seeing his face, Dragon's face, had affected her. The curses rang in his ears from his last waking moment in front of Ector's house. Far from being an emotionless mercenary, she possessed feelings running deeper than many others.

Tearing his gaze away from her, Arthur looked at his own image. Truth sat like a rock in his guts. As much as he had wanted to know his origins, he now wished for the return of innocence. Why couldn't he have taken his looks from the grandfather whose hide he wore? Why hadn't he seen himself in Dragon? How could he have been so blind? He wore the face of the man who'd sworn to kill her.

Arthur wondered what thoughts raged through Shadow's mind at this meeting. If only she could have found him as an infant, before his face formed into adult lines. Her pain showed clearly in her eyes after days of knowing he belonged to her. How she must hate him.

"Boy, names don't register on consciousness in mind link."

Shadow's voice cut through his misery like a stone dropped into still water. "The others wouldn't talk of you around me when we brought you inside. Say your name. I never knew it."

Her reflection grew larger in the console screen as she neared him.

"Arthur. I am called Arthur." Somehow he managed to speak in a voice resembling his own. He had the small satisfaction of not a single waver in his words.

"I like that. It is a blending of my lost name and your father's." Shadow's hand touched his shoulder. "Arthur, I can see that this is a shock to you. How are you feeling?"

"Sick." He spat the word out.

"Ector wanted to ship you out because he feared you had come for me. He and Ambrose consider you too dangerous to be amongst us. I don't agree. When I reversed the damage done to you, I sensed fear and a desperate desire to belong. Will you tell me why you reviewed my life?"

"I had dreams of places I had never seen, and I thought I might learn enough from you to live on the surface. I didn't intend to become a seer." Arthur took a deep breath to get control before he continued. "No one else came close to my psi-level but you. I had to know if you shared the dreams, and then I thought you might know of my parents, so they could claim guardianship until I reached adulthood."

"You almost paid for your quest with your life. Do you still feel a need for sensory playback?"

"No. Not ever." Shadow's grip on his shoulder closed to cause pain. He welcomed it. He needed another focus.

"And how do you feel about the Archive?"

Rage began to build. Anger upon anger until his body shook with it. The Archive knew his origins, and it had played him like a fish caught on a hook. He wanted to smash his fist into something, anything.

"Easy, boy." Shadow's arms came around him in a quick hug. "It has taken us all for fools. Are you interested in payback?"

Arthur found himself beyond speech. He could only nod.

"Hold onto that thought. Use the anger. You are a fighter, like your father."

Emotions raged through him, leaving him as limp as seaweed. He swiveled his chair to face her, breaking their contact. She opened her arms to him, and he let her hug him, needing to fill a void in his soul.

"Everything is all right now," Shadow told him as she held him close. "We can make this work together."

Arthur heard the comfort in her words as much as her gestures. He found courage to face whatever future she planned. Shamed by his lapse, he released her, not meeting her eyes. He wasn't sure how to act around a parent he'd just found.

"Do you want to ship out after Morgan, or do you want to join me in the battle zone?"

"Ector shipped Morgan out?" He worried at the scab on his hand where the tube had entered his flesh. "Why? Surely no one threatens the child, irrespective of what Ector does."

"She is as much at risk as you were, for similar reasons," Shadow said, turning away from him.

So, he'd hit a sore point had he? She'd dropped her defense. What did she mean by similar reasons? "Morgan is rated head blind."

"Many exceptionally gifted are, until puberty. If seers get their hands on her, they will find she has unlimited capacity to block intrusion."

"Assuming they are interested enough to investigate."

"Arthur, we must accept one of us will succumb if we are captured. They have always speculated, but knowing her parentage will cause them great anxiety."

"Why? Everyone thinks—"

"She's my child with Ector." She sighed and then faced him defiantly. "I would have kept her with me if she didn't look so much like him. As it was, we agreed Ector should raise her. You didn't get very far with your retrieval did you?"

"Does the Archive know?" he asked, thinking of Morgan.

"Undoubtedly it does, if you spoke the truth about comm-links."

"Every word. Our one chance of escape lies in surprise. The Archive will assume I went to Ector for help, even if it didn't pick Ambrose's mind clean before you captured him. I guess our prison was shielded from seer mind sweeps?"

"Yes and the house has a security alert system. We'd know if any attempted a probe. You're taking our exposure very calmly, Boy."

"My name is Arthur, and I'll deal with the future when I'm certain I have one." He thought for a moment. "We will be expected to leave Avalon any time now. Continuing with your quest is unwise in the circumstances, so that is what we will do. When did you plan to start?"

"As soon as Tarvi signals Morgan is safe. We should hear in two days."

"Then we act now."

"We?"

"You're going to need a shield." He squared his shoulders, comfortable with the thought that he could die fighting. "The Archive searches for me. It will be diverted if it thinks I am within grasp. If it breaks through the images I will create, then I shall be where I can warn you and help block it."

"Perhaps." The hardness flitted across Shadow's face again. "We will see what your brother decides."

31

SHADOW'S HUDDLED GROUP of dissidents argued in low tones from the other side of the central atrium in Ector's house. Behind a short screen of potted plants, one or another occasionally glanced over in Arthur's direction, as if to make a point. He'd expected there to be more of them, although dividing forces into small groups made sense. Copper's lookalike son and Ector he'd anticipated, but Ambrose – an intentional inclusion or a last minute addition? He guessed the latter, as Brethren group tactics tended to crescent formations as fighting units. Tarvi must have formed a third of another unit, now safe on the surface.

Voices rose for a few moments, and then the auburn-haired lad he'd first taken for Copper detached himself from the rest. He headed over to Arthur looking more amused than angry.

"Verdict reached?" Arthur straightened.

"Stalemate, brother mine."

A thrill ran through Arthur at those words. This one had the right to claim such kinship, but that he did . . . at this time? Was Kai on his side?

"You've decided?"

"That I want you along, whether we go ahead as planned, or

make a break for freedom? The odds are increased to a marked degree in our favor with your inclusion." The young man grinned in a friendly, half tentative fashion. "I'm Kai—did Mother tell you I have the fey gift?"

"She spoke of you. Who's against?"

"Ector and Ambrose for different reasons. Ector wants you safe on the surface, while Ambrose is afraid, though he'll not admit it. We are going after an access code for the Archive, one that will open sealed files. Ambrose thinks having you along with us will make the Archive look in our direction."

"And you?"

"A psi with seer or near-seer standing is a useful, but not essential addition. An Elite cadet of recent enrolment isn't a warrior, which leaves your claim of an ability to divert the Archive. My fey instinct for our survival odds intensifies near you. I cast my vote for continuing with the quest, if you join us."

"Shadow?"

"She needs to believe in you, because the alternative is unacceptable." Kai looked down at his hands. "My father told me about your existence—not my mother. He feared she would lose touch with reality if she ever found you. Ector is also very wary. She's hurting, has been hurting ever since you reappeared. If you let her down, I'll personally dismember you, very slowly."

"Kai, I didn't know, not about her, when I needed help. The one sense of family I've ever felt has come from Ector."

"You came here for him?"

Arthur nodded. "I got caught in a trap I should have seen. Ector and I were working together on one another's projects, so I hoped he'd help when I got sick. I was trying to find out if all life died on the surface, and he was looking into why the Archive wouldn't give Shadow or me access to information about the Terran slaves she found. I guess those codes are the ones you're after." He stood up to stretch and regretted his action when three pairs of eyes gazed at him from across the room. Settling down, he tried to ignore them.

Kai frowned, leaning forward. "Someone is leaking information to the Nestines. That or the creatures have found a way to help themselves. We found other systems like the Archive in the ruins of ancient cities on the surface. Those ones weren't working, but we did find plans for a skyship and a map of a city on the moon. What if they have an Archive system and it links with ours? What if those codes are the key to stopping the raids? What if we can't trust the Archive?"

Now Arthur understood why they risked their lives. Not just for opening a restricted area, but because the Archive could shut down Avalon if controlled by a hostile force. "I trusted the Archive at first, before it began to addict me and then cut me off from sensory playback. I had to get a fix, although I didn't realize it at the time, so I turned to another to provide protection from becoming lost in the system."

"What other?" Kai demanded.

"A dream-creature—or a nightmare—I'm not sure, except it exists."

"Describe." Kai tensed, leaning forward.

"A cave . . . always there is a cave. Sometimes a fire, and water drips endlessly. The creature . . . I can't put an age on it—both old and young. Eyes as black as night . . ."

"And a presence of hidden majesty?" Kai broke in.

"Yes." Arthur caught the wonder on Kai's face.

"Arthur . . . I share your dreams. I've seen him, but never the eyes. They always looked elsewhere." Kai clenched his fists. "I was raised Brethren. I'm a warrior, and yet I am afraid of that creature."

"Your gift protected you, as mine did not." Arthur came to a decision to trust again. "I've a feeling, an instinct, that this creature and the Archive are connected. They both encouraged direct sensory playback, and they both tried to destroy me. That's too much of a coincidence to ignore."

"Shared this gem with anyone else?"

Arthur shook his head.

"I agree it's far too neat to discount. But Arthur, why volunteer for a suicide run when you could use your gifts to escape?"

"Retribution. I'd like to deserve a death sentence already given." Arthur fingered the access port behind his ear as memories of pain and sickness renewed. "Besides, I'm curious. Any elaborate security measure in a peaceful society raises interesting questions."

"Mother's concern also, and why we're suspicious. Were you aware we lost six forts in as many weeks?"

Shock washed through Arthur. Brethren had controlled a good quarter of those in the Northwest. To lose six forts couldn't happen without inside help. Shadow would not leave a war zone at a critical stage unless she thought . . . He looked at his brother, reading confirmation in the body language. She came for the traitor.

"Yes," Kai said in answer to unspoken comments. "Ector said you were very smart. Still want to go along for the ride?"

"Just try stopping me."

"I think I've gotten enough to sway the holdouts. Excuse me, Arthur."

"This was all continued interrogation?" Arthur said, now aware of being used.

"No, brother, not entirely; this may be the only time we have to know each other." Kai stood up, regarding Arthur without a trace of guilt on his face. "Thank you for your honesty. It's appreciated."

Arthur watched the departing back of his brother in amazement. Kai possessed undeniable depths, and as he said, they might not have another chance to talk. For the very first time in his life, he felt a sense of belonging. It seemed so natural to share with Kai, almost as if they were meant to be together. Lost in a whole new inner world, he didn't realize the meeting had broken up until Shadow slumped down in a seat opposite.

"Kai's very persuasive when he sets his mind to a task. He said you might stay open for a while." Shadow glanced at the departing men. "They go to prepare an immediate sortie." She sighed, straightening in a replica of Kai's earlier action. "We didn't get off to a very good start, and now there's no time. What we do is too important for personal consideration, or I'd prefer that you join Morgan."

"The safe path perhaps, but maybe not the wisest, and I'm not a child to be protected."

"No, my son, Ector tells me you wear the mantle of manhood well. This shield you spoke about—will you need help?"

"The Archive will know if others aid me by the flavor of my mind."

"Then you must open totally to it?"

"There's open, and there's open. Expected behavior patterns will not be cause for suspicion, and it doesn't know I suspect it."

Shadow leaned forward, frowning. "Arthur, I think you had better tell me what it is you're planning."

"If the Archive finds me, then it can see and hear what I experience, yes?" He paused as she considered this. "If a false set of actions fall into normal behavior, it will assume where it thinks I am is where I actually am."

"You're suggesting effectively splitting your mind in two. I agree it can be done on a limited basis as you already showed me, but what you intend— *who* you intend to deceive, requires total concentration of effort. No one can be in two places at once."

"I can. I've had lots of practice in Sanctuary. I can keep up a shield for approximately three hours. Will that be sufficient?"

"How will we know if the deception is successful?"

"It gloats when it thinks it's scoring points. I can detect traces of its emotions." Arthur looked her full in the eyes daring her to argue more. She looked away to the entranceway and then stood up.

"I'll make sure the others leave you alone. Please begin."

Arthur began to build memory sequences into a journey around Avalon as he followed her out of Ector's house. He included details he would notice with the same frequency normal for him. He'd had time to decide what he would have done if he hadn't been helped by Shadow; now he followed through. One such as himself could be expected to slink back to Sanctuary, after a certain degree of soul searching. He would have to pay the price for escaping their clutches – they would expect no less. That meant he needed to access the mind of a seer to validate this mobile dream.

Circe's psi rating was about average for a seer, and she had a personal score to settle with him. When he'd contacted her from Elite barracks, she told him what she thought of his stupid decision and that she didn't want to see him again, unless he changed his mind, surrendered to Sanctuary, and fulfilled his eugenics duties with her. Her betrayal hurt more than he wanted to admit.

Sanctuary kept the surface world hours, so she would be sleeping, and thus an easy target. All he had to do was start a dream sequence, and then hang on tight while she played it out for the Archive. He reckoned it gave about three hours grace in all, if he had to activate it.

Since the Archive would imagine him dead or dying, it probably wouldn't be looking for him. Boasting to gain admittance to the quest was one thing, delivering, entirely another. Seers presented easy targets, but the Archive? The thought broke him out in a cold sweat. What if he was wrong and the end of that dark passage led to moldering construction records or obsolete secrets? The picture of Ector dozing off in front of his eyes as he tried to discuss racial survival surfaced. Another image of the Archive reverting to an archaic mechanism when confronted by Shadow and himself with details of inner Nestine activity blazed into his mind. Kai's disclosure of an inside agent betraying years of hard won victories in weeks weighed the scales further. Ector, Shadow, and Kai were real, living people. Who was he, with his pathetic half-life, to put his own fears before their safety?

Fear was the enemy. Fear could also be friend. Fear produced adrenalin rushes to enable flight or fight. He'd fight. He'd use it. Arthur finished his internal dilemma at the same time he emerged behind Shadow in the alley. Ector's ground runner waited with Ector in the driving seat, Ambrose beside him and Kai behind. He followed Shadow to the rear seats.

"Is your shield up?" Ambrose said.

"It isn't necessary yet." Arthur strapped himself in. "The Archive will be monitoring exits from Avalon on a routine basis, and will not expect accelerated plans. Please do not think of these, or of the enemy. I know this will be difficult, but the longer it remains in ignorance, the longer I'll be able to shield."

"Arthur gives us three hours after activation," Shadow said. "As I have no idea how far the dark zone stretches, I suggest we all think of the most boring routines imaginable. Perhaps Ambrose will give us a weapon cleaning drill."

"A blade rusts on constant exposure to water," Ambrose began. All except Arthur and Shadow joined in the automatic training response.

She nudged him in the ribs, but he shook his head.

'I need to be watchful,' he thought at her. She nodded, joining in the second response when it came.

Arthur let himself sink into meditation as they traveled. He didn't know, or want to know, their route. He did need to cast his consciousness loose to scan for that great mind. It had a unique flavor he'd come to recognize from frequent exposure. He couched his thoughts into the sort of general wish most residents of Avalon subconsciously expressed on retiring; that the being would continue to watch over them, adding to that thought a general sweep sent out for the reassurance of its presence.

Arthur's heightened abilities detected it engaged in fishery controls, while at the same time involving itself in an extensive sweep of outlying medi-tech stations. Not what he'd hoped for. A second later he almost lost his concentration when a presence touched his mind.

'Don't,' he thought back at Shadow. *'It's busy, and maintaining secrecy is too delicate a line to walk for distractions.'* The pressure desisted.

The Archive switched its venue to another station, also on the periphery. Arthur started to sweat. He guessed it acted so because his body hadn't been discovered; thus he could have turned up at a station as comatose without identification. It had visual recordings of all exits to barracks, so it must assume he'd changed clothes somewhere in the city without its knowledge. When it couldn't find accomplices, it attempted to backtrack whenever it found his location. Interesting that it must think him so smart.

Arthur reined in his thoughts as he realized he was doing the very thing he asked the others to refrain from doing. The sentience continued its intensive search with increased vigor when several of its workloads diminished during night hours.

Arthur tried to concentrate, but again his thoughts strayed. He began reviewing the number of medi-tech stations that had facilities for in-patient care and reckoned seven as the Archive started on the third. At the rate it sifted, he had about ten minutes before it began re-evaluating its strategy. With a guilty start, he paused in his speculation, but the sentience didn't waver.

Deliberately now, Arthur let himself think of the times he had evaded seers. It occurred to him that he had long ceased to keep his full attention on deception. As if triggered by this discovery, his mind jumped to a higher level of awareness. Every nerve tingled, every sense sharpened, and that small part of him keeping watch on the Archive registered no increased interest as the sentience moved onto the fifth venue. Even as he acknowledged this factor, his will grew beyond any level he'd previously experienced.

As Ector pulled into barracks parking lot, he knew, without accessing others that they intended to use his own escape route from Sanctuary as an entrance. A logical choice, since the least expected action gave an advantage. Ector's calculated selection of parking had to be admired; out in the open in his usual lot looked normal. Much better a ploy than trying to conceal the transport in an alley to shout of some nefarious action in progress. Arthur noted the Archive moving on to the sixth station.

Ambrose, Ector, and Kai shouldered backpacks, confirming Arthur's suspicion the quest was intended for three. Shadow stood rearguard while each slid down the exact same garbage chute Arthur had used weeks before. He recognized the pattern of Brethren training overlying strategy: put in the lead one who knows the way, who is competent and expendable. Save for yourself the hindmost place to both deal with pursuit and analyze ongoing problems ahead. Ambrose led, followed by Ector, Kai, himself, and then her.

They had almost reached Sanctuary by underground ways when Arthur turned to Shadow, signaling for a halt. The Archive had finished the seventh station. He didn't want to be surprised in Sanctuary cellars, or the dark zone. The others grouped around him, each face betraying anxiety.

"Arthur?" Shadow's crisp voice came across in the semi-gloom.

"It searches for me, and is about to change tactics. I need—"

but he didn't get the chance to finish. The Archive directed every shred of its capabilities in a search and locate pattern aimed at him. He didn't attempt to block it; instead, he willed himself into deception, letting his senses register his predestined route.

"It's found us," Ambrose said.

"Be quiet." Shadow's angry whisper silenced him. "He's under attack. Blank your minds of him, the quest, each other and where we are."

*

In his carefully constructed vision, Arthur's phantom self ran along an overhead walk in the eastern quadrant to leap onto a passing railpod when it slowed at an intersection. He registered mild amusement from the faces of fellow travelers at the pranks of an Elite recruit, bent on stretching rules. He had seconds until it reached an obligatory pick-up point. He boarded another pod, traveling in the opposite direction, again having substance in his own mind. The Archive gleefully alerted security at each stop point for any incoming transport. Round one to him.

Arthur refocused on a group of worried faces, picking out Shadow. "The chronometer has started ticking. I've twelve minutes before I need another halt. Can you get us through to the dark zone before?"

"Yes, in seven. Is there anything else I can do to help you?"

"Continue as you did. I don't need distractions."

"You all heard him. Move!"

Arthur concentrated, aware of Kai steering him around obstacles in physical reality, and then helping him climb down into the darkness. He couldn't try the same deception with transport hopping again, since the Archive wouldn't be fooled a second time. Now he needed to give it something it wanted, before it destroyed him. He gambled the acquisition of his seed was worth the stay of execution, having noted security sent by the Archive to catch him on his mind journey had their weapons set to stun.

Kai put shields on his eyes. "Arthur, if you can hear me, prepare for high-pitched sounds and a burst of light."

"What's he going to do?" Ambrose asked.

Shadow pried up the rusty entranceway with Ector's help. "Kai's made a study of ancient pyrotechnics. He modified a certain type to detonate with a whine rather than a bang. We need noise, light and movement to trigger sentinels I found at the first gateway before we risk passage, but not enough noise to bring seers running."

A flash followed by a hurtful sound set five laser bursts at the target object. Ector took aim and fired at the apertures. Kai sent another incandescent burst through the gateway. This time, all remained peaceful.

"Quickly, we have less than four minutes," Shadow urged.

Smells of ancient must assailed Arthur's walking corporeal body as his astral self waited for the final pod stop. They reached sight of the next gateway with one minute to spare.

"I'll scout ahead," Ector volunteered when Shadow joined the rest.

"No, I miscalculated the distance. We must wait. Arthur can't have any feedback from any of us until he's through with the trail he's laying. Meditation everyone."

Intent on his image-self, Arthur waited on the Archive's action before he continued to the next false trail. When the last stop failed to produce a captive from the innocent railpod, the Archive let its rage surge to unimaginable levels for a split-second. It now searched for an echo, rather than a presence, so Arthur released a picture of him sneaking into Sanctuary from the eyes of a passerby. The Archive began to pick through every mind within, starting at the ground floor up. Arthur obligingly left a trail to Circe's room, having accessed her sleeping mind moments before.

Fear of failure released adrenalin, but not to strengthen Arthur's will as he'd gambled. His mind made a peculiar flip, moving up into new realms, where he could feel rage as a hot wave of hate and power.

Hate was irrelevant, but loathing such as he felt represented constructive use of emotion, since it didn't impair his judgment. He activated the Circe program, letting it run while he dealt with the problem in his physical world.

"It's been too long," Ambrose said. "We have to move, or he'll take us down with him."

"Ambrose—" Shadow started.

"Look, we can't keep stopping for him. We must continue without him, or abort."

"Shadow, either keep him quiet, or remove his ability to vocalize, I don't care which," Arthur ordered. He heard, rather than saw, Shadow's sword drawn.

32

Earth Date 3892

CIRCE RESPONDED to his phantom kiss. Her dream sequence altered to his suggestion. The Archive entered her mind seconds later. It wanted him badly yet . . . it backed off to wait until he'd finished, satisfied he couldn't escape.

Arthur looked up to find Ambrose pinned against a wall with the point of Shadow's blade brushing his neck. She released him at Arthur's nod.

"We have at least forty-five minutes of uninterrupted progress," he said. "You can let him go now."

"How do we know we have that long?" Ambrose demanded, red-faced.

"Because I'm currently visiting with Circe," Arthur said.

"Less than five before security raid her room and find her alone." Ambrose dismissed the notion.

"Who's Circe?" Kai wanted to know.

Arthur grinned. "She's a seer breeding mistress who's wasted a large amount of her valuable time trying to get viable seed out of me. Now she dreams of gradual success."

"I've had enough of this fabrication. No one manipulates seers, and this lad claims he's controlling the Archive. Whose word are we taking for truth that the Archive is aware of our quest anyway? Do we have any corroboration? No." Ambrose shouldered Ector aside to continue. "I say this boy is merely voicing precisely what he's supposed to say to implicate us all beyond redemption."

Part of Arthur's mind registered irritation. He relaxed the barrier sealing away his ongoing encounter with the Archive to release a confined broadcast, cutting straight through privacy shields of all within his vicinity for the space of sixty heartbeats. Each face registered shock, and some looked embarrassed, while others were awed by the time he ended the transmission.

"Not . . . one . . . more . . . word," Shadow glared at Ambrose. "He's more than proved himself. Interrupt him again, and I remove your ability to interrupt, permanently."

Ambrose looked away; his shoulders slumped, unwilling to face a circle of hostile stares.

"Mother, I make it forty minutes now," Kai said.

"Keep together and no one move near any sentinel until we have tested it for activity. Same formation as before."

A more cautious group edged forward in almost total darkness for fifty paces until Kai called a halt. He fumbled in his backpack for a moment to withdraw a metal ball. "On your knees, everyone," he called, rolling it ahead of them. Nothing happened. Kai rummaged again for a pyrotechnic. He lit the fuse and hurled it as far as he could. A brilliant blue cascade would have temporarily blinded the party without eye shields. Again, no response to the prod. Kai unhooked a flashlight from his belt. They stood no more than ten meters from an obvious portal. It remained inactive.

"Advance slowly," Shadow called. "Let's have more light."

Ector and Ambrose both unhooked flashlights. At Shadow's signal, all removed eye shields. They moved forward with caution.

Ancient walls oozed malevolence around them. Ancient dust rose from every step to coat their lungs. They passed Shadow's first barrier and traveled unknown territory. Two more sentinels proved identical to the first and Kai disarmed each with ease. Ahead, a faint break in the wall alerted Ector. He caught Ambrose by the shoulder to halt him. The others grouped behind.

"What have you seen?" Shadow said.

"Maybe nothing. An irregularity. Kai . . . would you please?"

Kai went through his complete repertoire to no effect. He looked at the rest. "I sense danger. Our odds have just plummeted."

All gazed ahead. The passage stretched into infinite gloom, but the walls looked clear and there laid the danger. No one imagined easy access after the elaborate traps behind them, not with Kai's warning still ringing in their ears.

"I guess this one's down to me," Ambrose said, by way of general apology.

"Don't go past that break in the wall unless you're certain—" Shadow began.

"No more than a body length near," Ector broke in.

One step at a time, Ambrose advanced, shining his flashlight on walls, ceiling, and floor, and then he stopped for a long time.

"I'm not sure, but I think I've found a difference," he called.

They joined him to stare where his light rested on the floor.

"I think I see faint patterns in the dust," he said.

"He's right," Kai said. "Luck is riding with us now."

"We don't know how deep the dust is, or what lies underneath." Ector hunkered down, to touch the surface. "Shadow?"

"I can't, not alone. Have you any idea how difficult it is to lift individual particles? Every single one has to be isolated for levitation. I'd need to see the next wall break to even calculate how much power we need."

"Lights, everyone," Ector ordered.

Darkness lifted, revealing the passage stretching ahead.

"Hells, that's about twenty body lengths." Kai relaxed his grip on Arthur's arm.

"One hundred and twenty feet," Ector translated for the benefit of Ambrose.

Shadow turned to Ambrose. "I know how Ector ranks in psi factor, and Kai can't help, so that leaves you."

"Levitation is not my strong point. I can lift myself when the need is great, but inanimate objects tend to slip. Besides, I think I might recognize those symbols if I could see them clearly. I can't lift and decipher at the same time."

"I'll do it. Three is only going to complicate matters." Arthur moved forward to stand by Shadow.

"Maybe we could lift half at a time," Ector suggested. "Look, I know you said you were a twenty on a good day, but this isn't one when you're carrying the Archive."

"It's busy gloating. I really don't like gloating. That's a most disgusting expression of feeling. However, I'm free for a space."

"Don't you need to stimulate Circe's dream?" Ector wanted to know.

"She has an active imagination. She's doing quite nicely all by herself. I just need to keep a light touch on her mind."

"You ever lifted multiple objects before?" Shadow asked.

"I know the principle. Give me a moment while I focus. I'll take the left side of central.

Arthur looked at the stretch before them while he calculated the distance, probable depth and absolute width. He knew he couldn't use all his will, as he had to keep tabs on both Circe and the Archive. The residue might just be enough, given the drain of linking.

"Ector, we may need a reinforcement of will. Don't try to help us lift. Just give us the strength we need if we seem to be faltering," he said.

Shadow looked once into his eyes as she reached out her hand. He made a conscious effort not to block her as the strands of their wills linked together, before immense power flooded through him when their wills combined to a single purpose. Their eyes turned as one, to the dusty floor. Together they focused on every particle. The drain sucked at his life-force by the time they assimilated each atom.

Slowly, so slowly the mass lifted. Sweat ran down into Arthur's eyes, blinding him. He could feel the lifting, and then it faltered as limits topped.

"Ector," they gasped in unison. Power flowed into the joining to magnify their wills. The blanket of atoms once more ascended.

"That's enough," Ambrose cried. "Hold it there as long as you can. I can see now."

Every fiber of Arthur's being cried out for relief, and he could sense Shadow's distress, along with Ector's rapid tiring. His link with Circe began to fail.

"Let go, I have it," Ambrose ordered.

All three of them relaxed, and Ector dropped to his knees to begin rubbing at his neck muscles, while Shadow stretched, and Arthur breathed deeply. Kai passed high-energy rations to each. Ambrose stood with his eyes half-closed in deep concentration until Kai finished, and then turned to him.

"Have you an eidetic memory, Kai?"

"A what?"

"Total recall. I know all original Brethren had such from the moment of banding, but not if children inherit."

"Some don't, I did. What data do you want to review?"

"None, I need to download while the floor patterns are still intact in my mind."

"Go ahead."

Arthur wondered at Ambrose's strength. Shadow and Ector didn't bounce back as swiftly as himself, and neither picked up on

Ambrose for his peculiar request. He decided to take initiative.

"Ambrose, why is Kai storing?"

"So I don't lose the pattern while I compare ancient symbols against the original. I don't possess your level of concentration. Please let me alone for a while."

"Arthur, how much time do we have left?" Shadow rubbed her hands over her eyes and sighed.

"Twenty minutes on my current program."

"Then what?" Her gaze skewered him.

"Depends on whether the Archive will be content to let the apparent me sleep. If not, you'd best go on without me."

"Can't you . . . ?" Kay grinned.

"No. If I'm not where it expects to find me this time, it will know for sure I'm misdirecting. I could possibly buy five extra minutes, seeming to be at an exit. Where I can't be is anywhere around the rest of you. If I get five minutes, I'll try to use them going back to Sanctuary."

"Supposing I stay with you?" She laid a light hand on his shoulder. "There will be three left to continue. It might gain us more time."

"And two certain deaths, instead of one. I knew the risks, and I was forfeit anyway. Much may happen in the next twenty minutes. We may reach the end of our quest, or we might encounter a barrier we can't penetrate and have to turn back—the possibilities are many. I'd like my life to have meaning."

"Leave him be, Shadow." Ector wrapped his arm around her waist for a brief hug. "As he said, the future hasn't happened yet."

"We can continue now." Ambrose looked up. "The symbols were based on ancient cartouches. Follow my exact footsteps until we get across."

They formed up to proceed. Ector moved sluggishly enough for Arthur to wish himself not removed by one from the weak link. Shadow also noticed Ector's fatigue.

"Change of order. I'll follow Ambrose with Arthur behind me, then Ector with Kai at the rear."

Ambrose started, with each of them following in order. Arthur focused most of his attention behind him, very much aware Shadow made conscious sacrifices. She wanted the strongest for the final conflict.

Ambrose crossed the next sentinel, then Shadow, followed by Arthur, but Ector miss-stepped. The entire floor vanished into a hole. Arthur joined with Shadow in a desperate bid to grab the falling bodies with their combined psi power. They made contact, fighting against gravity and their own limitations to slowly levitate those two. Ambrose stood ready to haul the frightened pair onto solid ground. Ector sagged to the floor a few moments before an ashen-faced Kai joined him in safety.

"He's finished, Shadow," Ambrose said. "We'd best leave him."

"Not while I can carry him," Kai objected.

"We can make a chair for him between us," Arthur offered.

"No, I can manage. I don't have psi powers needed here." The auburn-haired Brethren got to his feet. His expression changed to shock, and he pointed.

"Ambrose. Come back!" Shadow started after the man, and then she turned, shrugging.

Arthur unclenched his will. He'd been preparing to turn her if necessary. Without Ector, they hadn't a hope of controlling Ambrose, who had walked away with supreme confidence. It meant he knew something he hadn't shared, a typical racial trait among Submariners. Unlike Brethren, they weren't very good team players, and the higher the ranking, the more individualistic they became. Arthur suspected Ambrose hadn't wanted inclusion in the first place if he wasn't the leader. Ector would automatically defer to Shadow on her own personal quest, but not Ambrose, who still considered Brethren as primitive death-mongers. He could see from the tension in her back that Shadow fought rage at this deplorable action. She'd let Ambrose go because she couldn't risk weakening herself further in a trial of wills and Arthur guessed she cut her losses by having Ambrose spring the next trap. The time lapse since Ambrose's departure confirmed his conjecture. He became aware of her intense scrutiny.

"Thoughts, Arthur? You probably know the man better than I ever will."

"His hobby is ancient forms of communication. I'd guess he learned more from those symbols than just how to get us across."

"Can you access his mind?"

"He'll be prepared for a fight. He wants all the glory," Arthur said. "I will if you really want."

"Kai?" she asked.

"I don't sense any danger for him, wherever he is."

"Then we go forward. Who cares who finds the quest end, as long as it's found?"

Arthur helped Kai get Ector up from the floor and settled into a carrying position, and then he and Shadow walked in advance. The passage elbowed to the right in the light of their torches.

"He walked with too much confidence for any traps," Arthur supplied. "We haven't heard any screams, so it's probably safe."

"How much time?" Kai huffed from behind.

"Ten minutes."

"Brother mine, you'll have to introduce me to Circe if we ever get out of this."

"Kai." Shadow glared back at him.

"Sorry, Mother, it's a man thing." Kai sighed. "I would like to anticipate some sort of reward at this point."

"If I can find a way to suppress your viability, we have a deal," Arthur offered, ignoring Shadow's outraged expression. As Kai said, this was man talk. "We wouldn't want seers to become augmented by fey qualities—they're bad enough as they are."

"If you two have quite finished?"

"We'll reconvene later, since the corner is just coming up. Where you can't hear us, I think," Arthur added, smiling to himself. If they survived this, if they could, he'd enjoy having a brother like Kai.

They saw Ambrose at once. He stood at the end of the passage in a rectangular room with a raised dais to the right and he studied a wall splattered with the same ancient symbols as on the falling floor. On the dais, a console invited more attention than the wall that Ambrose scrutinized with such concentration. The other walls appeared sculptured with scenes from a long-dead surface world, if Arthur judged the lack of saurians and other mutations aright.

"Leave Ector here," Shadow ordered. "One of us must return, if possible. He has enough psi power to call for help when he recovers."

Kai laid Ector down against a wall with Arthur's help. Shadow strode over to Ambrose with Arthur just behind her. They passed the dais before he realized Kai wasn't following.

"It looks as if—" Ambrose began, turning to them, and then his face froze in horror.

Arthur spun around. "No, Kai!" he yelled, too late to prevent Kai taking the steps up to the dais.

His weight already committed, Kai tried to turn. Lethal blasts of plasma bolts shot from ports in the stairs. Wet smacks sounded. Blood gushing from his body, the young Terran crumpled instantly.

33

"Kaɪ!" Shadow sprinted to her younger son's side, dropping to her knees. She pressed her hands over the bleeding holes in a desperate effort to stop blood loss. Tears streamed down her cheeks.

Arthur knelt down beside her to help. A spurt of blood shot between his fingers to hang, motionless. Time slipped out of sequence. A rushing sound in his ears drowned out the death rattle in Kai's throat. Shards of darkness flew at him as his awareness shattered into a sudden vision of the cave-sitter. His soul wrenched free from his body, while the damp cavern of his dreams encased his essence like a tomb.

"Sacrifices for the common good are a harsh burden." The young-old man's matte-black eyes appeared to radiate a red light from some inner source. The smooth skin of his face glowed above a snow-white beard. "Let your sibling go."

"No!" Helpless, Arthur wished for the strength to strangle this being. "I know you now. The Archive knows who Kai is and what his powers are. Only the Archive—*you*—have reason to want him dead before he plays his part. I can save him. I won't let go. I won't cede his life."

"He is forfeit," the cave-sitter said, raising those terrible eyes to Arthur, bringing an intractable will to bear on him.

"Too late." Arthur clenched his teeth. Beads of sweat began to drip off his brow. *He hasn't killed me. Why?* He was at the Archive's mercy, so why did the creature hold back? Why want Kai dead? A glimmer of understanding produced a motive: "If my body dies, you lose. You wanted to take over my mind. Well, I won't relinquish Kai." He drew a deep breath, fighting against the being with his entire telepathic ability. "Sacrifice unacceptable. Every last shred of my strength, I bequeath to him." Arthur directed his energy at Kai.

"Nooo . . . oo . . . o . . . " the cave-sitter wailed. A fading sigh and darkness closed around them. The scene whirled into a tangled mess of black fragments spiraling into light.

Arthur opened his eyes to see his brother still breathing, but Shadow? She looked as if she stared through stone, a Brethren expression that frightened him.

Kai's wounds were beyond any emergency supplies in their packs. Arthur's hands aligned with his mother's to stem the flow while he thought. If the organs weren't too badly smashed, an octet of seers could instigate tissue regeneration by telepathy. They used their own life force as raw energy if the victim were important, or one of their own. An octet ranked a combined psi power of approximately forty, since they wouldn't commit all their will. It left him at least four points short, even with Shadow's help.

"Ambrose, get over here will you?" he yelled.

"Can't. I'm trying to stop every other weapon being discharged. Kai triggered all of them."

Ector groaned as Ambrose called his warning. He lurched, stumbling with fatigue, to Shadow. Arthur committed in that second. He used seer techniques to body scan. The damage looked bad, with many deep puncture wounds, but if he used every ounce of his will . . .

"Shadow, link with me. I need everything you've got for Kai to have any chance."

She raised her tear-drenched face to his in misery. Arthur wondered, for a split-second, if any other woman cried without sobbing, or getting a red, splotchy face. Her tears just flowed, a liquid grief he couldn't bear.

"I can't lose two of you." She grasped his arm in a painful grip. "You'll be open to attack the instant you commit to saving him."

"I already have." Arthur gently pried her fingers loose, aware she hadn't realized which hand she used in the grief. "My brother is more important to me than your quest. Even now, the Archive searches for me. You don't have to choose between us. The choice no longer exists."

Hope, followed by determination flashed across Shadow's face. Arthur plunged into her now open mind, taking from her and Ector. Every hair stood on end when he focused. Will flowed from energy into matter. The body under his hands glowed as it healed. Tissue and organs regenerated at a far greater rate than had ever been achieved by an octet, but then the outcome meant nothing to them compared with Arthur's determination to save his brother.

Too much blood loss needed a life-force correction. Arthur didn't require Shadow's frantic warning, coming just before he sucked the last of her strength out, to know his blood type wasn't compatible to Kai's, any more than Ector's, or hers. He had to make Kai work with him, and for that, he needed a proscribed joining. Arthur didn't hesitate. His mind severed connection with the others to blend as one with Kai. Full flow of life started to return to his brother moments before Arthur ceased to be an individual. There was a second of exultation, followed by a moment of pure horror as a force reached out to snatch his essence from Kai. Molten fire flickered through his nerves. If he let go now, Kai would die and what would happen to Arthur? He sensed the Archive's presence trying to claw him through his brother. In that moment, he committed totally. If it wanted him that bad, it would have to pull him back from death, for he would not return without Kai.

The force wavered and Arthur merged with Kai.

The creature that arose from the floor of the chamber wasn't human. Tentacles of light emerged from a brilliant glow of pure energy. It stretched, feeling the power flow through its essence, aware of being a gestalt, an amalgam of two living creatures, but not disturbed by this knowledge. Almost as an afterthought, it directed two of its eyes at the man still trying to circumvent weaponry no longer of interest. It gloried in resources others couldn't even begin to imagine. Graceful beyond human capacity, it levitated to the podium where its many limbs activated a program previously buried in antiquity. An ocular magnifier rose from the center of the structure to focus on the projection of a combined retina pattern.

"Security scan approved. Voice-coded password from ruling planetary council now required," a disembodied voice requested.

"Armageddon." The gestalt's multi-toned answer came from the depths of its racial memory.

"Access granted."

The experience of direct sensory playback paled into insignificance before the wealth of data the gestalt absorbed. Centuries of history rolled into the awareness. Terrible facts registered in the gestalt's mind in those moments. At the end, a single voice screaming one word burst forth:

"*Free . . . !*" Then the cave-sitter's voice faded away into nothingness.

For an instant, the gestalt glimpsed the creature breaking its ancient bonds before it, too, spiraled into darkness.

*

Sound came from a long way away, a faint clicking accompanied by a clinical smell. Pain pounded with each tiny noise. It grew with the volume until Arthur writhed in agony.

"Easy, lad. Can you hear me?" Ector's voice came at a nerve grinding intensity.

Arthur wanted to scream, but sound pulverized him. He whimpered as a door rumbled open and someone thudded across the plas-glass floor. The sound of a slap-shot against the skin of his upper arm hurt more than medication being forced deep within. His temporary link with reality faded into silence.

Smell returned first: the dry, sterile odor Arthur associated with Sanctuary. He wanted to retreat before sound came, but there was nowhere to hide.

"It's all right now. Just take your own time," Ector said, his voice coming at a bearable level.

Arthur tried opening his eyes. The room lurched enough to make him feel sick, but compared to the results of an interrupted sensory playback, it seemed mild. Ector sat by his bed wearing deep blue infirmary sleepwear with a glyph standing for Sanctuary on the right sleeve. *Caught, and they have Ector, too.* Despair swept through him, and then he remembered Kai's hurt, his own commitment and a sense of absolute horror.

"Arthur, do you recall what happened?"

"Kai?"

"He recovered quicker than you did, maybe because he doesn't possess psi powers." Ector's expression creased into a frown. "You're both lucky to be alive. We are still unsure how you managed to separate yourselves. Now, what did you see after you formed a gestalt?"

Arthur wondered who really asked. He reached out to the Archive in a deliberate challenge. His questing mind met emptiness. Disturbed by his apparent loss of ability, he tried Ector next. This covert probe gained instant access. Ector's fear hit him hard. The man wanted answers. That fear overrode all other thought processes to the point where further, deeper sifting held no purpose.

"I wanted Kai healed. I don't remember beyond that until I woke up here," Arthur said.

"Are you sure? Kai says he remembers floating."

"I don't. What happened? Why are we in Sanctuary?"

"You know where you are. That's good." Ector took a deep breath. "The Archive has gone. All high rank psi powers are detailed to central control, and I'm to report as soon as I have enough strength to help run Avalon. It's chaos."

"Can I see Kai?"

"Absolutely not. He's to return to the surface where he's needed."

Whoever ruled now didn't want Kai and Arthur joining up. What had they done that made them so dangerous together?

"This gestalt . . . who witnessed it?" Arthur asked.

"Ambrose. He's still wetting himself every time he's asked to recount. Will you try very hard to remember? If we don't get some answers, we can't restore the Archive, and we'll be stuck with assuming all its duties ourselves.

Arthur didn't like the sound of that, nor the Archive's restoration. He feigned fatigue, shutting his eyes and Ector left him to sleep.

Scanning the building, he touched the thoughts of some seers, running around in collective hysteria. They were picked off, one by one, for administration duties, despite heated argument. To see seers forced to bow before the overwhelming needs of the community amused him. The heartbeat of Avalon fluttered while order gradually restored essential services with the conscription of psi powers. They didn't need him, not really.

His contribution would simplify matters, but it wasn't essential, which left him open for other possibilities.

Kai had said Brethren-controlled forts had reverted to Nestines and suspected a traitor. So, without the presence of the Archive as prime suspect, how did matters now stand? Arthur wanted to see for himself. He reasoned he wouldn't be requisitioned until he could prove all his powers had returned, and this meant he would be tested. After a supposedly fatal gestalt experience, expected to kill both of them, some damage might be expected.

This set off another strand of thought. What happened to them both? What scared Ambrose so much? He remembered Kai reviving, and a sick sense of melting. The rest ran through his mind like a sensory playback speeded to the point of making all the data meaningless. He couldn't get a glimpse of those images to make any sense of what happened. Arthur considered raiding Ambrose's mind, but something held him back, some reluctance to see the gestalt as others had witnessed it. Another streak of flashing images in his brain tired him. He let sleep come on soft wings.

A faint aroma of soap with an undertone of leather warned Arthur of another presence as he awakened. No one else smelled quite like her, he decided, as he lay with his eyes shut, feigning sleep. That unique mixture of cleanliness coupled with the tang of Brethren battledress identified Shadow as his guest without any need to touch her mind. Arthur shied away from a mental probe to raid for the reason she visited. He had an uncomfortable feeling she possessed a psi factor strong enough to block him and instigate a counter raid. Best not to tempt fate.

"Arthur?" Shadow's voice sounded half-amused and half-irritated. "Boy, will you stop trying to hide from me? I know you are awake."

His eyes snapped open to meet her steady gaze. "How? My

breathing didn't change."

"Your expression did." She leaned forward, reaching to brush a tendril of hair from his eyes. "A slight tightening of facial muscles betrayed you."

"My thanks," he propped himself up on one elbow to give her an ironic neck bow. "I will bear that in mind for the future."

"You're still evading me, Boy."

"My name is Arthur," he said, annoyed for rising to her bait. "How is Kai?"

"Regaining his strength. He will be shipping back to the surface in a day or so."

"Can I see him?" Arthur wanted more time with his brother. They had plans.

"We don't think that is a good idea." Shadow looked away, a firmness settling around her mouth. "We want to be sure you have no mental connections remaining before you meet each other again."

"What if I want to go to the surface?" Arthur let it come out as a general, disinterested inquiry.

"Not possible." Shadow met and held his gaze. "Kai is trained as a warrior in Brethren style. He can live off the land and blend in with surface-dwellers. You can do neither."

"Other Submariners work with Brethren," Arthur objected, guessing she expected argument.

"They are not the son I lost, and have now found." She caught his hand in her small one, exerting a gentle pressure. "This is not a punishment, Arthur. I am not asking you for more than I am prepared to give. Avalon needs all the strongest of us in order to function."

"What if I don't want to become a second-rate Archive?" He glanced around his sterile room, taking in the blandness, the lack of odor and color. He thought of Circe, and how she had tricked him into caring.

"Perhaps you should have considered the consequences of destroying the Archive. Now, what do you remember of the joining with Kai?"

So here it comes, another interrogation attempt. He let his facial muscles slide into a vacuous searching mode as if he wanted to remember. Looking her straight in the eyes, he said, "Nothing beyond what I have already told."

"Surely some memory?"

"I remember sucking in strength from all of you, a few fragments after that, and then waking up after." Arthur yawned.

"Enough for today." Shadow released his hand and stood up, preparing to leave. "Maybe you will remember more tomorrow."

Arthur closed his eyes as he settled back in his bed. He needed to think through all possible strategies. Did his need to surface stem from selfish reasons? Did he possess the strength needed for turning this war to the death around? Brethren, with Rowan in command, lost ground. What if a splinter group formed, a third independent force to strike at random? Nestines concentrated on Rowan and his Submariner allies; Arthur had found a blind spot in their vision.

The change of air pressure alerted him to a medi-tech coming to check up on him. He relaxed his face muscles to endure an examination without betraying his consciousness. The plan worked, and the man left.

Rolling over on his side in apparent sleep mode, Arthur continued to explore his problem. Returning dribbles of horrific data sucked at his soul, demanding action. Now if he had Kai at his side . . . there was a thought: one brother to recruit Brethren and the other to suck in Submariners. With Kai around, he could live off the land. All depended on how much Kai retained of their shared experience. He refused to alert others of his plan by trying to contact Kai. Shadow feared their joining as something dangerous. What if the links between them directed Kai to the same conclusions? They both needed to recover for what he had in mind. He let himself drift down into healing sleep once again.

A bored-looking seer sat by Arthur's bed when he awoke. He knew this man, Anwar. A high-ranking individual with delusions of grandeur he couldn't possible fulfill.

"Now you're alert, I need to see if there are any lasting effects from your criminal behavior, apart from the temporary madness caused by gestalt. No, don't argue with me," he said, as Arthur opened his mouth to protest. "No sane individual would even think of destroying the key to Submariner existence. Were you aware the purpose of Shadow's mission was to discover data to control the Archive? Open your mind to me, or I'll call in as many seers as I need to force the issue." Anwar locked himself into a probe trance in preparation.

Arthur countered by burying his secrets in great wads of trivia, while still leaving enough to satisfy.

By the time Anwar had finished, he looked at Arthur with pity. "Well, I can report you're physically recovered, if not mentally. Perhaps recreation might trigger the higher awareness into response without a return to insanity. Is there anything you would like to do?"

"Maybe if I could revisit some of my haunts as a cadet in the Elite," Arthur suggested, opening his eyes wide to assume a look of innocence.

"I'll make arrangements," the man agreed.

34

Earth Date 3892

FIVE DAYS OF POINTLESS wandering earned Arthur freedom from a discreet observer. Each new day brought a return of more memories and increased the urgency of his mission.

A small food dispenser by a docking port had a few tables and chairs arranged to the side of the walkway. He had been sitting facing the port for over an hour, working on the individual responsible for external traffic processing. Not a strategic port, this facility took one man, and that one was just about ready for what Arthur planned. The man neared the end of his shift in a low traffic time and showed every indication of boredom. He had cleared and restocked a transport that now sat empty, and he plodded through deliberate make-work in an attempt to keep himself amused. He even started rearranging furniture.

When the little man ran his hands through his thinning hair again, Arthur guessed the work placement was one deemed suitable for a low psi rating of limited concentration and intelligence. No doubt someone far sharper would replace him for busy periods. Timing mattered for his plan to work; he had just begun to concentrate when another sat at his table.

Kai grinned across at him. The building lights gave deep

tones to his copper hair.

"What took you so long?" Arthur smiled back.

"Have you rummaged through my mind, Brother?" Kai made a play of running his hands over his head.

"No. I guessed you would resent your allotted role as much as I resented mine." Arthur settled deeper into his chair, stretching out his legs. "I figured that you'd use your fey ability to find the best way out. I would have been worried if you hadn't shown up soon."

"Now what? Do we blend in with the next outgoing load?"

"This port is a cargo bay. We take a ship that's empty." He pointed to the dark outline of a transport latched onto a docking bay nipple, a twelve-man craft, from the shape seen through Avalon's dome shield.

"Won't a theft alert security?" Kai scanned the dock for officials.

"Answer yourself. Have the odds of success just gone down? I'd doubt it. No one steals in Avalon, so the security force isn't equipped to deal with it." Arthur looked at the little man in his glass booth and sent a sleep suggestion. The man began to yawn. "I think we are almost ready to make our move. Traveling light, or have you kit stowed nearby?"

"I'll supply any needs for both of us once we surface." Kai swiveled in his chair to punch in his credit code and collect a handful of protein bars from the dispenser. He grinned. "My father insisted each of us had several hidden caches. He assumed any captive from a fighting triad would crack under torture, if he didn't manage to fall on his sword first. Even Mother doesn't know the location of mine and yes, I am aware she can mind raid as easily as you, but I can sense her presence when she does. She respected my father's wishes on this one." He looked up from stowing his rations. "I know Elite often have implants. I assume . . . ?"

"I don't need power packs. What I have will function on normal electrical body discharges." Arthur watched the little man's head slump on his hands at his desk. "We're away."

They sauntered onto the craft as if by right. Once aboard, Arthur loaded a false destination with central departure, completed docking formalities and had them powering away from Avalon.

*

A door hissed open behind her, but Shadow kept her attention on her console, where the image of a vessel slid away from Avalon through the deep waters. She knew who entered her office. Ector had a certain way of walking when he was angry, as now.

His hands rested on her shoulders. "The boys are missing. I'm sorry. I have four squads out looking for them."

"I know." The tail light of the craft dimmed with distance. "They stole a submersible." She gestured at the screen. "That one."

Ector reached over her for a comm-switch. She caught his hand, stopping him and turned in her chair to face him.

"No." The word struggled for freedom. Shadow wanted Ector to have them brought back; the pair of them being together frightened her after the gestalt. Evegena thought they should never meet. More than the fear, she needed to bond with Arthur. Their last meeting still held a flavor of discomfort from both her and the boy.

Taking both her hands in his, Ector drew her to her feet. He frowned, his mouth compressed. "Why?"

"Arthur needs an escape from the seers, and he isn't going to get one if he stays." A hard knot formed in her chest. "Kai should have a clean break from Rowan, too. Haven isn't the place of safety it was since Rowan considers Kai a threat."

"What about you?" Ector hugged her. "Damn it, you've just found Arthur. He should be spending time with you."

"If I force his return, will he think of me kindly? Arthur and Kai want to be together. How will they feel if I separate them?" Tears blurred her sight. "They made a choice and have accepted a hard life by their actions. This is a man's decision from both of them. I'll not stand in their way."

*

"Smooth, very smooth. The next time I need to steal, I'll make a point of inviting you along," Kai said, his face lighting up with a wicked grin.

"This wasn't a challenge." Arthur shrugged. "Where theft is norm, it would be different."

"Not really, it's all in the right approach. Start sneaking when attempting to steal, and that's an open invitation to get caught. Attitude is everything."

"Kai, can you pilot?" Arthur asked as he considered a problem with the craft.

"I've seen it done . . . why?"

"Automatic pilot mightn't be a bright idea. It used to be fed into Archive terminals. Transports leave a faint ion trail, which we can fix if our passage is erratic. If pursuit misses one twist, fails to pick up the next for a while, they have lost us. I can handle that part, but it will take time. Can you take over for the run to shore, so I can get some sleep?"

"Any particular zone for landing?"

"You've that many caches?" Arthur said. "I am impressed. The southern landmass, with a deep layer of sand, if you can manage it. Pursuit won't reckon I'll use Shadow's landing points. As it is much too obvious, that's what we'll do."

"We're going to keep this transport?" Kai guessed. "I suppose stasis devices are standard equipment for all vessels?"

"Usually, in case of a medical emergency, but using one is a bad idea, since they may be open to a tracer. Kai . . . did you lie when you told them you had no recollection of our sharing?"

"Not entirely. I get a few brief flashes now and then. Too little information to be of any use." Kai peered into the darkness ahead of them. "Just a small point: I don't have an aquatic adaptation."

"There's an old way used long before the innovation of stasis. I'll breathe for both of us, so just pick a location close to shore." Arthur pulled up detailed maps on his screen as he began maneuvering.

"But what if . . . ?"

"Get rest. You'll need it. I'm taking us out into very deep water."

Kai gave up watching and settled into a somewhat restless sleep while Arthur gave his full attention to direction. He wanted it to seem as if they headed to lands deemed irremediably lost, to the far west. At a set point in his plan, Arthur sent a deeper sleep suggestion to Kai than he had previously activated. He wanted absolute concentration for his next series of maneuvers. Hours later, Arthur relaxed the command and Kai joined him soon after, looking rather sober-faced.

"What's troubling you?"

"Conscience. We spent so much effort evading the roles we didn't want, and we wrecked the Archive. What if it wasn't our spy? The quest . . . well it's over, and we're running away."

"Pay more attention to the little details, Kai. We have enough evidence to justify what we did. As for the quest, it has just started. Submariners are neutralized for the moment, and Brethren wallow in the sea of orders Rowan issues, while the Nestines take full advantage. They won't be watching for a small attack unit striking at their strongholds." Arthur paused to set direction for their general destination. Kai could fine-set it later. "We recruit until we have a workable force, and then we play strike and run."

"An independent army? I like the sound of that. Brethren are traditionally shock troops, not defenders. We create havoc, while Rowan and the Submariners consolidate. Now I understand why you want to keep this transport. It will give us the advantage of speedy relocation."

"Exactly. While I'm resting, you can make a short list of those tested in battle, who also possess technological knowledge. I want people who don't follow blindly. Wild cards are acceptable though. When we get them, we'll train them in our own way. You have Copper's knowledge of warfare, which we'll combine with my Elite program. Both sides have kept very much to their own tactics, making a combination unexpected."

Arthur yawned and stretched as he prepared to give up controls to Kai. He kept to himself his intention to recruit from forts as well as from Brethren. Kai couldn't even begin to imagine how busy they were going to be. As soon as he had enough manpower, he would switch tactics to hold, but not for the alliance. They'd had their chance and flunked it. His army needed one loyalty – to him. He wasn't going to rest until every Nestine served a more useful purpose by fertilizing crops with its ashes. If his plan worked, he'd turn authority over to the civilian population, so that he could devote his life to exploring the bad zones proscribed by Sanctuary. Kai might like a wandering life too. They'd make a great team. With that happy thought, Arthur willed himself to sleep.

As consciousness faded, a faint sense of being watched alerted Arthur, but he couldn't rouse, he couldn't move. His will pushed against a barrier too strong to break through. He fought against a black nothingness, and it won.

35

Earth Date 3892

THE WINGS OF NIGHT swirled around a trapped spirit, engulfing it in a dark vortex. The captive essence landed in a group of insubstantial apparitions – those warriors from the Wild Hunt who waited with eternal patience for another angry soul to join their legions.

Memories returned like a flood tide and a silent scream formed. Each soul wore a mantle of pain, all of them trapped by self-inflicted corporeal errors, or those of others' making. They sucked at the fury of a disrupted spirit to feed their own hunger for existence. He remembered the dreadful craving from his own waiting times.

Once more he stood with his comrades. So many lives remembered here, and every life and death in exact detail. Arthur had never died in his sleep before, though. Perhaps Kai, dozing at the controls, had caused a crash, or pursuers found their tracks despite all his efforts. Maybe someone picked through Kai's thoughts. Locating their vessel, a seer could rig self-destruct or disable it for their easy reacquisition. Whichever didn't really matter anymore, since here he stood, in this half-life, to continue his endless quest.

He bit down another scream, wanting peace, a final peace denied until he found the talisman. Sometimes he could remember a need to search for something in his corporeal form, but never for what, until this latest incarnation, where he had seen the sword. His almost-victory was snatched away.

The old one responsible failed to reckon on the species evolving so fast. Each incarnation brought Arthur closer to acquiring the talisman: his sword.

Viewing time as cyclic, he stood witness to land changing, developing beyond recognition, and those same developments crumbling into dust. Now the land resembled a time when the talisman throbbed in his hand. He knew, with blood running rivers deep from all the dead and dying, his rebirth must be imminent. Perhaps in the next life, he'd find it.

A breeze pushed at his robes. No tree or blade of grass stirred. The robes of other watchers belled out as their eyes became hungry in anticipation of another new spirit coming to join them. Souls sometimes burned out by whatever held them earthbound, or rejoined flesh to fulfill a quest, and then a gap in the ring of warriors appeared. Stronger winds pushed at him, whispering of new life. Unable to fight, he let it happen.

A gust took him, propelled his essence outward, away from the others. He rushed through night, over stunted moors, where even stars hid behind a thick blanket of cloud. Ahead, a fire like a beacon snared him as a shark to blood. He saw the face of the one who tended it as he drew closer . . . that one, from his dreams in this recent incarnation.

The cave-sitter turned matte-black eyes upon him when he reached the circle of light. Trained warrior responses sent Arthur's hand to reach for a weapon never there in these waiting times. Frustrated, he tried to channel the will he enjoyed in corporeal flesh, during his recent incarnation, and accomplish the same end.

"Resistance is an exercise in futility, Arthur."

"Should I enjoy watching you gloat?" The forces holding him pushed down on his shoulders. Arthur resisted, arranging his legs to squat instead of kneel. From that position, he managed to sit cross-legged. A chilling guess had become reality in those moments. The cave-sitter had used the same words to warn against resistance that the Archive uttered. He knew now with certainty they were the same entity.

"Interesting." The cave-sitter threw another branch on his fire. "So you think yourself defeated, and a captive?"

"I'm here, aren't I? Waiting with the Wild Hunt again, in between entertaining you."

"You dream, nothing more." Another hunk of wood joined the blaze. Sparks flew skyward.

"I'm alive?" Arthur squashed down a surge of hope, aware of how devious his companion was. "What do you want?"

"There are truths you must learn." The black eyes met Arthur's over the fire. "I intended to use your body as a vessel for my essence to escape from Archives. I needed the neural pathways without your essence cohabiting, and I almost got my wish, but then you joined in a gestalt with your brother. I thought I had prevented such a possibility when I directed his steps into death. I underestimated your need to belong. The forces you released smashed through my bonds and I now wear the form I wore when I first visited your world."

"Who . . . what are you?" Arthur resisted naming this being. He wanted more than a convenient handle. He wanted answers. The figure of power he remembered from a past life did not claim spacecraft skills, however restricted his wording in the language of those times.

"Later. For now, watch and learn." A gesture from the being sent a huge wall of flame between them. It flattened to form a golden mirror-like surface that smoothed into multifaceted moving images.

Arthur, trapped and horrified, writhed as it pulled him into glowing light. A helpless spirit without substance, he saw the actions of others through many windows. A tug in any direction that caught his attention brought him into the head of the person responsible. Full sensory playback paled into insignificance beside this experience. He *was* the Archive. Windows flashed before him, data surged into his memory base.

*

Gregor swallowed another stim tab, so close to victory that he dared not sleep. He walked over to a window, looking down, while he waited for the effects to kick in.

Did those endless lines of people who shuffled on the sidewalk just trying to move really care what he did, or how he did it, as long as they benefited? Did anyone care what the black-band wearing proletariat thought? Did ethics have any place in a world drowning under the weight of its own population? Would anyone find out that he bartered his skills to be on the first hibernation ship to leave Earth for another world? Did he care?

He fingered the metal band of his own silver identity wristlet. It gave him access to better quarters and medical facilities. He had received an education, and he might even receive permission to breed one day, unlike the sterilized black-bands. He wanted more. The right to walk down a street, and not have to share that same space with another living soul.

A comm-unit buzzed, calling his attention back into his laboratory. He depressed a button on the console. The face of a fat, balding man flickered into view.

"Wojuk, how long do you estimate your drones will take to hatch?" Director Greenley asked, wiping a sheen of sweat from his shiny pate.

"Around a year. I base that on the longest normal gestation period of all the species used in this amalgam." Sweat started under the collar of his white lab coat. Not from heat in his air-conditioned paradise, but from fear. Who else worked in similar fields of research? Had they made a breakthrough? Would he lose his place on the ship?

"We don't have a year. Speed it up. Do whatever." The screen went blank.

Gregor let his breath out in a hiss. The species he used, the genomes spliced together with so much care to create the greatest intelligence, and it came down to 'Do whatever'. And if he didn't, who else would, and steal his place? He plucked a hair from his dark brown thatch and fixed the root to a microscope slide. So, they wanted fast, did they? They wanted smart?

Ian Greenley was only a silver band, too. Gregor wondered who controlled the controller. What price did Greenley pay for the power he wielded?

Five minutes later, Gregor added human alleles to the beginnings of a new race. He sent a short current pulsing through haploid cells. His mouth curved up in a smile when he saw activity through the lens of his microscope. Aiming the comment at a now absent Greenley, he said, 'Let there be life,' and giggled at his own blasphemy.

*

"What do you mean, Dexter? The drones aren't viable? What good are they if they can't perpetuate themselves?" The fat, be-ringed hand banged down on a rare, real-wood desk. "Didn't you read Wojuk's data?"

"His notes stopped short." Just before you had him terminated, John Dexter thought but did not say. He wondered if Greenley had another geneticist waiting to take over from his research for a place on the first ship. How many of us vying for the same berth? How many prepared to step on dead men's shoulders, like he had with Wojuk?

"Fix it."

John saw his death in those black, pig-like eyes. He knew then what alleles he must use. The drones needed invertebrate characteristics to reproduce. They needed a queen. The solution wasn't perfect, or natural, but who expected natural in a Harvester? He cast a guilty look at Greenley, aware that no-one was supposed to name the drone species before the Director decided on a handle. That was what everyone called them, though.

*

Ian Greenley cast one last look at his home-world from the screen of the moon shuttle. He hated it and all who lived there. Five of his Nestines remained out of a hatching of twenty. Five plus the queen egg. Not necessary, the Ruling Planetary Council said. No more hibernation ships. No-one trusts those. Look what happened on the Saturn mission. We will pour resources into underwater cities instead.

Have you seen the first one? We've called it Avalon. No, we don't need the Nestines for that project. Oh, we're sorry, there isn't room for you in Avalon. We need physicists and chemists there, so you do see that your skills are redundant. While we are on that subject, we would like a full report on the whereabouts of six prominent geneticists. Tomorrow will do fine.

Greenly saw his mortality on their smug, soon to be safe faces.

His Nestines had killed thirty humans to get him aboard this shuttle. Enough of them survived to pilot the craft, and it held a fresh cache of weapons. Humans on the moon base were about to learn who ruled. He wouldn't kill them. The Nestines needed a source of fresh meat.

How much stock did each of the five hibernation ships contain?
Greenley needed an answer before he acted. Animal life and insects,
plants and fungi, as well as human sleepers. All must be on hand
to sustain the moon base. Then . . . Greenley giggled, imagining his
finger pressing the button. Nuke the bastards. Nuke all of them.
And in the beginning, there was one. *He giggled again.* Ian the
Almighty. Ian the Most High.

*

Ur-ar paused on the threshold of the passenger cabin, listening. He
sent his thoughts to the other four, so they also heard. Their minds
merged while the human raved. Let the human do as he wishes
until we are in control. Ur-ar must pacify and flatter the one
we Nestines call Fat Food. Let the fresh meat build a gestation
chamber for our Queen, and then . . . he shall be our hatching
gift to her.

*

Golden light swirled, shifting in the breeze, a feeling of wind
on skin. The skin of a body. Arthur opened his eyes to meet the
black gaze of the cave-sitter across firelight. The same horror was
reflected in those eyes. He wanted death. He wanted oblivion.

"Now do you understand?" the former resident spirit of
Archives asked.

"How am I going to tell them?" Arthur tried to imagine how
Terrans and Submariners might handle the horrendous truth
that the Nestines were created by humans.

"You don't." The cave-sitter held up one hand for silence
when Arthur opened his mouth to argue. "Remember the lesson of leadership. A leader is he who would serve his people by
protecting and guiding them. Protect them from a truth they are
not mature enough to handle. Guide them into paths of safety,

so that they may grow."

Arthur bowed his head to the wisdom of these words. Responsibility crushed down upon him.

"Arthur, keep faith strong. You are very much like your original incarnation. He put others first, as you do." A faint smile lifted the features of that old-young face. "Apart from hair color, you look similar too."

"What are you?" Arthur demanded, as the cave sitter's cloak flew back in the sighing wind. Other sounds too started to return.

"I suppose I could be eligible for the vacant Nestine mantle of deity," the cave-sitter mused, staring deep into flames, flames that did not reflect on those matte-black eyes. "I wouldn't make much of a god. I tried that once and became terribly bored with all the genuflecting and other forms of groveling. You'd be amazed how quickly worship palls and how close a watch on you all the devoted keep." The cave-sitter yawned, a very human gesture. "I prefer the life of a traveler and probably always will."

"What are you?" Arthur asked again. The wind sounds grew louder, and he began to float back, pushed by it.

"Think of me as Emrys," the being he had known in other times as Merlin called, fading to a shadow. "I've always rather liked that handle."

"Arthur? Wake up." Someone was shaking him. Arthur opened his eyes a fraction, trying to keep the dream, but it was gone in an instant.

"Do you feel sick? You made some peculiar sounds." Kai squatted down by his bunk.

"Only a dream. I dreamed a dream of long ago, of places far away. Yet, it seemed in my dream to be now. I spoke with an old friend, or an old enemy. I'm still not sure which. I'm going to miss him."

"Maybe you'll meet again," Kai said, still looking concerned.

"I hope not, and I rather think I'm going to revise an old religion, just so I can have someone to pray to that it never happens." Yes . . . even *he* would appreciate the irony of that. And there would have to be intricate, ornate gestures . . . and groveling, lots and lots of groveling.

Epilogue

EARTHRISE STRETCHED SHADOWS over the dusty, pockmarked ground, lending a faint touch of indigo to the airless surface. Kiri Ung's claws unsheathed the moment the black disc-shape of an incoming vessel appeared on his monitor, slicing through the tranquility like a bug heading for a fresh corpse.

What had gone so wrong during the return flight to Moonbase? Commander Te Krull's first report detailed a successful mission, despite resistance from the chosen targets. The Nestine patrol unit had captured an unbanded Terran without causing it physical damage.

Te Krull knew how important it was to question one of the free-ranging creatures, and for that they needed a healthy specimen, one capable of anticipating pain. Kiri Ung's crest pumped into full erection for the third time since receiving the last infuriating message. He waited for the buzz of the comm-unit, willing it to spew out Te Krull's voice. Nothing. Not a word since his second-in-command had sent out the urgent request for medical aid to meet the ship at docking bay. The captured Terran was hurt.

This prey-beast must be both coherent and articulate, because Kiri Ung needed to see if the Terran would lie to him. If it did, he would know it had free will; crucial information for the safe farming of the Terran race on the planet. These creatures must not be immune to Nestine mind control.

The ship approached Moonbase much too fast, and yet Te Krull would not disobey protocol without good reason. Just how damaged was the captive? And how, in the name of all creation, had a group of Terrans managed to override their programming? They shouldn't be able to see Nestine farmers, let alone attack them.

A cold claw of fear ripped down Kiri Ung's back, standing his fur on end. He turned to his desk console, sitting down to punch out a series of commands for the bot drones to start cleaning the outside of Moonbase as soon as the ship cleared docking port. Dust eroded every moving part, and Te Krull knew better than to leave a coating of dust when the ship bore no cargo but the captive.

Kiri Ung ran his paw over the smooth leather surface of his favorite chair. So soft and always difficult to acquire, Terran skin was almost impossible to cure in large enough sheets. The Terran on that ship had better be able to communicate, or Te Krull would suffer. Unable to settle, Kiri Ung returned to the window port to watch the incoming ship. He wanted answers, and as Queen's Mate, he was responsible for the continuance of healthy food for the hive. Had he missed some genetic abnormality emerging in the Terran herd? If so, a hard culling must be done.

The ship deployed forward thrusters and angled up for a position over a landing platform out of his sight. Kiri Ung now contemplated the emerging blue planet, partially shrouded by clouds; so beautiful from space and yet ugly on the surface. The primitive, stench-filled dwellings of the Terrans marred the scenery, but worse, the vast quantity of bugs seemed to prefer the taste of Nestine over Terran. He didn't envy Te Krull's role as planetary governor, not compared to his own clean work-station on Moonbase. Gradually, his crest deflated because he didn't want to confront his second-in-command with a threatening posture; that could wait. He picked up a soothing, intricately shaped crystal, enjoying the play of light on its many facets. Ironic that his most prized possession came from the first Terran a Nestine had ever eaten.

A rumbling stomach reminded him of the breakfast he had postponed to solve this disturbing turn of events. He wanted to eat in peace, without thoughts interrupting such a pleasant pastime. Maybe, after questioning, the Terran would make a tasty snack, if it was not too old; he liked his meat tender.

Behind him, steel doors hissed open and from the reflection of the thermo-glass window, he saw Te Krull advancing into the room. The Terran, hanging limp in his second's massive fur-sheathed arms, resembled a pallid worm where its naked skin showed outside of clothing. Of course, all the surface-dwelling ones needed clothing, lacking both fur and scales, unlike the clean and naked beasts kept in Moonbase's holding cells until meal time rolled around.

Te Krull advanced with his burden past a bank of monitors, approaching Kiri Ung's desk with a certain hesitation in his steps. Still Kiri Ung didn't turn. The Terran's chest wasn't moving: it was dead.

The buzz of Te Krull's thoughts brushed against his mind, but Kiri Ung blocked the telepathic link. His urge to dismember the commander was best kept to himself, though he maintained his turned back as a studied insult. He was safe enough, as his second would have to drop the corpse to attack. "Your orders were?"

"You said to go find Terrans capable of breaking through mind control to see us and to bring one of them back alive." Te Krull's crest remained a pink, fleshy bulge on the top of his head.

Kiri Ung turned, studying the Terran in Te Krull's arms. "Explain the deadness."

Te Krull looked away, refusing to meet his gaze. Whatever had happened wasn't going to make his second look good.

"We weren't expecting the ferocity of their resistance. That is why we only took one alive." Te Krull's head lowered.

"You top any Terran by at least two feet." Kiri Ung made a point of running his eyes over Te Krull's powerful physique. "You all had weapons. What went wrong?"

"They had weapons, too." A shudder ran through Te Krull. "Weapons like ours. I lost two Nestines for the six Terrans we took down. I hit this one on the head."

"Didn't you think to hold back on your blow?" Kiri Ung kept his tone mild while he mentally reviewed potential replacements for Te Krull.

"I was gentle." Te Krull made eye contact. His crest stirred, throbbing into a deeper red as the blood surged. "He woke in transit, and then he just shut down. I have never seen the like. I tried everything to keep him alive."

Kiri Ung released his own rage. His crest erected within seconds. "You are now telling me it willed itself to death? That they make weapons to rival our own, when they have no technology?" His stomach growled. It was long past his feeding time.

"These Terrans are different. Look at him. He has gills, and his skin is scaled."

Kiri Ung moved closer. Te Krull was right. Although all Terrans generally looked the same to him, this one was indeed different. Hunger pangs gnawed, upsetting his concentration. He reached out for a dangling leg and took a bite. It tasted fishy. He hated fish. He spat it out. "What is this? It isn't Terran."

Te Krull's crest deflated. "They are not surface dwellers, Queen's Mate." He dumped the dead Terran on Kiri Ung's pristine desktop, sending the priceless crystal artifact skidding onto the floor where it smashed into a million pieces. Both of them inhaled sharply. This was a singular tragedy. Kiri Ung leaned over his console to send out an order for a cleaning bot. He would deal with the loss later. Te Krull would pay for it once he outlived his value. That time might be fast approaching.

Together they examined the cooling corpse. This creature had webbing between his finger and toe digits. He had gills, and his skin was covered with transparent, watertight scales, something Kiri Ung had missed with the hunger upon him, despite Te Krull's observation. His fur bristled. "We didn't eradicate all the old ones. We must have missed some, and they have mutated over time. Search out and destroy all of them. You said aquatic? Look under the sea. I got a mouthful of saltwater fish."

Te Krull's breathing pits flared. "You're saying an underwater base with high tech?"

Trying to be patient and not rip his second's head off, Kiri Ung sighed. "They have advanced weapons from your own report. These are not our prey-beasts, who wave swords and daggers at each other. Program our Terran priest-drones to search out all Terran forts for possible infiltrators. They will make themselves more useful if they are allowed greater mind control over the others, so give them the ability. Dispose of any suspects without upsetting the herd, and then do a sweep of all continental shelves under the sea for trace signs of tech in operation. I want these mutants eradicated before they start causing problems with our stock. Is there any part of this you don't understand? If I find I need to revisit these orders, someone else will be listening to me repeat them."

"Did you want any brought to Moonbase for analysis?"

Kiri Ung grabbed a handful of the dead Terran's light-colored hair, raising the head up to eye level. "Kill them. Kill them all."

Coming in 2014

Sword of Shadows

by C.N. Lesley

Arthur and Kai have escaped the threat of Emrys but now must face life on the surface world, and all the fearsome creatures that dwell there. But just as they assemble the beginnings of a fighting force, they discover a vital component to their safety has been compromised. This means a return to Avalon, where Arthur has an unexpected encounter with the untrustworthy Merlin. The magician's orders are clear: Arthur must find the sword to save the surface-dwellers and Avalon. There is no alternative.

Kiri Ung, leader of the Nestines and ultimate controller of the Terran slaves on the surface, needs Arthur in order to ensure the continuance of his species. With the Nestine Queen dying, failure means ultimate extinction. Wherever Arthur goes, so goes Kiri Ung.

Whoever finds the sword first gains control over all humanity. But simply gaining possession of this powerful artifact is not enough to wield its power. Let the battle commence.

About the Author

C.N. Lesley is the pen name of author Elizabeth Hull, who lives in central Alberta, Canada with her husband and cats. Her family lives close by. As well as writing, Elizabeth also likes to read, paint watercolors, and is a keen gardener, despite the very short summers, and now has a mature shade garden. Once a worker in the communications sector, mostly concentrating on local news and events, she now writes full time.

Elizabeth's first book, *Darkspire Reaches*, was published in March 2013 and is an Amazon bestseller. For more information, check out her website at cnlesley.com

Acknowledgements

Thank you so much to Sammy H.K Smith, Zoë Harris and Ken Dawson from Kristell Ink. Thank you also to Evelinn Enoksen for a wonderful cover.

Many thanks to a wonderful bunch of friends who helped make this book what it is now. In alphabetical order: Treize Aramistedian, Lindsay B, Corrie Conwell, Carlos J. Cortes, Jeanette Cottrell, Susan Elizabeth Curnow, Jennifer Dawson, Linda Dicmanis, Crash Froelich, Rhonda S.Garcia, Giacomo Giammatteo, Ilona Gordon, Zoë Harris. Lisa Hartjes Jeanne Haskins, Kendra Highley, Elissa Hunt, May Iversen, Victoria Kerrigan, Raven Matthews, Lisa Smeaton, Sammy H.K Smith, Linda Steel, Dena Landon Stoll, P.J Thompson, Stelios Touchtidis Sylvia Volk, and Ursular Warneke

Other Titles from Kristell Ink

STRANGE TALES FROM THE SCRIPTORIAN VAULTS

A Collection of Steampunk Stories edited by Sammy HK Smith

All profits go to the charity First Story.

Published October 2012

NON-COMPLIANCE: THE SECTOR by Paige Daniels

I used to matter . . . but now I'm just a girl in a ghetto, a statistic of the Non-Compliance Sector.

Shea Kelly had a brilliant career in technology, but after refusing to implant an invasive government device in her body she was sent to a modern day reservation: a Non-Compliance Sector, a lawless community run by thugs and organized crime. She's made a life for herself as a resourceful barkeep, and hacks for goods on the black market with her best friend Wynne, a computer genius and part-time stripper. Life is pretty quiet under the reigning Boss, apart from run-ins with his right hand man, the mighty Quinn: until Danny Rose threatens to take over the sector. Pushed to the edge, Shea decides to fight back . . .

Published November 2012

HEALER'S TOUCH by Deb E. Howell

A girl who has not only the power to heal through taking life fights for her freedom.

Llew has a gift. Her body heals itself, even from death, but at the cost of those nearby. In a country fearful of magic, freeing yourself from the hangman's noose by wielding forbidden power brings its own dangers. After dying and coming back to life, Llew drops from the gallows into the hands of Jonas: the man carrying a knife with the power to kill her.

Published February 2013

DARKSPIRE REACHES by C.N. Lesley

The wyvern has hunted for the young outcast all her life; a day will come when she must at last face him.

Abandoned as a sacrifice to the wyvern, a young girl is raised to fear the beast her adoptive clan believes meant to kill her. When the Emperor outlaws all magic, Raven is forced to flee from her home with her foster mother, for both are judged as witches. Now an outcast, she lives at the mercy of others, forever pursued by the wyvern as she searches for her rightful place in the world. Soon her life will change forever as she discovers the truth about herself.

A unique and unsettling romantic adventure about rejection and belonging.

Published March 2013

GUARDIANS OF EVION, VOLUME 1: DESTINY by Evelinn Enoksen

Numak believes his destiny is to be a Rider; but he learns that he is far more important.

A strange and compelling narrative which encompasses philosophy, adventure and romance within a richly imagined world, embellished with the author's own extraordinary art.

Published April 2013

SPACE GAMES by Dean Lombardo

The cameras are on and the gloves are off in this battle of the sexes on the new International Space Station.

Say hello to Robin and Joe—contestants in 2034's "Space Games," a new, high-stakes reality TV show from Hollywood producer Sheldon J. Zimmer . . .

Space Games is a compelling story and a biting satire about reality television: those who make and participate in it – and those who watch it.

Published May 2013

THE ART OF FORGETTING: RIDER by Joanne Hall

A young boy leaves his village to become a cavalryman with the famous King's Third regiment; in doing so he discovers both his past and his destiny.

Gifted and cursed with a unique memory, the foundling son of a notorious traitor, Rhodri joins an elite cavalry unit stationed in the harbour town of Northpoint. His training reveals his talents and brings him friendship, love and loss, and sexual awakening; struggling with his memories of his father who once ruled there, he begins to discover a sense of belonging. That is, until a face from the past reveals a secret that will change not only Rhodri's life but the fate of a nation. Then, on his first campaign, he is forced to face the extremes of war and his own nature.

This, the first part of The Art of Forgetting, is a gripping story about belonging and identity, set in a superbly imagined and complex world that is both harsh and beautiful.

Published June 2013

THE RELUCTANT PROPHET **by Gillian O'Rourke**

There's none so blind as she who can see . . .

Esther is blessed, and cursed, with a rare gift: the ability to see the fates of those around her. But when she escapes her peasant upbringing to become a priestess of the Order, she begins to realise how valuable her ability is among the power-hungry nobility, and what they are willing to do to possess it.

Haunted by the dark man of her father's warnings, and unable to see her own destiny, Esther is betrayed by those sworn to protect her. With eyes newly open to the harsh realities of her world, she embarks on a path that diverges from the plan the Gods have laid out. Now she must choose between sacrificing her own heart's blood, and risking a future that will turn the lands against each other in bloody war.

The Reluctant Prophet is the story of one woman who holds the fate of the world in her hands, when all she wishes for is a glimpse of her own happiness.

Published August 2013

Non-Compliance: The Transition by Paige Daniels

Three months have passed since Shea Kelly and the rest of Boss's crew eliminated Danny Rose from the Non-Compliance Sector, but their troubles are far from over. A new, more dangerous opponent has emerged, causing those once considered enemies to strike a tenuous truce. Secrets about the vaccine, the chip, and the past threaten Shea's budding romance and even the very existence of the crew.

All titles in print and as e-books.